A DRAGONS OF SINUA

WAYWARD WINGS

S SLOTTJE

Wayward Wings

S SLOTTJE

Flintlock & Fluke Publishing

Content Warning

Wayward Wings contains scenes of torture, graphic violence and death including of children and animals, some sexual scenes, nudity, PTSD and physical trauma, fat shaming, misgendering, and depictions of bodily functions. It features smoking, alcohol use, and drugging.

Discretion is advised.

ACKNOWLEDGEMENTS

Writing and publishing a book is harder, and took longer than I had thought, however it has been more rewarding than I could have imagined. This book wouldn't exist without the help of the following people:

First and foremost, Jarek Adams, writer and guru of the Wordmaids writers' group, who as good as functioned as my writing coach over many years with her wisdom and encouragement. Her expertise and insights were invaluable in shaping my writing style and honing my storytelling skills. Additionally, I would like to express my heartfelt appreciation to my beta and sensitivity readers. Their generous feedback and criticism helped me to refine the direction of my novel.

I should also mention Rebecca Maeve Hartwell, Mindy Dwyer and Liz Bradley for setting up and running the Facebook groups Fantasy Virtual Critique Group and Fantasy Writers' Guild. These groups proved to be invaluable resources, especially during the challenging times of the Covid-19 pandemic.

Thank you to the British Fantasy Society who provided me with the kick in the pants I needed to get this project over the line.

I want to extend my appreciation to Richie Billing and my fellow authors who follow his excellent podcast, *The Fantasy Writers' Toolshed*, and gather on Richie's Discord to provide support and inspiration.

ACKNOWLEDGEMENTS

I owe my editors Nick Hodgson, Claire Rushbrook, and Eleanor Smith, as well as the team at Miblart, a debt of gratitude for their help in making this book as good as it has turned out to be.

And of course, thank you to my husband for his forbearance, and being the closest thing to magic I'll ever know in real life.

For Sarah T who inspired so many characters
and who would have enjoyed this book

CONTENTS

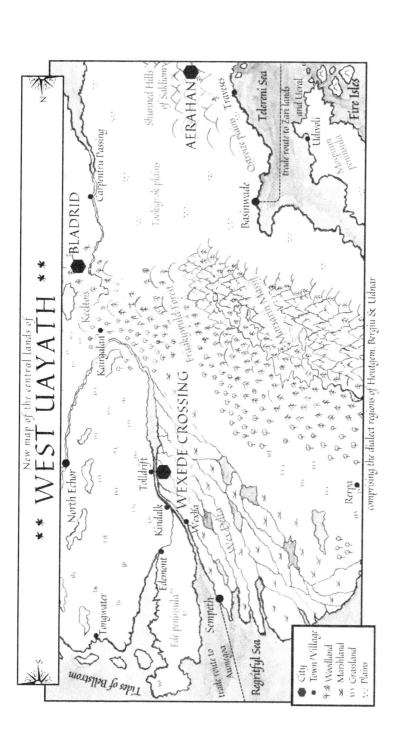

New map of the central lands of
✶ ✶ WEST UAYATH ✶ ✶

comprising the dialect regions of Houtgem, Bergiu & Uldnar

City
Town/Village
Woodland
Marshland
Grassland
Plains

BLADRID

AERAHAN

WEXEDE CROSSING

North Echor
Tongwater
Edemont
Kindalk
Tolldrift
Weyba
Sempeth
Rerya
Karagalan
Redtres
Carpentra Passing
Basinwade
Truvesca
Udivoli
Shunned Hills of Saklianru
Taskigrok plains
Friadypwld Forest
Marsarin Wassili
Ostrase plains
Telereni Sea
Morgum Peninsula
Fire Isles
Ede peninsula
Wax Delta
Regrifyl Sea
Tides of Balstrom
trade route to Aumega
trade route to Zari lands and Ueral

N

S

Part I

ONE

UNTIMELY EMERGENCE

Tearing through the husk of her cocoon, the dragon blinked, mystified by the golden clouds and the dark green pine needles that swayed overhead. After each prior iteration, the world had been bathed in silvery light. This time, the brilliance of a sunset surrounded her, not the light of a full moon. Caizhiu narrowed her eyes and realised she had four of them now.

Flexing her upper shoulders caused the brittle husk of the cocoon to split further, and as she shook it off, it slunk against the trunk of the tree. Caizhiu yawned, let the profusion of aromas on the evening breeze caress the receptors on her tongue. Scents of pine, primed gunpowder, and decaying meat swirled around her. When her senses untangled, a sudden but persistent pain welled up in her. The twisting of her insides was familiar; she tried to remember what it meant. She searched for a scent she could use to quell the gnawing discomfort. A whiff of fear – a delicious promise – caught her, and then it was all she could smell. Saliva dripped down her long teeth when her ancillary eyes spotted the human.

He stood a mere fifty paces from her, an aged farmer caught in the open of the field that surrounded the pine tree. Caizhiu remembered hearing his faltering footfall, running from the cocoon towards the dirt track and the safety of his auto carriage. But when the husk burst open, the man had stopped, the brim of his hat fluttering in the breeze and the legs of his trousers fluttering with fright. Though he had aimed a large flintlock rifle, under her gaze he was unable to fire.

When she lunged towards him, her foot snagged on the remnants of the cocoon. In an unfamiliar reflex, she extended her wings to keep upright. They tangled through the web of pine twigs, and one of them struck a weighty object suspended from a branch. She snapped at it and sank her teeth into the carcass of a ram. The animal had been gutted, stripped of its hide, and beheaded. Caizhiu searched her hazy mind to recall how it came to be hung here. Perhaps it was an offering from the old man. How had she known he was a farmer? Did she know him? The ram was an easier meal than a living human, and she bit down. Rhythmically shaking her head, she tore off a chunk of dead meat and gulped it down. The hunger lessened, and so did the frenzy that had gripped her. She sheared off strips of muscle and with every mouthful felt calmer – more like herself. Whoever that was.

The man took a quivering breath, lowered his rifle, and backed away. *{You are early.}*

His soul song was faint, but familiar. He struggled to form it through the fog of his fear, yet it flooded her with impressions in a way human speech could not. It warmed her, filling her with memories of a lifetime of affection, a family, a farm, a community, a friend. Morailo, she thought. He was her friend, Morailo. And she had nearly killed him.

She crunched up the neck bones and savoured the marrow. The sound carried, causing Morailo's heart to hammer in his chest. *{I barely had time to put up that damned ram!}*

Though Caizhiu felt as much a stranger to her mind as she did her body, she was able to organise her thoughts into a coherent song. *{How... long?}*

{Ten days.} Accusation tainted his affection. *{You're ten days early.}*

A Fabled would have reined in their level of intimacy but, though Talented, her friend was only human. Unable to keep from over-sharing, visions bled into his song: her looming over him, the dragon's gaze that had rooted him, her fangs that he imagined jabbing into his flesh, her talons slicing through his abdomen. Visions to haunt his nightmares.

The Keeltois weren't the hills where Caizhiu had first crawled out of her egg, not where she should have returned for her iteration. She'd had no desire to walk halfway across the world to a lonely mountaintop, and the Keeltois were the closest she had to a home. But she hadn't intended for her friend to be faced with her true form. She remembered now that she'd asked him to hang the ram to quell her hunger. Still, she had warned the family to stay away from the cocoon near the time of her emergence. It hadn't occurred to her that it could happen early. That was impossible. She wondered if her refusal to return to Jitren had been considered defiance of Sinuation, and that this may be its retribution. Morailo had almost paid the price for her hubris.

Despite lowering his rifle, he never once turned his back on her as he walked to his auto carriage. He opened the door, and a brown and white blur ran up the field towards Caizhiu. Morailo screamed. The cry of wordless panic turned into a name. "Mitzer, no!"

The dog dashed backwards and forwards around the dragon, assaulting her with high-pitched yips. Caizhiu extracted her claws from the ram's flesh and slowed the dog's movements until she could see each hackle quiver, each blade of grass bend underneath his paws. The dog rolled several times when she knocked him over with her tail.

{Caizhiu!}

Her jaws found the dog's throat, her fangs eager to pierce the windpipe and spinal cord.

{Don't harm my grandsons' dog. Please...}

His desperation hit her like spears. Her friend shouldn't have to plead with her. Reluctantly, she opened her mouth and raised her head. The dog whined and licked his chops. Caizhiu took her claw off the animal.

"Mitzer!" Morailo attempted to sound authoritative as he called the dog, but his voice trembled. "Get yourself back here, you daft pup!"

The dog limped down the hill, recovering his gait, as if to check all his limbs were still there. His ears flapped when he shook his head and his tail wagged hesitantly when he jumped into the cabin. Morailo followed him and slammed the door shut.

The contraption rattled, shook, and steam billowed from between the tall wheels as the carriage pulled away.

Caizhiu couldn't countenance that this might be the last time she'd see him, or worse, that this would be the way he'd remember her. She had to ensure she'd visit him in human form, however hard that might prove to be. *{I'll see you on the morrow.}*

The auto carriage slowed, and before he was too far away, Morailo's hesitant song reached her. *{Take as long as you need.}*

Once he'd gone, Caizhiu stripped the carcass to the bone, stroking the inside of her mouth with her tongue, trying to make sense of the displeasing flavour. The ram had been dead at least a week and it spoiled the taste. The human custom of charring food made her gag, but until today, she had always enjoyed raw meat. She didn't know if it was her early emergence, the challenge of the dog, or simply her new iteration, but she needed to make a fresh kill.

She stretched to get the last twinge of stiffness out of her neck, limbs, and tail. Her head brushed against the branch. How tall was that? Without the weight of the meat, the branch had returned to its normal height. She was considerably larger than she had been. Taking care of another urge, she aimed a stream of urine at the remnants of the cocoon, which dissolved into a black stain on the tree trunk. A stain that would remind Morailo of this evening for the rest of his days.

The sun sank below the Keeltois' peaks and the long shadows melded together into dusk. The concert of cicadas grew louder. Thin streaks of clouds broke to reveal the thinnest sliver of a waxing moon. She'd always been an impatient dragon, but ten days early was ridiculous. Bats and night fay darted about, feeding on moths and other flying insects of the wet season. Too agile for her to snatch from the air, but they reminded her of her 'appendages'. Tentatively, she unfolded her wings. They were enormous, finally large enough to enable her to fly. She would have to experiment with them. But not tonight, not in the dark.

She walked up the hill towards the treeline. Because of her longer legs, she reached the forest edge quicker than she'd expected. Twigs brushed her face, and she ducked to avoid the larger branches. The trees grew closer and closer together, driving out the grass for a layer of needles and fern mulch. She tripped over a tricky patch of brambles. Four eyes, and not one that could see in the dark. She had to rely on her other senses for her hunt. Her tongue tasted the air. Among the flavour of tiny rodents, burgeoning fungi, and pine trees, she found the pungent trail of a badger clan and followed it to avoid bumping into the trees. A bubble of silence formed around her as critters ceased their activity until the predator had passed. In the distance, a stag bellowed to attract mates and ward off rivals. Thankfully, she needn't kill something that big. Recent rain – the first of the season – had formed a stream nearby. It would be the best place to quench her thirst and offered an easier path through the woods. A break in the canopy allowed faint moonlight to shimmer on the narrow ribbon of water. Occasionally, the pinprick light of a night fay darted through the clearing. Caizhiu clambered over the rock bed and bent to the crevice in which the water flowed, scooping water from the creek and lifting her head to let it pour down her throat. It was cold and tasted crisp, carrying the minerals of the mountain.

She followed the riverbed up the hill. Six years ago, the storms had transformed the little creek, making it so powerful it had deposited a path of rocks that shrubs had not yet filled. The previous decades of wear had disappeared from the soles of her feet, and Caizhiu felt each pebble with renewed intensity. She reached the dam that the people of the Keeltois had repaired. No matter how long the dry spell might last, they had learnt to keep plenty of water in reserve. Caizhiu climbed past a trickling waterfall over the dam to a small lake beyond. A young vixen stood by the water's edge. When the fox noticed the dragon approach, she scurried into the woods.

There, where large rocky fingers stretched from between the darkness of the pines into the lake, would be a perfect place for an ambush. She could corner prey against the water. Unable to resist, she stole a glimpse at her reflection and froze in shock. The creature in the rippled mirror looked disastrously large. How could she transfigure *that* into a shape small enough to look human? But she had to. If she wanted to face Morailo and prove to him that she was still his friend, not a monster. And if she was ever going to be able to interact with neath humans again, she would need to disguise herself as one.

Caizhiu closed her eyes and concentrated on a human form. Naturally, the first one that came to mind was Morailo, but he was too short and slender to emulate. There wouldn't be enough room for her body parts. She tried not to get rattled and remember what larger humans looked like. When she'd controlled her perceptions so she could hear each individual drop of water leave the lake and join the creek below the dam, she inhaled and began to reshape her structure. Fortunately, her body still had its post-iteration flexibility. Shifting her organs, she condensed her flesh and bones, squeezing herself smaller and smaller. Her muscles twinged as she contracted them. It hadn't hurt this much before, had it? She rounded her head and flattened her snout, giving prominence to the nose over the mouth. Then she shrank and smoothed the hexagonal scales that covered her body until they had the texture of human skin. Her minor eyes she moved to the back of her head, and she drew in her neck. She pulled her teeth into her jaws and wrapped her long tail around her expansive waist. Extraneous folds of flesh she moulded, as best she could, to resemble the clothes humans covered themselves with. Lastly, she folded and refolded her wings over and around her, emulating a cloak to conceal her bulk. She included a hood to help hide her second pair of eyes.

The dragon stood upright on her shortened hind legs. She drew in her claws and shaped her feet like those of booted humans. For a moment she teetered on her now narrow, clawless feet to balance her bulk. Was this small enough? Reeling with each step, she shuffled to the water's edge. Her mass was so dense that, should she slip, she would sink straight to the bottom. Once she felt sure she wouldn't lose her footing, she tried on some expressions: she broadened her jawline so she could open her mouth, and when she grinned, she remembered to square her teeth. She was still too tall, too wide. But she could shrink no further. At least she looked human. To complete her facade, she changed the colour of her front eyes from black to white, leaving just the dot of her pupils dark. The rest of her colours she would take care of in daylight. Compared to maintaining her solidity, adapting her skin colour was easy. Stepping back from the water, she let the sensation of her new shape seep into her muscle memory. Ears, she remembered; humans had skin flaps for ears.

Her stomach gurgled. Contracting into her human form took a lot of energy and concentration, especially the first time. And she was still recovering from her emergence. She would need this shape later, but it'd be useless in her current hunt. Caizhiu walked back to the rocky formation and relaxed against it. She sighed with relief as her body returned to its natural shape. Her scales and eyes dulled to a mottled grey until she was indistinguishable from the granite.

And she waited.

The night breeze brought a drizzle that coated the woods and the dragon. The wind picked up and Caizhiu let her temperature drop with that of the stone. A brace of deer came to the lake but stayed too far away. When the earliest rays of dawn dyed the sky a drowsy pink, and the birds began their chorus, a mountain hare appeared. It was a large male with a mangy coat. He hopped stiffly along the waterline, right over Caizhiu's tail, and stopped between the rocks to drink from the lake. She moved so quickly the hare barely had time to react, and she caught him mid-jump. With one tooth, she punctured his lungs, with another she broke his neck.

Exultation flooded her when his warm blood ran over her tongue and the animal's heart silenced. The dimming of the ember of life sated her, at last. It was incomprehensible to her that humans could kill without this pleasure. To them, it was a cold act, a practical means to feed themselves. She had learned, though it made no sense, that if a human experienced a thrill like Caizhiu felt, they'd consider such a person ill.

Killing a hare, a neath being, was one thing. How would it have felt had she not just killed but eaten Morailo? It was true, he was human, but his Talent made him kin as well – neathkin, for want of a better term. Hunger might have blinded her to guilt, but only until it was satisfied... until it was too late. The dragon she had become was still a mystery, but at least she hadn't burdened herself with such a mistake... yet.

Two

Closest Thing to Home

It was well past noon when Caizhiu stepped onto the long drive to the Hilleram hotel. Though she had emerged early, she could feel her muscles, ligaments, and bones stiffen already. She had only a few hours left to improve her facade, so it was time she tried it out on actual humans. By the next dawn, she would be able to shift from her own form to her human one, but from then on, she could only adjust her pigment.

The gravel cracked as she wandered towards the large farmhouse. Stones split under her steps. Morailo and his wife had converted the building when their sons had taken over the running of the actual farm. For the past few years, their daughter and her husband had run the hotel. It looked as it always had: grey stone with shutters and doors painted in the red, black, and white that were considered welcoming in the Keeltois. She noticed they had fixed several bhodine carapaces to the roof, replacing the ruddy-coloured tiles.

A little boy on a wooden tricycle froze when he saw Caizhiu approach. She raised her hand. "Well met, Moro."

The boy returned the gesture. Then he looked at a woman with a swollen belly who appeared at the kitchen door. She wiped her hands on her apron and, with a tight smile, said: "Go get Grandpa. Tell him his friend is here."

Moro jumped off the tricycle and darted off, shouting the exact phrase his mother had told him. "Your friend is here, Grandpa!"

Eslonya was the spitting image of her mother. Short and stocky, with light brown skin and long black hair tied into a braid spiralled into a knot on top of her head. Her multicoloured headscarf draped over her shoulders. She walked into the shadow of the dragon and looked up at Caizhiu.

"Indeed, you have changed. Will you remove your hood for our house?"

Caizhiu obeyed and watched Eslonya study her. The scrutiny made her uneasy. "Is it... not right?"

Eslonya clicked her tongue and sucked in her breath. "I didn't know you could be a man. But you're so tall now. It makes sense. You look ridiculous without a beard, though. What are you, a boy? And bald! No hair?"

"Loose hair is tricky." Caizhiu enviously eyed Eslonya's towering braids. In her previous iteration she had hidden skin folds in a mimicked braid, but outside of the Keeltois, human customs changed fast. Loose hair was now the norm in most places.

Eslonya placed a hand on her arm and, with a slight squeeze, invited the dragon to follow her to the house. Caizhiu was about to, but then Moro skidded back into the yard, bouncing on his toes in excitement. Morailo followed at a calmer pace. He looked stern, but at least he wasn't carrying his blunderbuss. Caizhiu moved her arm out of Eslonya's reach. "I only came to collect my... things."

Morailo strode towards her and stopped between Caizhiu and his daughter. "So, because you come dressed as a big man, you think you can insult us?"

Dumbstruck, Caizhiu shook her head.

"You pay us good coin and you expect us not to fulfil our end? You want people to say we don't have good hospitality at this hotel?"

Caizhiu opened her mouth to explain that the use of their field and the ram were all they'd needed to provide, but then she noticed the twinkle in his eye. His feigned frown turned into a broad grin. He slapped her arm and hugged her. The switch from being scolded to the embrace was too sudden, and Caizhiu failed to accommodate his gesture. Instead of pulling her close to him, Morailo staggered as he pulled himself to her. The top of his hat tickled her bottom chin. Caizhiu gave a gentle hug back.

"Come on in." Morailo nodded at the kitchen. "Eslonya is preparing a welcome-back meal. The boys should be here soon, too."

The door seemed smaller. Caizhiu ducked as she followed Eslonya through it. Moro grabbed his mother's hand and pulled on her arm. Eslonya, hindered by her belly, squatted next to him. Without taking his eyes off Caizhiu, Moro whispered something in his mother's ear and Eslonya whispered back. The little boy squinted at Caizhiu, then darted out of the kitchen. Caizhiu helped Eslonya to her feet.

"Not just a man, but a gentleman." Eslonya raised an eyebrow.

Cooking wasn't Caizhiu's forte, but with Eslonya's exasperated and increasingly detailed instructions, she could just about manage to set a table. The kitchen lamp took quite a few knocks as her head bashed against it. At one point, she had to stop to bend the metal back into shape.

The door from the hallway into the kitchen opened and Eslonya's husband entered, followed by their eldest son, Torbel. The brown and white dog stuck his head around the door, looked at Caizhiu, and left with an affronted whimper.

"Mitzer!" Torbel shouted. "It's only Caizhiu."

But the dog was unpersuadable.

Torbel studied her with the same unashamed curiosity his mother had. He had been Moro's age when Caizhiu had last seen him.

"You've grown," she said, and he retorted whip quick, "So have you."

"Torbel! Mind your manners." Eslonya scowled at her son. "Caizhiu is a guest."

There was a muted roar coming from the yard. Alarmed, Caizhiu walked towards the kitchen door, but no one seemed to share her concern. The roar was replaced with cheerful voices. She reached for the handle when the door flew open and two men, mid-argument, tussled to get in. Osobayo was first through the door and stood so close to Caizhiu that their toes nearly touched. Slowly, he moved his eye-level gaze from Caizhiu's chest up until it met her eyes. He managed a strangled: "Mercy-of-Six."

Right behind him, Raccio let his widened eyes glide over Caizhiu's bulk. He cleared his throat and asked: "Just how many rams did you eat?"

Caizhiu stepped back to allow the brothers to enter. Under Eslonya's disapproving gaze, both quickly snatched their hats off. Simultaneously, they remembered their wives were still outside.

Raccio, having retrieved his composure, pulled a young woman forward. "Doriana, this is Caizhiu. Caizhiu, this is Doriana, my wife."

Caizhiu remembered Morailo had mentioned when she'd arrived that his youngest's nuptials had taken place, but she had been too focused on her impending iteration to pay attention.

"Well met." She bowed her head in the regional custom.

Osobayo and Raccio burst into laughter.

"Yeah, you're gonna have to deepen your... ehm..." Raccio pointed at his throat. "Your voice. That squeakiness doesn't work with the new look."

Caizhiu modified the shape of her throat and tried again at a lower register. Doriana bowed her head and smiled timidly.

"Apologies." Raccio jumped forward again. "Dor, Caizhiu is an old friend of the family. She's a... Is it still she? Ahem. Yes, he, she, whatever, is a, well, a dragon for want of a better... yes, a dragon. And—"

"Can we do this at the dinner table?" Eslonya asked. "And close that door!"

"Sorry, sis." Osobayo held up his hands and ushered his wife and daughter to the table.

Caizhiu looked for the sturdiest chair, avoiding the one at the head of the table, which was reserved for Morailo. She chose a corner seat, where she'd be able to uncoil part of her tail unobserved to partially take her weight.

Morailo and Moro joined the gathering. Though called, Mitzer stayed out of sight.

Eslonya frowned. "What's wrong with that dog?"

Caizhiu studied the floral design on the rim of her plate to avoid Morailo's glance in her direction.

Raila took the seat opposite Caizhiu, and they stared at each other for a while, internally listing the changes in each other's appearance since last they'd met. Osobayo's daughter was only a year older than Torbel, but though she still wore her hair short in a juvenile style, she was almost a foot taller than her cousin.

"Do your female young mature faster than your male ones?" Caizhiu asked Osobayo, and Raila grinned wickedly at Torbel.

The adult humans sniggered, and the girl took the advantage. "Boys are slow."

"They take some growing up." Eslonya eyed her brothers, rubbed her belly, and gave them a mischievous grin. "Glad this one is going to be a girl."

"A girl?" Torbel and Moro said in unison, faces twisted in disgust.

"That's what Heort said." Eslonya winked at Caizhiu, who sensed she had been included in a joke but was unsure what it had been.

Caizhiu moved a piece of boiled meat around her mouth and tried to find the muscle memory for mastication. Swallow it, she commanded her throat. The ball of food seemed to grow in her mouth with her chewing. Finally, she forced it down.

"So tell us, Caizhiu," Raccio said, tearing off a bite of bread and continuing with a full mouth. "What creatures and scoundrels have you been chasing these past years?"

Relieved she could stop eating for a minute, Caizhiu told them of the frost drake, Tipvigut, whom she'd battled and defeated on behalf of Magistrate Withervale, the band of raiders she'd rounded up for the town of Benru, and the hunt for the werecat of Alorabridge. Torbel and Moro listened to the tales with wide-open eyes and had to be reminded to finish their dinners. Raila frowned sceptically. She rested both elbows on the table and her chin on her fists.

"If you really are a dragon," she said, "why didn't you use your fire breath to defeat the frost drake?"

"If?" Caizhiu raised an eyebrow, but the girl didn't back down.

"You don't look like a dragon. Why don't you do something dragony, breathe fire?"

The conversations around the table fell silent, making Morailo's cough sound even louder. He wiped his mouth and had a sip of wine. His eyes found Caizhiu's, and she saw something she'd never seen in her friend's face before. His terror made her lower her gaze, and she moved the food around her mostly full plate.

"I'm not that kind of dragon."

"I believe you're a dragon," said Torbel, prompting a disgusted look from Raila.

"No, you don't, you suck-up!"

"I do. She was a woman, now he's a man. Why not a dragon?"

With all eyes on her, Caizhiu had no choice but to finish her meal. The stew was easier to eat when it was cold. At least it didn't imitate the life it no longer possessed. Luckily, there was copious wine to wash it down. What humans lacked in their cuisine, they more than made up for with their fermented fruit and vegetable drinks.

Eventually, Eslonya told the boys to get ready for bed, and when they lingered, she accompanied them.

"Suppose we'd better get going too." Osobayo stretched his back as he stood.

"Do you want me to walk you home?" Caizhiu was surprised at the laughter her offer provoked.

"Walk?" Raccio scoffed. "We can do better than that."

Caizhiu frowned. She hadn't smelled horses. Then she remembered the roar of their arrival and rolled her eyes. "Not you too."

Raccio and Osobayo exchanged amused glances.

"It wouldn't be good form for bhodine farmers not to have auto carriages. Come see!" Osobayo motioned for her to join them outside, his eyes shining with excitement. She followed them to the yard. "We are no longer dependent on your tales of strange lands, dear friend. We can travel there ourselves now."

Not one but two of the monstrosities stood parked, or rather abandoned, on the gravel. Like the brothers themselves, the carriages looked identical. They were sleeker than Morailo's, with rounded cabins and room for two rows of humans to sit three abreast, high on top of the mechanical heart of the things. The narrow wheels had dug in where the drivers had braked hard.

"I think," Osobayo's wife, Becarra, said as she unfolded the ladder to climb aboard, "we'll take it a bit steadier on the way home, shall we? No more racing."

"Can I drive?" Raila piped up. "Please, I'm old enough."

"You don't look old enough," said Caizhiu.

Raila harrumphed. "What would you know? You're a dragon." She looked at her parents and tilted her head to the side.

"Not in the dark." Becarra ushered her to the left of the central driver's seat. Osobayo straightened his hat and sat to the right of his wife. Becarra pumped the lever by the steering wheel and the contraption growled as if alive.

"Sorry we didn't get to chat, Caizhiu. Will you be around for a few more days?"

"Yes, she will," answered Morailo before Caizhiu could. "Until she's used to... well, these recent changes."

Father and daughter waved through the tiny side windows while Becarra carefully turned the auto carriage through the gravel. The bhodine carapace roofs gave the contraption the appearance of a giant wheeled insect crawling up the path.

"You drive steady too," Morailo warned his youngest. Raccio shrugged, and in a mock gesture of assistance, he touched his wife's backside as she climbed into the cabin. She giggled, tutted, and reached back to steal his hat.

"That boy will be the death of me," Morailo whispered as the auto carriage sped up the drive and disappeared into the inky black of the night.

Caizhiu let the sudden peacefulness wash over her. Her head swam in wine and residual noise. "I'd forgotten how much you humans like to talk."

"Yes, and I fear my lot are worse than most." Morailo pulled an ornate little box from his pocket. "You wanna smoke?"

"Not that kind of dragon."

"Mind if I have one?"

She shook her head. He went back inside to fetch his pipe. Eslonya, and her mother before her, had always hated him smoking in or even near the house, and since it wasn't worth the argument, he'd put a little smoking bench by the well. The whiff of smoke made Caizhiu feel uneasy, especially here in the Keeltois. Some memories she wished her iterations would swallow, but this had never happened.

Sat on her haunches, she rested her back against the well. Morailo sat next to her and smoked thoughtfully. Old age had grooved his features and marbled his long hair.

"You know..." He let out a lengthy puff of smoke. "When I was younger, I used to have a crush on you."

Caizhiu nodded. His mother had told her at the time. He'd been barely more than a child, gangly and gauche. This first infatuation had started and ended almost ten years before Lonnuta had caught his eye.

"I mean, I knew what you were. But back then, I was young, and you were so... exotic. Beautiful." He laughed at his own foolishness, but there was no mirth in his voice. "I thought I knew what you were. But I didn't have a clue, did I?"

Caizhiu picked up a little stone, studied it, and tossed it back among the gravel. His look of alarm at the dinner table was etched in her mind.

"I am truly sorry for... before, in the field," she said softly. "I don't understand how that happened."

He puffed on his pipe and patted her shoulder. Caizhiu put her hand on his and switched to her soul song. Human words wouldn't cut it and she needed him to understand.

{And I deeply regret not being here for you when she passed.}

She let him flood her with memories of Lonnuta: the teenager, the young woman, the farmer, the mother, the hotelier, his soulmate. And she shared hers with him: the conviviality, the sense of belonging Lonnuta had always imparted.

Morailo cleared his throat, and she heard his knees crack when he got up from the bench. He shook the ash out of his pipe onto the gravel and stepped on it. Without looking back, he walked to the house. "We've kept your hoard in the backroom on the ground floor. Dream well, my friend."

"And you." Caizhiu hoped he would dream of his wife, not of the dragon in his field.

THREE

HEORT

"Have you ever driven an auto carriage?" Torbel swayed a stick back and forth as he walked through the tall grass beside the track. While a little surprised, Caizhiu was grateful that Morailo had no objections to his grandson accompanying her to the bhodine shelters. It was a sign of trust she wasn't sure she deserved.

"I haven't even been in one," she said.

The boy swung the stick over his shoulder like a miniature copy of the wooden beam Caizhiu carried. "Trueso? I've driven Grandpa's. Only around the farm, but I didn't crash. You think Uncle Raccio would let me drive his auto carriage?"

"Probably."

"Why don't you have an auto carriage? You have loads of gold. You could buy one."

"What makes you think I have gold?"

He shrugged. "You're a dragon. Isn't that what you keep in your room?"

She stopped and turned. "That was meant to be a secret."

Luckily, the beam passed so far over Torbel's head he barely noticed.

Caizhiu did have a modest hoard. Gold was what she demanded for her services, and she had no intention of spending it on a human contraption that wouldn't even hold her weight.

"If I had gold, I'd get an auto carriage and drive all over the world!" Torbel ran ahead to open the gate for her, which reminded her of a young Morailo, though she couldn't recall Morailo having been this talkative. Perhaps she'd chosen to forget.

Try as she might, she couldn't pretend that time had stood still. Torbel looked like his grandfather, but he wasn't him. It seemed only a few years ago that the farm had kept sheep. Now, blue-and-purple-striped bhodine ambled up and down the undulating fields instead. The creatures stood tall as oxen with broad withers that tapered in a teardrop rear. Occasionally, they would extend their long necks from under the carapaces that covered their backs to look around or munch on a clump of grass. Inoffensive creatures, more plant than beast, that spent the day peacefully basking in the sunlight. Horses, cows, or even sheep might have bolted, but bhodine paid little heed to a dragon walking among them. The taste of their flesh was so revoltingly waxy they had no natural predators and no need for fear. Osobayo and Raccio's decision to replace succulent sheep with such useless beings was incomprehensible.

The brothers' animated voices reached her before she arrived at the shelter.

"Hey, Caizhiu!" Osobayo waved at her. "You've been to Ucral, haven't you? How sunny would you say it is there?"

"Extremely sunny. It's a desert isle."

"Right," Raccio crowed. "It's a desert, no grass. When they graze, they produce runnier verve; better verve. Let those poor Ucralian bast—"

He noticed Torbel, swallowed the rest of his words, and held his hands up in apology.

"This thing isn't getting lighter," Caizhiu said. "Where do you want it?"

Osobayo rushed forward to help her put down the beam, but Torbel stepped in between them, waving the bag he'd been carrying.

"What's this? Your ma make us lunch?"

The boy nodded.

"We'll have it in a moment. Let me help Caizhiu first."

Caizhiu carefully let Osobayo take a little of the beam's weight so they could lower it gently. She stretched and rolled her shoulder, ensuring it stayed in its human shape.

"Thing is," Raccio set a ladder against the front post, "they might get more sunshine down south, but they'll still need to milk the bhos and store the verve. You know how sticky it gets when they've not been watered for a while. So I reckon they'd be better off investing in those ones with larger carapaces for roof use. You know the ones. And we get more of the Osos type, smaller backplates but runnier verve and more of it. If that order of Sibrand's Mechanised Carriages is anything to go by, we should be able to sell... well, Caizhiu's weight in verve, no problem. Whatta-ya think?"

"I think you should go into business with the Ucralians," Osobayo said wryly. "You clearly know more about their business than they do. I'm sure they'd appreciate your advice."

While Caizhiu lined the strengthening beam up between the front and back post of the shelter, Osobayo threw a line over the centre beam. Raccio picked up the drill and climbed the ladder.

"Hold on. I didn't quite get it." Osobayo tried to grab the other end of the rope that was clearly out of reach – even for Caizhiu. It was tantalisingly close. With a little jump, she made up the difference and grabbed the rope. The whole shelter shook with her landing. The old centre beam, already sagging, creaked ominously. Inversed fountains of dust dropped from the ceiling, and Raccio nearly dropped the drill in his sudden grasp of the ladder.

The brothers exchanged a wide-eyed glance, and Osobayo turned to his nephew. "You unhurt, Torbs?"

Torbel, clutching the bag, answered with a huge grin. "Do it again!"

"No!" Raccio hastened to say. "At least not when I'm up a fu... up a ladder!"

Osobayo shook the dust off his hat. "You understand we're trying to strengthen the shelter, not bring it down on our heads, yes?"

"Apologies," Caizhiu said with a roguish smirk. "I'm not quite used to this body yet."

She lifted the new beam so he could tie the rope around it. They repeated the procedure at the other end of the beam. This time, Caizhiu was careful to catch the rope without causing another tremor.

"You lift this end and I'll take the other. Torbs, keep one foot on the bottom rung and hold the ladder, and you..." Osobayo pointed at Raccio. "Try not to fall off and break your neck."

Raccio mimed losing his balance and then waved away his brother's concerns.

Caizhiu was careful to lift the beam at the same pace Osobayo could manage. Once Raccio had it lined up with the original beam, he got the drill and rotated the turning handle so the steel bit into the wood.

"I hear," he said between several curse words, for which he apologised, "Sibrand's are working on an apparatus small enough to carry, so, you know, you could have a verve-driven drill."

"Anything for an easy life, eh?" Osobayo mocked.

It took considerable time before Raccio was satisfied the holes were deep and wide enough. As his brother was immobilised by having to hold the beam in place, he instructed Torbel to toss the wooden pegs and then the hammer up to him to catch. His approach to the exercise seemed to be geared towards causing his older brother maximum anxiety and frustration.

When at last Osobayo was free to move, he walked over to Torbel. "What's your ma packed for us then?"

"Oi!" shouted Raccio, but it was Osobayo's turn to torture his brother by getting first pickings at the food and divvying the best bits between him and Torbel. Their nephew, acquainted with having a younger brother, played along.

"Torbs," Raccio pleaded while drilling out the last of the holes, "save me some of that cheese. I'll let you have a go in my auto carriage."

"Sis will kill you," Osobayo warned.

"I'll worry about her later. Just now I have to prevent my starvation!"

Torbel held out a hunk of bread and cheese to Caizhiu, but she declined. Above her, Raccio hammered in the three pegs with intemperate urgency. Caizhiu grabbed the ladder to steady it and felt the vibration from each hammer blow. If she concentrated on it, she could even feel Raccio's breathing and the beating of his heart. When he let himself slide down the ladder, Caizhiu stepped back.

"Job well done." He slapped her arm and walked over to the lunch, rubbing his hands. "We've earned this."

{Morailo said I'd find you here.} Silhouetted against the light and dwarfed by the large shelter doors stood a delicate creature who smelled of woodland and friendship.

{Heort!} Caizhiu walked up to meet her friend so he wouldn't have to enter the structure. Though he didn't let it stop him from visiting his human friends, buildings made the cervitaur uncomfortable.

Heort planted his hands on his front-hips and leant back as he looked up at her. This year's antlers were still partially covered in velvet but shaping up to an impressive set. Antlers and all, he only reached up to her chest. *{That is quite a change.}*

{I'm not the only one.} She tilted her head and rolled the fabric of his lapel between her fingers. *{Since when do you wear clothes?}*

He spread his arms proudly, flaunting the fawny coat with light blue stitching. It reached to just above his knees, was tied at his front-hips with a blue belt and opened at the back to leave room for his deer-like hindquarters. *{Since I discovered the convenience of pockets.}*

Caizhiu pointed at the harness of leather straps and hessian pads around his waist and across his rearback. *{You look like a pack horse.}*

{I'll take no mockery from a dragon shaped like a human.}

"Oi!" Osobayo said sternly. "It's rude, having your silent conversation, leaving us out."

"Apologies." Heort swallowed the 'p', forcing his tongue along the l-sound and finally mangling the 'g' into a 'zz'. Most Fabled felt human languages were beneath them, but he had mastered the local dialect of Uayathi and plenty of Trader Talk too. Though his snout was not as pronounced as it was in deer proper, it was not a human mouth. Unlike Caizhiu, he couldn't alter his shape to accommodate human speech. It was solely due to his determination, as well as years of practice, that he'd learned to form words.

Osobayo walked over. He smiled, but his eyes were serious. "How is she?"

Heort took the man's hand in both of his. "Your sister is well. I'm not foreseeing difficulties."

There were many reasons why the cervitaur might visit, but since Eslonya was expecting, the elder brother's concerns had leapt to the worst possibility. Caizhiu hadn't picked up on the quickening of his heartbeat when Heort appeared, but now it returned to a steady rhythm.

Heort let go of Osobayo's hand and asked: "May I borrow your dragon?"

***

D ragon and cervitaur made their way towards the edge of Hilleram lands, passing through the bhodine herd. Compared to them, Heort looked especially slender and nimble.

{What do you make of these things?} Caizhiu asked. *{Why keep something you can't eat?}*

{You're asking the wrong person. Keeping sheep made as little sense to me.}

He hopped over the fence and waited for her. After her experience in the shelter, she wasn't keen to try to jump it and she'd struggle to climb over the fence without breaking it.

{This would be easier in your true form.}

Though Caizhiu couldn't see any humans, she said: *{We're too close to the farm.}*

{That bad, eh?} Heort's song flooded with concern, and Caizhiu felt a little sorry for herself. She tried to shrug it off and awkwardly crawled through the gap between the fence's upper and the lower slat.

She realised how ridiculous she must look as she felt Heort's stifled mirth. *{Don't you dare laugh.}*

{I make it a rule never to laugh at big scary dragons. Even when they are stuck in fences.}

{I'm not stuck!}

Goaded, Caizhiu pushed against the slats that pinched her belly, and she ended up face down in the grass. She got to her feet and wiped the dirt off her knees as if that was exactly the level of grace she had intended to display.

They walked uphill until Heort finally stopped her. The vegetation cleared, revealing a rocky terrain before them, but the thinning conifer bushes behind them still provided shelter. Neither of them could smell even residual human presence.

He put his hand on her arm. *{Show me.}*

It occurred to her it had been decades since even Heort had seen her dragon form. Using his nudge to overcome her reluctance, she transfigured. It took a minute to unfurl herself, and as she loomed over the cervitaur, he let go of her arm and took a few cautious steps back. He didn't emanate fear, and she was grateful for that, but his sympathy was almost as bad.

{Maintaining human form must be terribly uncomfortable for you.} His fingertips caressed her scales as he walked around her. With an approving nod, he ran his thumb over the edge of the arrow-pointed caudal blade and tail spikes. He made his way around and stood on his hind legs to reach up to her upper shoulders. *{Look at your glorious wings. They're enormous!}*

Caizhiu gave a half-hearted beat, and the gust caused Heort's front hooves to slip. Instinctively, she extended a steadying hand to him. Both of them froze. The cervitaur licked his nose and carefully reached behind him to unhook the parts of his coat impaled on her talons.

{How did you manage not to kill that dog?}

{You heard about that.} Caizhiu hung her head. *{I didn't mean to. And Morailo... I can't believe what I nearly did.}*

Though she had intended not to, she poured every bit of her loss into her friend, for the person she'd been, and her confusion over who she was becoming. He ignored her wave of emotion, let it wash through him. Then he let his eyes glide over the wings whose shadow engulfed him and held her claw in both hands. *{All that may be true, but look at your beautiful wings. You really ought to learn to fly. After all, what is a dragon without flight?}*

{I've always managed before. Besides, I can barely walk without breaking things... and you want me to fly?}

Heort spread his arms. *{Nothing but mountain here. Break away.}*

{You're here.}

{I'd be obliged if you could do this without breaking me.} He winked. *{But, as we know, I'm quick enough to dodge one clumsy dragon.}*

Four

First Flight

Caizhiu leant forward towards the chasm and extended her wings. The breeze, carrying the aromas of granite and pine, played with her membranes. At the last moment, she pushed her wings forward and backed away from the edge. She roared in frustration at her nerves and felt the flash of alarm it provoked in Heort. Dread even stirred in her when the echo reached her.

Heort winked at her. *{You can do this.}*

She leant towards the edge again, raised her wings, gave a couple of faint beats to get a feel for the air currents, looked into the gorge, and balked.

{Perhaps you should take a run at it?}

She paced towards the edge and back, beating her wings to shake off her trepidation. Her tail hit a rock and sent it into the ravine. The pause until it finally hit the ground did not reassure her. Stepping back from the edge, she stretched the tension from her muscles, raised her wings, and ran, getting into a steady stride, each propelling her forward faster. Taking one last step, she beheld the chasm beneath her and the enormity of the sky above. She tried to put another foot down but found no ground. Her tail whipped to find balance. She turned to return to the safety of the cliff, but it was too late. The wind twisted her, depressing her right wing. She saw sky, then rock, and then her left wing hit her in the face. She thrashed to free herself. Her right claw screeched over rock until it found purchase and she slammed into the mountain. For a moment she could only hang there, winded, blinded, and trapped in her stupid wing.

So as not to lose her grip, she tried to find a foothold. Her right foot found nothing but void, but the talon on her middle-left toe hooked into a crevice. This gave her enough stability to move her left wing out of her face. The wind pushed her from her foothold, and she slid, but now her other arm was free, and she dug into the mountainside with both claws. Caizhiu folded her wings flat against the rock so the wind wouldn't catch hold of them again. One wing-thumb was positioned just below a horizontal crack. She raised it slightly to hook the wing-thumb into it. She doubted it would take her full weight, but it gave enough support to her left claw to allow her to reach up with her right and get a better grip. Despite not being able to see the ledge, she climbed towards it. Though they didn't take as much weight as her lower shoulders, her wing shoulders ached just as much. She didn't know how much further she had to go, but she had no choice but to climb on. Finally, she'd crawled high enough to give her legs a hold, so she wasn't reliant on her arms and wings.

{Caizhiu?}

She looked up and saw the antlered outline of Heort's head peek over the edge. The sudden rush of anger and relief spurred her on, and she climbed up with renewed energy. She scrabbled over the rocks to get the rest of her onto the flat and collapsed, gasping to catch her breath. *{What?}*

Heort had his face in both hands. *{There are pigeons laughing at you right now. Pigeons!}*

Caizhiu chuckled through her wheezing. *{I wonder what cervitaurs taste like.}*

{Don't blame me. You're the one dumb enough to jump off a mountain.}

Caizhiu got to her feet. Her legs felt as if they might drop off and she struggled to stand.

Heort jumped onto the stone she leant on and examined her upper shoulders. Despite the pain, she extended her left wing for him to check over. It instantly felt better under his touch. *{Your shoulder's a bit wrenched, but you've not broken anything, and your wings are tear free.}*

It amazed Caizhiu it wasn't more serious, and Heort seemed to have similar thoughts. A dull ache pulsated through her muscles, causing her to put off the transformation to her human form for a few hours. She didn't want to let her muscles stiffen after their ordeal, so rather than rest she began a slow trek back down the hill. Heort stayed by her side, flowing ease into her through his fingertips. He hadn't smelled this anxious since their first meeting. He must truly have been scared when she plummeted into the ravine.

After half an hour of walking, she realised that concentrating on not falling over and accidentally crushing her friend had taken her thoughts off her discomfort. But the energy she'd exerted, the energy she was using to heal, was taking its toll and her body was demanding payment. Upon hearing her stomach growl, Heort tried to step aside, but Caizhiu arched her tail to guide him back. Even this little gesture of toying with him increased the desire to go hunting. The forest was alive with potential meals, innumerable beings to appease her hunger, and she yearned to kill a few.

{That scent you're fixating on...} Despite Heort's disgust with her eagerness, he stayed by her side. *{That's not mine, is it?}*

She shook her head. It was a doe, and she'd walked this way not two minutes ago, with a few fawns old enough to survive on their own. Perfect. Caizhiu's movements changed, becoming more deliberate and quieter.

They reached a clearing where conifers grew small among grasses and brambles. Caizhiu halted when she saw the doe at the centre. She hadn't envisaged running into the animal this quickly. The fawns scattered, disappearing between the trees, but the doe stood in the open as if rooted.

Perhaps the sight of the dragon petrified the creature. Caizhiu took a few steps forward, expecting the doe to snap out of her stupor. But she didn't bolt.

Oppressive silence filled the clearing. The surrounding conifers swayed, but the grass within didn't move with the wind. The Sinuation-infused air prickled with dread. It radiated from the doe and captured both Caizhiu and Heort simultaneously. If either of them had wanted to flee, it was impossible.

"Caizhiu."

At the distorted sound of her name, the dragon's scales quivered in shock.

The deer's eyes rolled, but her legs remained motionless. Bones in the doe's jaw cracked and her throat twisted to force it to produce sounds it was never meant to. And still the animal lived. Whoever controlled her used her breathing, playing her like a musical instrument.

"Caizhiu, the Wayward One. You will answer me."

She had not had enough time to recover from her aborted flight, but she had to take her human form to answer the speaker in a verbal voice. Prying her joints into human form and condensing the tortured fabric of her being was excruciating and forced her "I answer" to erupt from her lips in a scream.

"I answer," she repeated with as much composure as she could manage. "Who is it I answer?"

"It is Ingrirath who speaks."

Caizhiu's legs gave way beneath her, and she landed on her knees in the tall grass. This shouldn't be. She couldn't conceive of the trouble she must be in for one of the Six Keepers of Sinuation to speak to her. She scoured her memory for a misdeed but could think of nothing.

Almost nothing.

But that had been a mistake, and so long ago. Why would Sinuation wait this long for retribution? Her hands grasped the dirt as if she needed to keep hold of the ground, cling to it as she had to the mountainside.

"Kneeling is not required," the Ingrirath-deer said. The forced voice was flat; Caizhiu could get no sense of the emotion beneath. She thought about getting up, but her body would not respond, and she could only hope the Keeper would not consider it insolence that she stayed on her knees. Surreptitiously, she opened her back eyes to take in her surroundings. If death was coming, she'd rather face it.

"I am not near you, or I would not have had to make use of this poor animal. Once I have finished, I trust you to despatch it. I had hoped to find you near the Magistrate, but I suppose I should have known better."

Relieved, Caizhiu concluded she'd survive at least long enough to do that for Sinuation's Keeper.

"Honoured Ingrirath, forgive my..." She didn't know. "Transgression?"

She forced herself to raise her head and look at the doe, though the image of the misshapen creature moving her jaws was stomach-churning.

"No need," the deer said. "I apologise for disturbing your iteration early. You have turned out well, though you may find your wings are not at full strength yet. But I have little time, and I have need of your service."

Caizhiu scrunched the grass in her hands. "You want to... hire me?"

"You have a reputation for finding things that have gone missing. A man called Ozcahar Nitt has vanished from my service, and landed on the Uayathan shore. He is lost and in need of justice. Will you bring him before Sinuation's Judgment?"

Ingrirath made it sound as if she had a choice, as if there was a possibility Caizhiu would say no. Caizhiu tried to order her thoughts, but her head seemed full of mud. It had been a Keeper of Sinuation who had pulled her out of her iteration. She had regarded their interference as a myth, a scary tale shared among dragons. Finding it to be true was shocking. However, if Ingrirath was willing to meddle in such a manner, perhaps she'd be able to help. Perhaps she could ensure that in Caizhiu's next iteration her mass would shrink, make it easier to retain her human guise. Perhaps she would; if she found Caizhiu worthy.

"Will you do this for me?" There was no mistaking the impatience in the deer's voice.

"Yes, of course, praised Ingrirath." Caizhiu bowed her head. "I wonder if in return, in your great—"

But, as suddenly as it had appeared, the Sinuation hold dissipated like a dream in morning's light. Beside her, Caizhiu heard Heort sob with relief. She grabbed hold of his coat to pull him close. Quaking, they held each other, Caizhiu's cheek pressed against the cervitaur's. In the clearing, the deer staggered, gagging and gasping through her broken throat. Her jaws flopped. Blood dripped down her long neck.

Caizhiu seeped an apology into her friend and let go of him. As she jumped forward, she transfigured. Knocking the deer to the ground, she tore the broken head from the body. The animal jerked and was dead. No lust was quenched by the kill. The doe's terror should have tasted good, but Caizhiu had never before smelled the sweet scent of fear on herself. She wondered if she'd ever be able to relish its scent with the same innocence again.

She ate perfunctorily, with the coldness of a human, just so as not to waste the deer's life. The expected disgust from Heort didn't materialise. Perhaps he too had more powerful emotions to deal with.

{I didn't recognise the language, but did I hear it say 'Ingrirath'?}

Caizhiu shuddered, and he did too. *{It was Aumegoan. And yes, it was her.}*

As if to compensate for his earlier immobility, Heort paced around the clearing with short and rushed movements. His tail twitched, and he fiddled with the buttons on his coat. *{But the Six only contact the Magistrates. What does that mean? What does she want with us?}*

{Not us. Me.} Caizhiu tore off a hind leg of the doe.

Heort backed off a little and straightened his coat, accentuating the difference between himself and the slaughtered animal.

{What does a Keeper of Sinuation want with you?}

{She wants to... No, she has hired me.}

Heort thought for a moment. *{We should talk to Gostawa, get the Magistrate's insight on this... strangeness.}*

FIVE

THE MAGISTRATE OF BLADRID

R attled by the encounter with the Keeper, Caizhiu had not returned to the hotel. Sleep had eluded the friends. Instead, they had spent the night under the star-speckled sky, watching the murmurations of the night fay's mating dances. Heort had mused how pleasant it would be to soar among the stars. Caizhiu had doubted her ability to fly to such a height, or even fly at all.

They had not discussed Ingrirath.

When they passed the Welcome Gate of Bladrid City, Caizhiu noticed how the dirt roads were now covered in smooth flagstones. Despite the early hour, the streets filled with humans. Bladrid had grown in recent years, much more so than in the previous hundred. Not that long ago, everyone would have greeted Caizhiu, but now there were many faces that she didn't recognise, scents of whole families she didn't know. They greeted her in a friendly enough manner, but as a stranger, reminding her that she had a new and unfamiliar appearance. By contrast, men, women, and children crossed the street to greet Heort, to shake his hands, run theirs over his rearback, or touch his antlers. It became difficult for Caizhiu to stay near him as the multitude managed, without any force, to work its way between them. If it hadn't been for her height, she would have lost sight of the cervitaur in the sea of hats, hoods, and headscarves.

{How do you stand this?} Caizhiu asked with something approaching pity.

{The burden of being a good luck charm.}

{A what?}

He shrugged and tried to pass a group of farmhands on their way to work, who all insisted on shaking his hands.

{It's a human thing.} He flicked his tail in embarrassment. *{They think touching me will bring them good fortune.}*

The man blocking his path smiled broadly and grabbed the cervitaur's cheeks. Heort touched the man's wrists. "May I pass, please?"

Caizhiu imagined how easy it would be to swat the irritating man and all his friends aside. But it was unnecessary. The farmhand stepped back without protest, and he even parted the crowd to clear a path for the little cervitaur.

{Does this happen every time?}

Heort nodded. *{Which is why I mostly chronochi through the city rather than walk.}*

They approached the largest building in Bladrid, the reason it had become a city rather than a town. Even though Bladrid had grown around it, the Magistrate's manse still looked extravagant compared to the other buildings. It had exotic red-brick decorations over the rectangular windows and a set of enormous double doors in the middle of the building. It looked designed to welcome larger Fabled, like hiisi or trezzohl, and was the only building that would be accessible in her true form. However, Caizhiu suspected that the reason for the entrance's extravagant size was to intimidate miscreants brought before the Magistrate.

They climbed the steps to the manse, and she put her hand on Heort's shoulder. He gave her a puzzled look.

{I'm just seeing if this good luck thing works. I might need it.}

One of the doors opened before Caizhiu could knock. They were greeted by a balding man who appeared the same indeterminate age he'd been when Caizhiu had last seen him.

It was unclear whether the Attendant recognised her, but with a glance at Heort, he said: "I will inform the Lady Azer you are here. Can I get you anything while you wait?"

Neither Caizhiu nor Heort needed anything, but politeness dictated they'd allow the Attendant to be kind. When they both requested water, the man bowed his head and disappeared.

Caizhiu looked around the enormous entrance hall. It perfectly reflected its current occupant, with ornate painted ceilings, tapestries, and statuettes of famous Fabled. Several doors on either side of the hall led to offices. The building, the centre of administration for the region, housed the council of the Trade Guild and the department of the Burgomaster. There were seats scattered between them where already people waited their turn. At the back of the hall, a bifurcated staircase twisted from the floor above their heads. Caizhiu grinned when she noticed the large portrait of a dragon on the wall of the landing. It wasn't someone she recognised and had probably sprung from the imagination of the painter.

Heort winked. *{It's meant to be you.}*

The painted dragon looked down menacingly at the wooden bench beneath it, as if it were about to devour the prisoners forced to sit there and await their fate. In Caizhiu's opinion it was an incredible amount of effort to daunt a couple of lowly pickpockets, which was the extent of criminality in Bladrid.

{I don't see any depictions of cervitaurs.}

{I'm just glad she covered that horrid marble.}

Unusually for the region, Lady Gostawa Azer had covered the floor with a myriad of Zarian rugs that must have cost her or the people of Bladrid a fortune. It made the building a muffled place, and much more comfortable for those with hooves.

{*Did you nudge her?*}

{*Of course not!*} He sounded offended but not entirely honest. {*But I may have suggested it.*}

The Attendant appeared with a tray with two cups of water and led them up the stairs to the Magistrate's chambers.

Gostawa herself opened the door to welcome them. Her headscarf, loosely draped over her shoulders, had a gold pattern featuring several types of Fabled. A dainty pair of spectacles decorated her face. By the delightful scent, both contained a trace of actual gold. Its aroma soothed the tingle of craving that had ignited within Caizhiu the moment she'd accepted her hunt.

The Magistrate walked to her side of the desk, but eyeing the delicate chair that Caizhiu wouldn't be able to sit in, she too remained standing. She let her Attendant put the tray on the desk and dismissed him with an exchange of nods.

{*The dragon Caizhiu.*} Despite standing on a raised floor and her high-soled shoes, Gostawa still had to look up at her. She pursed her lips. {*I see you've completed your latest iteration. It would have been courteous of you to inform me of your intention to have it here before embarking on it.*}

{*Courteous, but not obligatory. I informed the farmer Morailo whose land I used.*}

Gostawa bit her lip as if to physically restrain her vocal voice. {*Morailo Hilleram is not the Magistrate.*}

Heort placed a hoof pointedly on Caizhiu's foot. This was not the time to remind Gostawa that she was Magistrate of the Keeltois because Morailo had refused the role. To make matters worse for her, Morailo had been very successful. Almost a third of Bladrid's population was employed on the Hilleram farm, and many of its businesses depended on them. And now a dragon, who by rights should go through the city's sanctioned channel, had chosen to circumvent the office and deal with Morailo directly.

{*I suppose I should be grateful that you grace me with your presence at all.*}

{It's better than that, Lady Azer.} Caizhiu smiled. *{I'm here to ask for your help.}*

The Magistrate sank onto her chair.

{It is a notable day when Caizhiu the Wayward comes to my door for help.} Gostawa's soul song softened. She was as Talented as Morailo, but far more practised. Caizhiu had surprised her and for a moment Gostawa slightly over-shared. Her song carried undertones of curiosity and suspicion. Though she apologised in advance, Caizhiu shared as much of the experience of meeting Ingrirath with her as she could, terror and all. She included her own wonder at what might have happened if she had been in the Magistrate's office as Ingrirath had hoped. Gostawa paled at the thought. She pressed the fingertips of both hands together and then her thumbs to her chin. When her skin had regained its normal shade, she opened her eyes.

{May I?} She reached for the cup Caizhiu hadn't touched and took a few sips. *{I must admit, I have never personally been contacted by a Keeper of Sinuation. Nor, by the sound of it, should I wish to be. My communications have always been via more conventional means, letters and the odd courier.}*

{But have you been told about this Ozcahar Nitt?}

The Magistrate shook her head. Although her face betrayed none of it, Caizhiu got a glimpse of the disquiet at the core of the woman as she stood and paced to the window.

{Things appear to be changing, Hunter Caizhiu. This office...} She raised her chin at the wobbly human figures below that walked from one white-rimmed rectangle to another. The world looked warmer and hazier from the Magistrate's office. *{It means less and less to them. That is worrying in itself, but now it would seem that it means less to the Six as well, for them to contact the Fabled directly.}*

{All that we know is that Ingrirath,} said Heort, making a small triangular gesture of reverence, *{chose to hire Caizhiu to find this Nitt person. It'd be wise not to speculate what her reasons might be. Some paths only the Keepers walk, as they say.}*

The cup he picked up from the tray had a concave spout to the left of the handle, allowing him, despite the slight tremor in his hand, to pour the water into his mouth without spilling it.

Gostawa gave a quick but unconvincing nod at her reflection. Caizhiu wondered if she noticed anew her Aumegoan pink complexion and her straw-coloured hair, so uncommon in the Keeltois.

{Well, it certainly pains me that I can't be of more assistance. But it would seem you are on your own, Caizhiu.}

{Not entirely,} said Heort.

Gostawa turned to give him a curious look, and she pushed her spectacles back onto the bridge of her nose. *{I hope you are not suggesting you will be leaving us.}*

Heort shrugged apologetically. *{Yes, if Caizhiu will have me. I was with her on the mountain and so it would seem only right I accompany her.}*

Caizhiu was about to tell her friend to stay put, that she worked better on her own, but Gostawa beat her to it.

"Absolutely not!" The Magistrate finally gave in and spoke aloud. Her vocal voice betrayed the accent she'd spent years shedding. "Have you no care for this community at all?"

"Respectfully, the apothecary can take care of the few people I help."

"I think you underestimate your importance to these people." Gostawa planted her hands on her hips. "You are a symbol of good fortune, and you can't abandon them. I won't have it!"

Caizhiu remembered the annoying crowd below and let darkness flow into her soul song. *{Lady Azer, I hope you are not suggesting that Heort is not free to go where he pleases?}*

{No, of course I'm not. But he is part of this community, and we will be diminished by his departure. As Magistrate, I am supposed to look out for the people's interests with regard to the Fabled. Am I not?}

{Quite so.} Heort reached between them to put his empty cup back on the tray. *{Indeed, there are people I would like to visit before we depart. Not least, of course, the apothecary about Eslonya.}*

{*Both of us will leave on the morrow.*} Caizhiu locked eyes with Gostawa, daring her to protest.

{*That would be fine,*} Heort said happily and bowed at Gostawa. {*Obliged, Magistrate.*}

Caizhiu restrained a snarl and dismissed Gostawa's attempt to summon her Attendant. {*We will see ourselves out.*}

When they reached the double doors, Caizhiu turned to Heort. {*In what way do you imagine you are obliged to her?*}

{*I'm obliged to her for helping me.*}

{*Helping you how?*}

{*Getting you to agree I could come with you.*}

The cervitaur chronochi'ed away through the crowd. Caizhiu watched humans occasionally catch sight of him from the corner of their eye, look again, and dismiss it as imagination. He had evaded her just as skilfully. Being outsmarted by Heort was one thing, but by a human, even a Talented one, for that there was no excuse.

SIX

THE RACE AND THE FAY

Caizhiu glanced over her shoulder when the clattering of iron-rimmed wheels on stones was interrupted by something that sounded like a toad being strangled. The auto carriage took up the width of the road. Sunlight gleamed off the carapace rooftop. The wood was painted in the same colours as the bhodine roof – a dull purple marbled with dark green stripes. The driver braked harshly, and Caizhiu wafted at the cloud of steam and dust that enveloped her. Raccio opened the door of the cabin and leant out. "You're in trouble, Caizhiu. Where have you been?"

Torbel was sat next to his uncle and beamed. "I blew the horn. Did you hear it?"

Raccio thumb-pointed at the small copper instrument hanging from the ceiling and Caizhiu nodded at the boy. "It was hard to miss."

"I'm dropping Torbs off at the hotel. You wanna lift?"

Caizhiu leant into the cab. Though the carriage stood tall, most of the height was from the wheels, and the cabin itself was cramped. The top of Raccio's hat touched the ceiling.

"Do you like this... contraption?" she asked.

"Yes, obviously."

"Then I don't think I should ride in it." Caizhiu stepped back and closed the door. "But perhaps you'd care for a race?"

Torbel pulled eagerly at Raccio's sleeve. Raccio squinted at Caizhiu, stroked his beard, and looked at his nephew. "What do you think?"

"Yes!" Torbel shouted. "We can beat him!"

Raccio pumped the handle by the steering wheel and raised his chin at Caizhiu. "You ready, Dragon?"

She raised her eyebrows in response and the auto carriage moved off, picking up speed as it straightened up. Though it was just a practice, her veins buzzed with the excitement of a chase. Since she was going to hunt one, it was probably a good idea to try running in her human form.

The road sloped downwards, and Raccio did everything he could to increase the speed before it would incline again. Caizhiu's pace matched the carriage and Torbel shrieked with excitement when she appeared next to the window. Raccio's eyes were fixed on the road ahead, occasionally glancing at the controls. His lower lip was clamped between his teeth as the carriage bounded over the dips and bumps. Ahead the sign indicated the left turn to the hotel. Coldness settled in Caizhiu's chest. The cabin was positioned high on the wheels and the turn was tight. Raccio had left braking too late.

The road cracked under her feet as she sped up. Stones tumbled from underneath the wheels into the grass at the roadside and she jumped past the auto carriage. It lurched towards her. Two of the wheels span free of the ground. The door flew open. Caizhiu grabbed the top of the carriage with one hand while, with the other, she reached for the boy, who was propelled from the seat. Her feet dug into the ground as she pushed back against the weight of the careening carriage. The varnish cracked along the height of the frame as the wood bent. As if plucking him from a tree, she took hold of Torbel's jerkin, swung him towards her, and tucked him under her arm. The auto carriage straightened up, and the wheels fell back onto the road. Raccio slid across the seat, his momentum forcing the door open. He tumbled out and landed on his back.

Caizhiu held Torbel up under his armpits, careful not to squash his ribcage. He blinked as if unsure whether he should cry. Raccio groaned and staggered to his feet. Coughing in the dust and clinging onto the carriage, he walked round it. When Caizhiu handed him Torbel, Raccio embraced his nephew and sank to his knees, burying his face in the boy's jerkin. After a minute he looked up and checked him over. Finding him uninjured, Raccio mumbled hoarsely: "I'm in your debt, Caizhiu."

"That may be, but if your sister hears of this, neither of our lives will be worth living."

"Trueso." Raccio wiped a smudge of blood off his lip and looked around for his hat. He rose stiffly, and running his fingers over the rim of the doorframe, he whistled.

"That's a bit of a mess you've made of my auto carriage. Let's hope Sis won't notice. Still, it could have been worse. No damage to the axles, the carapace, or the engine. She'll run."

"She? Next, you'll be naming the damned thing," Caizhiu grumbled.

He accepted the hat that Torbel had retrieved from the verge. "Excellent idea. After all, they name ships, don't they? What do you think we should name my carriage, Torbs?"

"Nearly-fell-over?" the boy suggested.

"No, no, that won't do at all. Your ma would kill me. Keep thinking. We'll come up with something."

He lifted Torbel onto the seat and held up a warning finger. "This time, you hold on."

Torbel nodded. While his uncle walked around the carriage, he studied Caizhiu. "You were behind us. How did you overtake us to catch me?"

"We call it chronochi. It's a way to move fast, but only for a moment. I don't know what you'd call it."

"We call it cheating," Raccio said and started up the auto carriage.

She watched the vehicle continue along the track.

***

When Caizhiu walked into the yard, Raccio was helping Torbel climb out of the cabin. Moro dumped his tricycle by the well and ran to hug his uncle and beg for a ride in the auto carriage.

Eslonya followed, carrying a filleting knife, which made her appear menacing to those with a guilty conscience. She looked her brother up and down. "What in blazes happened to you? You're filthy."

He flicked a speck of dust from his shoulder and pretended not to notice the rest.

She frowned and, adopting a stern tone, said: "One of you'd better tell me what happened."

Raccio and Caizhiu exchanged a furtive glance.

"We raced Caizhiu!" Torbel bounced on his toes. "And we won!"

"I told you to drive carefully." Eslonya pointed at Raccio. "No more racing."

He held up his hands. "I won't. I promise."

"And you!" She pointed the knife at Caizhiu. "Where have you been? Do you think we don't worry, just because you're a dragon?"

"Caizhiu!" Torbel grabbed her hand. "Come see my collection."

She shrugged apologetically at Eslonya and pretended that she had no choice but to follow the boy to whatever he needed to show her. Moro said nothing but held Caizhiu's other hand. She allowed them to lead her through the kitchen and hallway into the sitting room. It was large enough to accommodate several adult humans in comfort, available to guests who stayed at the hotel. Today, only Morailo sat in one of the cosy chairs. He wore a small pair of spectacles on the tip of his nose as he re-hemmed a set of trousers. The pup by his feet got up and slunk out of the room.

Caizhiu ducked to avoid the ceiling lights. Despite the small windows, the room was well lit. With every bhodine carapace the family had placed on the roof, more of the flameless lamps had appeared through the house. Humans abhorred the dark.

Torbel gestured to Caizhiu she should sit on her heels. Careful not to lose her balance, the dragon squatted in front of the old fireplace. She had not seen it lit once. After the Great Blaze of the Keeltois, Kartarra had blocked the chimney. Recently, the fireplace had been screened off by a foursome of glass panels that resembled the Magistrate's window, making it into a cabinet.

"I only have three," Torbel warned so as not to raise her expectations, "and they don't shine."

The frame of the upper right window had a handle and the smallest keyhole Caizhiu had ever seen. Torbel fished the corresponding key from beneath his shirt and wrestled the necklet over his head, catching his ears several times before he freed it.

"Put on your gloves," Morailo warned without looking up from his sewing. Torbel sighed theatrically and took the set Moro handed him from the mantelpiece. They were too big, probably an old set his grandmother used to wear, and he struggled to turn the key in the lock. He opened the panel and reached in to retrieve a creature not even half the size of his little finger. It wriggled to escape the folds of the glove. Caizhiu had seen night fay many times. They were common throughout most of Uayath, Osos, and Aumegoa, darting dots of light that hunted nocturnal insects or danced in murmurations through woods and fenlands. She had never considered what they might look like up close.

"This is Iefyri," Torbel said. "I only got her one moon life ago."

The fay pushed herself through a gap between his finger and thumb. She slid onto his palm and turned over so that her claws could find purchase. Torbel stretched out his hand and held it closer to Caizhiu. It was hard to focus in on the minuscule creature. From the corner of her eye, she could see Morailo smirk and wave his glasses, but she shook her head. Standing upright the fay looked amusingly human, a similarly proportioned bipedal creature with two arms. What Caizhiu had mistaken for a mop of untamed hair turned out to be feathery antennae, and the tiny torso was covered in bristly and brightly coloured fur. But where her glassy wings should have been there was only a single torn stump.

Caizhiu extended a finger. Initially the creature stepped back, then grabbed her fingertip to pull herself up. There was no weight to the fay. She stood on the tip of the dragon's finger and her shoulders twitched, but her remaining wing-stub jerked uselessly. Instead of taking off, she tumbled backwards onto Torbel's hand. She tried again and flopped forward when her body wouldn't react as it was supposed to. Torbel folded his other hand over the top of her and placed her back in the cabinet.

He pointed at another fay who'd rushed in to pull Iefyri free from his hands. "I've named that one Artyni."

The two scurried and disappeared between the twigs at the back of their enclosure. A few of the larger twigs had been placed vertically against the cabinet window and bound together with strips of bark. The intricate tower nearly reached up to the access. Torbel picked it up by the tip. While he snapped the strips and twigs, one of the night fay climbed up. She beat, bit, and kicked his thumb, but he flicked her with his other hand, and she landed in the layer of sawdust on the bottom.

"Don't be mad," Torbel cooed at the fay, reaching into his pocket. "I brought you something."

He showed Caizhiu a heap of dead bees and put them into the cabinet. "From Aunt Doriana's hives."

He picked one bee from the pile and held it out to the night fay. She snatched it from between his fingers and hurled it back at him. The throw fell short, and the bee bounced off the window. Moro giggled and Torbel closed the cabinet door, locked it, and put the key back around his neck.

"I've had Siorri since last dry season. She's the reason I have to wear these." He removed the gloves. "It's really itchy when they bite you."

Moro looked at his grandfather. "Are they sisters?"

Morailo shrugged. "I don't think so."

"Do you have any brothers or sisters?" Torbel asked Caizhiu.

Morailo winked at her. "Don't tell them. You'll frighten them."

"We won't be scared. Will we, Moro?"

It seemed like yesterday that Morailo himself had sat cross-legged, staring up at Caizhiu, and asked the same question. He'd always been keen on siblings, possibly because his mother had only managed to carry him to term.

"May I tell them?"

"Go ahead, but if they wake up from nightmares, you'll have Eslonya to answer to."

Caizhiu stroked her chins as if contemplating it thoroughly while the boys jumped with eagerness to hear. She hunched forward and motioned for the boys to come closer. Folding her hood over the children's heads, she formed a conspiratorial tent.

"Dragons," she whispered, "don't have families like humans do. They lay their eggs, in a desert, in the woods, or on a mountain... anywhere. And in the eggs baby dragons grow."

"You were in an egg?" Moro asked with a naughty chortle. "Like a chicken?"

Caizhiu pursed her lips and frowned, but then she gave a nod. "The eggs were on the tallest mountain of Jitren. That's very far away. I grew and grew, and my egg became smaller and smaller. I knew I had to get out of my egg as quick as I could. Do you know why?"

They shook their heads.

"Because when a dragon hatches, they hatch very, very... *very* hungry."

Torbel cocked his head, trying to understand what she meant.

"So when I finally broke through the shell of my egg, what do you think I did with my brothers and sisters?"

Caizhiu licked her lips.

Torbel squirmed and scrunched his face. "You... ate them?"

"Yes!" Caizhiu tapped them on the back.

The boys shrieked, then giggled and fell about laughing.

Caizhiu pulled her hood back.

"So if I were a dragon, I should eat Moro?" Torbel grabbed Moro and tickled him. Moro screamed and ran away from his brother, who gave chase, smacking his lips.

"If you boys are going to eat each other, you'll have to do it outside," Morailo said.

The boys darted through the door. Caizhiu heard Mitzer's excited bark, happy to accompany them in their game.

Morailo chuckled. "After you told me that story, I went around for weeks telling people I'd eaten my siblings. When my ma heard she gave me such a walloping."

Caizhiu smiled. Eslonya might be formidable, but she had nothing on her grandmother. Kartarra Hilleram could have scared the naiad from the sea.

"Would you be honest with me?" he asked and shifted in his chair. She worried he might talk about her post-iteration lapse, but he pointed his glasses at the fireplace-cum-cabinet. "The night fay. Are they, as you'd call it, otherkin?"

Caizhiu frowned her confusion at him.

"I didn't mean a soul song," he clarified and rubbed his beard. "Sometimes, I wonder: are they talking, and we just can't hear them?"

"Even if they were, it wouldn't make them otherkin. Your dog barks, but you would not regard him kin." She faltered, realising her words could easily be interpreted as an insult. The Six had not seen fit to gift his offspring the ability to form a soul song.

She changed the topic. "Why does Torbel keep them?"

"He finds them, usually after a storm. One he got from a spider's web, I think. If their wings are intact, he releases them. If not, he brings them home."

"Why? They are not jungle fay, too tiny to make a meal of."

"He rescues them." Morailo's chuckle ended in a deep sigh. "I'm afraid he has yet to learn that sometimes compassion and cruelty are the same thing."

Seven

The Spell Spinner and the Thief

E ven the rain was different here, Ozcahar concluded. Of course, they had rain in Thirdburg, long periods of it, but inside the city it didn't affect you the way it did in the wilds. At home he could have traversed the entire city and never got wet. Until his hasty departure, he'd thought the whole world was like that. But here, rain came in waves. He watched it lash past the window of the dinky inn as if the world were on its side. Perhaps it was.

He'd never imagined such emptiness. Even from this first-floor vantage point, as far as he could see, there were only fields, the barrenness broken only by a row of willow trees lining the riverbank that meandered through the landscape. A desolate landscape through which he had to find his way alone.

There was barely any traffic here, and in this weather the few travellers he had met on the road were disinclined to talk, never mind pick up a hitchhiker. He'd been forced to walk. He didn't know where abouts he was, only that he was moving slowly – too slow, painfully slow. The backs of his heels were raw with broken blisters. The outsides of his feet and his little toes were red too. He'd been lucky to find this inn last night, but he had to keep moving and he could not continue on foot. He watched boats work their way up the river. That was it. He'd made himself useful on *Prosperity*; he could do that again. Those boats must be going someplace. It was probably his best chance at finding whatever passed for civilisation around here.

He'd make for the village harbour, but his first priority was to get sturdier clothes that would keep him dry. Still wrapped in the warmth of the bedding, he glanced at the dark patches beneath the chair over which he'd hung his doublet and trousers. Between the chair and the bed lay his socks and shoes, spaced erratically where he'd hastily removed them in the dark. Yesterday's soaking had warped the flimsy leather. The mere sight of them made his feet ache.

His underclothes were almost dry to the touch. He removed the belt from his damp trousers to put it on the other pair, but when he pulled them up, he noticed the set of buttons and no belt loops. Piss it! He hadn't taken the braces. The trousers hung around his legs and there was slack at the top; their previous owner had a larger physique. Ozcahar pulled the trousers up to his waist and tied the belt around his hips to hold them in place as best he could. Half-dressed, he hobbled to the sink. He wet his face and rubbed the worn piece of soap to a lather.

A knock on the door made him jump. He kept his razor in one hand as he cautiously unbolted the door. It was the innkeeper's son.

With an expression of embarrassed boredom, the lad asked: "Require you morning-food, sir?"

"Yes," Ozcahar said, but before he could think of the Trader word for 'please', the other had retreated down the stairs.

The lad had been the only man Ozcahar had seen without a beard. He touched his jawline with its day-old stubble. Perhaps he should leave it to grow, blend in. He dropped the razor in his bag and washed the soap off his face.

The blisters on his hands after his first day aboard *Prosperity* had healed already, which was due to the salve a shipmate had given him. Given him... in a way. Ozcahar had figured the seasoned sailor didn't have much need of it and had slipped the little pot into his haversack along with the man's spare trousers.

Walking down the stairs was agony, not just because of his feet, but also the aching of his calf and thigh muscles. He gritted his teeth and wiped the sweat off his forehead. He straightened up before entering the barroom, which was empty but for the landlord and his son.

"Good morning," Ozcahar greeted, pleased he'd remembered the Uayathi term. The landlord raised his eyebrows and repeated the greeting. He beckoned him to come over and sit at the table he'd just wiped.

Breakfast was a generous selection of bread, slices of cold meats, smoked cheese, and a boiled egg. It came with a fragrant herbal drink he didn't recognise. The taste was pleasant enough, but it left a filmy feeling on his teeth. He took several bites of the bread to get rid of it.

"Tasty-food?" the landlord asked.

"Yes. Good." A hollow answer. Ozcahar realised he'd polished off the meal with the rapaciousness of someone who didn't know when, or if, he'd eat again.

He inhaled deeply, releasing it slowly as he stood up and walked to the bar to settle his bill. His wages from *Prosperity* were shrinking far too rapidly, but he didn't have a choice: the road was too cold and wet to spend a night there.

"Require coat. Require..." He pointed at his shoes.

The landlord closed the till and said something Ozcahar didn't understand, but he interpreted the circular motion the man made as an instruction to walk around the building, back towards the village square.

"Grateful." He lifted his haversack over his shoulder and hobbled out of the inn. The sun was shielded by a thick covering of clouds that looked as if they had plenty more water to unleash. Daylight revealed the village to be little more than a collection of weathered buildings, the square a mere widening of the road with an oak tree in the centre. Only the inn and the chandlery looked well-maintained. Ozcahar noticed a shop that, in faded signs, advertised an incoherent assortment of items for sale. He entered and was greeted by an elderly woman he remembered seeing in the barroom the previous evening. She had remarkably red lips and grey hair that she wore in a complicated knot. Last night she'd sat alone in the corner, nursing a single tiny glass with a clear liquid.

"Aha!" she exclaimed in a raspy voice. "Require coat and hat."

It wasn't a question. She mimicked him walking into the bar last night, dripping over the floor. Before he could say anything, she'd darted through a curtain to the back of the store. Now that his eyes were used to the gloom of indoors, he looked at the eclectic collection of wares. Small iron items, assorted lengths of rope, a basket with root vegetables, and beneath the glass countertop he could make out a haberdashery of all sorts. There was an inviting jar of boiled sweets on the counter, next to the register.

The shopkeeper returned carrying a coat and hat. Given her sprightliness, she probably wasn't as old as he'd assumed.

The coat was heavy, a decent fit, though a little baggy around the shoulders. The shopkeeper straightened it. As she did so, the coat hugged him. It reached to his knees, and he figured the waxy material would keep the rain out. He tried on the hat. She tutted and took it off him to turn it the right way round. The price of the hat wasn't too bad, but the coat was as dear as he'd feared. It was a quality coat, but it cost him a third of his earnings from *Prosperity*.

As she handed him the pitiful change, the shopkeeper noticed his shoes and shook her head with a sigh. "Require boots."

"No coin," Ozcahar said.

"Little coin," she answered, pointing at his coin pouch. "Better no coin than no feet."

He couldn't argue with that and watched her disappear behind the curtain once more. She'd left the register open. She must have noticed he had limited means. This was her way of helping him out. He wouldn't take all of it, not even as much as he'd handed over, just take a few coins back. Not enough for her to miss.

The shopkeeper returned with a pair of rugged boots. Ozcahar felt embarrassed to take off his shoes, but she pressed a pair of thick, dry socks in his hand.

"With boots," she said and patted his hand. It felt wonderful to be able to put his clammy feet in the warmth of the soft wool. He sat a moment enjoying the feeling before trying on the boots. They seemed too large, but once they were on his feet, they felt snug and lighter than expected.

"Grateful." Retrieving his pouch from the haversack, he handed her the coins she asked for.

She held open the door, but as he passed her, she grabbed his wrist with such force it hurt. Ozcahar didn't catch her mumbled words, but he realised in that instant she couldn't be True Human because, though he wanted to, he couldn't move his arm, nor his feet. Not one single muscle. A spell spinner, he thought. He was caught.

"No do well here, thieves do." Her voice was a low hiss that echoed through his mind.

He wanted to protest, but his lips, tongue, and throat would not obey. He felt her other hand press on his middle, slide underneath the new coat to the pocket of his doublet. She retrieved the coins he'd taken as well as the boiled sweets. He wanted to explain, to apologise, but he could only stand there and suffocate. Would she kill him over a few sweets? His vision drew in for the lack of oxygen.

"Free you, yes?"

He couldn't answer, only hope for clemency. And then the shopkeeper released her grip. Ozcahar gasped to get air into his lungs.

"Be heedful, foolish thief."

Ozcahar stumbled backwards towards the door. "Y-you no human."

She took hold of the lapel of his coat and raised a warning finger. "No thievery from humans also."

He shook his head like a child scolded, and she shoved him through the doorway. "Be away from here!"

He landed on his backside, scampered to his feet, grabbed his haversack, and ran. Despite the pain, he kept running until he had left the village far behind him and the curse of the spell spinner began to wear off. His plan had been to go to the harbour and see if he could persuade his way onto a river boat. Instead, he was again on the dirt track, being rained on, and he'd have to walk for hours. Curse her! It wasn't as if she'd needed the coin. She had a roof over her head; he didn't. Curse her and curse his own stupidity. Jorganyon had called him an idiot, and he was right. The instructions had been clear: get as far away from Thirdburg as you can, and don't get caught. That was all he needed to do, and it seemed pretty straightforward. He couldn't trust anyone – not even his own instincts, it would seem – and he couldn't rely on his big brother to get him out of trouble. The last bit of help Jorganyon had been able to provide was to get him onto *Prosperity*. Ozcahar was on his own now. He'd better get smart quick if he wanted to survive.

EIGHT

ON THE ROAD FROM THE KEELTOIS

Three days after leaving the Hilleram hotel, Caizhiu and Heort reached the edge of the Keeltois. At the bottom of the slope, a small herd of bhodine trudged along a path that followed the river. When Caizhiu saw a few horses and a pony-drawn wagon too, she realised they weren't bhodine but a caravan of auto carriages. The train of travellers carried an enticing odour that caused a flutter in her core. She walked slowly, so as not to alarm those below.

By contrast, Heort nimbly skipped down the steep slope, waiting for her to catch up. *{How are we going to find this Ozcahar Nitt? We don't know where he might be, or what he might look or smell like.}*

{Normally I get more information from my employers, but I was... distracted.}

Heort cocked his head in recognition, agreeing to the euphemism for the existential terror from which neither had yet recovered. Normally Caizhiu negotiated via a Magistrate's soul song full of vivid details, not a human voice from the contorted throat of a deer.

{Ingrirath said...} Caizhiu felt her hand make the triangular movement. She had never felt the need to pay tribute to the Six before. *{She said he'd landed on Uayathi shores. He likely sailed from Thirdburg to the harbour of Sempeth. Travelling inward would lead him to Wexede Crossing, a city from where he could disappear in any direction. I hope to pick up his trail there.}*

They had nearly reached the tail end of the small group of horses and wagons: three auto carriages, three horse-drawn ones, and a few riders with a pack horse in tow. Two of the riders broke away from the caravan.

"Halt your approach!" bellowed a gravelly voice in Trader Talk with a strong Spao twang.

One rider approached them while the other waited. The horses were only lightly packed, but both saddles had at least one gun-scabbard; the approaching rider had two. Both riders held their reins with one hand.

Caizhiu stood still, folded her hood back with her hands and then held them up to the advancing rider to show she was unarmed. The rider on a large piebald horse came closer. Her hand rested on her flintlock pistol, but she hadn't primed it. The other rider had, but he kept it at his side, not quite out of sight. It was a warning, not a challenge. The odour of the approaching rider carried a blend of the southerly regions. Her eyes were hidden, but Caizhiu could make out a dark brown chin and long grey locks. The guide shook back her hood a little and squinted from Caizhiu to Heort. Her companion scanned the surroundings in case these two were only the diversion.

"Well met, friend. Be this road to Wexede Crossing?" Caizhiu asked, testing how well the guide knew the local roads.

"We travel to North Echor." The woman rasped it as if it were an order rather than an answer. "But ahead road splits. If you trek left there, you reach Crossing."

Despite her far-flung accent and mixture of scents, she carried herself with the confidence of someone who'd taken this route several times. "My name be Dysleer, and my men and I guide Nellepeth and Company."

Her horse snorted and walked back a few steps. She urged him forwards again. Caizhiu intensified the layer of human body odour in her own scent to trick the animal into tranquillity. The guide, sensing the calming in her horse, relaxed a little, though she kept her expression stern. "If you desire, you may trek-with till road splits. Friend."

She made the hand gesture that meant payment would be expected.

"Grateful," Heort said in Trader, and the woman raised her eyebrows.

Dysleer looked at her colleague and laughed. "You ever known one such as him that can talk?"

She'd switched to Spao, a vernacular that contained so many Zari words it could barely be described as part of the Uayathan dialects. Heort, struggling to understand the guides' exotic speech, cast Caizhiu an edgy glance.

"I never known any like him at all," the other answered with a sassy grin. "But I heard they live in the Keeltois and are meant to bring good fortune."

"Then you and your guardsman be welcome to trek-with," the guide said with a polite bow to Heort.

She trotted her horse past the vehicles that hadn't slowed while they'd had their conversation, to catch up with her spotter up front. While Heort bounded forward to mingle between the travellers, Caizhiu struggled to keep pace with the carts and riders without revealing her inhuman nature. She broke into a jog as if she needed to warm up.

On the right of the valley, grey clouds shrouded the Keeltois. The blanket rose and fell with the heaviness of the rain. Here and there the river water swamped the track, and the procession slowed to pass single file. Rain did not make for talkative humans. Caizhiu aided a horse-drawn cart by pushing a wheel out of the deepened groove, but the driver didn't turn around in the rain, only waved in gratitude. The clouds descended and covered even the valley road in fog. Caizhiu felt the tremor a few seconds before the distant thunder brought the entire caravan to a halt.

Her soul song found Heort, who, as she'd suspected, stood alongside the guide. She agreed with every impression he sent as the rumbling grew to a roar.

{Mudslide. It'll land a few hundred leaps ahead of us.}

While the people around her peered into the dense clouds around them, scarcely daring to breathe as they waited, Caizhiu chronochi'ed around them towards the front. The guide looked only mildly surprised. Then her attention was drawn to the crashing of sludge and stones hitting the valley floor. Mist obscured their vision, but the impact was close enough to shower the caravan in flecks of mud and tiny stones. After the barrage had quieted, Caizhiu shoved Heort forward. In the dense mist they could easily slip away unnoticed.

{Are we not going to help them?}

{They chose the road.} She could hardly be expected to stop for every idiot who underestimated the conditions. *{They'll be fine.}*

"The Six favoured us today," the guide said with faked bravado.

Heort cocked his head and gave Caizhiu a stern look with his dark-pool eyes. She hadn't realised he could muster that expression; it looked comical on him.

{They will not be fine. Surely you can discern what they are up against.}

The creatures' scent was hard to distinguish from the rocks and the dirt, but Heort was correct, as he usually was. Hunters waited in the hills. The least Caizhiu could do was warn the guide.

"Mud cut off your route, and you be trapped against a river rising," she whispered so the rest of the company wouldn't hear.

Dysleer's swallow was laboured. "Explain your meaning."

"It's hiisi that have you trapped."

The woman looked sceptical, but mostly to convince herself. She closed her eyes for a moment and then hinted at her underlings to approach. There were only three of them, one so young he struggled to grow a beard. Even if several of the travellers too were able to hold their own in a fight, the group was chanceless against the creatures.

"Be you certain?" the guide asked. She cursed under her breath, looked over her shoulder at the collection of riders and carts, and cursed again.

Dread infused the wet human smell and Caizhiu bit her lip to keep her focus on Heort. *{I have a job. Rescuing humans stupid enough to venture out in their flimsy contraptions isn't it.}*

Heort looked around at their temporary companions. *{I'm sure Ingrirath would forgive you that distraction.}*

The door of the cabin of the most ornate auto carriage swung open and a short, circular man climbed down. The metal honey scent Caizhiu had noticed as they'd approached the travellers wafted with him from his vehicle. He waddled over to the guide, positioning himself between her and Caizhiu. He spoke Spao. "What is the hold-up, Dysleer? When can we trek on?"

"Apologies, Mr Nellepeth, but our friend..." She nodded at Caizhiu and spoke Trader. "... think this be hiisi work. He well be correct."

The man crossed his arms. "What does that mean?"

"It mean we back-trek to Carpentru Passing—"

He interrupted her with spittle-filled expletives that shook his puffy jowls.

"Or we trek onward," she continued. "And, at dark fall, we face attack by hiisi."

"But you said we'd reach Kairgalan before nightfall."

The gruffness in Dysleer's voice hid her impatience. She switched to Spao, presumably to save her employer embarrassment. "Trueso, but that was before our path was obliterated, sir."

"It took us two days to get here from Carpentru." His tone vacillated between ire and sulk. "We can't take the mountain road in this weather. You said so."

Caizhiu cleared her throat and her mind. The scent around Nellepeth was intoxicating, better even than that of his fear. Ingrirath had made no mention of payment. She hoped Heort was right, and the Keeper would forgive her adding to her hoard.

"No back-trek to Carpentru," she said in Trader. "I offer help."

The man half-turned towards her, as if she had only now become important enough to notice, and glared at her from underneath his ornate hat. Caizhiu tapped her middle and ring finger on the palm of her hand to indicate payment would be required. She watched the river creep up the bank and was about to remark on it when Nellepeth sighed and asked: "You, fat man? What action be you able to do?"

"For only a tenth of the gold coin you carry, I take care of hiisi."

Dysleer bent to her employer as low as her mounted position would allow, let her hood fall to cover her face, and told Nellepeth that they had little choice but to let the stranger try. Caizhiu pretended not to have heard the words.

"Have we an agreement, sir?" she pressed him. Nellepeth was the only one who carried something she desired. "Have an agreement, you and I?"

Nellepeth rolled his lips from the inside of his mouth outward until they were pursed. Eventually he spat: "Yes, we have an agreement. But I warn you. If this situation was by your design, I report you to Magistrate quicker than you blink."

Caizhiu suppressed a smirk and turned to Dysleer. The guide reached under her cloak and held out a scabbard. Caizhiu nodded appreciatively but declined the weapon.

"Grateful, but maybe you require it yourself. You have a lot of people."

Dysleer raised her eyebrows, shook her head, and hung the scabbard back on her belt. "You be brave or fool, friend. May the Six aid you."

"Better move your carts up higher, away from the river."

Dysleer followed her glance at the rising water. She was going to say something, but Caizhiu had disappeared into the wall of clouds.

The air filled with the scents of freshly upturned earth and splintered tree trunks. Caizhiu took care not to trip over the stones that had rolled away from the path of destruction. She knew Heort was beside her before he appeared from the dense grey.

{Ah, now that there's gold in the game you want to help. What's your plan?}

Caizhiu handed him her haversack. *{My plan is that you look after my hoard and find the easiest way over the mudslide for the caravan, while I talk with the hiisi.}*

NINE

THE HIISI

In the silence of the shrouded hills, Caizhiu heard the beat of droplets that fell off the vegetation under the slight tremors of approaching hiisi. Every so often a bush or branch snapped back when something large walked past. Though they were close, she couldn't make out how many there were. The hiisi were a secretive race. Caizhiu had encountered them only a handful of times. They were formidable, at least as tall as she was in her human form, and likely they sensed her approach as well as she could theirs. This was their terrain, their hunting ground.

Had she not chronochi-sidestepped it, the boulder that landed next to her would have flattened her. The hillside shook with its impact. Had they seen her or merely reacted to a sound she'd made? Caizhiu crouched beside her unexpected cover and adapted to the enveloping white. Their footsteps could be felt more than heard. As they neared, she made out the scraping of claws on stone. The two hiisi slowed when they approached the enormous boulder. As she blended herself against the rock, she heard their snuffling, seeking her scent, and she caught a sense of their confused song. One of the hiisi emerged from the fog. The silhouette looked humanish, but as the creature approached, Caizhiu saw the characteristic horns spiral away from the broad head, protecting the neck. There were few marks on them. Caizhiu guessed this was a junior member of the troupe. It wore a leather breastplate and a horse's hide across its shoulders.

The hiisi walked up to the boulder and placed a calloused hand, big enough to encompass half her head, on the stone right next to Caizhiu's face. Three protuberant eyes took turns retracting into a puckered blink as it tried to find its victim. The hiisi slowly opened and closed its wide mouth, masticating the mist. She caught a glimpse of a blood-red tongue and serrated teeth. As far as Caizhiu knew, hiisi didn't predate humans. They showed more interest in their livestock and other possessions, but since they had no qualms about killing humans during a raid, she wasn't sure. It wasn't uncommon for travellers to go missing. Who knew what happened to them?

{Greetings.}

The hiisi jumped back like a startled cat and crouched in anticipation of an attack. The horned head whizzed round, eyes blinking furiously, in its attempt to find her. Though she couldn't hear their conversation, Caizhiu felt the prickling of their soul song as it flew back and forth. It pinpointed each hiisi, one two paces away, the other behind the boulder, a couple a little further up the hill. From the concentration of song, a fifth, standing on their newly created boulder field, was the troupe's leader.

Caizhiu chronochi'ed next to it, but the leader wasn't as easily startled as its minions. In no previous encounters had a hiisi engaged her in a physical fight, but this one attacked with surprising speed, wrapping its hands around Caizhiu's throat. She dropped herself backward, grabbed the hiisi's arms, and placed her foot against the creature's crotch. It didn't have the debilitating effect it would have done on a human male, but she managed to lift the hiisi, and as they tumbled down the field of stones, she broke its hold. A stone-filled fist struck her jaw, knocking her head against the ground. She rolled to the side, and a boulder smashed against the rock, narrowly missing her. She got up and fended off a stone thrown from the opposite direction. The troupe leader cornered her between two towering boulders with a rock in each hand. She ducked as one smashed above her, raining smithereens upon her. Snarling, she shoved her opponent to the side so that it, not she, caught the full barrage of stones its troupe hurled at her. A rock the size of Caizhiu's fist hit the hiisi in the temple. It staggered and shook its head. Caizhiu didn't wait. The creature was positioned downhill from her. She transfigured into her true form, then spread her wings and used them to propel herself towards it. The force of her impact knocked her opponent off its feet. They landed hard, her weight winding the hiisi. Before it could recover, Caizhiu clamped her jaws onto its horns. The bruise where the hiisi had struck her stung as she bit down. The hiisi howled, then grabbed hold of her jaws, cutting its fingers on her teeth. Blood and saliva dripped onto its face. Her claws slipped through the chinks in its leather armour to find the flesh beneath. Her jaw muscles strained to crush the horns, and with a pop, a tip broke off.

{Are you willing to talk now?}

The hiisi squirmed. *{Yes.}*

She placed a claw on the creature's throat, two talons feeling the throbbing of its pulse. *{Tell your friends to sit and be still. If so much as a pebble falls near me, you die.}*

She let go of the hiisi's head and looked to see the others obediently plopping onto their backsides. One sat on its haunches but, under her baleful gaze, got all the way down. Now that it was no longer staring up into her glowing gullet, the troupe leader gasped for breath.

Caizhiu didn't wait for it to regain its composure. *{You will not interfere with the human travellers below.}*

{Are they yours?}

She spat out the tip of its horn and flooded her soul song with conviction. *{They are.}*

{Is it just these humans, or is the road yours?}

{Just these humans.}

The hiisi sniffed and considered whether it could live with the loss of one quarry and tried a proposition. *{Would you take the gold and leave us the rest?}*

The smell that wafted from the valley was tempting: the aroma of hot horses and humans intermingled with gold overtones and a smattering of cervitaur. She conceded that, under other circumstances, it was a good offer, but not for her.

{These humans are under my protection.}

There was a brief pause and a flutter of conversation between the hiisi. She felt the leader's throat gulp against her claws, and it sang: *{You'd be the dragon Caizhiu then.}*

{I am she.} Caizhiu removed her talons from its throat and stepped back.

As their leader got to its feet, the other hiisi shuffled, unsure whether they too would be allowed to get up.

The troupe leader rubbed its throat. *{These humans are yours.}*

Caizhiu transfigured into her human form to show off her lack of injury. It was agony. Even when the muscles had settled, her face continued to throb.

The hiisi looked at her in puzzlement. Then it sighed in relief as if it had figured out why she'd chosen to diminish herself.

{The humans are unaware you walk among them,} it said admiringly. *{And you can devour them when you please.}*

***

The cloud cover retreated up the hill and, despite the approaching dusk, her vision cleared when she approached the caravan. The humans hadn't progressed as far as she'd hoped, but further than she'd feared. They'd managed to climb up out of reach of the water, but having left the road, moving the vehicles over the trees and boulders strewn haphazardly by the mudslide was arduous. Each rider had dismounted, and the horses were utilised to either pull wagons or carry luggage, lightening the load. Humans pushed and pulled vehicles or busied themselves moving debris out of the way. She even espied Heort with a rope attached to his harness, attempting to pull an auto carriage out of a cleft in the rocks while humans pushed it.

She looked for the piebald horse. She couldn't see him, but she did spot Dysleer at the front. The guide was coaxing two exhausted ponies to move forward. Caizhiu joined the two women, looking as worn out as the animals, who were pushing their wagon. With her help they passed an enormous boulder, half-buried in the earth. It had been there a long time before the hiisi had created their boulder field, and had diverted the onslaught of mud, trees, and stone into two streams, creating a small clearing in its lieu.

Caizhiu walked to Dysleer. The woman stood bent over, hands on her knees, gasping for breath between bouts of coughing. She spat a glob of phlegm on the ground and winced as she straightened her back.

"The hiisi no be trouble." Caizhiu had meant to sound authoritative but had forgotten the state of her face and how painful using her vocal voice would be. "We must use here for place-to-rest. You no can dark-trek."

Dysleer took a swig from her waterskin and, after clearing her throat, addressed the company. She instructed the women with the wagon to pull it to the side. As Dysleer rasped instructions, Caizhiu made her way to the last carriage, the one Heort was pulling. The rope attached to his harness was strained tight. Caizhiu grabbed the rim of the auto cart cabin and leant forward, her weight helping to shift the vehicle.

Half an hour later they'd managed to get the last wagon to the clearing. Caizhiu had surmised from the conversation between Nellepeth and Dysleer that the group had anticipated they'd reach the village of Kairgalan and spend the night there. That was before the mudslide. Though the vehicles were designed to carry freight and didn't have living quarters, the humans were too tired from their ordeal to care about the poor sleeping conditions.

With his legs folded beneath him, Heort had propped himself up against the wheel of the carriage. His eyes fluttered open, and he smiled weakly when Caizhiu sat down next to him. She leant over to untie the rope from his harness, and he nestled against the warmth of her condensed body.

{I think I might experience muscle ache tomorrow.}

{Trueso for us both.}

He studied the side of her face and tenderly reached up. *{I see you had a good talk.}*

Her wry smile exploded a throbbing ache across her face and even down her neck. His touch eased the pain, and she wondered if that would work on his own body too.

Awkwardly, he reached behind him to find the right pocket. With a triumphant smile he fished out a little glass jar and grabbed her hand. He folded all but one finger into a fist and smeared some of the ointment from the jar on her index finger. *{Daub it onto your gum, as high up as you can manage.}*

The bitter taste almost covered the stinging she felt when she touched the swollen flesh.

Dysleer and Nellepeth walked over. Their unsteady pace sounded as if both were in physical discomfort and trying not to show it.

"Your return suggest success." Nellepeth crossed his arms. His demeanour notwithstanding, he looked even less imposing than he had earlier on. His lavish head covering was gone, revealing a bald cranium surrounded by a wreath of wispy hair.

Caizhiu sighed and said: "The hiisi be dealt with."

Dysleer looked at the half moon occasionally visible between the rushing clouds. "We crave fire, but I no want people to dark-walk for dry-wood."

"Good-thought. Hiisi no likely be only ones prowling misty-hills. Where be your spotter?"

"He ride to Kairgalan on fast horse. In case you no return and those-who-live, if any, require aid."

Even in the low light, Caizhiu saw Nellepeth's eyes widen. Perhaps he only now realised the life-and-death situation he'd been in. How long would that comprehension last once the immediacy of their peril had passed?

"I do first watch," the guide said. "I wake you in three hours."

Caizhiu nodded and watched them stumble away. She wouldn't be able to sleep without losing her human form. She would just sit and heal.

Dysleer stopped, stood for a moment, then turned and walked back towards her. Carefully she lowered herself onto her haunches and whispered: "Who be it that join this company?"

"He be Heort. I be Caizhiu."

Dysleer swallowed hard and avoided Caizhiu's eyes. She looked at Heort instead. "Apologies, your name have no meaning for me."

There was little energy in his dismissive shrug.

Moonlight caught her eyes as Dysleer glanced up at Caizhiu from beneath her grey curls. "But you... they tell us you appear as warrior woman, Honoured Caizhiu. I no foresee I ever walk a path to owe you my life."

"My form be new. And you no have debt to me, Guide Dysleer."

Dysleer stood up and rubbed her chin. "Grateful. But perhaps advice be of value to you. You ought let your companion do-speaking, so people think you be his servant. People give fewer questions."

She bobbed her head and wandered off to watch over her charges.

Caizhiu's gaze followed her until the guide was one with the shadows of the camp. Gold or no, she was pleased she hadn't left the caravan to their fate.

Ten

Shadows in Kindalk

Despite the rain, the dock of Kindalk was aflutter with activity. Villagers and sailors milled around the ships, hurriedly loading goods from and to carts. Fierce gusts of wind whipped over the low buildings and threatened to rob them of anything not strapped down. *Wexede Wanderer* was coming in fast, heading into the wind. Her verve engine thumped at full strength against the current.

Ozcahar stood a few paces forward from midship and kept his eyes fixed on the rapidly approaching quay. He tightened his grip on the rope and his legs caught the rolling of the ship. The water jumped up at him as it sloshed between the hull and the quayside. He counted down the distance. To his right, a man called Detrone, with dark brown skin and a reassuring smile, leapt forward, and Ozcahar followed. Beneath him a ball of rope rolled and creaked as it was squeezed against the jetty. It was an easy step off the barge, but he still felt relief when his feet touched the solid wood.

He rushed to the cleat and tied the rope fast, glancing at Detrone, who was doing the same at the front cleat. The engines had slowed and Ozcahar ran towards the stern to catch the line the first mate, Narastien, threw him. Her tense expression softened and broke into a grin once he'd secured the third line.

"Good-work, Baby Face."

He wasn't entirely sure what had earned him the nickname, but he guessed it was his lack of whiskers. He'd stopped shaving, but his fair hair took a long time to make a visual impact.

Narastien hopped over the side of *Wexede Wanderer* and landed gracefully next to him. The first mate was short and slender. He liked her. She looked more Aumegoan than anyone else he'd met here. She wore her blonde hair not only loose, but short, without the complicated braid structures he'd seen on other Uayathan women. She checked his knots and showed him her fist with the pinkie finger raised. The gesture that was an insult in Aumegoa seemed to mean something positive here.

The crew spoke a mixture of Trader and Uayathi, fluidly switching mid-sentence, which made it impossible for Ozcahar to follow. But the skipper, Tijs, was precise in his orders, making sure his newest crewmember understood what was expected of him. He stepped away from the wheel and caught their attention. A wiry man with silver hair and a neatly trimmed beard, Tijs was most times softly spoken, unless the situation required a louder response. Then he managed a volume incongruous with his slender frame. Ozcahar only made out a few words, but one of them was 'verve'. Since Narastien jumped back aboard, and disappeared below deck, he surmised the skipper had told her to check the engine which had been running for longer than he'd anticipated. As indicated by his curses along the way, Tijs had pushed them harder than he'd have liked on account of the racing current.

"Ozcahar, you aid Detrone."

He was getting used to the local pronunciation of his name, with the 'uh' sound instead of the 'oh' and emphasis on the final syllable. The skipper never used their nicknames.

Ozcahar nodded and joined Detrone securing the plank to the quay as gusts of wind pushed it back up. Once they'd managed to strap it down, they made their way to the hold. In his melodious voice, Detrone indicated which crates contained the vegetables that were intended for the cart. There were a lot of crates and it took a good half hour for them to unload and aid the driver of the cart with the covering of the wares. Then there followed more freight that needed to be shifted onto carts, and equipment for the vessel itself that needed to be brought on board. They weren't finished until dusk set in. All the while, rain fell steadily, spreading the lights from the buildings in rivulets snaking to join the raging river.

A sharp whistle attracted their attention, and Ozcahar and Detrone turned to see Narastien and Tijs walk off *Wexede Wanderer*. The first mate waved them over.

"Pissing weather no quit!" Narastien grumbled and steered the group towards an alleyway where the overhanging roofs would protect them if they walked single file and dodged the odd waterfall. It was dark between the buildings, but the first mate never hesitated, confidently turning left and right. Not that long ago, Ozcahar would have been able to navigate Thirdburg's web of walkways with similar ease.

Finally, Narastien stopped at a small recess between two buildings with a worn metal door. It swung open, and they walked in. As they entered, the patrons greeted them with excited clapping and hollering. At first Ozcahar thought the enthusiasm was due to the popularity of his shipmates, but then a trio of musicians in the far corner started to play.

It was pleasantly warm. People stood shoulder to shoulder in the snug barroom. The first mate indicated they should take off their wet coats to hang them in a niche by the door, and she grabbed his hand to pull him through the throng. Ozcahar felt his pockets and realised he'd left most of his coin aboard *Wexede Wanderer*.

Narastien noticed his expression. "No need for worry, Baby Face. We provide hardy-food." She squeezed his bicep and grinned. "We require you be strong. No hungry-hand."

They used the area between the musicians and the patrons to head to the bar. The gaunt barmaid acknowledged them with a quick smile and continued serving the waiting customers. Just then the flute player, a plump woman with bronzed skin and shiny black hair, broke into an intricate and catchy solo. Over the metal of her instrument, her deep brown eyes caught those of Tijs, and she danced around him, closer and closer. His eyes never left hers and he matched her movements, revealing a playfulness that surprised Ozcahar. They swayed for a few moments, pelvis to pelvis, until she spun away from him, back to the depths of the other instruments. Tijs exhaled through pursed lips, watched her for a couple more seconds, then continued to the bar. Most of the people were on their feet, unable to resist the music, so Narastien easily found them four bar stools. Detrone grinned, nudged Ozcahar, and chin-nodded at the skipper. Tijs rested his cheek on his hand, elbow on the bar, and stared back at the flautist.

"Careful, Skip," Detrone whispered with a smirk. "I wager she have nixes blood."

Tijs cleared his throat and grinned at his sniggering crew. He tapped the bar, and the barmaid walked over. She wiped away a wisp of hair that had escaped her braids, slapped Narastien on her forearm, and asked Tijs for the order. Obviously, this was a regular stop for the *Wanderer*'s crew.

Ozcahar couldn't believe his luck at having found them. When he'd reached the village of Wexba yesterday late in the afternoon, he was ready to collapse. He had sat slumped against one of the upturned sloops by the side of the single jetty that was the harbour, watching the river racing past. Having found the weather more than a match, a fair number of ships had sought shelter. Just as he'd groaned to his feet to look for shelter himself, he'd noticed *Wexede Wanderer* and Detrone struggling to hold her. Without thinking, he'd dumped his haversack and joined the man on the rope. Together they'd kept the vessel from drifting into the one next to her. It turned out to be his best decision in a long time.

The barmaid set a tankard of foaming ale in front of him. He held it up to Tijs and gave a nod. "Grateful, Skipper."

Detrone growled at him, baring his teeth. "Rrrr," he said. "Grrrate-fyl."
Narastien laughed and corrected Detrone's own accent: "Grrrah-tfyl."

The three of them tried their versions of the Trader word and decided that, since there was no authority on the matter, and they'd all understood the meaning, they must all have pronounced it correctly.

After his days on the road and the work today, Ozcahar had thought he'd be exhausted, but he didn't feel tired at all. He turned to face the room and to watch the three musicians. Closest to them stood a man with a rich-sounding violin. He wasn't as flamboyant as his two comrades: the woman with the flute and another with a higher-tuned violin. The women moved gracefully as they played, twirling amid the undulating crowd. All three had the same shiny black curls. The women had theirs piled up high and the man's cascaded down his back, nearly to his waist. Occasionally he shook it out of the way of his instrument. People tapped their feet and swayed, breaking out into dance where space allowed or intoxication demanded.

Narastien touched his arm and pointed at the crispy bread, nuts, sausages, cheeses, and items he didn't recognise fried in batter that had appeared on the bar. Detrone reached over and grabbed a handful of nuts. One by one he skilfully flicked them into the air and caught them in his mouth. Proud of his accomplishment, he beamed at Narastien.

"Impressive." The first mate shook her head and handed Ozcahar a tiny spear and demonstrated her own stab, dip, and munch technique.

The food tasted delicious, though one of the dipping sauces was spicier than Ozcahar would have liked, and, to the hilarity of his companions, he drained his tankard in one go. It was quickly filled up again, and it took some restraint not to gulp that one down too.

"What name has this?" He pointed at the sauce.

"Maspho," Narastien said.

He practised the word, hoping to avoid the stuff in the future, though he doubted he'd remember the name in the morning. There were too many things. Sailing on *Prosperity* and *Wexede Wanderer*, the names of the towns, the Trader words, the workings of a river barge, and strange bar food. And always looking over his shoulder.

Though the crowd thinned out as the evening went on, the enthusiasm of the remaining clientele only increased. The female violinist held her instrument and sang. The tune inspired cheering and several people joined in, with various degrees of success. Narastien grabbed both Detrone and Ozcahar by the hand and led them to a space in front of the musicians. Ozcahar watched Detrone rock awkwardly from one foot to the other, realising he looked just as silly. Luckily someone joined an arm with his so he could follow, or at least attempt to follow along. Narastien locked her arm through the other and pulled in Detrone as well. She managed the footwork well, but either through drink or inexperience, most of the dancers resembled bumbling bhodine more than night fay. This only seemed to heighten the merriment.

A few songs later, Ozcahar felt a tap on his shoulder. He turned to see Tijs wearing his hat and coat, indicating it was time to go. Ozcahar manoeuvred himself through the dancers to the niche where he'd left his own. The floor was wet, but the cloth of his coat was mostly dry. He turned and collided with Detrone as he struggled to get his arm into his sleeve. Awkwardly they passed each other in the confined space, and Ozcahar headed for the doorway. Tijs and Narastien already stood outside in the alley, collars raised against the fierce wind. Above the doorway of the establishment, a single verve lamp swayed. Shadows danced away in both directions and disappeared into the blackness of the alley.

Ozcahar stood swaying as he tried to fix the misaligned buttons of his coat. It struck him that he should have visited the outhouse before he left. After he hobbled a few steps after his companions, he decided nature wouldn't wait. He found a corner untouched by the lamp light and hurriedly removed the minimum amount of clothing to allow him to pee. It took a long while for him to empty his bladder, and when he was finally able to tuck himself away, he stood in an empty alley.

Barely any light shone past the shutters of the buildings. Even when the moon deigned to show her face, the overlapping roofs shielded her light from the narrow passageways. They no longer reminded him of the airy walkways. Thirdburg was a bright city even in the darkest night, a shining jewel by the coast, a beacon. This place was a dark maze. The walls that earlier had provided shelter appeared ready to topple over on him.

He sloshed through leftover puddles by the sides of the alley. The narrow streets echoed. More than once, he found himself listening out for footsteps that turned out to be his own. He pressed his fingernails into his palms, and it was as if his clothes fit tighter around his chest. He cleared his throat, ready to call out without letting his voice betray his unease, when someone beat him to it.

"Ozcahar."

He quickened his pace, letting his fingers slide over the wall and keeping his other hand out in front of him. He found a turning and went left, following the noise.

"Ozcahar!"

He was getting closer. Was that Detrone? His fingers lost the rough brick feel of the wall. He found a corner and rounded it. Fleeting moonshine illuminated a small square. He walked into the light and studied the buildings around the square for familiarity. Buildings looked different with their shutters closed. From the corner of his eye, he caught a shape separate itself from the blackness.

On the edge of the buildings' shadow stood Jorganyon. The recognition that surged through him felt like relief. And then terror. This was not, could not be, his brother. He alone had boarded *Prosperity* for Sempeth. Even if Jorganyon had left Thirdburg, via whatever route he had taken, he could not be here, now. Could he? Jorganyon, or whoever this was, held out his hand towards Ozcahar as if to beckon him, then ran down an alleyway. He was about to follow when a hand grabbed his shoulder.

"You be... huh... like frightened fish," Detrone said with a half-smile. "I shout for you. Why you no come?"

Ozcahar bent double to catch his breath. He tried to laugh but didn't quite manage it. The sound he produced was like the whine of a startled dog.

"I see…" He pointed to the alleyway the apparition had disappeared into, but he remembered in time not to mention Jorganyon. "I think I see someone… Go that way."

"See you somebody you know?" Detrone frowned. "Somebody who no here? Maybe you see nixes."

"What be nixes?"

"River wraiths," Detrone said darkly, but with an incredulous smirk and a teasing twinkle in his eye. "No mess with nixes."

Gingerly they walked into the alleyway. It was hard to tell in the darkness, but the narrow street seemed to be deserted and Ozcahar sighed with relief when the street opened up to reveal the docks. Clouds covered the moon, but the area was lit faintly by the mast lights. Ozcahar looked around, but the only human shapes he saw were Tijs and Narastien standing by *Wexede Wanderer.*

"Next time," the first mate said, "you muddleheads, piss before we go."

Ozcahar looked over his shoulder at the empty harbour. There was a lot of movement in the shadows, but it was just the breeze playing with coverings and the oscillation of the mast lights.

"What problem has Baby Face?"

"He be chasing nixes."

Ozcahar shook his head and blushed. "I be drink-fool. There be nobody."

Detrone soft-punched Ozcahar in the arm and the first mate laughed. She held out her hand to help Ozcahar sway over the plank.

"Definitely drink-fool," she said.

Narastien opened the door to the down below and turned to step onto the ladder when there was a deep splash in the river, as if something the size of a man had jumped in between the ships. The first mate looked up at the others with a wilted smile. Nobody said a word as Tijs locked both doors before they went below to their cabins.

Eleven

Nellepeth's Payment

Compared to the haggard company he was in, Nellepeth looked remarkably stylish in a clean dark green leather coat and hat with a gold trim. The raindrops bounced off them in the same way they did off Caizhiu's own wing cloak. At last, the hillside ahead of them was boulder free, and Nellepeth puffed as he climbed onto the driver's seat. When he pumped the lever, the engine hummed to life. Vehicle fog enveloped the wheels, and he carefully steered the contraption towards the clear road, his helper scurrying to keep up on foot. Once the carriage was on the road, Nellepeth rubbed his hands together and made way for the younger man to do the driving. He himself took a seat in the luxurious compartment. The compartment Caizhiu knew also contained his gold. *Her* gold.

Thanks to Heort's ointment, her face was hurting less, but one of the women she'd helped with her ponies insisted on constant conversation, which Caizhiu could have done without. The woman had no useful information to give and spoke mostly nonsense.

"You be true folk," she said, patting the seat next to her, "to kill hiisi and keep human road safe."

Caizhiu thanked her but declined the ride.

The woman pulled a face. "You want work for Dysleer, not for..." She made fists with her index fingers stuck up and put them to either side of her head. "Them."

Caizhiu decided to walk to the front of the caravan, where she found Heort in cheerful discussion with Dysleer. She noticed that whenever the guide's eyes threatened to meet hers, Dysleer looked down. By contrast, Nellepeth glared at her out of the little window in the carriage door.

Heort and Caizhiu walked between the two groups, auto carts in front of them and horse-drawn ones and pack horses behind.

{I've found a use for you.}

{Other than patching up your face?}

She tried to think of the right word to use. "How is it going... boss?"

{Are you feeling quite well?}

Caizhiu tried on a grin, but residual pain dampened its vivacity. *{Something Dysleer said last night, about how for humans it is acceptable if I was your... What do they call it?}* She sent him an impression of the young man following Nellepeth around. *{Your servant.}*

Heort continued with slightly bouncier steps, his hands in his pockets. Had he been human, Caizhiu felt sure he would have whistled.

When the road diverged from the river, the muddy track became firmer underfoot, and the company fell into single file, lining their wheels up with the two grooves on the grassy trail. Fraakywuld Forest stretched all the way west to the Rerpa river, between the Marsarin Massif and the marshes of the Wex Delta. Without a word, the group bunched together. Even though the road only skimmed the large forest, Caizhiu smelled apprehension in many of the humans. They called it the Dreadwoods.

She knocked on Nellepeth's carriage. "Turning to Wexede Crossing be soon ahead."

He unbolted and removed the piece of glass from the window in the door, releasing the honied scent of gold from within. Caizhiu had the impression he knew exactly what she meant, but as he'd decided to play dumb, she elaborated. "Soon we part company, and we have an agreement."

He leant towards the window. "The so-say hiisi on the mountain."

"The agreement be that I take care of hiisi so you onward-trek unharmed. I keep my word."

Nellepeth smiled, but his eyes remained in a scowl. "You say it be hiisi. But nobody see hiisi. You only little be present to help us cross landslide. How know I you encountered hiisi? How know I you defeat them? Trueso, you no even bring a head for proof."

"I no say I kill hiisi, only I take care of them." Caizhiu put her hand on the edge of the window, leant towards it. "I do so."

He laughed and gave a challenging half-smile. "You agree I no can know if you keep our agreement. Perhaps you wish we consult the Trade Guild at North Echor."

"I have business elsewhere, and I no trek to North Echor. You pay me what you owe." She opened the carriage door, grabbed Nellepeth by the front of his fancy coat, and yanked him out of the cabin. His eyes bulged in his sallowing face. She held the heavyset man close, enjoying the aroma of gold and fright. After the hiisi, he felt like a feather in her grip. Nellepeth pushed against her chest and stretched his legs to touch the ground, the tips of his boots skimming the grassy path. The wind took his ornate hat, and as it landed on the trail, it was trampled beneath the ponies' hooves.

His face reddened and the man's gurgling sounded loud in the sudden silence. Caizhiu kept walking but realised she was overtaking the carriage that had slowed and stopped. The riders upfront halted and turned to block the path. Dysleer turned her horse around. She held her pistol trained on Caizhiu, but her hand was shaking. A confrontation with Dysleer was not what Caizhiu wanted, nor had she intended to embarrass the guide. She set Nellepeth on the ground and held her hand up to Dysleer. The woman didn't lower her pistol until Caizhiu lifted an eyebrow at her and released her employer's lapel.

Dysleer let out a wavering breath as Nellepeth made a show of coughing and gasping as if Caizhiu had held him by his throat. He glowered from Dysleer to Caizhiu, but now that his life was no longer in danger, the guide holstered her pistol.

"Pay me what you owe."

Nellepeth balled his fists.

"I pay!" Under his breath in his Spao dialect, he added: "But I will also raise a grievance with the Trade Guild at North Echor."

Caizhiu stepped aside, and Nellepeth boarded his carriage to retrieve the gold. She flowed the scent of gold over the roof of her mouth. When he re-emerged from the cabin, he dropped a little satchel in Caizhiu's hand. She felt a warm glow spread from her lungs through her whole body. For a split second she wanted to uncoil herself, let the glorious sensation fill every inch of her. Instead, she opened her eyes, decided that the amount he'd handed her was close enough to a tenth, and dropped the satchel into her bag. She grabbed his arm and pressed something into his palm with enough force to make Nellepeth wince.

"When you arrive at North Echor," she hissed in Spao, "give my compliments to Khost Bartos. I hear he is still head of the Trade Guild there."

She patted his shoulder, almost knocking him off balance. As she walked past Dysleer, she tossed the guide a couple of coin for the journey and looked around for Heort, who was already right behind her and followed her into the trees.

With a puzzled expression, Nellepeth held up the tip of a hiisi horn.

Part II

TWELVE

THE BRIDGE OF WEXEDE CROSSING

With the Fraakywuld to their backs, grassland stretched out before them like a beige blanket. Here and there pools of rainwater had gathered in shallows, mirroring the pale blue of the sky. Black and white birch trees, their delicate leaves still deep in bud, were scattered among the swaying reeds. For the first time in three days, Caizhiu managed a grin without pain shooting up her jaw.

{You're in a happy mood.} From his lower vantage point, Heort couldn't see the horizon, as the plumes of grass reached up to the cervitaur's chin.

{Once we've crossed this plain, we'll get to Wexede Crossing.}

Heort placed a hoof between the tussocks. Caizhiu laughed at his cry of disgust when it sank into the mud. He fell forward and both his front legs bored into the sucking sludge. He clutched at the tall grass but struggled to pull himself out. After watching him fail for a few moments, Caizhiu squatted and placed her hands under his arms, raising him up until he could place his hooves back on solid ground. With a stroke of her thumb, she wiped a fleck of mud from his cheek.

{This would be so much easier if you'd mastered your wings,} Heort grumbled. *{We've got a nice open space before us. I'd get to keep my hooves dry.}*

{And I would end up face down in the mud instead. I think not, my friend.}

They were far too close to the road, and in this wide-open space, would be visible to any travellers. She'd rather jump off another mountain than expose herself here.

Caizhiu trudged through the sea of blades, leaving deep footprints that quickly collapsed into a muddy furrow. Heort tottered after her, jumping from tussock to tussock, muttering all the way. Once they reached the road – a sandy track fortified with slats to allow the distribution of the weight of laden carriages and wagons – their progress quickened. The sun hadn't yet reached its zenith when the outline of Wexede Crossing appeared on the horizon. Its bhodine roofing and the blue sky made the town shimmer as if covered in jewels. Caizhiu imagined how glorious it would be to approach the city from the sky.

When they reached the Welcome Gate, they were overtaken by a pair of large auto carriages and an ox-drawn wagon. From the rear of the covered wagon, a little girl with long brown braids poked her head through the cover. She looked Heort up and down. He waved, and she returned the gesture. Caizhiu rolled her eyes. The canvas flap opened wider and a firm hand on the girl's shoulder guided the child back into the wagon.

Wexede Crossing welcomed trade from far and wide, and humans of all complexions and cultures thronged in the streets.

Heort sniffed and snorted. *{Does this place always smell so bad?}*

Caizhiu nodded. The pong was caused by the multitude of perfumes and powders with which the humans cloaked themselves, and it had grown worse over recent years. It wouldn't be easy to find the right Aumegoan trace in this hodgepodge of fragrances, especially since she didn't know what her quarry smelled like.

Though the city was busy, it surprised Caizhiu the humans barely gave Heort a second glance. His appearance was so unusual that it had to startle them. Instead, people walked by with less purpose than normal but greater haste, like panic but with a different undertone. When the friends reached the city centre, the source of the consternation became apparent.

The pride of Wexede Crossing was the three-arched bridge across the river that had lent the city its name. However, where the famous bridge should have stood, only stone stumps remained, the river raging over the ruins. The harbour was filled with barges and smaller vessels unable to depart due to the rubble left in the river. On the downstream side, vessels were fastened to improvised moorings and people were trying to offload the cargo via tenders.

"When happen this?" Caizhiu asked a woman carrying a heavy bag of foul-smelling linen from the quay to the road. The woman dumped the linen onto a little cart with a patient-looking dog.

"Two days before." She spoke Trader with a Houtgem accent so thick Caizhiu guessed she originated from the Ede peninsula. "Praise to the Six that nobody be hurt. So much rain. Terrible. Require you river crossing? These skippers, they charge too much... too much... It no be fair on merchants. They be raking in coin, but they no pay me more."

The woman shook her head and walked back to the quay to get more soiled clothing and bedding. She was busy with her washing service, but it was little wonder that the city was full of aimless people. Barges and other river ships had arrived from Sempeth and Edemont and were either unable to dock or were trapped in the harbour. Merchants continued to arrive by road, expecting to cross or offload their wares onto the ships. Locals stood around and clicked their tongues at the sight of the damage.

{Are you enjoying this?} Heort sang her some disapproval.

{Wexede Crossing has become a perfect trap. My pr... my target's options of escape have halved.}

{Unless he's on the other side of the river.} He nodded at the row of bridge stumps.

{There is no harbour at Tolldrift. That's why they built the bridge. From Thirdburg, Ozcahar Nitt will have *to come through Wexede Crossing.}*

No doubt the Trade Council had their collective hands full with the travellers that gushed into the city, but it would still be polite to advise the Magistrate she was here. She'd made that misstep with Gostawa and didn't want to repeat it. Human they may be, but Magistrates were also the representatives of the Six.

In Bladrid, the Law and Trade Guild building was a grand purpose-built affair. Here, the Trade Guild had repurposed one existing building, then another. It now occupied four houses, gutted to form a single dwelling. As they approached it the crowd swelled. Several times she lost sight of Heort. Eventually Caizhiu grabbed his harness and lifted him up as if he were a carpet bag. Once they were in the lew of a backstreet, she set him down.

{I do not appreciate this!} He straightened his jacket and flicked his tail.

Caizhiu tried not to smile at his annoyance. *{I'll make it up to you in a minute. Time for you to be my boss.}*

{Don't suppose there is a way to dismiss you, is there?}

At the far end of the alley, Caizhiu pressed her shoulder against a locked door and forced it open. She preceded Heort into a wide office with a low ceiling and three rows of clerks that turned as one to look at the intruders. Surprise, confusion, and anxiety filled the room and fixed the clerks to their seats. One of them cursed when a drop of ink landed on the paperwork they were transcribing, and the clerk closest to them, a weary woman with tightly wound brown hair, stood up.

"Apologies for this disturbance." Heort walked from behind Caizhiu.

The woman glanced at her colleagues then genuflected to him. "May we help you?"

"My boss seeks an audience with the Lord Magistrate," Caizhiu said.

"The reception is that way, sirs." The woman pointed at the double doors across the room, but then decided to escort them. There was a slight waver to her voice when she said: "I will ring Attendant Tannermere to alert her to your presence."

She eyed Caizhiu warily to see if that was acceptable.

Caizhiu bowed her head in gratitude. "That would be helpful."

To her dismay, she found that the inside of the building was as busy as the street outside was. Ushers tried to corral the mass into order, but agitated merchants moved backwards and forwards, trying to tussle past each other to a Guild representative. In the far corner, a little brass bell chimed on its metal coil, but Caizhiu thought it unlikely it would help.

"Shut up!" The voice was so high-pitched it cut through the noise yet powerful enough to arrest people. Sensing her authority, the throng obeyed and as one turned to look at a woman in a purple dress, the bright-coloured garment compensating for her short stature. It narrowed severely at her middle and widened at the hips. She cocked her head and flashed the crowd a smile that was just a little too wide. Her pile of golden hair jiggled with the movement.

"Obliged." With a simple hand gesture, she quieted any objection and continued in her penetrating sing-song voice. "Now, you people will sit on the floor if you cannot find a seat and you will await your turn without causing further hassle to my staff. Or you may leave."

Heort wormed past Caizhiu, catching the eye of the woman in purple. She strode towards them through the parting crowd, a cloud of dead roses accompanying her.

"Welcome, Esteemed Guest." She curtsied to Heort, gracefully bending at the knees, and raised her eyebrows at Caizhiu.

"I—" Caizhiu caught herself and, with a sideways nod at Heort, said: "My boss is here to see Lord Magistrate Veentar."

The woman waved for them to follow her. In her wake they bypassed the crowd. Caizhiu expelled the flower aroma from her nostrils before it made her sneeze, noticing Heort shake his head too. The maze-like corridor took random turns, led up and down steps, as it followed the structure and unmatched floor levels of the different buildings.

They followed the Attendant until they reached what had once been the grandest building in the street. The walls were decorated with portraits of former Magistrates and Burgomasters, all the same size.

"A moment, please," the woman said to Heort. "Who may I say is here to see him?"

Her eyes flitted to Caizhiu, who answered with a straight face: "The cervitaur of Bladrid."

The frown passed over the woman's face and she studied Caizhiu, even stepping back to get a better angle. Then she disappeared behind the office door.

{You know her.}

Caizhiu allowed her mouth to curl into a half-smile. *{Myrta. Yes, she's a good sort.}*

{Yet you don't mind toying with her. Perhaps you are not... a good sort.}

{Perhaps.}

The door opened, and the woman stepped aside to let Heort enter. The room was expansive and brightly lit. Its carpet was the same purple colour as the woman's dress and the wall opposite was lined with broad-leaved plants in copper pots. Papers were piled up across the office floor in neat but haphazardly placed stacks. Gigantic, detailed drawings of the late bridge, or possibly a new one, covered the Magistrate's desk. As Heort stepped forward his hooves sank in the raised shag.

The region's Magistrate, Lord Yullorik Veentar, straightened up from the drawings and walked towards him. He was a broad man with unrestrained brown curls, and he held his arms wide in greeting. Then he closed his right hand over his left fist and bowed. Heort copied the gesture.

Caizhiu stepped forward, and the Attendant coughed. She gave Caizhiu a pointed stare and arched her eyebrows. Without an explicit invite, as a servant, she'd be expected to retreat and wait outside in the hallway. Caizhiu hadn't considered that aspect of her ruse.

{Heort!} she urged.

He turned and only then noticed she was not right behind him. Unaccustomed to deceit, he licked his nose and stammered in worse Trader than usual: "Please join-in, Caizhiu."

From the corner of her eye, Caizhiu saw Myrta's mouth fall open.

"I knew there was something familiar about you," the Attendant hissed under her breath. "You cad!"

Yullorik coughed and frowned at his Attendant. "That will do for now, Myrta."

Her dress restricted the movement of her back, so she gave a little curtsy and retreated backwards, closing the door as she left.

{I see my Attendant has recognised you, Hunter Caizhiu.} His soul song betrayed his irascibility and his exhaustion. *{Though you have a new appearance and I freely admit I struggle to see the resemblance to the woman we knew.}*

Heort sighed. *{She is the same.}*

He bowed at Yullorik, even placing one front hoof behind the other. *{My name is Heort and we're grateful you can see us at this no doubt busy and fraught time.}*

{And you bring business from Bladrid?} Even when they didn't use them to speak, humans found it difficult not to let their thoughts reflect on their faces. Caizhiu saw the Magistrate's lips form a taut line. Rather than dealing with Fabled, he wanted to concentrate on the bridge, the responsibility of the Trade Council. She remembered this about him.

Caizhiu raised her eyebrows, but the Magistrate barely noticed. She didn't bother with sympathy. *{I am here to inform you that we are hunting a man called Ozcahar Nitt.}*

The Magistrate squeezed his eyes shut and ran his finger and thumb over his forehead, then shook his head. *{The name is not familiar. I'll have Myrta check our records.}*

Yullorik looked at Caizhiu and his forehead creased. He stroked his cheek with his thumbnail as if he wanted to say something but wasn't sure how to. *{This man... Does he bring trouble?}*

Yullorik's head was full of images. Seven years ago, she'd grappled with an incubus called Naayanax at Wexede Crossing and the hunt had caused damage. She remembered it as trivial. However, the owners of the wrecked boats and demolished buildings had disagreed. The Magistrate's memories agreed with them. Part of him even wondered if the destruction of the bridge was somehow connected to her reappearance.

{We'll certainly try to keep out of your way, Lord Magistrate,} Caizhiu assured him, barely able to keep indignation from her song.

Thirteen

The Surprise in Narastien's Garden

Ozcahar's back ached, his legs ached, and his arms ached, but finally they had reached the warehouse. Since the *Wexede Wanderer* couldn't enter the harbour, Tijs had resorted to hiring a cart. The crew pushed the cargo up the riverbank, the slow trek towards the city involving pulling and pushing the cart along the road. It had taken all day. Only in the last hour had the road become firm enough for their feet not to slip on the mud and grass. Ozcahar let out a sigh of relief as he sighted the warehouse. It was the sweetest thing he had seen in a long time. With renewed energy, he helped to unload the goods off the cart and stacked them as directed.

"Well done." Tijs looked at each of his crew with a broad grin. He walked over to Ozcahar, who respectfully got up from the crate he'd slumped on. The skipper counted out the agreed upon payment into Ozcahar's palm and asked: "You sure you no travel longer with us?"

He spread his arms at the cargo and the warehouse beyond. "The river be difficult, and I require good-crew. You be good-crew."

His own desire to agree surprised Ozcahar. Would he be able to stay hidden on this little barge, keep his head down and live a wholesome life? No, it was too close to Sempeth, too close to Thirdburg, too close to what he had done.

"I must travel further. Grateful for work."

Tijs slapped his shoulder. "Good-trek to you, friend."

Loneliness flooded Ozcahar as he walked towards the doors, and he almost changed his mind. Then the bustle of people that moved up and down the street swallowed him. The sun was setting and bathed the scene in an orange glow. Ozcahar looked in both directions to get his bearings. He ran his fingers over the Trader symbol for Harbour that was carved into the wall and decided he'd follow the flow of people in that direction. Wexede Crossing might only be the size of one district of Thirdburg, but on the street it made little difference to his experience. He missed the ladders and high-level walkways, but the sensation of people engrossed in their business was the same.

He jolted when he felt a tap on his shoulder. Grasping his haversack, he turned around to see Narastien.

"Still a frightened fish, Baby Face. Many-people frighten you?"

He shook his head. If anything, he felt more at home than he had since he'd set foot on Uayathan soil.

"Know you where-to you go?" There was a lightness to Narastien's step, as if she hadn't been grafting her guts out. As if she wasn't carrying her heavy bag over her shoulder. As if she wasn't twice his age.

Ozcahar looked around and shrugged. "Require place-to-sleep."

She bit the side of her bottom lip. "City be busy with no bridge. Little space for place-to-sleep. You no be good-crew, no more. I no be boss. I have home-house. You require place-to-sleep."

The little Trader Talk he knew went for a short wander, and he mumbled incoherently. He hoped his surprise didn't show. How embarrassing it would be if he misconstrued her meaning. Such a mistake might be considered an insult, or even a crime. He didn't know. He felt the weight of time passing as he searched for the right words, any words.

"I... I... ehm... no stay in Wexede Crossing. I travel further."

"You no travel further this dark. You seek place-to-sleep." She winked at him and indicated that he should go with her. "You wish bed-company?"

He had not misunderstood her, and an errant smile spread across his face. He straightened the haversack over his shoulder, and with a cautious look around, he followed her through the melee to a curious-looking building. It was situated on a broad three-way intersection with the front facing the middle of the junction. Three broad stone steps led up to a set of rounded double doors, on either side of which the walls of the building receded into the buildings next to it. Where it stuck out above the surrounding buildings, it formed a full hexagon.

Narastien walked up the steps to the front door and set down her bag.

"What be this place?" He took a step back and almost knocked into a velocipedist, who cursed, swerved, then continued up the street. Mumbling an apology, he looked up at the building. It wasn't high enough to describe as a tower, but it had a second floor. The surrounding houses only had one.

"This be home-house."

Ozcahar whistled to himself as she unlocked the doors. She went ahead of him into a shallow anteroom and disappeared through a set of heavy curtains. He felt a brief sting of hesitation before he followed her, wondering who or what might await him. Floral perfumes permeated the house. He rubbed his nose and glanced around the trapezoid lounge. Two tall windows looked out on the streets leading to the junction, their angular tops mimicking the building's shape.

Narastien shouted something he didn't understand, and after a moment of listening for a reply that didn't come, she shrugged. She pulled shut the wine-red curtains with their gold embroidery and turned on bhodine lamps on the back wall. Between the two lamps hung a large painting that reached to the ceiling. It depicted some sort of winged monster, a theme that was followed in a collection of statuettes on the low cabinet that stretched the length of the back wall. Ozcahar ran his finger over the polished surface and stroked a few of the precious objects. They were made of silver and gold; a few had jewels for eyes. He wondered if he could slip his nail underneath the tiny ruby on a gilded horseman.

Narastien picked up a small piece of paper that was placed between two figurines. He couldn't read the writing, but the message brought a satisfied grin to her face. She stood so close to him they nearly touched. He noticed that, unlike her, he hadn't left his muddy boots in the anteroom, and he felt the weight of the filth that covered him. He clamped his arms to his sides. "Apologies."

His companion seemed to guess his thoughts and chuckled. "I be equal mess." She stood on her tiptoes, put a hand on his arm and her lips to his ear. "Require wash, you and I."

She took his hand and led him through a little hall into a courtyard at the back. It was unexpectedly large, with two lights that illumined stone steps leading to flower beds. Their colourful cascade had not yet reached its full glory. The third light lit steps up to a waterless fountain. He watched Narastien climb up to the fountain and empty a layer of rainwater and the odd petal from it. Sitting on her haunches, she looked at him over her shoulder and smiled. She removed her doublet and beckoned him to come closer. While she pulled her tunic over her head, he adjusted his trousers and obeyed. Her short blonde hair stuck out at funny angles. She looked small against the budding blooms and the stone basin. The lights played over her pale shoulders and breasts, and the rest of the courtyard dimmed into shadow.

"You also, Baby Face," she said, unclasping the belt from her trousers. He hoped it was too dark for her to notice his blushing. Silently he cursed his embarrassment. As if that stupid nickname wasn't bad enough.

He cleared his throat and walked to her, leaving his coat and, after a struggle, his tunic on the steps. When he'd taken off his boots, he hesitated and looked up. He tried to imagine where he was in relation to the streets beyond, but the oddly angled building and the shadows made this difficult. Narastien stood stark naked by the empty basin of the fountain. If a husband was going to jump out of the shadows, she wouldn't likely have stripped. He took off his trousers, but remembering the note, he arranged his clothes so that they were easily grabbable should he have to make a hurried departure. She beckoned him to come closer, directing him to get into the basin. He covered his penis, less timid than he, with his hands. Careful not to slip and fall on his ass, he stepped into the basin. It was so deep that, sat on the side, Narastien's eye level was only slightly higher than his.

"Sit, sit," she said.

"W-why?"

"Be surprise, Baby Face."

Ozcahar wanted to point out that as he no longer worked on *Wexede Wanderer*, she had no business using his nickname. But it was probably better if she remembered him like that.

"I no like surprises," he grumbled, glancing at his pile of clothes.

She trapped the tip of her tongue in her grin. "You like this one."

As soon as he sat, Narastien pulled on a rope. He heard a clink, the rush of water. He held his breath to brace himself against iciness that was about to crash down on him. Instead, he was drenched in wonderfully warm water that filled the basin.

"Best feeling after harsh travel. Trueso?" She beamed at him.

He laughed in relief and lowered himself in the steaming water to escape the chilly air. "How this heat?"

She pointed at the roof, but it was too dark to see what she wanted to show him. "I no good know. Verve power, like *Wanderer*."

She dipped a toe in, flicked water at him and he let his gaze drift up her leg. Aware he should show gallantry, he sat up and reached out to help her step into the basin. As his hands moved up from her hips to her waist, to her breasts, his earlier hesitation dissipated. Straddling him, she bent forward to run her fingers through his hair. He kneaded her buttocks, and she pressed her lips to his. Her thighs squeezed his sides. Ozcahar wanted to be careful not to hasten the finale, but as she lowered herself on his crotch, he knew he'd have little control over that. And that was fine by him.

FOURTEEN

THE THIRSTY DRAGON

Despite the approaching darkness, the sound of conversation filled the air. Usually as evening set in, travellers would find shelter or rest for the day ahead, but with the prospect of an unproductive day, they stayed in the bars and the streets. Wexede Crossing had become a trap. Solemn patrons occupied the long tables outside The Thirsty Dragon. Two men walked out just as Caizhiu and Heort approached the door. Their faces were grim, and their luggage seemed to weigh heavy on their shoulders.

"No trouble yourselves," the one said with a shrug, "no place-to-sleep here."

Some taverns had signs stating people were welcome to spend the night on their floor, an attractive offer for a traveller soaked on the river or the road, but The Thirsty Dragon did not. Caizhiu held the door open for Heort and she sensed him push down his discomfort at the confinement and smoke-filled air. He coughed, which drew stares, and then, one by one, the clientele turned their attention back to their conversations. Caizhiu picked out only the distinctive Crossinger drawl in the muffled voices.

Most sipped their drinks and smoked in silence. Three men were engaged in a game of Long Shot. One moved an icon over the spiral board that covered their table. Another eyed him, stroking his beard, as he shook the dice, hoping for a turn of fortune.

Caizhiu swallowed a string of curses when she walked into one of the ceiling beams, obscured in a layer of grey. She was forced to crouch to navigate her way through the cramped room. Apart from smoke, the hoppy scent of spilled beer, road dirt, and stale human sweat filled the air. The low light emanated from scattered candles on the tables.

Caizhiu walked to the bar, placed two hands on it, and chin-nodded at the barman. He was lanky, but with some podginess around his middle. Over the years she'd noticed the receding of his hair until it was all gone and only his bushy eyebrows remained. The lines around his dark eyes hinted at a lifetime of forced friendliness.

"Greetings. You know me as Caizhiu," she said and nodded at one of the pumps. "My friend will have a Sinuation's Kiss and I will take the Dark Oblivion."

The man bit one side of his lower lip and studied her face. "I used to know a woman by that name. How did I know her?"

"You are a friend of hers. Seven years ago, you helped her track an incubus and she paid you with a rare gold coin. Your father told you he named this establishment after her."

"He never told me why, but it is true that he did." The man put two large tankards in front of her. "It is a title then, rather than a name. My apologies, sirs, I have no rooms available. What with the destruction of the bridge, there are lots of travellers looking for places to stay."

"Anyone of them called Ozcahar Nitt?"

"Is that Aumegoan?" The line between his brows deepened. "Can't say I've had any Aumegoans in here lately. Do you want me to keep an ear open?"

Caizhiu put the coin for the drinks on the bar, ensuring she gave more than the required value. The bartender met her eyes, took the coin, and nodded.

"Well met again, Caizhiu."

Caizhiu and Heort turned to see Myrta standing in the doorway. She'd ditched the restrictive purple dress and changed into an indigo frock coat over a pair of pantaloons and donned a tall thin-brimmed hat. The sweet aroma that covered her scent was even stronger than before, stronger than the smoke. She grinned and tipped her top hat. "I thought we might find you here."

She strode in, dragging a woman in an ankle-skirting grey dress and a blue jacket behind her, and ordered two drinks. Caizhiu smiled at Heort's double take at Myrta's hair. She had undone the elaborate pile and tied it with a simple ribbon at the base of her neck. Her companion, who hadn't looked up at them yet, had a red braid that peeked from under the hood. The loose styles would be considered scandalous in the Keeltois region.

"Let us sit and catch up properly." Myrta found a free table at the back. "Oh, I nearly forgot. This is Euvie." She pulled round a chair for the woman to sit. "Lovely, these people are Heort from the Keeltois and the hunter Caizhiu."

Euvie bowed. If possible, she looked even more out of place in the bar than Caizhiu, and more uneasy in it than Heort. Her auburn hair was matched with thousands of freckles that covered her face. Her grey dress had a frilly collar that covered most of her neck.

Heort looked at the chairs and scanned the room. Finding a lack of stools, he tucked his legs under him so that the table was level with his chest. In the shadows of the corner, and out of sight of the humans, Caizhiu uncoiled part of her tail to sit on her chair.

"Have you found any record of Ozcahar Nitt?"

"Straight to business, eh?" Myrta took a swig of her drink. "No 'how have you been', 'it's good to see you', or 'when did you get married'?"

She nodded at Euvie and Heort. "I see this new iteration didn't give her more manners. Is it still 'her', or should I say 'him'?"

Caizhiu shrugged. "I have not changed, just grown. How you speak of my human appearance is of no significance."

Myrta frowned, chewed the inside of her lip, and took a sip of cider. She played with a strand of her long hair. "So, out of curiosity... Trueso, which are you?"

Caizhiu's eyes narrowed, and she gave a lopsided smile. "A dragon."

"So I've been told, but I've yet to see any evidence of that."

Caizhiu handed Heort his tankard and he looked sceptical as she drained half her own drink in one gulp.

"Did you say they named this tavern after you?"

She grinned and wiped her mouth with the back of her hand.

Heort held the heavy tankard with both hands and tried to coax the liquid into his mouth without spilling most of it onto his coat. "What is this?"

"Sinuation's Kiss, a honeyed birch wine. I thought you'd like it. You should take a cue from the sign," Caizhiu said and nodded at the emblem behind the bar depicting a green dragon with its head in a barrel of beer. "I've never seen a drunk cervitaur. Expect you look like you did earlier, on the mud."

Heort hesitated, but then dipped his snout into the tankard. Caizhiu turned to Myrta. "So, did you find any trace of my pr... of Ozcahar Nitt?"

"I have clerks checking our records, but so far we have found no one called that on any crew list or making any application. But we've had a lot of travellers stranded here. It'll take us a while to catch up." Her eyes lit up. "What you want him for?"

"I've been hired to find him."

"That's dragon for 'I don't know'," said Heort.

"I like him." Myrta elbowed Euvie, who nearly spilled her drink. Touching her tankard to his, she asked: "What are you doing with old sourpuss here?"

"She's my friend. I think she'll need my help."

"I don't." Caizhiu emptied her tankard. "Unless it's to get another round in."

The others stared at their near full drinks. Still, Myrta stood up to go to the bar and came back with more drinks. Heort looked at the second tankard in front of him, rubbed his face, and blinked.

"I would guess," Myrta said, "that the ship from Thirdburg has arrived in Sempeth as it does every two moon lives. Normally, we'd expect an influx from there. But with the weather we've been having, anyone transporting cargo up the Wex might have been delayed. And if he travelled by road... Well, who knows?"

"You have contacts with the skippers. Perhaps you can have a word with a few friendlies."

"I already have, but it would be helpful if you told me a bit about your target. What he looks like, his age?"

"Unfortunately, we know only his name."

"Forgive me for saying so," Myrta said, "but isn't tracking a mere human beneath your skills?"

Caizhiu shrugged. "Trueso."

"Were it not for the fact that the human is wanted by the Six Keepers of Sinuation," Heort added.

Myrta snorted her cider out of her nose. She ducked under the table to cough, and her face was bright red when she re-emerged. "What did you say? Did he say the Six?"

Euvie had a far-away look on her face and dragged the tip of her finger through the ring her tankard had left on the table, drawing the interlocking symbol of triangles in the cider and condensation.

After a moment of heavy silence, Myrta whispered: "Did... Lord Veentar say that? Is that why he sent for you? He didn't say anything to me." She glanced at her wife and added: "Of course, you don't have to tell us. I mean... if it's a secret."

"Lord Veentar did not send for me, and he seems to have enough on his mind not to trouble him with this," Caizhiu said, glaring at Heort.

Myrta whistled. "You didn't tell him. You are placing me in an awkward position, and you've only just got here. Was it, what's her name, Lady Azer, that sent you our way?"

"It's not a secret, but I'd choose my moment to tell His Lordship if I were you." Caizhiu gulped down her ale. "And no. Gostawa knows, but the message did not come via her. It was more direct."

Myrta speechlessly listened to Caizhiu's tale, her hand finding Euvie's on the tabletop. Once Caizhiu had finished she sat back, frowned, and said: "I thought the Keepers of Sinuation weren't to contact the Fabled directly."

"So did I." Caizhiu stared into the flame of the candle in the centre of the table. It flickered, and she snuffed it out between her finger and thumb. Its sting lasted only a moment as a ringlet of smoke ascended to join the haze that covered the ceiling.

Despite being neath, the woman had an uncanny way of getting information out of people. It was the reason that Caizhiu preferred Myrta to the more official way of dealing with Yullorik. She would have made a fantastic Magistrate, if only she had been Talented.

Myrta cleared her throat and smiled at Euvie before addressing the other two. "So listen, where are you staying? All the taverns and hotels are jammed. And we have a front room with a carpet and everything..."

It had been days since Caizhiu last ate, and her hunger was reaching the sweet spot where her senses were heightened, but craving hadn't taken hold yet. She'd rather not waste the night on Myrta's floor.

Heort smiled at her. The liquor fatigue was upon him. *{Go, search the city. I'll look after your friends. But... don't leave me with them.}*

{I'll find you before the night is done. If you doubt me, hold my gold. I won't leave without that.}

"We'd be grateful to accept your offer," Heort said to the women, "but our friend has business to attend to."

"You won't cause us difficulty, will you?" Myrta asked.

Caizhiu scoffed. "Is that why you offered us your roof – to keep an eye on me?"

Myrta's face turned red with restrained fury. "I don't care if you are a dragon or a fraud; you are an ass, Caizhiu! My offer is genuine, as is my company."

"I know. Just look after my cervitaur."

Before Heort could protest, Caizhiu affirmed she'd see them later, knocked back the birch wine and stood up. By pure luck, her head missed the beam.

FIFTEEN

FOOD AND FAMILY ENTANGLEMENTS

Drizzle descended on the garden and the lovers' afterglow. Narastien sat on the rim of the basin, with her legs dangling in the tepid water. Her skin was covered in goosebumps, and Ozcahar placed his hands over her hard nipples. Cold as she was, she still took her time rinsing the soap from his hair. He kissed her chest. She moved his head back and ran her thumb over the stubble on his cheek.

"You require shave." She pouted. "You be much pretty with no beard, Baby Face."

His whiskers itched where she'd played with them, forcing him to scratch his chin. "It be cold. I require beard."

Without warning she turned round and felt about her on the steps to retrieve her clothes.

"Trueso, it be cold. Come." She beckoned as she got to her feet. "We require heat and food."

Ozcahar got out of the basin. The chill of the stones bit the soles of his feet and the mizzle lay a mantle over his shoulders. He hurried to pick up his clothing and followed Narastien to the house.

In the hallway she tossed him a towel and laughed when he dropped his clothes to catch it. She watched him dry himself, but as he gathered his damp clothing, she pulled two garments from a cupboard and handed him one. It was a downy wrap-around tunic, pink, and too small. The sleeves reached halfway down his forearms, and it was so short it barely covered his backside. Yet the fabric felt comfy and freshly washed.

Narastien wore a silken robe. It had a fancy pattern and reached to her ankles but didn't seem to provide much in the way of warmth. He wanted to wrap his arms around her, but she led him to a room off the hall. It was scarcely furnished with a bed on one end and a flimsy wooden door on the other, behind which he suspected he'd find a collection of practical garments. The rug that covered most of the floor was faded and frayed at the edges. To the side stood a writing desk and stool.

Narastien took his bundle of clothes and placed them on the desk. She waved in the direction of the bed. "Sit, sit."

The softness of the mattress caught him out. The bed might be simple, but it was the most luxurious he'd ever known. He leant against the headboard and hugged his chilled legs.

"Be you cold still? Wait."

Narastien disappeared, and he examined his surroundings. The room was narrow with high grey walls and only one small window above eye level. He pushed away the thought that it looked like a prison cell. Prisons didn't have comfortable mattresses or warm blankets.

Narastien reappeared with two steaming tankards. She cocked her head with a smile and handed him one. Curious, he smelled the contents.

"Spiced wine." Narastien gave him an encouraging nod, and he took a sip. It tingled his lips and seemed to warm his body from the inside out.

He pressed his hand on his stomach but couldn't prevent it from rumbling.

"I get tasty-food." She placed her tankard on the bedside table and rushed out again.

Ozcahar took another sip of the wine, listening for her footsteps. Thinking himself foolish, he shook his head. Still, he swapped the tankards before she backed through the door, carrying a tray of mouth watering food. She set it between them on the bed. It was stacked with bread, cheeses, pickled fish, and cold meats.

He watched the precision with which she cut cubes off a hunk of cheese. It was hard to believe this was the same woman who over the past few days had bellowed commands at him. She sat with a carefree grace, one leg folded in front of her, the other dangling off the bed. It wasn't a word that would have occurred to him before, but she looked girlish, without the weight of her conscience to drag her down. She looked free and beautiful. Ozcahar leant forward and kissed her.

"You no hungry?" she asked with a sly smile.

The grumbling of his stomach answered for him, and he crammed a piece of bread into his mouth. He tried some of the fish, which was not as terrible as he'd feared. After a few mouthfuls he found the flavour quite pleasant. Narastien stuck the knife into one of the cubes of cheese and held it out to him. It was a delicate blade with a decorative handle.

"Your home-house be much..." He tried to recall the word she'd used. "Much pretty. River be rewarding?"

She laughed and shook her head. "No so much rewarding. My father-father build home-house. Build lot of Wexede Crossing."

"Your room be small."

"I no require big room." Narastien shrugged. "Most times on boat."

He nodded at the spread of food and the drained but still warm tankards. "You no live-alone."

"Live with sister. Since..." She counted on her fingers. "Two-ten years almost, when mother die. Father die before. She has spouse, and home-house be theirs. They be welcome to my visits."

A lump formed in his throat as Ozcahar listened to her. It was as if he were being shown a life that could have been his, if only he had been able to conceive of it. A life where people left valuables for anyone to take. Where people had food enough to share with strangers. Only now did he realise this was what Jorganyon had tried to achieve. Why he'd got him the job serving Ingrirath. He'd always aimed for a better life. And Ozcahar had fouled it up.

Narastien stroked his forehead with her thumb, and he noticed the deep frown that had set there. She cocked her head to read his face.

"You no like think of family," she said and, for a moment, was again the first mate looking after a crewmember. Perhaps it was the wine, but he was briefly overcome with melancholy that threatened to well up in his eyes. He tried to sound breezy and change the topic back to her.

"Your sister work river also?"

"Takes after father-father, hard-work long times. Sister be... alike, ehm..." Narastien chewed on a piece of bread, looking for a Trader term he might know. "Alike first mate to Magistrate."

She beamed him a grin, happy at having found wording he would understand. His skin tingled with tension and his mouth went dry. The Magistrate. That was the last thing he needed. Jorganyon had been right; he should have kept moving. He breathed out slowly and made sure his hand wouldn't shake when he took a piece of purple fruit off the tray.

Narastien grinned and shook her head. "Be you cold still?"

He shrugged and bit into the leathery peel, careful not to let the juice drip onto the bedding. Perfunctorily, he moved food to his mouth, the tastes and textures barely registering on his tongue. Her chattering was drowned out by the rushing of his blood.

Narastien got up to fetch a refill of warm wine and at last he could make his escape.

Sixteen

Wylthren Mudridge

Caizhiu darkened her hue to match the night, but the sheen of the drizzle on her skin betrayed her movements. The city wasn't as vacant as it seemed. From their scent, most of the wild sleepers around the harbour were strangers to the city. Any one of them could be the person she was looking for.

The footsteps that followed her were soft and placed with care. She listened out for the scraping of flint on steel, but it didn't come. The footsteps kept their distance.

Caizhiu stopped by the quay wall. The river sloshed between the boats and their ropes squeaked with movement. From one of the ships in the darkness below, she heard the brief clatter of a man relieving himself, followed by the closing and bolting of a door. In the jungle of sound, she found the place where her shadow stopped. She ran her breath over the roof of her foreshortened mouth. Her pursuer concealed his scent with a cigarette.

Caizhiu spun round, deliberately billowing her wing cloak to increase her size. Startled, the man dropped into a defensive stance and reached for the weapon under his cloak. She covered the distance between them in one chronochi'ed leap. How easily her hand now wrapped around a human throat. His heartbeat pulsed against her index finger and thumb, quicker with each beat as his body caught up with the turn of events. She grabbed a handful of his tunic with her other hand and raised him off the ground. In the time it took his eyes to widen and his breath to catch, she had turned and lifted him over the quay wall.

"W-wait!"

A roll of paper dropped from his lips and bounced off her wrist. Its glow extinguished in the water below. When his hood fell back, Caizhiu realised this was not the man she was hunting.

"Wylthren Mudridge?"

"Who else would I be? Let me go. No! I mean, set me down." His left hand grasped her arm, and he tried to hook his heels on the wall edge, to get back to solid ground.

Caizhiu looked down to find the barrel of his pistol quivering over her chest. She should have been quicker, more clear-headed. In her dense human form, it was unlikely a shot would have wounded her, but it was still careless. She twisted the weapon from his hand, causing the man to groan in protest more than pain. Shuffling in the shadows told her that, underneath the upturned sloops, wild sleepers were pretending they hadn't seen a thing. Dread mixed with rainwater all around the harbour. Caizhiu took a drag of this appealing undertone in the city's stench before she stepped backwards, pulling the man away from the edge. Holding him by the collar, she used his pistol to guide his chin towards the harbour light. "You've changed."

"*I've* changed?"

Wylthren had been a scrawny youngster when they'd last met, and she found the memory irreconcilable with the man before her. He was nearly as tall as she was, and his biceps were bulbous, stretching the fabric of his sleeves. It was a metamorphosis almost as remarkable as her own.

His gaze flicked towards the pistol. "You know how to use that?"

"Not a clue."

"Then…" He wet his lips to retrieve the strength in his voice, then held up his hands. "Would you mind not pointing it at my head?"

She let go of him, took a large step back, and held the pistol out in front of her. It looked puny in her hand. Hard to believe it could deliver such a nasty sting. Seeing that she held it like one might a stick, her fingers wrapped around the trigger guard, Wylthren let out a long and tremulous breath.

"Six's Mercy, I forgot how fast you move, my friend." He wiped the drizzle off his face and jerked his shoulders to straighten his knee-length cloak.

"I wouldn't have described us as friends."

"Aw, come on – of course we are. I'm a bit hurt you didn't look me up. We worked so well together last time."

"Worked together? All I remember is an impetuous child who was constantly underfoot." Caizhiu's voice took on a dark tone. "One who managed to deprive me of my hard-earned gold."

Wylthren flexed his fists and took the pistol, like a wild foxling reaching for an offered morsel.

"I was mature for my age." He fiddled with the hammer mechanism to make sure she hadn't bent the weapon out of shape. "And the Magistrate agreed my help had been *invaluable*."

Caizhiu frowned at his high-grade tunic and the emblem on his waterproof cloak. "Are you impersonating the city guard?"

"I *am* a city guard," Wylthren said with a lopsided grin. "An apprentice one, anyway. So, when I heard you had returned, I thought… perhaps I could be invaluable again."

Caizhiu relaxed her scowl but didn't smile. "And as part of your apprenticeship, didn't they teach you not to sneak up on a dragon?"

"I wasn't sneaking. I just wasn't certain it was you. Anyhow, not messing with the Fabled is basically the first rule they teach us. It's what the Magistrate is for. If the Magistrate can't handle it... they get you."

He stared into the blackness of the river before he continued. "Are you here because of our bridge?"

He sat down on the quay wall. After a brief pause, Caizhiu joined him.

"We've had some difficulties with the nixes. I'm not saying they... you know, destroyed our bridge... But I thought perhaps, if that was true, that Veentar – I mean Lord Magistrate Veentar – had contacted you to take care of it."

Wylthren bent forward to shield his knees from the drizzle. He took a leather pouch from a pocket on his belt and fished a piece of birch paper out of it. He loaded it with the pungent strings from the pouch and rolled the paper into a narrow cylinder. Placing it between his lips, he looked around and, with a frown, muttered: "All due respect to the Six and the city council, but these verve lights don't make lighting a smoke easier."

He shrugged and played with the useless cigarette. "Don't suppose you've learnt to breathe fire?"

"Not that kind of dragon. What did you mean 'difficulties'?"

Wylthren glanced over his shoulder and lowered his voice. "Some skippers report strange breakdowns, thefts, and being held up for no reason. They say it's like the river isn't behaving like she should."

"What does Yul..." Caizhiu grimaced and corrected herself. "Lord Magistrate Veentar say?"

His desk had been covered in drawings. He had been concerned with nothing but the practicalities of moving people through the city, helping the traders, and ultimately rebuilding the bridge. There had been no thought of the nixes in his mind. That itself was surprising, even a little worrying. Had Yullorik even consulted the nixes about the bridge?

She stood up. After the ingratitude Nellepeth had shown, the last thing she wanted was to get embroiled in another conflict. Especially one based only on river rumours. Wylthren would need to look elsewhere to make his mark.

"I'm tasked to find a human called Ozcahar Nitt. I doubt he has anything to do with the bridge, but I'll ask him once I have him."

When he rose to his feet, Wylthren placed the prepared cigarette in the pouch on his belt. He raised an eyebrow. "But if he has come via the river, perhaps the nixes know something about your man. I mean, however unlikely, would you not want to check that?"

***

Heort balled his fists in his pockets and climbed the steps to the home. Though he would never tell her, he was grateful Caizhiu had found them before he had to enter the building. The room had a dizzying number of walls. Everywhere he looked, even above, his view was blocked. The air was thick with the simulated scents of dead flowers. He shuddered at the click of the door lock behind him. Caizhiu opened the curtains, and though the outside was hidden by darkness, the knowledge it was there made the confinement bearable. He licked his nose, flicked his tail, and reminded himself that he had spent many times in human dwellings and had always survived.

To distract himself, he concentrated on the interior: the warmth of the carpet enveloping his hooves and the impressive portrait on the back wall. It was large and detailed, and he pretended it was another window. The work depicted 'The Last Iteration of Ujojen the Conflicted', who stood with their wings outstretched. One was covered in feathers, gleaming in the sunlight. The other had a translucent membrane between a clearly visible bone structure terminating in claws on each finger. One head, the one with the beak, was looking up at a threatening sky while their second head, bearing rows of bloodied teeth, glared at the fiery mountains at their feet. Both faces were twisted in despair as they realised that nevermore would the sky be theirs to command. Over the horizon their shadowy pursuers broke away from the landscape. It was an exceptional portrayal of the legendary tragedy.

Euvie disappeared through a door to the left of the portrait. Heort was tempted to follow her serene aura, but then Myrta strode to her guests. "My great-grandfather painted it."

He pointed at the collection of figurines on the chest of drawers below the portrait and asked: "Did he create all these pieces too?"

Caizhiu picked up a golden horse and rider as if to examine the craftsmanship. She closed her eyes and inhaled with an enraptured expression. Myrta exchanged a frown with Heort, who gave Caizhiu's foot a kick. The dragon opened her eyes and, noticing their quizzical looks, put the statuette back.

Above them the floorboards creaked, and a rumbling came towards them from behind the wall. Ujojen's portrait trembled. The door to the right of it swung open and a naked woman with a sateen robe flowing behind her like a cape burst in.

"Myr!" Her face paled as she looked at each of them with growing horror and hastily wrapped her flimsy garment around her. "Oh blood and piss! You have company."

Myrta sucked in her reddening cheeks and rolled her eyes. Deliberately audible, she released her breath and positioned herself between the woman and her guests.

"And by the look of it, so have you."

The other woman blushed and smoothed the shiny fabric of her robe. She lowered her voice, though it was still loud enough for Heort's hearing to pick up. "Well, yes, I did. But I seem to have misplaced him."

She looked around the room as if expecting to find her caller among the gathered strangers. "I went to get some drinks and when I returned, he'd vanished. I've looked everywhere, even went upstairs. Nothing."

"That's quick work." Myrta crossed her arms. "Even for you."

The other grimaced. "That was uncalled for."

"Not entirely. You pick up another stranger from some bar?" Myrta rubbed her forehead and hissed: "Did you check the silverware?"

"He was no stranger. He's a good kid." The other woman combed her fingers through her short hair. "I'm sure he wouldn't..."

Her eyes flitted to each of the statuettes on the side as if to count them.

At last Myrta softened. They hugged, and she whispered: "I'm glad you're home. You had me worried. This weather..."

They broke their embrace when, from the other side of the room, a door opened and Euvie poked her head round. "Naz? Did you eat the supper I'd prepared?"

"Piss it," Naz muttered under her breath and bit her knuckle. "Apologies, Euvie. I didn't realise you had guests."

She ducked past Caizhiu and smiled feebly at Heort as she walked round him.

"And my spiced wine?"

"Honest apologies." She followed Euvie to the kitchen. "Myr's note only said you were out late."

Myrta turned towards her guests. She stroked her neck and slowly opened her eyes. Her expression was inscrutable. "May I introduce my sister, Narastien."

Seventeen

The Dweymin Curse

Before this iteration, Caizhiu could keep her human form for days. Now, her lungs ached to inflate fully, her wings longed to unfurl, her tail twitched to straighten, and she regretted the copious amount of liquid she'd consumed. At last, the sound of Myrta leaving for work signalled that it was appropriate to rise. She extended an arm and leg towards the ground and rolled over the edge of the bed. The floorboards groaned and the bed returned to its original shape. She had not intended – in fact, had argued against – taking Myrta and Euvie's bed while they spent an uncomfortable night on the floor of the front room in a misguided gesture of hospitality.

When she made her way down the dainty stairs, her every step caused the treads to creak. Behind her was the room from where she heard the gentle snoring of Myrta's sister. To her left was the door to the garden, and the rush of falling rain. She twisted her insides in a vain attempt to make more room for her bladder.

The door to her right opened. Daylight brought out Euvie's bronzed complexion, dappled with brown freckles. A few strands of curly hair had already escaped her loose braid. If she was fatigued from a sleepless night, it didn't show on her face. "Would you care for breakfast, Hunter Caizhiu?"

The woman noticed her hesitation and the corner of her mouth quirked up. "Don't worry," she said with a wink. "I think I have something that you would enjoy."

Intrigued, Caizhiu watched her don a cloak and followed her to the garden. Rain fell steadily from the white sky, occasionally whipped up by a gust of northerly wind. Euvie walked to a coop to the rear of the garden and opened it. A cockerel and three chickens stepped out onto the ramp, blinked at the light or the rain, and clucked their way to the ground to forage for insects. She grabbed the fourth hen as she emerged from the coop. The chicken folded her legs beneath her and calmly bobbed her head. Euvie held the bird out to Caizhiu.

"I suppose you'd prefer to despatch her yourself."

Caizhiu took the animal, and the hen gave a piercing squawk that sent the others in a flutter. She ripped off the head and put her lips to the ragged neck, so the heart pumped the lifeblood down her throat. Nerve pulses trying to reach the detached brain tickled her tongue.

Her hoodwing shielded her lower face, and she wiped the blood off with the heel of her hand before turning round.

Euvie was gathering eggs from the coop. As she looked up to Caizhiu, she bowed her head. "If you'd excuse me, I will leave you to your breakfast and go prepare mine."

Euvie proved to be far more robust than Caizhiu had taken her for. But then she'd married Myrta, so she must be made of stern stuff.

Caizhiu cracked open the chicken's ribcage, fished out the crop and the liver, and popped them in her mouth. The other birds seemed unperturbed by the sight of their sister being devoured as they scratched and pecked around for their own meals. When Caizhiu discarded the leftovers into the pen, the others came running for their pick. She sucked the strings of meat from between her teeth, then used the rainwater that had collected in a shell-shaped fountain to wash the blood off her face.

Euvie was brewing a hot drink with a strong and alluring aroma. Caizhiu recognised it as chalkar, a Sarfi drink, which was usually mixed with milk and honey to ease its bitter taste. Heort stood next to the oval table. He had been more persuasive than she and had convinced their hosts to let him sleep in the garden. Wrapped in a horsehair blanket, he had the ambivalent look of a puppy who had just been bathed.

"I'm grateful for the breakfast," Caizhiu said. "But I am surprised. Humans don't usually serve live food."

Euvie answered without turning round. "My people make a point of knowing those we mix with."

"Your people are the Sarfi." Heort struggled with the difference between the 's' and 'f' sounds. It was unclear whether he'd asked a question or made a statement.

"So even in the Keeltois you have heard of us."

"Of course we have." He looked at her with a puzzled expression, studying the chilling of her aura. "You are the Wanderers, the bringers of tales and goods from afar, the originators of Trader Talk."

The woman handed Caizhiu a cup of chalkar and added honey and cream to her own.

"Not many people know it was us who brought Trader Talk to the world."

"Not many people's memory is as long as ours," Caizhiu said between sips of the hot liquid.

Euvie stared into her drink. "They say we brought a common tongue to the people because we can't be Talented."

Caizhiu wasn't sure this was true, but as she recalled the many Sarfi she'd met, she couldn't think of any that had been able to hear a soul song, let alone use any other Talent such as soothsaying, willhexing, or chronochi'ing.

Euvie took a sharp breath and looked at Heort. "You are a healer, trueso?"

"I try."

"Perhaps it is true that we can't be Talented, but unfortunately, we can be cursed." Euvie unbuttoned her blouse and Caizhiu heard a breath of shock catch in Heort's throat. Unable to resist, she cast a glimpse in their direction. Euvie leant against the worktop with her back to the window. The rain had temporarily ceased, and although the sun hadn't quite broken through the clouds, the light formed a halo through her red hair. Her blouse hung open, revealing her neck and right shoulder. The freckles that covered her face continued down her neck. Where her neck and shoulder met, her light brown skin was interrupted by a spider's web of scar tissue. The rutted threads ran over her collarbone and up her neck, to her jawline.

"Dweymin bite," Heort said. "It looks old."

"I was a child. They attacked. My family was killed." Her voice was empty, rehearsed, the sound carefully distanced from the memory. She sighed and closed her blouse. "I've got used to the scars and obviously... the other thing isn't of immediate concern, but I wondered if there was anything you could do. Is there?"

"Though the scars are old, I can give you something to lessen the markings." Heort reached into one of the many pockets of his harness. He put a vial on the table and hung his head. "Lifting your blood curse is something beyond my abilities. Any offspring you bear would be theirs. It might look human at first, but it would be dweymin."

"That's what I thought." Euvie shrugged and flung her braid over her shoulder. She picked up the vial and studied its simple shape. "But it couldn't hurt to ask."

The heavy silence was interrupted by the opening of the door. Even though she was still in her nightshirt, Narastien appeared refreshed. "Is it still morning?"

In the blink of an eye, the pain vanished from Euvie's face, and she smiled warmly at her sister-in-law. "It is. Do you want eggs on your toast?"

"Absolutely! Honestly, I expected to sleep till midday after that journey. That pissing rain!"

Euvie scowled at her and Narastien apologised for her foul language but pointed at the window. "Well, look at it; it's pouring down again."

Euvie handed her a cup of sweetened and creamed chalkar that she eagerly accepted.

Caizhiu released a breath. She hoped that her sister-in-law's distraction would allow her and Heort to leave without feeling like they had let down the woman who had given them shelter.

***

T he voice was gruff and loud. His sleep-fogged mind couldn't work out what was being said, so Ozcahar wrapped his arms around his head. The beating didn't come, but someone grabbed his coat and dragged him from his hiding place underneath a parked auto carriage.

"No-harm," he stammered in Trader Talk, still unsure whether it meant he intended no harm or if it was a plea for mercy. "Please. No-harm."

A night on the wet streets of Wexede Crossing had left his body aching and stiff. The warm bath, sex, and food of the previous evening seemed so distant they might as well have been a dream.

The man who held his lapels was broad of build with thick arms and a sizeable belly. His tawny-brown face was marked with a scar that ran from the top of his right cheek across a bulbous nose to disappear into a bristly auburn moustache and beard.

Ozcahar blinked the rain from his eyes. Over the man's shoulder he saw two others. One was of the same build as the first with similar features, minus the scar. The third was slimmer, shorter, and twice as old. They glared at him as they cocked their rifles.

He held up his hands in a pitiful plea. His fingers were yellow with cold. "O-only place-to-sleep. N-no-harm."

One of the men ducked underneath the carriage to retrieve Ozcahar's haversack. He repressed the urge to protest and stared longingly at his worldly possessions.

"Release him, Darjani." The older man lowered his rifle and uncocked it. "He be vagrant only."

The strong man let go of one of his lapels but continued to hold him up against the auto carriage. Even in the dark, when he had sheltered beneath it, it had looked an impressive vehicle. The early dawn brought out the red, blue, and gold of the paint job. It was the biggest auto carriage he had ever seen with no less than six wheels. And there were two of them. A little way down the road stood a cloth-covered wagon with two oxen. Next to it a woman was rubbing the animals. He tried to catch her eye for help.

"This be no vagrant's coat. This be no vagrant's hat." Darjani's scowl deepened as he patted Ozcahar's pockets. "We have plenty trouble without thievery also."

"I buy coat and hat. No thievery, sir."

Darjani fished something out of Ozcahar's coat and wiggled it in front of his face. "Be this yours?"

The delicate silver knife looked out of place between his fingers and out of keeping with Ozcahar's appearance. Shit, they would hand him over to the City Guard for thievery. Narastien would be called to identify the object. The possibility he might have to face her oddly seemed a worse fate than whatever terrible punishment awaited him for the other thing.

Darjani pressed his thumb on the knife's squared point. Stolen or not, it was a pathetic weapon, and the man snorted as he placed it back in Ozcahar's pocket. His lookalike ceased his rummaging through the haversack, dropping the pink tunic back in the bag. "If he be thief, he no be good one."

Ozcahar felt a sting of insult that dissipated when, at last, Darjani let go of his collar. His hope for freedom grew as a chorus of voices shouted at them from up the street. A group of Crossingers approached them. He counted at least nine people, mostly men, and all with an aggressive demeanour. Perhaps these people had seen the altercation and were coming to his aid.

The elder of his three accosters stepped forward, his hands raised in a pacifying gesture. He spoke in an even tone. Ozcahar didn't catch every word, but the gist was that the man understood those gathering were unhappy at their presence. The crowd didn't seem appeased. A short man with his hands clamped on a rifle stepped forward. "Day-before-dark you be told to leave!"

"We no do crime," the older man said. "We only came for bridge."

A gasping murmur cascaded through the gathered at something behind the four. A woman emerged from the second carriage's side door and stopped halfway on the steps. She wore an ankle-length flowing dress, sturdy boots, and held a baby in her arms.

"Go back in!" Darjani shouted and waved at her. But the crowd had already surged forward. The woman turned, her motions too hurried, and she lost her balance. Clutching her infant, she flailed and grabbed onto the doorframe. Startled, the baby burst into breathy sobs.

Ozcahar felt the world closing in on him when the short man with the rifle stopped next to him, aiming it at the woman. The killing of a woman and child would attract an endless amount of attention, so Ozcahar crashed his elbow into the man's temple and his foot against his knee. The rifle fired into the air and the man dropped to the floor, Ozcahar landing on top of him. He grabbed the weapon and pushed it to the ground so the man couldn't raise it again. He winced when the man kicked his shins, but he clutched the rifle. Someone wrapped an arm around his throat, and he was pulled backwards. Though he struggled to breathe, he managed to plant his knee in the crotch of the man beneath him. The man let go of the rifle in favour of his knackers.

Darjani punched the one who had his arm around Ozcahar's throat and ran towards the carriage to make sure others didn't follow the woman inside. Ozcahar twisted round and used the butt of the heavy rifle to break his assailant's nose. All he could hear was incomprehensible but furious shouting. A fist glanced the side of his face. He stepped back to avoid a second blow and bumped into the back of a man about to throw a rock at the carriages. The thrower turned and brought a stone-filled hand down onto Ozcahar's head. He deflected most of the impact, but the blow shoved his hat over his eyes. Half-blind, he twisted, kicked, and swung the rifle around to keep his attackers at bay. They were everywhere, their rain cloaks making it hard to tell one from another. One he recognised was the man whose nose he'd broken. Undeterred by his bloodied face, he charged Ozcahar, shoving him backwards against the second carriage. He heard the whine of the engine starting. Using this distraction, the man punched Ozcahar and grabbed the rifle. As they tussled for the weapon, his head collided with the wood of the carriage, but he refused to let go.

Three shots rang out. Ozcahar checked to see if he'd been hit and, on finding he had not, lifted his hat to see where the sound had come from. The other man let go of the rifle and backed away when two guards on horseback approached. City Guard. Just what he'd hoped to avoid. Hoofbeats resounded in the streets, so though the vehicles blocked his view, Ozcahar guessed more approached from the other side. There was nowhere to run. One of the riders placed his horse in front of him, cornering him against the carriage.

"You mustn't be here," the guard said in an authoritative tone. Ozcahar was searching for an answer when he realised it wasn't him who'd been addressed.

Seated on the carriage driver's seat, Darjani replied: "We no do wrong an action. City hospitality be terrible."

The guard looked at the crowd of sheepish-looking citizens and back at Darjani. "Bring you curse to our city?"

"There be no fault in curses, just misfortune."

"Trueso. But fault or no, you no share misfortune. You must leave Wexede Crossing."

Darjani gave a stiff nod, and at a flick of a lever, the auto carriage whined to life. The guard turned his scowl to his colleagues. "Note down particulars of this rabble." His stern eyes glanced over the griping crowd. "We have no lenience for vigilantes. You people have problem? You see the Guard."

Ozcahar shuffled forward to avoid the moving wheels. He kept his head down, but the horse's snort caused the rim of his hat to flutter. A drop slithered over the bridge of his nose, and he wasn't sure if it was rain, sweat, or blood. The oxen-drawn wagon creaked over the cobbles behind him, two mounted city guards bringing up the rear and blocking Ozcahar's escape. He couldn't slink away without drawing attention. They'd make him give his name, explain how he'd come to be here, and he couldn't think what story he could tell. His accent would betray him.

"Here, friend!" a voice called out. It was the older man. He was sat on the driver's seat of the covered wagon, holding the reins in one hand, and the other he held out to Ozcahar, who grabbed it and pulled himself up. Keeping his head down and his face hidden from the city guards, he leant the rifle against the footboard and took a seat next to the stranger. The wagon rolled on.

He exhaled.

EIGHTEEN

COLD ENCOUNTERS

Wylthren sported a broad grin when he met them outside their hosts' home. His bouncy gait reminded Caizhiu of Morailo's young dog.

"This is Apprentice Guard Wylthren Mudridge. Lord Veentar must think little of us to saddle us with someone so junior."

Wylthren bowed to Heort. "I'm at your service."

"From that introduction..." Heort extended his hand. "May I assume our surly friend thinks highly of you?"

As he wrapped his hand around the cervitaur's, Wylthren smirked at Caizhiu.

"I'd think more highly of you if you weren't so foolish as to allow a cervitaur to touch you. Honestly, do they teach you nothing in the Guard?"

Wylthren groaned as he looked from his hand to Heort's friendly smile. "Willhexing?"

"I call it nudging. But have no concern; I only use it when I absolutely have to."

They strolled past the dry dock, wandering through the alleys between rows of warehouses. At least the tall and slender buildings sheltered them from the wind, if not the rain. As they headed away from the hectic city centre, Heort attracted more curious glances, but the people parted respectfully to allow the city guard and his odd companions to make their way down the street.

"Excuse me," Heort asked, "but why are we moving away from the harbour if we're looking for nixes?"

"Because they avoid our city." Wylthren gave a grunt of satisfaction when he found the towpath passable. "Besides, there will be plenty of skippers who didn't make it to the city and had to moor up along the bank. We can ask them too."

Typically, a flotilla of boats would navigate the river, but now, only the most robust vessels ventured to make the trip. The bank was dotted with smaller ships wherever it was firm enough to secure them. Local crews waited at home for a change in the weather, leaving many vessels unmanned. Of the people they did speak to, no one had heard of an Aumegoan traveller.

Caizhiu wished she could walk on all fours, to distribute her weight, and use her claws to grip the muddy track. Heort skidded multiple times before he leapt onto the grassy verge. Wylthren slithered along the towpath, though he tried to hide it with confident strides between slips. On their right, the grey torrent of the Wexede raged to the coast. The ceaseless gushing intensified the discomfort in Caizhiu's bladder.

"That'll teach you, Thirsty Dragon," Heort said with the closest expression to wickedness his face was capable of.

Wylthren raised an eyebrow.

"I need a piss," Caizhiu clarified.

The young man shrugged. "Don't hold back on my account."

"Impossible in this form, unfortunately."

His eyes darted towards her crotch. "Didn't you give yourself a... you know."

She grinned at his discomfiture. "This isn't a male body. It's not a human body. It just looks like one. I've had to make considerable accommodations to fit myself into this small shape. One of the things I've had to forfeit is access to my bladder."

Though the most acute, it wasn't the only sacrifice her human shape demanded. Her human form had always been too dense to swim, and this had worsened exponentially in her current iteration. She tested the riverbank but found the edge too waterlogged for her to stand on. Catching Heort's eye, she said: *{I have an idea. But I don't think you'll like it.}*

He shook the rain off his ears and cocked his head. *{I'm sure you're right, but tell me anyway.}*

Caizhiu ran the procedure by him in a series of imaginings and he rolled his eyes.

{I hate that idea. But I don't have a better one.}

"As good a place as any." Caizhiu had found a grassy peninsula protected from the Wexede's current by a barge moored upriver. Heort prodded the squishy grass with his front hooves, sinking further with every step. His hearts sped up, and he took long breaths to keep calm. Caizhiu sat on her haunches, her feet digging into a knotty muddle of mud and roots. She ran her hand over Heort's rearback, her fingers testing the straps of his harness.

"Better hold my legs, Caizhiu. I'll get more reach then." He looked around at her. "Oh, and just in case you'd get the notion to be funny, I won't appreciate you pretending to let go."

She gave him a lopsided grin and infused her song with reassurance when she wrapped her hand around his hind legs and carefully lifted them off the ground. She let them twitch between her fingers, waited for Heort to suppress his instinct to flee, then gently tightened her grip. The cervitaur took jittery steps towards the water's edge on his front legs.

She was about to tell Wylthren to watch her haversack, but when she saw him holding out his hand to form a chain, she grabbed his wrist. His weight was insignificant compared to hers, but it was cute he wanted to help.

{We seek the nixes of the great Wexede river. Will you answer us?} Heort stretched his upper back in line with his rearback and dipped his fingertips into the river to extend his soul song to the nixes.

{Who is it that calls to us?} came the response from the river. The voice was reminiscent of rain hitting water. Caizhiu and even Wylthren could feel the cervitaur's shiver, as chilly tendrils snaked up Heort's arms.

{The dragon Caizhiu seeks your audience.}

{Why does she insult us with her human outfit?} The river voice dripped with contempt. *{Does she speak for them?}*

Wylthren whimpered as Caizhiu, too absorbed in the nixes' conversation, failed to filter out the alien acuities that engulfed him. Touch-telepathy did not usually affect humans that strongly. Not unless they were Talented.

{No. She is here for her own pursuit and would be grateful for nixes' assistance.}

"Only a little grateful," Caizhiu muttered to Heort. His concentration fluctuated, and he told her to be quiet.

{Why should we trust a dragon dressed as a human? If she wishes to meet with us, let her prove she is not here to do their bidding. Let us meet on more equal terms; meet us on the water.}

The nixes let go of Heort's arms and the cervitaur blinked. He took a couple of rapid breaths as if he'd been unable to and rotated his arms to lift his upper back away from the water. Caizhiu released Wylthren to focus on Heort, and the human scampered up the verge. She steadied Heort as he awkwardly walked backward on his forelegs until she could put his hindlegs on solid ground.

He shook the rainwater off himself. With greater attention than usual, he wiped his fur and coat in an attempt to dry himself. He rolled his eyes at Wylthren and tilted his head. Caizhiu sighed. She walked over to the young man, who tried to hide the tremor in his hands by clamping them on the clasp of his rain cloak. "They say we hear the Fabled before we die. Am I going to die?"

Caizhiu realised she had never found someone so completely raw before. Although humans seemed to grow up fast, she should have remembered that Wylthren was barely out of childhood.

"No, you are not dying." She hooked her right arm under his left, wrapped her other around his back, and helped him to his feet. "You're just Talented. It usually emerges a bit earlier in life. I'd have thought the Lord Magistrate would have noticed your development, but I guess he was busy."

Wylthren opened his mouth, and fearing a torrent of questions she had neither the ability nor the time to answer, she said: "Come, we need to find a boat, talk to those damned nixes."

***

Ozcahar sat silently, slowly massaging his hands for warmth, and watched the landscape move past. He found it impossible to work out where the sun was in the diffuse grey sky, and he could only hope he wasn't being taken back the way he'd come. The ceaseless rain added to the marshland on either side of the road. With every turn of the creaking wheels, he could feel the weight of the wagon depress the wooden slats and hear the mud squelch up between them.

His heart jumped when the fabric of the covering behind him opened. He scooted towards the edge of the seat when two heads appeared, one above the other. The image of the monster in Narastien's painting flashed through his mind.

The upper head belonged to the woman he'd seen earlier tending to the oxen. Two silvery blonde braids hung on either side of her head. Between them, like a tiny copy, the lower head was that of a little girl. She eyed him suspiciously. "Who be he?"

The driver smiled at Ozcahar, and though he took care with the pronunciation, when he repeated his brief introduction earlier, the man didn't quite get it right. "He be Karri."

Relieved he'd been quick-witted enough to garble his name, Ozcahar nodded.

"Grateful for help, Karri. I be K'Netta," the woman said, tapping her hand to her chest. She pointed at the driver. "And that be Mihai."

She repeated the names, slowly enunciating the syllables, and each time with the hand gestures.

"I be Roovie," the girl chimed in and whispered loudly: "Be he slug-minded?"

The woman inhaled sharply and put her fingers to her lips. "Roovie, that be unkind. Karri be foreign, not slug-minded."

She ushered the child back between the flaps of the wagon's cover and tutted at Mihai. "Why you take him? Ask you Darjani?"

He patted the hand she'd placed on his shoulder and, noticing the auto carriages in front had stopped, drew the oxen to a standstill. "We ask him now. Come, Karri."

Mihai climbed from the driver's seat, and K'Netta took his place without a word.

The road had veered away from the river, but they were surrounded by swampland so waterlogged it looked like a gigantic lake. Only the tufts of tall grass and the occasional tree stuck up from the watery mud. Where the tilt-cart had stopped, the slats of the path were submerged. Mihai bounced on them and seemed satisfied they wouldn't sink further. As the two men made their way past the parked carriages, Ozcahar made sure his steps matched Mihai's exactly, heedful to keep them on the wooden path.

The two stout men he remembered from earlier stood ahead of the first carriage where the road split. Their scowl deepened when they spotted Ozcahar. It occurred to him that the marshes would probably hide his body forever. Mihai noticed him fall back and took Ozcahar's elbow, gently urging him to keep up. "These be friends Darjani and Brayshen. They no-harm you."

"Why be he here?" Darjani asked and placed his fists on his hips, making him seem even broader.

"I no leave behind Karri. He help us, so Crossingers be angry with him."

"Be mistake, my friend." Darjani shook his head. "What do we with him?"

Mihai gave a dejected laugh. "What do we with ourselves?"

The silence was heavy and unwelcoming. Darjani walked towards Ozcahar. There was no escape, but Mihai seemed to have been right. The earlier aggression had left the man.

"You no can trek-with." He spoke slowly, pointing at the right fork. The slatted track disappeared into the haze where sky and marshland met. "You go-walk there. You go-walk through marsh, long-long trek to Rerpa."

Ozcahar was already cold, and the prospect of a long walk was uninviting. He didn't know what or where Rerpa was. At least it wasn't back. He hung his head, then looked at Brayshen. "Hand my bag?"

Brayshen paled and rubbed his beard.

"Lose you his bag?" Darjani asked.

"Deep apologies, Karri. I drop bag when Crossingers attack." Brayshen spread his arms at Darjani and extended his hand to Ozcahar. "Now he must trek-with. He no can go-walk alone, with no clothing, coin, or food."

Ozcahar nodded eagerly. "I be no trouble. I promise. I no thief from you."

"You be as choice-poor as we be, Karri." Darjani looked up, letting the rain land on his face, and shook his head. He pulled a large paper roll from under his arm and spread it against the carriage. "No can trek over river. If we trek west, we walk into marsh. We come from there. We know it be no good for carriages. We must trek south."

"Into Dreadwoods," Brayshen said with a deep frown. "Be bad idea, Brother. Too much danger for us, for..."

"The choice-poor must trek Dreadwoods." Darjani rolled up the map. "That be us. Hope if we trek fast, we be safe."

He turned to Mihai and Ozcahar with a sad smile. "At least Karri prove he fight with us."

Ozcahar wondered if he'd have been better off staying in Wexede Crossing.

Nineteen

Ingrirath

At the sound of hoofbeats and sloshing wheels, Caizhiu turned to see a pony trotting towards them. The animal had been white. Now half was the ruddy grey of the dirt, and the rest was dappled in muddy specks. The driver of the buggy expertly balanced speed and caution while travailing the slick towpath. They could slip off the path at any moment. If they landed in the water, there would be little the dragon could do to save pony, driver, or the buggy's passengers. Not in her human form.

She, Heort, and Wylthren climbed up the embankment out of the way, though Wylthren waved at the driver and yelled a warning that the path ahead was impassable.

Just before the path descended completely into sludge, the driver pulled the pony to a stop. Damp rose from her back and her eyes rolled with unease at the roaring water.

Wylthren slithered towards the carriage. He gave a polite bow to the person or persons inside and opened the door. He lowered the steps and removed his rain cloak to lay it out onto the grass.

Hindered by her narrow pencil skirt, Myrta descended from the buggy. With an almost imperceptible shrug, she stepped off the rain cloak onto the wet grass. She marched to the top of the embankment, an effort that wasn't aided by her heels, which dug into the soggy ground. She stood as straight as was possible on sunken heels and, with two impatient fingers, motioned for Caizhiu to approach. The dragon raised her eyebrows at Heort and climbed up to the First Attendant.

Myrta turned her back on the company and waited for Caizhiu to reach her. "I have... disturbing news," she whispered. "We've had a message that Ingrirath is dead."

Caizhiu staggered a few steps down the slope and grabbed a handful of grass to steady herself. With devastating clarity, she recalled her fingers digging into the dry, rocky ground of the Keeltois when she had beheld the Sinuation-wrought deer.

"W-what did you say?"

Myrta stared ahead at the horizon and slowly breathed the words again. "Ingrirath is dead."

"Do you... Does Yullorik... Does Lord Veentar know how?"

Myrta turned towards her. While the dragon was on her knees, the two were at eye level and Caizhiu felt the weight of the human's stare.

"She was killed."

For a moment she feared the very substance of the world had changed so that she was unable to know which shape she held. She pulled a clump of roots from the embankment, stared at her human hand as dirt squeezed from between her fingers. Human hand. Human shape. Human mouth. She felt her tongue, her throat, her vocal cords, and tried to form her thoughts into words.

"How... how is that possible?"

She felt Myrta's hand on her shoulder. "However powerful they may be, the Six are human. Evidently, they are as mortal as I. According to the report from Thirdburg, despite good health, Ingrirath fell into an unarousable sleep. She remained such for days, and half a moon life ago, she died."

Half a moon life ago… That aligned with her early emergence. Remembering her encounter with Ingrirath's deer, her breath caught as she recalled how abruptly it had ended. Caizhiu got to her feet, careful not to slip. "What is Lord Veentar's assessment of the situation?"

"Ah," said Myrta, "I didn't quite get round to telling him about your affiliation with Ingrirath. I was going to, but he caught me off guard with that news. Frankly, I was too shaken, and he was very busy."

"So you agree he is a terrible Magistrate."

Myrta pouted. "Those words would never pass my lips. Nor is it your place to speak them, Dragon."

Caizhiu grunted. "He has Talented sprouting up under his nose without noticing, a city about to flood, and he has not spoken with the nixes for the Six only know how long."

"Five," Myrta muttered as her fingers followed each of the interlocking six triangles on the symbols embroidered on her dress. Even Caizhiu felt the urge to tie the blade of grass between her fingers into the intricate pattern. Instead she let it drop to the ground and wiped the dirt off her hands. She turned to her companions. Heort, she had no doubt, had heard every word, but hid his shock better than she. Wylthren and the driver had carefully averted their curious gazes. They would not hear of the news from Caizhiu.

"It seems your hunt for Mr Nitt has gained in significance," Myrta said. "How are you getting on with the nixes?"

"Not as well as I had hoped." Caizhiu held out her hand to steady the First Attendant's descent from the embankment. "They want to meet on the water."

Despite her wobbly walk down the hill, Myrta gave the dragon a haughty little smile. "I might be able to help with that."

She stepped onto Wylthren's cloak, held her hand out to the buggy. "You'll remember my sister, Narastien. She has a position as first mate on one of the river barges."

"How did you know we'd have want for a boat?"

"Because I'm no fool, Caizhiu. I can't recall the last time we've had any dealing with nixes. It stands to reason this is because they are disinclined to meet. If they were to agree at all, well, there was a good chance it would require a boat."

Not for the first time, Caizhiu wished the woman had been Talented. What a Magistrate she would have made.

Narastien, dressed in simple black breeches, a shirt, and jerkin with a short cloak hung over her shoulders, stepped down. She grimaced a smile.

"The eh… the *Wanderer* is moored just up ahead. She's not my ship, you understand, but the skip – I mean, Captain Riverson. I'm sure… if I ask, I mean… he'll…"

"You're wittering, dear," Myrta interrupted. "Just lead the way."

Narastien pointed at the flooded towpath. "You won't get this fancy-ass carriage over that."

Myrta looked back up the embankment and turned to the driver. "We'll have to continue along the crest. There is no path, but the ground is fairly even, so if you take it steady, do you reckon it's possible?"

The driver squinted. "The problem will be to get us up there, First Attendant."

She turned to Caizhiu. "Would you mind giving us a little push?"

"It'd be easier to put you over my shoulder and walk."

Caizhiu smiled at the withering look Myrta gave her, and she held up her hands in mock submission. The sisters climbed back into the carriage. Caizhiu motioned for Wylthren to approach and handed him his trampled cloak. "Make yourself useful."

The driver coaxed the pony to walk up the steep slope. The mare shook her head in confusion, but it was as far as her protest went, and she dug her hooves into the wet grass to pull the buggy up the hill. Side by side, Caizhiu and Wylthren put their backs against the rear of the vehicle, feeling it slither to the side as the pony struggled to find purchase. Digging their heels into the embankment, they pushed carefully. Gradually the buggy scaled the slope, and enthused by the prospect of even ground, the pony rushed towards the crest, causing both Wylthren and Caizhiu to fall backwards. The ground gave way beneath Caizhiu's feet, and she slid down the embankment. The icy water gripped her feet, causing a sting into her bladder. Turning as she slid, Caizhiu clawed at the mud with her inadequate human hands. Mercifully, she came to a stop when only ankle deep into the river. She tried to put her foot down, but it disappeared into the gooey riverbed. Her breath caught in her chest. Unless she could find leverage, her strength was of no use. She didn't want to subject the humans to her true form, but if the ground gave way, she'd sink. Would she then have time to transfigure? Moving slowly to prevent the riverbank from crumbling, she positioned her knee beneath her and pushed herself free.

Wylthren sat on the bank with his arms draped over his knees, trying to suppress a chuckle, but Heort gave her a close-call nod. The three trudged up the hill after the buggy. Caizhiu grumbled at the muck that covered her head to foot and flicked some into Wylthren's smirking face. He punched her arm playfully, then examined his knuckles with a pained expression.

"Keepers' Mercy, it's like punching brick."

"And she floats just as well," Heort added.

They followed the buggy along the crest of the embankment until it sloped to a crossroad leading to the river on one side and a farmhouse on the other. The slip was entirely submerged. Caizhiu wished she'd known of its existence; it would have been a much better place for Heort to contact the nixes. By the look of the muddy tracks, the farmer had recently moved goods out of the cellar and lower floor. The building looked abandoned and was surrounded by a wall of sandbags. On the other side of the slip, two barges were tied to a wooden jetty. The choppy waves lapped at the planks and there was a gap between the slip and the jetty where a set of steps had been swallowed by the river.

Narastien didn't wait for the driver to open the carriage door for her. She ran across the road, jumped onto the quay, and made her way to the first of the barges. To Caizhiu's relief, it looked robust. She had worried that the boat would turn out to be a dinky dory that would barely take her weight, but *Wexede Wanderer* was the length of seven humans and the width of three, with a reassuringly high bow and stern. Midship she had large boards to stabilise her and, just for once, Caizhiu was pleased to note the bhodine carapace on her roof. Perhaps there was something to the human's obsession with automation after all.

Caizhiu noticed how Narastien had lifted away part of the railings, creating a gap that would allow them to step easily from the jetty onto the ship.

A slim man with long silvern hair opened the door to the wheelhouse, his expression a jumble of delight and confusion. "Narastien? What are you doing here? I thought you'd have at least a few days Crossing's side with—"

"No such luck, Skip."

"Apologies." He mirrored her shrug and looked over her shoulder. "You... eh... you've brought company."

His eyes lingered on the emblem on the buggy and the city guard. "Are you in trouble?"

Narastien laughed. "No. It's my sister, Myrta."

"Ah, the First Attendant." He frowned at Narastien. "Am *I* in trouble?"

"Also no. Her... friends have need of a ship."

He walked past her and elegantly leapt from ship to quay to solid ground. His fingers were verve-stained green, and he wiped them on a cloth hanging from his belt. He had the unkempt air of someone who had not expected to get visitors.

"First Attendant," he said with an awkward bow. "My name is Tijs Riverson, captain of *Wexede Wanderer*. I understand you want the use of my vessel."

"Not me exactly," Myrta replied as she descended from the carriage. "It is the bounty hunter Caizhiu who has need of your ship."

Tijs did a double take at Caizhiu's size. "You have no cargo. To where do you want to go?"

"I have business with the nixes of this river."

The captain took a step backwards and bit his lip. "Nixes. I don't know. I generally try to avoid getting involved with…"

He was going to say something else but swallowed it. He looked at Myrta with a pained expression. "Attendant, I make my living on these waters."

Caizhiu felt herself grow impatient with the man, as if he embodied the deficiencies of the people of the Wexede. Humans were the only species where most of them couldn't soul sing and who, despite intelligence, walked through the world as unaware as animals.

"Then you should be pleased we're seeking an audience with them," she said. "It is long overdue. The nixes have requested we meet on the water; hence, we need a ship."

She pointed at his hands. "Is it not in working order?"

Tijs straightened his shoulders. "Of course she's in working order. I just finished giving the engine an overhaul."

"We don't need to go far, just the middle of the river."

"A little way upriver there are some poles towards the east side of the river. They are not in the centre but are now surrounded by water, so they won't be used by anyone who needs to reach their ship. We could moor up to one of those. Would that suffice?"

Once they'd agreed on fair recompense, she followed him towards the ship. She let the others jump onto the jetty and proceed onto the barge before attempting it herself. If the structure were to give way beneath her, at least only she would fall in. With a twinge of jealousy, Caizhiu watched them hop over the water one by one as she walked on the slip. Even though the stone underfoot was sturdy, she felt dread well up as the water sloshed around her knees. The slats bent into the water as the jetty sagged beneath her. A glance passed between the humans on the ship, and they backed away from the boarding point.

Wexede Wanderer dipped and creaked when the dragon stepped aboard. Balancing on the tilting deck, Narastien loudly voiced the curses Tijs and Wylthren had only mumbled.

"What have you got us into, Naz?" the captain said softly.

Narastien rolled her eyes in the direction of her sister and mouthed an apology to Tijs. "It's not like I had much of a choice."

Caizhiu walked to the centre of the ship and *Wexede Wanderer* levelled out. Tijs drew a deep breath and walked towards her, sporting a civil but tense smile.

"I'm guessing that you don't spend a lot of time on ships. While we're in motion, it would be helpful if you did not move around... at all."

She wondered if the humans were aware that for once her trepidation surpassed their own. Those damned nixes had better tell her something.

TWENTY

THE NIXES

*W*exede *Wanderer* moved away from the jetty in a billow of steam, her engine working at top capacity to make headway against the river's flow. Skilfully, the crew aligned her with two pikes mid-river and tied her on. No one spoke when the deck slanted as the ship dipped beneath Caizhiu when she moved towards the boarding point. It had been bad enough at the jetty, but it was worse in the middle of the river, battered by the current. Before opening the gunnel door, she breathed in the flavour of human fear and let it roll over her tongue to quell her own unease. The rim of the deck was a few finger lengths from the grey water.

Caizhiu knelt and stuck her hand into the river. The current seized her with a grip like iron, and had she not held onto the railing, it might have unbalanced her. Water sloshed onto the deck, running down the inside of the gunnel.

{I have met your terms. Give me the audience I requested.}

{Join us.} The vortex of voices sparkled in her mind as it crashed over her. They were lively and mirthful, mocking and light. *{Let go of your raft. Prove that you have not come to do the humans' bidding.}*

From somewhere above her she heard human shouting and Heort's hooves skidding on the deck. Wylthren grabbed hold of the cervitaur's collar to prevent him from sliding towards her.

{Let go, lest you wish to endanger your human masters.} The nixes' grip held her wrist and moved up to envelop her up to her elbow, drawing her down with all the force of the torrent. *{Meet us here, in our realm. We will be gentle with you, Dragon.}*

{That's good to know.} Caizhiu focused on a single ripple in the rush, a single spin of the maelstrom, where the cold was separate from the water. The spray slowed until she saw each drop separate and then rejoin the whirls. She tightened her grip on the boat and the wood groaned beneath her fingers. *Wanderer* tipped further and then, when she had concentrated her mass and with all the speed she could chronochi, Caizhiu pulled back. For an instant it felt as if the full strength of the water resisted her. The coldness slithered from her arm, twisting to escape her grasp, and then it was almost weightless, no longer the river, but a drop. Liberated, *Wexede Wanderer* lurched and then dipped again under Caizhiu's weight. Crew and ship groaned in unison. Careful not to add to the rocking, she stood up and smiled at the nixe she held by a green-grey tentacle. *{I'll be gentle with you too.}*

An assault of panic flooded her as she watched the creature flail to free itself. Clammy tentacles coiled and uncoiled around her arm. But without the force of the river, there was no power to them. Too frightened to form a coherent song, the nixe could only engulf her with raw emotion. Caizhiu felt the tentacle shrivel and become rigid in her grip. Exposed to the air, the nixe turned bipedal with a small, sleek body and elongated limbs. Hazy colours rippled over her skin and settled into a yellowish belly and a grey back with large dull green splotches. The round head was covered with blistered tendrils that moved of their own accord, twisting and rolling as if searching for something. They left a tingling imprint when they curled around Caizhiu's hand, causing tiny jolts to shoot up her arm. The nixe's bulbous eyes blinked constantly, and the pinprick pupils darted in aimless terror. Instead of a nose she had quivering slits where human cheekbones would be, two on each side. Her mouth was a fleshy beak.

The river surged around the ship.

{Release our sister, Mighty Dragon. We were but teasing. Please. We meant no harm. Release our sister.}

Even though the vessel was tied fast, she jerked in the current as if trying to free herself. Caizhiu growled and dug her fingers into the wooden gunnel. A moment of doubt as to the competence of *Wexede Wanderer*'s crew flickered through her mind.

Caizhiu ignored the creature's twisting and her vain attempts to pry open the fist around her arm. She turned and walked towards the others, away from the gurgling river.

{Give me your name, nixe.}

At last, the creature looked at her. Caizhiu's mind filled with the purling of water flowing among stones, the sparkling of sunlight on its surface, and the fresh taste of dew.

{Is that your name?}

The nixe's nod was uncannily human.

Tijs forced a smile. Despite the juddering of the deck, he shuffled forward. He caught Caizhiu's eyes and spread his arms, holding his palms up to show the nixe that he was unarmed. Regardless, she slunk away from him, her tendrils squeezing Caizhiu's arm while she kicked and twisted to get free from the dragon's grip.

{Don't give me to the humans.}

Mildly annoyed, Caizhiu realised that the creature was more frightened of her companions than of her. She lowered her captive and placed the nixe's newly formed feet on the deck.

{I'm going to release your arm, but if you force me to catch you again, it will not go well with you. Do you understand me?}

Caizhiu opened her hand and the nixe slowly withdrew her arm. The tendrils released their hold on the dragon and twitched around the nixe's shoulders as she observed the crowd on the deck.

{I wish only to talk.} Caizhiu flexed her hand and tried to ignore the itching where the tendrils had touched her. She glanced round at the others. Wylthren stood furthest away, one hand on the gunnel of the shuddering ship and his other on Heort's shoulder.

Myrta tried to get closer but was hindered by Narastien, who stood between her sister and the nixe. The first mate occasionally scanned the ship, anticipating an attack that could come from any direction. She held the boathook as if it were a quarterstaff.

Caizhiu took a step back. The nixe looked small and forlorn on the deck. Now that she was free, Tijs' earlier confidence seemed to have paused. He bit his lip and, though he tried to sound affable, his voice trembled when he said: "I'm the captain of this ship. Welcome aboard."

The nixe flinched away from him. Her beak quivered as she gasped to get air into her rudimentary lungs.

{Please, Dragon, give me your protection.}

{In exchange for my protection, I want two things. Firstly, tell your kin to cease their jostling of this ship. And secondly, though you are known as the tricksters of the river, when I ask you questions, I wish you to be truthful.}

Wexede Wanderer settled on the waves. The calmness was so sudden that the humans nearly lost their footing.

Tijs bowed his head to the nixe. "Obliged. I'm Tijs Riverson. May I know your name?"

"This is..." Caizhiu tried to distil the nixe name into a single human word. "Purling."

"This is Purling," Purling repeated slowly, forming the syllables not via her beak but the slits on the sides of her face.

"How are you doing this?" Tijs gasped. "I know you are not my wife. But you look and even sound like her."

Caizhiu looked at the mottled green creature with her slick skin, tail, and writhing tendrils. She cocked her head and raised an eyebrow at the captain, but his gaze was fixed on Purling.

The other humans had a similarly bewildered look, but Heort sported a broad grin. *{An admirable mirage.}*

Caizhiu frowned. *{Do they all see a human, not a nixe?}*

{I think so, though it would be good to find out how Talented our young friend is.}

Heort turned to Wylthren. "Is this the first time you've seen nixes?"

"How would I know?" came the mumbled reply. "They look just like us. That... that could be my mother. She's been dead nigh on eight years, but that's... that's what she looked like."

"Look again." Heort slipped his hand in Wylthren's. "See them for what they are. See through the mirage."

The young man gasped and bit his thumb knuckle in an effort not to cry out. "I don't think I want to."

"You may as well get used to it, being Talented."

"W-will I see Caizhiu's true form too?"

"Not unless she wants you to." Heort patted his arm. "So, best not to upset her."

He smiled wanly and looked away from both nixe and dragon.

Myrta fixed the strands of her hairdo and straightened her hat. She stepped forward and her sister grabbed her arm. "Pay heed. Many a sailor has been lured to their grave on account of the voice of a loved one."

Undeterred, the First Attendant's heels clip-clopped on the deck. Myrta was only slightly taller than Purling and bowed to the nixe. After a glance at Caizhiu, Purling mimicked the gesture.

"Have they seen your target?" Myrta asked Caizhiu and chin-pointed at her hand. "Are you hurt?"

Caizhiu realised the prickliness had persisted, and she'd been rubbing her thumb over the irritation. Where Purling's tresses had touched her, the skin had reverted to her scales and her talons had forced their way through the skin. She folded her wing cloak over her hand. "It's nothing."

{A human travelled on this river,} she sang. *{His name is Ozcahar Nitt. Have the nixes seen or heard of him?}*

Purling cocked her head to make sense of her meaning. How ridiculous her query must seem to nixes. All Caizhiu had was a name, and that was a concept they struggled with. Why would an individual human have significance to them? Then Purling's blistered tendrils surged with excitement. *{Ozcahar! Frightened fish. Why you no come?}*

{Do not toy with me, nixe. You saw him?} Caizhiu nearly forgot about her hand and only just refrained from grabbing Purling in disbelief.

The tendrils convulsed around Purling's head. *{We hear them shout 'Ozcahar'.}*

Together with the echo of his name, the nixe song dowsed Caizhiu's mind with the image of a human male: hair like sand and sky-blue eyes.

{Where was this? When was this?}

Purling looked around to orientate herself and pointed down river. *{A human dwelling downstream. Two nights ago.}*

"Truly? It has seen him?" Myrta laughed and beamed at Narastien, who returned a wishy-washy smile.

Caizhiu lowered onto her haunches so she was at eye level with Purling. *{Can you give me his scent?}*

The nixe blinked, uncertain what she was asked for. It was a perception too far. Caizhiu held up her intact hand. *{Never mind. You've done well. I'm obliged.}*

{Now that you have what you want, may I rejoin my kin?} Purling hugged her arms around herself. *{Or do you intend another end for me?}*

{You'll have my protection until I return you to the river. But perhaps we can be of further help to each other.}

Caizhiu stood up and gestured for Wylthren to approach. Reflexively he looked behind him, and, realising she meant him, his eyes found Myrta. She placed a hand on his arm. As an apprentice guard he was part of the

Magistrate's responsibility, and by extension hers. "What are you planning, Caizhiu?"

"I won't kill him."

From the reaction of Wylthren, Myrta, and even Heort, it was obvious her words were not the comfort she had intended them to be.

"Did you not want to be, how did you put it, *invaluable*?" Caizhiu grinned at Wylthren. "You should be wary with your wishes. You never know when the Six may be listening."

Myrta pointed at Caizhiu. "I trust you not to harm him. Don't make me regret that."

She didn't stop the dragon guiding Wylthren to the gunnel. Purling followed and observed. *{The human is frightened of you.}*

{Yes, he is.}

Purling placed a hand, cold and slender and without a thumb, on Caizhiu's arm. The dragon stifled her instinct to pull back, but this touch didn't have the same tingling effect as the creature's tresses had.

{Dragon, we don't trade in human lives. We have no interest in them.}

{Have no fear. I'm not about to offer him to you.}

Wylthren stopped dead. "I should hope not!"

{Your perception is improving.} So as not to overwhelm his senses, Caizhiu used her flattest soul song. *{That will make the next step easier.}*

She placed her good hand against his back and gently urged him to walk on. By the gap in the gunnel, where she'd fished Purling from the river, she got the young man to kneel, and she squatted by his side. The deck dipped, lowering them to the river's surface. Purling stared at the water longingly, but she stayed put. It would be extremely difficult to pluck the creature from the river a second time, but even the slim chance that she might be able to prevented the nixe from absconding.

{Before I set you free, would you and your kin consider how curious it is that you are frightened of the humans, and the humans are frightened of you?}

With liberation in sight, vivacity returned to Purling's song. *{Why are humans frightened of us? They are so plentiful and so fast with sturdy rafts like this.}*

{Most humans are neath. It makes them afraid. But there are some that are otherkin.}

Purling cocked her head at Wylthren, who sat slack-jawed, trying to untangle the assault of impressions that washed over him.

{Which is he?}

{He's becoming otherkin.}

Caizhiu gently closed Wylthren's mouth. "Let's try with something basic. All you need to do is request help."

"Help with what?"

She placed her finger on his lips. *{Not with your verbal voice.}*

Careful not to let her claws slice into his skin, she grabbed his neck and dunked his face into the whirling Wexede. Expletives resounded between Narastien and Tijs. Wylthren flailed his arms to get purchase either on the ship or the hand around his neck. His desperate blows barely registered against her scales. Bubbles exploded around the submerged face. Caizhiu raised him up enough for his spluttering cough and breath, before dunking him back down.

{I don't think he can breathe in the water.}

It took Caizhiu a second to realise Purling had made the observation in earnest.

Wylthren stopped struggling and let himself go limp. His strategy of conserving his breath allowed him to stay under longer, but his reserves weren't unending, and he squeezed her wing cloak with increasing intensity.

{Come on, Wylthren. You can do this.}

His waterlogged pleas were unintelligible. Caizhiu wished she hadn't said she wouldn't kill him. Perhaps it would have been quicker if he thought she would.

"Enough of this!" Myrta sounded shrill, frightened. "Let him go."

Caizhiu told her to be quiet. She hauled Wylthren up, heard his frantic release of breath, and pushed him down before he could draw a new one. His response wasn't exactly a word, not even an impression, but she felt it nevertheless. Like Purling earlier, it was merely an emotional surge, a primal desire to live. She had perceived it. As had Purling, Heort, and probably every nixe up and down the river.

Caizhiu stood up, hauling Wylthren with her, hacking, wheezing, and puking river water onto the deck. His breathing came in jagged sobs as his hands and feet tried to find purchase on the deck. Inadvertently she'd snapped the restraint on his braid and his black curls drooped about his shoulders. With her good hand she wiped a strand from his face, but he pushed her away.

"This..." His eyes were closed, and he slumped against the gunnel, gasping for breath. "Is because... of that gold... isn't it? You've... never forgiven me... for that."

Caizhiu smiled and ruffled his wet hair. {*Not terrible for a first attempt. I'd suggest you practise your soul song with them... and Lord Veentar, of course.*}

She cocked her head at Purling, who scrutinised Wylthren in wonder and cautiously approached him. Wylthren's earlier alarm at the sight of the nixe had evaporated. Purling seemed fascinated at the concept of a Talented human and Caizhiu repressed her now familiar surge of annoyance at Yullorik. With a smug grin, she turned to Myrta, only to receive a look of impotent fury. It was then that she realised the others did not share her satisfaction at a job well done. This is what she got for dealing with neathkin. She should have taken her own advice and steered clear of the brewing conflict, left the humans to sort out their own mess.

{*You're free to return to the river whenever you please,*} she told Purling, and the nixe bowed to Wylthren before disappearing into the grey water.

He went to spit over the side, thought better of it, and wiped his mouth on his sleeve. "Caizhiu? Purling wondered..." He searched for the translation of soul senses into words. "Is the Ozcahar... of this ship... missing?"

TWENTY-ONE

A TRACE OF OZCAHAR

"Ozcahar? They're looking for Ozcahar?" Tijs turned to Narastien. "Did you know about this?"

"Naz, I asked you if you'd heard of him," Myrta hissed. "Why didn't you say something?"

Narastien's knuckles paled as her fists tightened around the boathook. "Why should I? Who is this Caizhiu that I should answer his questions?"

For a moment no one aboard drew breath; even the waves and the reeds seemed to hush. Caizhiu walked towards the first mate. None of this had been necessary. She hadn't needed to get on this damned river. She hadn't needed to get embroiled in the human–nixes conflict, if only this woman had spoken up. Slowly, but surefooted, Narastien retreated towards the other side of the barge, where there was a narrower gap between the wheelhouse and the gunnel. Too narrow for Caizhiu.

Myrta's fingers brushed her wing cloak and Caizhiu moved it out of reach.

"We didn't realise who it was you were looking for," Tijs said and stepped forward, conciliatory hands raised.

"*She* did."

"That's my problem to deal with." Tijs refused to move back. Caizhiu was standing so close that she could feel the rapid beating of his heart. "She's *my* crew."

She picked the captain up under his arms and set him aside.

The *Wexede Wanderer* listed to the other side as Caizhiu followed Narastien.

"It would have saved me a lot of trouble if you had been honest with your sister. You had better tell me what you know of Ozcahar Nitt."

"Oh death upon you!" If the woman was frightened, she overshadowed it with anger. "He never wronged me. Why should I help the monster that's chasing him?"

From behind her Caizhiu heard Myrta utter a pained groan, a muttered curse, and Naz's name.

{*Tread carefully, my friend.*} Heort was right, of course. Myrta had been upset at witnessing her treatment of Wylthren. She would consider seeing something similar with her sister, however embarrassing she was, unforgiveable.

Narastien kept upright on the tilting ship by walking backwards over the gunnel. She held on to the wheelhouse with one hand and the boathook with the other.

"Come on then," she goaded, and, at the slightest movement of the dragon, she added, "I'll throw myself overboard rather than help you."

"Your life is yours to squander." Caizhiu shrugged and opened the door to the wheelhouse. She waved her hand to waft the indoor air past her nose. To the back of the small room, she espied a hatch that led to the living quarters and cabins.

"Besides," she added with a sardonic grin, "what makes you think I couldn't simply get the nixes to deliver you back here?"

Narastien glanced at the water. That was the moment Caizhiu chose to duck and take a large step into the wheelhouse. Shifting her weight back to the centre of the ship caused the *Wexede Wanderer* to heave upwards. The scooping motion unbalanced the first mate, and she lost her footing. The boathook clattered to the deck. Her hand slid down the wheelhouse, so that she managed to slow her fall, but her knees still thudded onto the deck.

Heort swayed towards her, adjusting his hooves to stay upright as the vessel rose and fell. Narastien grabbed the boathook and staggered to her feet. Her face was twisted in pain, and she pointed the hook at Heort.

"Don't you approach further!"

He held his hands out. "If you be hurt, maybe I can help."

"Obviously, I'm hurt," Narastien spat back. "Just keep away from me."

Caizhiu stuck her head through the wheelhouse door and gestured to Heort to join her. She turned to Tijs and said: "Did you not refer to her as your problem to deal with? I suggest you do so."

She led Heort into the wheelhouse.

{I have no salves for the friendships you wounded.}

{Humans are resilient creatures. They'll get over it.}

She pointed at the hatch at the rear of the wheelhouse to the down below. It was too cramped for the dragon to get through, let alone move around inside the ship. But she could catch the scents from within: acrid verve, food in various states of preparation and decay, and the body odour of four humans that lingered in the mattresses of their berths.

{I need you to get down below and get me a scent profile.}

His earth-brown eyes were white-rimmed with fear as he stared into the dark hole. Caizhiu placed her hand firmly on his shoulder. As her fingers fanned over his shoulder, he looked at her thumbnail that punctured his jacket at the edge of his collarbone.

{By the Grace of the Six, what happened to your hand?}

{It was the damned nixe. Don't concern yourself with that now.} She pushed him towards the entrance and felt his back stiffen under her grip.

His hooves skidded on the polished wood of the floor, and he licked either side of his nose.

{*It's got one of those ladder things. I don't do well with ladders.*}

Caizhiu stroked his downy ears and added contrition to her song. {*I'll help you in and I'll help you out. You have my word I won't leave you in there.*}

He gave an audible gulp and a curt nod. She lifted him up under his arms, dangling his long, slender body over the entry. He kicked his four legs for purchase and winced when his ankles and shins found the runs before his hooves did. Once he had a foothold, Caizhiu gently lowered him. His hands gripped her arms, and she felt him squeeze them all the way until they held hands and his hind legs stood on the lower deck. She could only see the whites of his eyes in the dark.

{*Promise me you won't make this floating contraption bounce around.*}

{*I'll try to resist the urge.*}

In response he shared a glimpse of the suffocating closeness of the walls and the slickness under his hooves. Someone walked around on the deck and Heort flinched.

{*The cabins,*} Caizhiu urged. {*The quicker you get this done, the quicker I can get you out.*}

He walked along the narrow hallway with the galley to his left and two cabins on his right. By the smell, the door in front of him led to the captain's cabin.

{*Find the familiar.*} Caizhiu closed her eyes to concentrate on his soul song, all the impressions he included.

{*Familiar?*}

{*We can discount the scents of the humans on deck. That leaves two unknowns. But I have a feeling we have come across Ozcahar Nitt's scent before, though we didn't know it.*}

Heort opened the door to the cabin where the berths reeked of young human males.

{*That one,*} Caizhiu said when he turned to the berth on the right. In her mind's eye she saw the golden horse and rider in Myrta's front room. She had breathed in the delicious aroma of the gold and, at the time, had not distinguished the fainter one beneath it. Here Heort had found the same scent. The scent of the sandy-haired man.

***

In the approaching dusk, Myrta had decided to discard the precarious path along the river and take the inland road back to Wexede Crossing. Caizhiu had never known her to be as quiet as she had been in the past couple of hours. Her sister had stayed behind at the ship. Neither she nor Tijs had mentioned Ozcahar Nitt again, even when they thought Caizhiu was out of earshot. Her initial elation at finding the scent profile had quickly turned to disappointment. Walking behind the buggy, Caizhiu realised they were following the same road to the city her quarry must have used, but little betrayed his passing. It had only been a day and the multiple downpours had dispersed the trail. If the man was in the city still, she had a chance of finding him. But he had evaded her once, either through wit or fortune, and most likely he had already departed. If she didn't catch up to him soon, his trail from Wexede Crossing would fade as quickly as the one here had.

The road was more solid than the muddy track on the riverside of the embankment. A soft rain resumed, landing in quivering balls on her shoulders. She watched them join into rivulets and run down her wing cloak. As she did so, Heort caught her eyes.

{Let me have a look at that hand.}

She glanced in the direction of the buggy to see if they hadn't acquired curious gazes, but neither of the occupants had stuck their head out of the window. She uncovered her hand and held it out to him. To her relief, the colour had returned to the brown of human skin and though the nails were still talonesque, she'd managed to retract most of their length. *{I can't quite get it back into shape. It resists, like it's asleep.}*

{Has this happened before?}

She shook her head. *{Never. Is it venom?}*

{Nixes aren't venomous.} He traced the faint ridges of her scales with his fingertips. *{It seems to be some sort of after-effect, a reaction to something. Did you feel anything?}*

{It... tingled.}

She withdrew her hand and tucked it under her cloak as they walked through the northerly Welcome Gate. The city lights had not yet come on, but it wouldn't be long. In the alley behind the Law and Trade Guild building, the buggy pulled to a stop, and the driver jumped off to open the carriage door.

Myrta had refashioned her hair, straightened her dress, but dark circles under her eyes gave her a haunted expression. "You and I need to have a word."

Caizhiu concluded from the First Attendant's tone that she wouldn't get the appreciation she deserved. Feigned contrition was likely expected, but she had never been good at that. Rather than waiting, she stepped forward to meet Myrta halfway and held out her good hand. The First Attendant lifted her face into the rain as she looked up at her adversary. Droplets formed a dark trail from her eyes and over her cheeks as if drawing tears.

"If you want your damned gold back, you'd better explain to me why you assaulted one of my guardsmen for, as far as I can tell, no reason." She took a deep breath and added softly: "I trusted you."

"You made it clear your loyalties lie with Lord Veentar and I respect that." Caizhiu diverted her glance at the buggy to the city guards that were milling around the building. Attendants and guards were readying themselves to go home or find the nearest watering hole. She bent to Myrta and tempered her voice. "But even you must admit that he has his limitations. I wager that you have done more than your share taking care of his business. Case in point; it was you on that boat today and not him, though he is the Talented one."

Myrta bit her lip as though physically restraining her riposte.

"As misfortune would have it, you are not Talented," Caizhiu continued. "Wylthren is. It might have taken months to determine that, had we used more... delicate ways. Moreover, the nixes needed to know that there is at least one human they can speak with, should they need to. If Yullorik can be bothered to tutor him, Wylthren might be useful to you... and the nixes."

Myrta sucked in her cheeks and, after a deep breath, said: "Are you saying that you tortured him for *our* benefit?"

"It expedited his Talent."

"Have you considered the possibility that the type of assistance you provide may not be necessary? That we don't need it?"

Caizhiu blinked but said nothing.

"You came to us for help." Myrta turned towards the buggy and glanced at Wylthren. "Don't presume we can't manage our own affairs."

The city lights had sprung to life, and Wylthren stood in their watery glow. Having exited the carriage, he had finally managed to light a cigarette. He leant against the buggy, his head lowered so that his hood kept the rain off his smouldering birch roll. He raised his chin at Myrta to acknowledge her signal and reached inside the buggy to retrieve Caizhiu's haversack.

Wylthren had got rid of the little birch roll by the time he got to them, treading it into the mud, and he'd tied his hair back to keep it from blowing across his face. His polite nod at Myrta was reciprocated crisply. She extended her hand, palm up, signalling for him to speak candidly.

Wylthren handed Caizhiu her bag and, meeting her stare, said: "You got what you came for. Please tell me you're leaving."

"Like last time, you were not completely useless." Caizhiu hesitated. "You have my gratitude, young Wylthren."

"I will remember that."

For the first time, he'd judged the weight of those words correctly. She hoped that, if they were destined to meet again, the animosity he felt would have eased.

She bobbed her head towards Myrta. "I assume we have overstayed our welcome, so if you'll excuse us, I'll continue my hunt and attempt to trouble the city no further. Please relay my gratitude to your wife for her welcome, and my... respect to Magistrate Veentar."

Myrta returned the gesture. She did not argue and did not try to persuade the dragon to stay at her house again.

Caizhiu was going to say something else, but then she caught the scent. She spun round, searching for the source. Closing her eyes, she ignored the comments from Myrta and Wylthren. When she opened them again, the lights around the building seemed to congregate, as if the falling rain reflected their glow in one specific direction. She took no chances and chronochi'ed across the road, weaving between the aimless people, scattering some like the raindrops in her wake. She grabbed the front of the hapless man's cloak. Pinning him to the doorframe with her bad hand, she folded his hood back with her good one. Brown curls sprang around his head and his face carried considerably more wrinkles than the man the nixes had seen. The guard's eyes widened, and cries of surprise and alarm were joined by the sounds of his colleagues fumbling with and cocking their pistols.

"Curse you, Caizhiu!"

Though lacking its usual grace, Myrta's voice carried enough authority for Caizhiu to let go of the man's cloak. The guardsman crumpled but caught himself. His trembling hands gripped the doorframe and the object he'd been holding landed on the floor with a dull thud. Caizhiu stepped back, causing the city guards around her to do the same. A hand landed forcefully on her shoulder, and she knew without needing to look that it was Wylthren's. He was one of the few people that could reach that high and still have some strength left. The gesture wasn't meant to impress her but to show his colleagues that she was under control.

"Apologies, Guardsman Huurik," Wylthren said to the cornered man and held his hand up to his colleagues. "He... ehm... thought you were somebody else."

"Your friend should calm his ways." The guard straightened up and adjusted his uniform. "Next time he might get his head shot off."

"I wouldn't describe us as friends," Wylthren muttered.

Myrta joined them and finally the guards lowered their pistols.

"Keepers preserve us, Caizhiu! What did we just talk about? Stop harassing the City Guard."

"I didn't want to risk him getting away," Caizhiu said with a shrug.

"Away with what?" Huurik sounded bewildered. "Honestly, First Attendant, I'm just now returning from my shift. I've done nothing."

Caizhiu picked up the haversack the guard had dropped and breathed in the smell that was unmistakably the same as the sandy-haired man's.

"We don't believe you have done anything wrong," Myrta reassured him.

Curiosity replaced wariness in his eyes as he looked Caizhiu over.

"We retrieved the bag from a ruckus in the southern quarter this morning." Huurik took a moment to build suspense, but not letting it linger so long that his audience had to prompt him to continue. "A small mob of citizens set upon a company of Sarfi travellers."

"That is not the behaviour I would expect from our citizenry. I hope you made some arrests."

"We issued warnings and some fines, but to be fair, the assault wasn't entirely baseless, First Attendant. The travellers carried a dweymin curse. We did refuse them entry, but it's been so busy it was easy for them to slip past. They were here only for a single night."

"And to whom did this haversack belong?" Myrta asked, but there was no doubt in Caizhiu's mind with whose aroma the content was marinated.

"I'm not sure. There was a scuffle going on when we arrived, but since none of the citizens claimed it, I guess it was left by the Sarfi. We escorted them out of the city, First Attendant. Made sure they left this time too."

"By which Farewell Gate did they leave?"

Huurik looked at one of his fellow guards for confirmation and said: "The southern one."

A quiet sigh escaped Myrta's lips. "It would appear that you know where to continue your hunt, Caizhiu. Keepers' Kindness, it is not within our city."

Caizhiu bowed to her. "I'm obliged to you, First Attendant."

Stuffing Ozcahar Nitt's haversack into her own, she walked towards the southern exit of Wexede Crossing. If fortune willed it, she could catch up with her quarry before daybreak. And, even more urgently, hidden in the darkness of the wilds, she could finally have a piss.

Part III

Twenty-Two

Into the Dreadwoods

Ozcahar was not sure how long he'd dozed, but when he opened his eyes, Mihai sat in front of him, a rifle across his knees. It was warm inside the covered wagon. Thick drapes separated different sections, muffling the creaking of the carriage. Soft furs and ochre and blue patterned throws covered the furniture. An elaborate bhodine light swung gently from the ceiling, scattering colourful triangles around the living room.

Mihai looked up. He wore a wonky set of spectacles that rocked when he smiled. Ozcahar spotted a satchel with tools on the table between them and that the man had removed the rifle's lock.

"Where be we?" Ozcahar's voice was hoarse with the dry heat.

Mihai pushed a tray across the table and grunted for him to take a cup. The creamy drink with a bittersweet aftertaste was still warm and lubricated his throat.

Mihai and K'Netta had taken turns to drive the cart, urging the oxen to keep up with the auto carriages that moved at a near constant pace.

After their brief stop, when Ozcahar had been allowed to travel with them, Roovie had returned to her parents, which he had learnt were Brayshen and his wife.

He no longer felt the spongy bounce of the wheels rolling along the marsh paths, nor did he hear the slurping and squelching as wooden slats were swallowed and spat out by the bog. The movements of the wagon were jerky and less forgiving.

"Where be we?" he repeated, stronger of voice.

Without looking up from his cleaning work, Mihai said, "We travel uphill into Dreadwoods."

He circled his finger at the soft scraping of branches on the roof. "Perhaps we stop-to-rest, perhaps we dark-trek. Darjani will say."

Ozcahar watched in silence how the man carefully cleaned the rifle. Mihai inspected the wear on the flint with an inscrutable expression, so that Ozcahar couldn't tell if the mechanism was in decent or terrible condition.

"Have you a..." He searched for the right word. "A no-friend away from city?"

Mihai reassembled the gun, testing the resistance in the movements and ensuring the hammer lined up. "A no-friend? Ah, you mean foes. Yes, Karri. Outside city, inside city; there be no difference. That be reason Crossingers want us away. Foes find us, always."

When the wagon jostled to a halt, he handed the rifle to Ozcahar and jumped to his feet. On his way out, he grabbed a bag and the rifle that was hung on the wall. Ozcahar gulped down the last of the drink, tightening his grip on the rifle. More and more he got the sense that he should have taken his chances with the City Guard in Wexede Crossing.

The wagon and the two auto carriages stood in a clearing. Ozcahar stared up at the impenetrable trellis of reedy trees that surrounded them, finding it impossible to tell how far they stretched. The road behind them and the one ahead vanished into blackness. High and wispy clouds glided past the moon and cast amorphous shadows among the bare branches that quivered in the breeze.

Darjani and Brayshen walked towards the wagon. They carried their rifles not over their shoulders but in both hands, though the barrels were pointed towards the ground.

"We must dark-trek," Darjani whispered urgently. "Clear Dreadwoods hastily."

"That may be," K'Netta answered, quiet but firm. "But oxen require rest and food."

She didn't wait for a response but climbed from the driver's seat, kicked a chock behind the wagon's wheel, and untied the foaming animals from the yoke.

Mihai shrugged at the others. "She be correct. Long uphill trek ahead. We too require rest and food." He pointed at the auto carriages. "Have you enough verve for a dark-trek? Enough till sun-up?"

Brayshen frowned and rubbed the back of his neck. "I think yes."

Darjani swung the rifle over his shoulder and squeezed the arms of both Brayshen and Mihai. "Agreed then. We rest and we eat. Afterward we dark-trek."

Mihai turned and motioned for Ozcahar to join them. "Know you how shoot that?" he asked, pointing at the rifle.

Ozcahar shook his head. As a boy he'd daydreamed about owning a pistol, but Jorganyon had joked he would likely shoot his own foot off.

Mihai scratched his beard cheek line, smudging it with a greasy mark. "I teach you."

"Kem and Uritta also," Darjani said. "They require repeats."

Ozcahar followed Mihai. When he was introduced to Kem and Uritta, it surprised him how young they looked. They regarded him with a mixture of poorly disguised scepticism and genuine curiosity. Kem turned out to be the son of Mihai and K'Netta. His flaming red hair was tied severely into the smallest ponytail Ozcahar had ever seen, and he had a face marked with the scars of adolescent skin. "You be that vagrant then."

It was a casual conclusion without judgement. He was oblivious to his father's frown until Uritta elbowed him and then the boy looked confused and offended.

Uritta looked about the same age. She travelled in the lead auto carriage, with Darjani, his wife, Shofranka, and their infant son. Ozcahar guessed she was Shofranka's sister on account of their matching mahogany ringlets. The girl smirked as she pulled a pistol from her belt.

Mihai was a good teacher and Ozcahar enjoyed learning how to load and fire the rifle. Once he'd got over his nerves, his fingers seemed better able to deal with the powder and shot. Kem and Uritta were quicker at the procedure. Though they mocked each other mercilessly, they gave Ozcahar only encouraging comments.

A plug of fabric in his ear muffled the crack of the rifle. He'd pulled the trigger and the target tree's bark shattered. He couldn't help but grin from the rush of power he felt. The second shot slammed the tree in almost the same place, as did the third. Mihai asked if he truly had not shot before.

"Lucky," Ozcahar said. It was the first time he could say that.

Uritta cocked her head at him and smiled. She was skilful at loading her pistols, but her hesitation at the discharge skewed her aim. Mihai said it didn't matter. In the darkness ahead their targets would have to be a lot closer than the tree in order to identify them.

"No shoot *us*," he warned each of them repeatedly.

Brayshen's wife, Pabelie, made use of a pause in their practising to bring them a bowl of a hearty but bland soup. Roovie skipped next to her and handed each a hunk of bread. As she waited for them to finish, Pabelie pulled her shawl tight around her shoulders. Kem giggled when she took his empty bowl before he had even swallowed the last mouthful. "We trek on already?"

Pabelie pressed her lips together, nodded, and grabbed Roovie by the hand so fiercely the little girl began to snivel. Her mother's frown silenced her, and she helped to bring the empty bowls to the carriage.

The exuberance at sharpening their shooting skills vanished with the darkening of a cloud that passed by the moon. Mihai placed his hand on his son's shoulder and looked at each of his students. "It be full dark soon. With luck we dark-trek in peace. Otherwise you must use your skills for good or bad. Kem, you travel with me. Uritta travel with Brayshen and Pabelie."

Mihai fished spare shooting paraphernalia from his bag and pressed them in Ozcahar's hand. "You travel with Darjani. May you stay lucky."

Ozcahar bowed. He felt able to hold his head high as he walked to the first auto carriage.

Darjani welcomed Ozcahar onto the driver's seat and started the lead vehicle. He pointed at the ammunition bag strapped to the seat between them and the powder flask hanging from the ceiling. They had ensured no light leaked from the living quarters, but there was nothing to be done about the noise of the engines, the hissing of the steam, or the scraping of the metal-rimmed wheels on the ground as they traversed roots and rocks. They had travelled in this compromised silence for half an hour when Darjani cleared his throat and, keeping his eyes fixed on the road ahead, asked: "Has Mihai told you of our danger?"

"He say you have foe."

"This be true. A foe who hunt us. Where you live, have you dweymin?" Seeing the incomprehension on Ozcahar's face, he searched for a better, possibly familiar, term. "Have you wolf-but-not-wolf, half-wolf, man-wolf?"

Ozcahar shook his head.

"Be Six obliged you have not. Dweymin be scourge of travelling folk. Monsters who curse our women and steal our children."

Ozcahar couldn't help but glance at the man, even though he wanted to keep his attention on the nebulous trees. "What look have they?"

"When first you see them, you think they be human. But when near, you see they be too broad, too full of fur. Like a man wearing thick rug, and... their face..." His voice changed. The tone had started as one telling a tale, but its vigour waned, and it shifted to a deeper level, one of unwelcome reminiscence.

"They have face alike..." He mimed an elongated snout. "With many cutthroat teeth, and yellow eyes."

A rasping scream sounded from the darkness. Ozcahar spun round so fast he nearly lost his balance. He cocked the rifle, moving it left to right at the trees, looking for the direction he thought the cry had come from.

"Be calm," Darjani said with a mirthless chuckle. "That be only night-bird."

Ozcahar lowered his weapon and licked his lips. His heartbeat took longer to quieten.

"Why hunt the..." He forced his tongue around the strange word. "Deemin... Why hunt they you?"

It took a long while before Darjani answered. "They come for my brother's child."

Whenever the moonlight allowed, Ozcahar studied the darkness in the woods on either side of them. Even though he knew them to be birds, the eerie echoed calls sent a shiver up his back. As they climbed, the trees grew sparser, and their roots and trunks contorted as they'd grown past boulders from the stony ground. They seemed to be covered in rough scales and the branches covered in a spiky fur. There were many trees in the rooftop gardens of Thirdburg, but in all their variety of foliage, he had never seen trees with needles before.

Darjani put more strain on the engine to get the carriage up the ascending road. Ozcahar shifted in his seat. He wasn't sure how long they had travelled, but the cold of the night had settled into his muscles. He wiped the condensation off the tip of his nose with his sleeve and flexed his fingers to make sure they would still be able to pull the trigger should it be needed. Stealing a glance at his companion he noticed the big man blinked repeatedly and patted his own cheeks to stay alert.

"Let me drive carriage," he said. "You sleep short time."

Darjani thought it over and then talked Ozcahar through the controls. "What distance behind be Brayshen's carriage?"

Ozcahar leant out from the bench to peer into the darkness. He could hear the creaking and hissing of the other auto carriage, but it wasn't easy to see in the dark. As his eyes adjusted, a break in the canopy of the furry trees cast pale light over the caravan. He could make out the outline of the auto carriage and beyond the shape of Mihai and K'Netta's wagon. Beyond that, he counted at least a dozen pairs of yellow eyes.

TWENTY-THREE

FIGHTING THE DWEYMIN

In the dark solitude of the marshlands, Caizhiu indulged in taking her own shape. Yet, whenever the clouds thinned to reveal the full moon, she glanced around for imaginary onlookers. Away from the stench of the city, she could concentrate on the more subtle aromas in the damp, heavy air of the night. Many travellers had trodden the marsh paths with their wares and livestock, and their miscellaneous odours lingered among the wooden slats. Among them were the scattered dashes of Ozcahar Nitt. She resounded his name in her head, using it to layer his details over: how his yellow hair reminded her of gold, how his odour reminded her of Thirdburg's lofty walkways, the sea, an ointment he'd used to treat broken skin and how it mixed with a hint of Narastien. No matter how many humans he'd surrounded himself with, she would know him.

Leaving the scents of the swamp behind her, she followed the trail of her quarry up into the aromatic fusion of the Fraakywuld. He had taken a track due south, climbing higher into the pines, towards the Marsarin Massif. Caizhiu moved at a quick pace, but not quite a run. She knew how far humans travelled in a day and expected to come across his encampment at any moment. The night was drawing on and he would have to rest at some point.

It was impossible to keep the light of the night sky from one of her four eyes, and it left the others blinded by comparison in the darksome shade beneath the pines. Winking was an ability she had often admired and never mastered. While gazing at the round moon, it occurred to her that tonight was the moment she should have emerged.

Heort appeared at her side. His eyes were far better suited for the darkness, and he appeared to be searching for something. He licked his nose. *{Have you noticed how quiet it is?}*

The dragon shrugged and inadvertently rustled the branches of the shrubbery with her wings. The sound illustrated what Heort had remarked upon. She was unconcerned; the landscape usually quieted as she moved through it.

{It's not you this time. There are hunters about. Dweymin, by the smell of them.}

Once he'd mentioned it, Caizhiu caught the canine-like reek of the creatures. It brought to mind the scar on Euvie's shoulder. She growled at the prospect that someone else might get to her quarry first, that he would be killed before she found him. Her patron might be dead, but that didn't mean she'd allow herself to fail. Her word had been given. The agreement stood.

She had hoped to ask Ingrirath whether, even if she could not reduce her size in the next iteration, she would halt her growth. That hope had shattered into pieces with the Keeper's death. But perhaps the other Five, or Ingrirath's successor, would be able to grant her that as payment. Dead, Ozcahar Nitt would be worth nothing.

Needled branches hit her face as she sped up the foothills of the Marsarin Massif. Her trail whipped through the shrubs. The dweymin scent converged with her quarry's. She smelled the lingering stench of discharged powder weapons. How long would human travellers be able to hold out against the pack?

***

Ozcahar dared not glance at Darjani. Afraid to blink, his gaze remained fixed on the dark woods ahead of them. The engine buzzed and roared as they climbed the precipitous path, shrouding the landscape in clouds of steam. While gripping the rifle with one hand and the handrail with the other, he couldn't prevent the bristling branches from lashing his face. His legs shook with the effort it took to push his back against the carriage to prevent being thrown. He wondered how well Darjani knew the roads, hoped he had a plan, but feared he was hurtling them up the mountain just to get out of the dreaded woods.

All around, the dweymins called their howling, growling phrases to each other. They had abandoned their stealthy tracking and tried to flank the caravan. Occasionally, he glimpsed hairy bodies running between the trees; sometimes they ran on two legs, lifting their heads to fix his stare with their amber eyes. Other times, they sprinted on all fours to catch up or overtake. One jumped towards the carriage, its paw wrapping around the handrail, and Ozcahar slammed the butt of the rifle into the snarling face. The auto carriage careered along the road. When the dweymin fell back, he nearly followed it.

A shot rang out from behind, followed by a yelp too filled with agony to determine if it had been made by man or beast. The trees ahead spread out, and by the light of the moon, Ozcahar could see the chasm they were heading towards. A cry of shock muted on his lips when Darjani veered the vehicle to the left to ride it alongside the ravine. Darjani raced the carriage along the ridge, higher and higher, bumping over the stone path. A dweymin sprang onto the road ahead of them. He couldn't tell if it was the same creature that had tried to jump onto the driver's seat. In the night, they all looked the same: a blur of dark fur with a pale stripe on either side of their back. It jumped aside when Darjani barrelled towards it while another leapt across the road and again the vehicle gave a wobble, causing it to slow and forcing Ozcahar to brace to keep his seat. A monster jumped onto the carriage, claws tearing at his trousers, scraping his skin before they dug in. Ozcahar let himself fall backwards and kicked at his assailant to give himself time to aim the rifle. He bumped into Darjani, and the carriage lurched to the right. The left front wheel dropped into a narrow cleft in the road, but their momentum forced the rear of the auto carriage onwards. With a loud crack and spray of rivets, the wheel split from the axle. Ozcahar was free from the dweymin's grasp, but airborne. The dweymin hit a tree with a nauseating crunch, but Ozcahar was fortunate to curl into a roll around the rifle. He came to a stop and staggered to his feet. The monster didn't move. The second auto carriage had not halted in time, and he saw Brayshen dive off the driver's seat as it smashed into the first. The front wheels collapsed under the force and the vehicle toppled. Supplies that had been strapped to the roof landed all about him, but it was Darjani that caught Ozcahar's attention. The big man had also been thrown clear. He shook his head, but as he got to his feet, a dweymin rushed towards him from the woods. Ozcahar's fingers found the powder flask. He aimed the rifle, followed the running creature with the barrel, and fired. The shot thumped into the carriage roof, but the dweymin skidded, veering to the side in case a second shot wouldn't miss. The ammunition pouch was still strapped to the seat and Ozcahar was as good as unarmed with his discharged gun. In the little time it had bought him, Darjani drew a curved dagger from its scabbard and leapt at the assailant. The dweymin lashed out with its paws to fend him off. Both withdrew with minor wounds, circling each other for the next attack.

Shrubbery exploded as a trio of dweymins sprang forth, one heading straight for Ozcahar. By zigzagging, he narrowly avoided the charge. He put his entire weight behind ramming the butt of the gun against the elongated jaw. Rows of needle teeth perforated the creature's tongue. He hit it again, as hard as he could, but the dweymin merely shook its head, blood and saliva spraying Ozcahar's face. Brayshen motioned for him to find cover. He ducked to avoid one of the creature's enormous claws as a shot rang out, and the dweymin fell backwards. Ozcahar ran towards the carriages.

Darjani stood backed against the roof of the toppled carriage. His assailant pressed his right hand against the wood so he couldn't use his blade, but the big man held his other hand around the creature's throat. Ozcahar swung the rifle to hit the dweymin across the back of the head. Though the blow was powerful, the creature didn't flinch. It moved fast, turning away from Darjani, its claw grabbing the front of Ozcahar's coat. In one smooth movement, it lifted him off his feet and threw him into Brayshen. Their skulls collided.

Ozcahar came to with his face in the dirt. His head throbbed and for a moment he thought he was back in the street with Brayshen's fists grasping his collar.

"Darjani!"

Ozcahar followed Brayshen's gaze to his brother, who had kicked the dweymin and freed his dagger. He swung it, intending to slice into its shoulder, but his opponent twisted, and he only sliced its arm. The dweymin buried its teeth into Darjani's throat and tore out a clump of bearded flesh. The big man fell to his knees, holding his throat with both hands. Then he slumped to his side and was still. Brayshen shook his head, his gaze turned inwards, and seemed unaware of the four dweymins surrounding them. Ozcahar shook the man's shoulder when thunderous explosions erupted overhead.

Kem had taken up a position between the two carriages and was firing pistols as quick as Uritta could load them. They held the dweymins at bay long enough for Ozcahar and Brayshen to dive between the wheels of the auto carriage into relative safety. Pabelie pulled the men to their feet and Uritta took the rifle off Ozcahar. The girl's headscarf was stuck to the side of her head. With a vacant expression on her bloodstained face, she loaded the rifle, handing it back to him together with a ramrod and ammunition.

Brayshen joined Shofranka, who stood by the gap between the two auto carriages, firing through the crack. Kem laid at their feet to stop any dweymins that tried to slide under the carriage.

"Go there," Uritta commanded, pointing at Mihai's wagon. The two crashed carriages formed a barrier between the humans and their attackers. K'Netta had parked their wagon behind the carriage, so completing a semi-circle. Behind the company was the ravine. The drop was too steep to attempt a climb down, but it also prevented the dweymins from climbing up. Ozcahar wondered how much shot they had between them. As long as they had ammunition, they might be able to hold out, but unless aid came, the dweymins only had to wait.

The oxen bellowed and arched their backs against their yokes. K'Netta struggled to get them within the half-circle, but the frightened animals resisted. In their desire to flee, Ozcahar had to move from his position so as not to get squashed between the vehicles.

At that moment, one of the dweymins spotted Ozcahar and grabbed hold of the rifle. They tussled nose to nose. The face of the monster was flatter, the teeth blunted and the ears less pronounced than the ones that had attacked him earlier. It was as if Ozcahar stared into rippling water and saw a distorted human face.

Behind him, one of the oxen jerked his head and a large horn caught the strap of Ozcahar's powder flask. He and the dweymin were tossed to the side, and slammed into the carriage with such force it winded Ozcahar. His assailant had let go of the rifle and looked around, bewildered at finding itself within the circle of vehicles with multiple enemies to attack. Its yellow eyes met Ozcahar's, who discharged the rifle. The creature stumbled back, swatting at the wound in its chest as it sank on its knees. The shot scared the oxen and the wagon's wheels rolled back and forth over the fallen dweymin. Ozcahar reloaded the rifle and aimed it at another one of the monsters that ran at him. The lucky shot caught it in the face at point blank range, killing it instantly. He started reloading when a paw grabbed his ankle, pulling his feet from under him. The dweymin writhed under the wagon. Blood oozed from its chest wound, and though it struggled to flee, its legs were crushed under a wheel. The grip on Ozcahar's ankle weakened, and its claws grazed his boot as movements slowed.

"Go," it gurgled in a blood-choked whimper. "Wish... go... home."

Ozcahar stared at K'Netta. "It talk Trader. Why talk it alike... alike us?"

"It be youth," she said, offering him her hand to stand up. "Be new changed."

He finished reloading the rifle and wanted to take up his position again, but K'Netta stopped him. "Aid us, Karri."

He tried to understand what she meant. He *was* helping. Sure, he wasn't the best shot, but he was getting better. The woman beheld the scene and wiped tears from her cheeks. He let her swap his rifle for a pistol and followed her to the second carriage.

She opened the door. "Come, child!"

When Roovie emerged, her eyes darted from K'Netta to Ozcahar.

K'Netta placed her hand in his neck and pulled his ear to her lips. "We be chanceless. You take Roovie child. You run."

Ozcahar wanted to protest, but she did not give him a choice.

K'Netta stroked the girl's hair. "Go with Karri."

Roovie shook her head and tears welled in her eyes. K'Netta took the child's chin between finger and thumb. "Be silent. Be brave."

She pressed the girl's hand in his and Roovie squeezed his fingers.

K'Netta manoeuvred the oxen free from the wagon. The animals snorted and bellowed at the chaos and predatory scent of the dweymin pack. K'Netta whipped their backs with a loose strap, and, freed from the weight of the wagon, the oxen thundered towards the trees. Dweymins jumped aside to avoid being trampled. The animals were still yoked together, and though thinner trees splintered beneath them, soon the animals both passed a trunk on either side, and they were stuck. Panicked, they bucked, twisted, and pulled each other to the left and right. In the turmoil, Ozcahar grabbed Roovie. With the pistol ready in his free hand, he ran to escape into the darkness of the woods.

Twenty-Four

Standoff at Ice Bird Falls

His thighs burned as he hurried up the hill, weaving between the trees, and only his sturdy boots prevented him from twisting an ankle amid the roots and rocks. Ozcahar stumbled and nearly dropped the little girl. She clung to him, wrapping her legs around his waist, and buried her face into his tunic. Thankfully, it muffled her snivelling.

Shots sounded. Dweymins yowled and howled behind them. Perhaps it was his imagination, but the ground seemed to tremble with the footfall of pursuers. He wasn't about to stop to check.

Roovie became heavy and slowed him down. How long would he be able to carry her? More and more frequently her legs slipped and bumped against his thighs. When she tried to climb back up, her foot came dangerously close to his genitals. That would be an incredibly stupid way for their escape to come undone. He wanted to put down the child, tell her to follow him, but knew she would not be able to keep up. Then he would have to stand still to wait for her, and that would be impossible. Perhaps it would be safer for the girl to run along a different path or find somewhere to hide.

He was barely aware of the sound of water when a root caught his shin and the ground sloped away beneath him. His weakened legs couldn't catch the jolt and his knees buckled. He pushed Roovie away from him and she landed on her side, splashing in a layer of the water. Despite his terror, Ozcahar cried out in pain as his knees hit the rocky bed of the small tributary. He stayed low for a moment, expecting to be pounced on, but no dweymin appeared. Roovie stood up, shook the water from her braids, and pulled on his arm. Biting his lip and blinking back tears, Ozcahar got to his feet. He listened for possible pursuers but could only pick up the gushing of water. In the absence of a plan, he took the child's hand and walked towards the source of the sound.

They reached the valley edge. The crashed carriages were somewhere to their left, shielded from sight by overhanging trees. Ozcahar moved slowly so as not to betray their position. The moon cast an ethereal glow over the valley. The little stream they'd fallen in turned out to be overspill from a larger river above them that ended in a spectacular waterfall. Roovie's tears stopped for a moment as she beheld in wonder the torrent that disappeared into shimmering swirls of spray below.

He stared at the gloom amid the trees for the yellow eyes, but there was nothing but the dark. Still, he felt certain their pursuers were on their trail. His legs protested the further climb, but he ignored the pain. He should have guessed from the amount of water pouring from the cliff, but when the woods opened, he saw how wide and wild the river was. There was no way to cross it and nowhere else to run.

Warily, Ozcahar approached the cliff edge to find a way down. Roovie inhaled sharply, and he spun round. With difficulty he let go of the girl's hand and fumbled for powder to put into the pistol's pan. A darkness separated from the trees. Ozcahar raised the pistol and blinked to get a handle on what was emerging before him. It was larger than any of the dweymins he'd seen, its black shape obliterating the woods and everything beyond. As Ozcahar stared up at it, the nothingness opened an enormous maw filled with glistening teeth. He aimed and fired.

***

Caizhiu had been elated when the scent trail of her target moved away from the standoff between the pack and the travellers. The dense needle canopy blocked almost all light and she couldn't see a thing, but his fear and exertion intensified his scent. His footprints lingered on the forest floor, leaving a fragrant trail. As they climbed the hill, the trees were widely spaced so she could more easily move between them, but their erratic pattern caused her to misjudge her steps. She banged her head more than once against a hefty branch or trunk and caught her wings in the shrubs.

She heard her quarry stumble, evidently having similar difficulty navigating the forest, but she held back, carefully driving him towards the Ice Bird Falls. The river ahead would form a barrier and a clearing, meaning she could avoid tackling the human in the tangle of roots and shrubs beneath the pines. At last her quarry stood before her, and she could relax. She had found him before the dweymin pack. They were approaching fast, but she had time to fold her bulk into her human form before they'd arrive. And then she was shot.

Luckily, the metal ball bounced off her teeth, but she roared in surprise, prompting a release of urine from both Ozcahar Nitt and the dweymin pup. They stood with their backs to the falls and Caizhiu was unsure how to proceed. She was almost four times the size of her quarry and had neither speech nor hands. If she tried to snatch him from the edge, he'd flee or fight. She was larger and faster than before, and if she wasn't careful, she'd knock both little creatures into the ravine. It would have been easier if he'd fainted, but the human stayed annoyingly upright. To speak to her quarry, she had to adopt her human form, but mid-transformation she wouldn't be able to dodge a second shot or defend herself against the approaching pack. With a wary eye on that damned powder weapon, she slowly circled the two to herd them away from the edge. Somehow, though it clung to his leg, she needed to separate the shrieking pup from her quarry. Had it not been for the dweymin scent, Caizhiu could easily have mistaken it for a human girl.

{The little one is frightened,} Heort's song reached her. *{I'll try to coax it away.}*

{The pup is not our concern.} Without turning away from her quarry, she searched the woods for her friend. *{If you want to help, use your verbal voice to tell the human to keep still.}*

{I think the dweymin pup is our bigger problem right now.}

The undergrowth burst alive with movement, forms separating themselves from the black. Heort sprang forward, dodging a dweymin that tried to tackle him. Caizhiu turned towards the new attackers, grabbing Heort by his jacket and yanking him out of the way. They missed the cervitaur and instead the dweymin jumped up at her. With her mouth full of jacket, she could only ineffectively swipe at the agile creatures. Sharp teeth and claws dug into her scales. Despite one of the heavy dweymins hanging off her throat, she jerked her head and tossed Heort across the raging river. The movement unbalanced her, and with a third dweymin hurtling into her side, she toppled. The creatures were swift and strong, and they could see her a lot better than she could see them. Evading her easily, they took turns attacking with ferocious fury. She beat her wings to get back on her feet and shook off her assailants. One plunged into the raging river and scrabbled at the rocks to escape its watery clutches.

{Be away, Dragon! No one attacks us in our domain. Not even you.}

She turned to a large individual with broad grey stripes running from the corners of his eyes along his sides to the flag-like tail. It didn't crouch or pounce, but straightened up to its full height and approached her at a leisurely pace. Although it was small compared to her, it exuded power.

{It is Windfur who speaks. You must be Caizhiu, the human-dragon.}

{Esteemed Windfur,} she said, sidestepping the insult, *{I have no interest in your pack or your pup.}*

The pack leader yowled an instruction, and the dweymins stopped their charges. They paced back and forth in a semi-circle, glaring at her.

{Who has sent you, Dragon? And why?}

Caizhiu realised she had come to their realm reeking of Wexede Crossing. As the pack had increased their terror on travellers from and to the city, it was no wonder they'd concluded that she had been sent by the Magistrate to constrain them. A different Magistrate might indeed have paid attention to their attacks, but not Yullorik.

Caizhiu spread her wings and bowed her head.

{There is no coin on your head. My interest is only with this human, who is valueless to you.}

Most of the dweymins kept their eyes on her, but one inched towards the girl. It was a young individual whose features still resembled its human stage. The soul song was so subtle Caizhiu couldn't detect it. But the pup went from being fearful to becoming cautiously curious. The dweymin squatted beside the pup, bowing its head so it could touch its fur. The touch was enough. Without further hesitation, it hopped onto the dweymin's back. The human raised his pistol. To show she meant the pack no bother, and to keep her quarry alive, Caizhiu swiped her tail against the back of his knees. He stumbled, and the pistol clattered onto the ground. He dropped onto his hands and knees, searching for it between the rocks.

As one, the pack turned and vanished into the blackness amid the pine trees. The dweymin she had shaken off her throat had found safety on the other side of the river, and she looked around to see if Heort was unharmed. It was a mystery how her friend had done it, but the dweymin lay prone, snoring.

At last she skulked to the human, who froze halfway to his feet. He raised the pistol, and she waited, ready to dodge a shot that didn't come. Perhaps he had no powder, or the weapon was defective. Desperately, the man threw the device at her and tried to run past. She spread her wings, and he skidded to a halt, a dry sob catching in his throat as he shambled backwards, resignation in his eyes. She hoped this was surrender, but then he turned and ran in the only direction he could. She chronochi'ed after him. He jumped. Her jaws snapped in the space where he had been, and her claws dug into the ground to prevent herself plummeting over the edge. The silvery rush of the Ice Bird Falls swallowed her human.

TWENTY-FIVE

FIGHT OR FLIGHT

What she had suspected from Morailo's initial revulsion had proven correct; she was too monstrous to the humans. She had been too impatient not to shield Ozcahar Nitt from that horror and he had rather faced death.

Caizhiu beat her wings to move herself back from the ledge over the waterfall. The valley below her was a grey blur. Across the fast-flowing river, Heort hopped to the ledge and looked down. *{Well, that didn't go to plan.}*

Caizhiu lifted her drooped wings off the ground and stretched them. With every beat, she could feel the weight lightening off her paws. A powerful beat and a jump later, she landed beside him.

{Well done,} Heort said with a beaming smile. *{We'll make a proper dragon of you yet, my friend. I knew you could do it. You can go after your human. It's not too far of a drop and the water sounds like it lands in a deep basin. There's a good chance he'll have survived the fall. With a bit of luck, he can swim. You'd probably be able to glide most of the way. Granted, your first attempt wasn't... a great success, but you're stronger now.}*

{I'm pleased you are so confident in my ability to fly.} The dragon put a paw over his shoulders, eliciting a sharply drawn breath. One talon curved round his neck, and the other four around his right arm. *{Because I'll need to borrow your vision.}*

{Unlike dragons, cervitaurs are not meant to fly.}

The sleeping dweymin choked on its long tongue, coughing and snorting through the snoring. As it rolled over, the creature shook its fur and drowsily got to its feet.

{Or would you rather stay here?}

Heort shook his head, fingered the claw that tickled his throat, and licked his nose.

Caizhiu moved one paw round to Heort's upper chest, hooking her talons into his jacket. The annoyance he leaked at the ruination of the fabric dampened her own nervousness. With her other paw she grabbed the straps of his harness and her bag that was strapped to his back and spread her wings. Wind struck the mountain and curved up in a brisk wave. The water thundered beside them, and its spray hit Caizhiu's face.

{Caizhiu, when... I mean, if we crash... please try not to land on top of me.}

She held her breath, leant into the wind, and hopped off the ledge. The wind filled her membranes as she kept her wings as rigid as possible. The descent was rapid, but as she exhaled and pushed the pinkie of her wings into the wind-stream, she felt the deceleration. She straightened up, gliding over the treetops below and holding her head straight. Her vision extended from the valley ahead of her, the tips of both wings simultaneously, and stretched further almost to her back, but it was blurry.

{You'll have to open your eyes if I'm to see anything,} she sang to Heort. When he finally forced them open, the valley glimmered in moon-kissed clarity.

Her wing muscles burned with exertion. She might not be able to beat her way up, but when she banked to the left, she caught a current to rise. The Fraakywuld was even more dense below than it had been on the top side. The treetops rushed by, and as the next mountain rose up before her, she banked with the wind. To Heort it looked like the Ice Bird Falls were a silver thread embroidered in the black velvet of the landscape.

{Wearing clothes is having a bad influence on you,} she sang to distract him. *{You're thinking like a tailor.}*

Despite his distress, Heort kept his eyes open. His legs kicked habitually with the air rushing past his face as if he were running. *{Can we please find your human so we can get down?}*

The river snaked down the steep hill, swilling around boulders and through rapids. Previous rainfall had cleared blockages, evidenced by the silt-stained branches and tree trunks deposited into its numerous bends. The dragon followed the ribbon to the valley. Despite their best efforts, Heort couldn't see the body of Ozcahar Nitt, living or otherwise, amid the river debris. Caizhiu soared in a large circle back towards the falls, not daring to fly low enough over the river to pick the scent of her target from the multitude of mountain smells. She might survive a hard landing, but she wasn't sure her delicate friend would.

A growing ache spread from between her upper shoulders until it expanded over most of her back. Her wings became heavier and increasingly difficult to control. Heort noticed her erratic movements and fidgeted between her paws, which did not help.

Below them, the river widened and turned into an ambling giant. Caizhiu spotted a small clearing on the river bend and swooped down, ignoring the anxious reaction of Heort. Approaching the bank, she forced her wings to brake, her stomach dropping as gravity found her. She let go of her friend and, with a last beat of her weary wings, moved herself out of the way. The ground approached fast, and she caught her landing in an undignified gallop. Her wings fluttered behind as she hurtled into the bushes, bruising a toe in the process. Once her astonishment at the lack of injury had faded, she shook the shrubbery from her crest and limped to the clearing. She lowered her belly into the soft grass, let out a long-held breath, and closed her eyes.

Heort placed his fingertips on her forehead. Although his soothing touch spread healing through her muscles, the beating of his hearts was deafening. He stood very close to her, and fright hadn't left her scent yet. Caizhiu raised her head to push him back and snorted to rid her nostrils of his aroma. Saliva dripped from her teeth onto the grass.

Heort took a few steps away from her. *{I'll... I'll go check the riverbanks for a sign of our human friend.}*

{That's probably best.}

She caught the white of his backside as the cervitaur vanished into the night. His hightailing caused a shudder of desire throughout her body, but even if she'd wanted to, she was too exhausted to give in to her hunting instinct. She had to kill something large, eat something with a lot of life to spill, but first she had to rest. By the time slumber had taken her, to all but the sharpest observer, her body had become part of the landscape.

***

The last thing Ozcahar remembered was being sucked down a rapid and thrown into a large boulder. Then the decision to let the icy water take his life had been a quiet one, easy and peaceful. But the river had not taken him. He was no longer flung around by the currents. A scaly surface scraped against his cheek. Weakly, he tried to kick his legs for solid ground, but they were caught on something. He thought the monster of the mountain had snatched him from the water, that it held his broken body between its jaws. Perhaps he had only moments to live before being torn asunder. Shivering with cold and terror, he opened his eyes.

What he had thought a monster turned out to be the scabby bark of an uprooted tree that had fallen over the river and netted him in its branches. He unhooked his legs and tried to swim. Moving his right arm caused such a spasm of pain he sank beneath the surface. He pulled himself up by a branch, but gulping for air caused further bolts of agony to rack his body.

Very slowly, taking care not to let the current pull him under again, he placed his left hand along the uprooted tree until he reached the shore. On one hand and his knees, he crawled onto the rocky bank. He wanted to rest, but if he did, he wouldn't get back up. His legs were wobbly, but not broken. He had to get away from here, find civilisation – if it existed in these parts.

With practice, Ozcahar found a balance between breathing shallow enough not to wince and not so shallow as to pass out. All around, trees towered over him; between them was only the blackness of the forest. He was completely alone – at least, he hoped he was.

If he put his weight on his right leg and took a long step with his left and then a short step with his right, the pain was manageable. It was easier when he climbed up a hill, harder when walking down. As long as he kept up the rhythm and the ground stayed steady, he set a pleasing pace, not as fast as he would normally walk but far from stumbling. If he were to trip, he only had one hand to catch himself. If he sprained an ankle, he could do little but sit and wait for a predator to find him. He tried not to think about how far into the woods he'd journeyed with Darjani's travellers, how far the river had taken him, and how vast the Dreadwoods were; tried not to think about Roovie, left on her own at the mercy of those monsters. The ground dropped away beneath his feet, eliciting a groan as he caught his misstep. The step down led to a flat area. On either side, the trees had parted in a line to his left and right. He'd stumbled upon a road, a human road. Ozcahar whooped and laughed out loud. He immediately regretted making the sound.

Walking was easier on even ground, and though he judged the chance of a passing vehicle very slim, he kept an ear out for the sound of a horse or engine. His careful listening alerted him to the sound of something moving through the undergrowth. It was following him, keeping its distance, but inevitably on his trail. Ozcahar didn't wait to see what it was. Perhaps it was a monster. Perhaps a poacher on his way home. He dared not look and sped up his laboured pace, the exertion sending a stabbing pain into his side. He sighed with relief when the creeping dawn revealed an oval of dwellings around the through road. Covered in branches, the buildings blended into the forest as if to hide their presence, and there was no sign of the inhabitants. It was early still, too early for night to have returned the colours it stole. Ozcahar hurried from building to building, looking for a door or window. At last he found the Trader symbol for Inn on the doorframe.

"Please, give shelter."

There was no response.

"I be human." His tapping changed to banging. "Trueso. Open door, please!"

But the door remained forbiddingly shut. He heard heavy footsteps approach from behind him, and he hobbled around the building to find a place to hide in the dwindling shadows. It was a mistake, as he found himself trapped between the building and the fence of the field next to it. He ducked between the slats of the fence. It felt like his right arm was going to drop from his shoulder as he threw himself onto the rugged dirt. He blinked back tears and crawled to his feet. He'd stumbled no more than halfway across the tilled field when a movement in the woods ahead of him caught his eye. A creature with branches on its head jumped over the fence. It looked as if it was partly formed from the trees, an emissary of the Dreadwoods.

Ozcahar backed away and turned to see a large man approach. At least he thought it was a man; it could be one of those wolf creatures. If it was a villager, he should ask for help, but then he'd have to explain what he was doing in this field. Would that be regarded as trespassing, to enter a field? He no longer had money to bribe nor a pistol to defend himself with, but he rifled through his pockets regardless. His fingertips found the cold of a metal object. He fished it from his jacket and held it out to ward off both assailants. It was the delicate cheese knife he'd taken from Narastien. He closed his eyes and tried to focus on that evening. It was as good a memory to die with as any he had.

"Ozcahar Nitt," the hooded figure said in a portentous voice that pronounced his name with an Aumegoan inflection. "You have run well, but now you are exhausted. Your only weapon is a blade that even if it were sharp would not pierce my skin and you are holding it in your unfavoured hand. Give me your weapon, and I give you my word that I will not harm you."

Ozcahar wasn't sure if what fell from his lips were words or just a cry that welled from the crumbling remnants of his defiance. He sank to his knees and let his hand drop onto the earth, the knife slipping from his fingers. The hands that grabbed his armpits and tried to lift him back onto his feet caused blinding pain to explode from his shoulder, making breathing impossible and engulfing his consciousness.

***

Heort did not think the human looked dangerous, stretched out on his back, covered in goosebumps and bruises. The hunters' blind sheltered them from the rain but was still cold, and the half-dressed man shivered in his sleep. Stroking his fingers over the plum-coloured clouds on the swollen and deformed shoulder, Heort felt how the arm bone had moved partway out of the socket. It wasn't the first time he'd dealt with this kind of injury, and it wasn't the worst case he'd come across. Heort ran alleviation from his fingertips and the muscles around the man's joint softened. He pushed the arm bone back into its correct place.

{Will he live?} Caizhiu asked. Even in her human guise she was too large to comfortably come in, so she leant on the doorframe.

The rest of the human's welts and grazes seemed minor, though Heort was concerned by the angry red and purple blotches that marked the side of his chest. He spread his fingers over it and concentrated on healing the muscles, tendons, and bones.

{Miraculously, yes. He's injured, but he'll live... If you don't make it worse.}

None of the ribs were broken, though the severe sprains would hamper his breathing. As far as Heort could tell, the human was a commonplace example of his kind, if not a lucky one. But as long as he was unconscious, he wouldn't be able to tell whether he was in any way Talented.

{Shall I wake him?}

Caizhiu grunted an affirmative. Aware that she blocked the exit, trapping him with the human, he hesitated a moment before taking some deyfaal leaves from a satchel. He crushed the tiny sprigs, rubbed their residue over his fingertips, and held the pungent salve close to the man's nostrils. Heort readied himself to jump out of reach if he needed to. He started when the human snorted, and the blue eyes fluttered open. The man blinked and squinted, his eyes wandering over the cervitaur's antlers, then Heort's face. The sharp intake of breath hurt enough for him to gnash his teeth.

Heort pressed a hand on the man's chest. "Move with heed."

He didn't exert enough calm to restrain him if the man put up a fight, but enough to halt an instinctive urge to bolt upright. He fashioned his face into the approximation of a human smile. It worked on the people in the Keeltois, and he hoped it would on this stranger.

Ozcahar's voice was raspy, and he spoke an alien language.

"Talk you Trader?" Heort asked.

The man frowned at him, an expression Heort was familiar with. He tried again, carefully forcing his errant tongue into the required shapes. He hated how stupid it made him sound.

Keeping his eyes fixed on Heort, Ozcahar carefully pushed himself backwards until he was sat up, leaning against the wall. He patted his chest and his eyes widened with a question for which he couldn't find the words.

"I mend shoulder and seek damage. Be easier with no shirt." Heort had to repeat it several times and still was not sure he was understood. He picked up the long coat and draped it over the man's shoulders.

"I no do-harm." Heort tried to flow tranquillity into the human as he stroked his youthful hair.

Unhelpfully, Caizhiu chose that moment to lean into the blind. "Look who be awake."

Ozcahar flinched within his coat. The manner in which she grinned at him reminded Heort of the look in her eyes at the Ice Bird Falls. Her face might be differently arranged, but the mien was the same: a hunter stalking trapped prey.

Caizhiu took the parcel Euvie had given them from her bag and held it out. "Be you hungry?"

Ozcahar glanced from Heort to the parcel and shuffled closer to take it. It looked like Euvie had been right in her choices of human treats, because he tore into the beeswax paper to stuff the bread, cheese, and meat into his mouth. He grimaced with the pain in his side his eagerness caused, but he didn't stop eating. After a few mouthfuls he seemed to become aware of his surroundings.

"Apologies," he said to Caizhiu. "Require you some?"

"I eat already."

She let a bit of the pleasure of her hunt flow in her song. Heort flicked his ears as his mind flooded with her images of torn flesh, the taste of blood, and wood pigs' death squeals. He felt sick, but Ozcahar did not react at all, blissfully licking crumbs off the paper.

{He really is just neath, isn't he?}

{As far as I can tell.} Heort shrugged. *{I found no song in him.}*

Caizhiu held up a leather canteen with birch wine. "Require some?"

Ozcahar rebuffed Heort's aid to stand up, choosing to hold on to the wall instead. He hugged his coat around him as he stepped out of the hut. Heort followed, relieved at leaving the enclosure behind.

"Grateful, friend," Ozcahar took the canteen from the dragon. He took a long slug and wiped his mouth clumsily with his wrist. He said something to Caizhiu that Heort didn't understand.

"I talk Aumegoan," she replied and chin-nodded at Heort. "But he no can. So we talk Trader."

Ozcahar let his eyes glide over him as if he only now truly saw him. Standing, he towered over Heort, and this seemed to surprise him. "Be it yours or be you its?"

Caizhiu didn't answer and handed him his haversack. "Dress. The day no grow warmer."

Ozcahar fished out a fluffy pink tunic and his fists tightened on his haversack. "This be my bag."

His eyes darted as if he was about to run, then winced when the pain in his ribs reminded him he couldn't. Trembling, he reached into the bag to get clothes more suitable for the cold, and without looking up he mumbled: "Track you me from Crossing? Be you City Guard? You speak Aumegoan. Track you me from Thirdburg?"

Caizhiu spread her arms. "See you insignia? I no be City Guard."

"Then..." He took another swig from the canteen; seeking courage or relief from the pain. Perhaps both. "Who be you?"

"Caizhiu."

"Be you bounty hunter?" Ozcahar finished the wine and tilted his head when he looked at her: "Alike dragon?"

Caizhiu rolled her eyes, but then she seemed to swallow her usual response. Maybe the image of the human jumping off a mountain was ingrained in her memory as well. She wouldn't want to risk him trying that again.

"Trueso," she said. "I be named after dragon."

Twenty-Six

The Food and the Flame

There was a watery chill on the wind that whistled through the mountains. The human walked at a sloth's pace. Several times Caizhiu had suggested she should carry him over her shoulder, but Heort thought she'd exacerbate his injuries. Since she'd told Ozcahar he'd be taken to the Magistrate of the Keeltois, his requests for rest became plentiful, probably a ploy to protract their journey. Heort, by contrast, skipped ahead, cheerful at the thought of returning home.

Was it the right thing to do, to take Ozcahar to Lady Azer? She couldn't return him to Ingrirath as she had planned. The Magistrates were the Six's emissaries. Gostawa would know what justice to do to him. Caizhiu couldn't imagine what that might be, if he had anything to do with Ingrirath's death. She watched him hobble along the track. Wouldn't the killer of a Keeper be stronger, smarter, harder to catch?

The sun dipped behind the peaks and the temperature dropped. When they reached a hollow in the rock face that flanked the path, Caizhiu decided it was a good place to rest. Ozcahar followed her to the back of the hollow and let his haversack drop from his fingers. Without a word, Heort picked it up and used the clothing to form a layer for the human to lie on. Ozcahar lay down, placed his head on the rolled-up bag, and within moments his face sagged as sleep took him.

Caizhiu looked at the fragile form by her feet. He looked delicious. With a sharp shake of her head, she banished the thought. It was just because she was hungry. She'd have to hunt. And she would have to get the human something to eat, too. He'd wolfed down all of Euvie's rations, and he didn't look like he'd survive long on air alone. She loathed the thought of leaving him, still unconvinced that he had not hidden a Talent that could harm Heort. But she'd have to.

***

When she got back to the overhang, dusk had long passed and clouds were gathering to obscure the waning moon, leaving the mountainside in pitch darkness. Caizhiu walked into the hollow, staying close to the wall so as not to step on the other two. She could hear the human's restful breathing and the chattering of his teeth. He hadn't moved.

Heort had curled up at the back of the bluff shelter next to him. He had removed his harness and laid his coat over the human. When he glanced at the stripped hunk of meat in her hand, Caizhiu regretted she had not removed the buck's hoof.

She cast her mind back to Eslonya's kitchen, but though she had endured many a meal there, she had no idea how the woman managed to ruin meat the way she did.

She nudged the human's leg with her foot. His eyes snapped open, and she heard him groan. "W-where be we?"

"We no be as far as I wish. Partway up mountain only."

She held out the deer leg to him, which he grabbed but instantly let go with a startled whimper. He wiped his hand on Heort's jacket.

"What be that?"

"Your evening-food."

The human shivered and got to his feet. He cocked his head at her, trying to figure out if she was joking, but she pressed the severed limb into his hand.

Caizhiu dropped a collection of twigs and branches by his side. "Know you how to burn it?"

Ozcahar looked at the deer leg. "Ehm... I no cook many time."

The human arranged the wood by state of dryness into a triangular shape.

"I be hurt. I no can make fire." He handed her two sticks and mimicked that she had to rub them together. It looked ridiculous, and she squinted at him, but Heort confirmed he'd seen the technique used. As she sat on her knees, Caizhiu became convinced the other two had conspired to play a joke on her, but eventually a sliver of smoke curled up from the gathered pine needles. Ozcahar blew on the smouldering kindling until it caught flame.

Her feeling of triumph was short-lived when she caught Heort's eye and the scent of smoke filled the hollow. She sat against the shelter wall, close to the opening. As the smell of the fire was bringing back memories, she reassured herself it had been over a hundred years ago. And that it didn't count if you used human means to create it.

{We're a long way from the Fire Isles.}

Heort picked his jacket up from the floor and retreated to the back of the hollow. *{The Keeltois are even further, but it found you there.}*

Caizhiu nodded and watched the human shiver in the fire's glow, wrapping his good arm around his knees. He'd noticed Heort's retreat. "Be it afraid of fire?"

Caizhiu shook her head.

The flickering shadows danced over the walls of the shelter. Five night fay floated into the hollow, attracted by the warmth and the shelter from the whistling wind. She watched them hunt moths among the incandescent particles that drifted up from the fire.

It took hours, in which Ozcahar fell asleep several times, for the meat to be charred enough, but finally the human took the meat off the fire. He dropped and caught it so as not to burn his fingertips. Caizhiu was mid-smile at his clumsiness when she noticed a spark that floated into the hollow and slunk into the fire's core like a suicidal night fay. She groaned and Heort sat up. He too had noticed the faint smell, like the eggs that humans would boil for their breakfast. Eggs that may have gone off.

The glowing woodpile stirred with a familiar soul song filled with images of an ancient firestorm. *{Do my eyes deceive me, or is this the mighty dragon Caizhiu?}*

The memories that came with the sardonic voice were something she could have done without for her entire life. Even Morailo was too young to remember the fire, but the stories from his mother had left a mark on him and his children. They had left their mark on the whole Keeltois region. Caizhiu answered the memory with the image of the diverted river, the sensation of cooling water on her skin.

Oblivious, Ozcahar picked a sliver of meat from beneath the charred layer, smelled it, touched it with the tip of his tongue before biting off a morsel.

"The meat be ready." He tossed a branch onto the fire. "We can raise the fire."

A flurry of glowing needles swirled up to the ceiling. The shelter filled anew with the smell of burning pine. He reached for more wood, but Caizhiu held up her hand.

"No."

Ozcahar looked at her, sensing the solemnity in her voice but not understanding the reason. She couldn't blame him. He could not hear the scorching soul song.

{Well met, Wayward One. I have missed you.}

The human picked up another stick and was about to throw it on when the fire stirred. At first it seemed merely the collapse of a burnt log, but then a ball of flame and charred wood rolled from the heart of the furnace. A creature jumped out of the roll and stretched into a snake-thin form that landed on four legs. It was the size of a wildcat, with a long snout. Silver-tinged ridges ran along its back and over the tail. They gleamed against the onyx-coloured body. Two spiralled horns protruded from the back of its head. When the creature sprang from movement to movement, an orange glow emanated from the fissures where the scales parted as if it consisted of fire itself. It opened its flame-blue eyes and observed the company. There was a depth to those eyes, a temptation to stare into them. It inhaled sharply and puffed out a fountain of sparks that lit up the shallow shelter.

At the far end, Heort sprang to his feet, slapping his hands over his jacket to pat out the flames before they took hold.

{And there you are too, Venison. To find you here is even more surprising than my esteemed friend.}

Ozcahar scooted backwards to the hollow's wall and raised the branch, ready to strike.

"What be that thing?"

"A fire drake," Caizhiu grumbled, not taking her eyes off the creature. It had grown to same size as Mitzer, but Ozcahar's fire had reduced. Having kept the fire low so as not to burn the meat had helped. Thankfully, there would be a limit to the danger it posed.

"Its name be Brekranez."

The drake hopped onto the human's knee, its paws leaving blackened prints on the woollen fabric.

{How kind of you, Caizhiu. You brought dinner.}

"Get off, monster!" Ozcahar poked the stick at the drake to push it away, give himself time to stand up. With a sly smile, the drake clamped its jaws around the stick, twisting it out of Ozcahar's grasp with such ease it seemed as if the human was feeding it. The wood sizzled, smoke bellowing from either end. A spider crawled from underneath the rugged bark, but before it could spin a thread to escape, it caught aflame along with the rest of the branch.

Ozcahar coughed at the smoke that accompanied the fire drake's movements. He winced and grabbed his pained ribs.

{I see you've already tenderised him.}

Caizhiu sighed pointedly. *{Leave him alone. He's my prey... I mean, he's my target.}*

Brekranez's chuckle ricocheted through the hollow as if it chose which wall to bounce off next and enjoyed the misdirection. It snapped the charcoaled branch in two and swallowed it, granting it a little more height. Ozcahar backed away and picked up another branch. Caizhiu wondered what the fool hoped to achieve other than stoke the fire drake. Standing on its hind legs, it now reached up to the human's chest. The flame-like tongue danced around its chops, and it assaulted her with its reminiscence of the taste of human blood as it sizzled on its tongue.

{He's a scrawny thing, but we can split him between us. I'll leave the kill to you; I know you enjoy it most. I promise I won't char your half.}

Caizhiu ignored the tempting sensation of soft human flesh. *{I don't eat kinfolk.}*

{When did you turn from hunter into herder?} sang Brekranez. *{Leave otherkin off your menu if you must, but this thing isn't kin. No more than that deer he's eating.}*

Caizhiu stood up and seized the drake by the tail, pulled it off Ozcahar, and cast it aside before it could burn her palm. The human dusted the ash off his shirt and knees, straightening up to make himself look taller too, as if that would help.

Brekranez slithered along the floor towards the smouldering fire and reignited the remaining wood. The heat allowed it to swell to the size of Heort.

{Let me see what's become of you since your iteration.}

Caizhiu had no intention of transfiguring. *{You will find me a more formidable foe, dear drake. I was but a dragonling when last we battled, and yet I won.}*

The part of the legend that had been forgotten was that none of it would have happened had it not been for a fire drake and a young dragon trying to impress each other. She would not make such a mistake again.

{I was never looking for a foe.}

The pile of burning wood was reducing steadily. If no wood was added, it would flame out within half an hour, and the drake would have to find amusement elsewhere. As if guessing her thoughts, it nodded at the collection of wood behind Ozcahar. *{Your human will get cold without my glorious flames.}*

Caizhiu scoffed. *{He'll be fine. Make no mistake, I will piss on your fire just to get rid of you.}*

As it withered, Brekranez let the flames carry it to the ceiling to lap up the night fay. The creatures crackled briefly on its tongue and were gone.

{Till next time, dearest Caizhiu, when you and I really should share a meal. You are, after all, more like me than you are like them.}

The drake cooled and blackened into smoke. She followed the sparks of its form but couldn't be sure at what point it had disappeared into the night, except that the air in the hollow seemed lighter and had lost the stench of over-boiled eggs.

TWENTY-SEVEN

THE SILVER ROSE

After five days traipsing along the damp mountain trail, the Silver Rose Tavern was a welcome sight. The building looked worn by the elements, but in otherwise good condition. Fields surrounded the house, a few tortured fruit trees, and a barn with an auto cart. Clothing was hung from long ropes between the building and a tree by the river's edge. Caizhiu smelled goats, chickens and saw a large pig laying on its side. But no ponies. She had hoped to purchase one for the human, so the onward journey might proceed faster.

Though he walked slowly, his talking cascaded like a river. Since Heort had treated the blisters on his feet, Ozcahar had not stopped. He told the patient cervitaur about the walkways of Thirdburg and asked him about his salves and potions. Upon seeing the tavern, he spoke excitedly, and with pleading glances in Caizhiu's direction, about the prospect of a warm meal and a soft bed.

Chickens and rabbits shot into their small pen when the dragon walked past. Caizhiu was about to knock on the patron's door when she heard the scraping of a latch on the other side. A stout woman, holding a hammer in one hand and a bag of dowels in the other, started when she noticed her three visitors and gripped the hammer a little tighter.

"You travel late in the season. Rains be upon northern lands and southern road soon be too hazardous to track." She emphasised the thick 'l' sound and the rolling 'r' of the local dialect in her Trader.

"Trueso," Caizhiu replied in Uayathi. "Our need has taken us to the road at a poorly chosen time."

The woman narrowed her eyes and curled her top lip. Caizhiu wasn't sure whether the woman distrusted her story or if she had not heard what she'd said, so she repeated her words a little louder and added: "My name is Caizhiu. I am told your tavern is a welcoming place."

The woman's sceptical expression softened.

"My name is Phiazola Rozar. I have heard of *your* reputation also. Bounty hunter, trueso?" She concentrated on the other two visitors and pointed at them with the handle of the hammer. "Which one is your target, or is it both of them?"

Caizhiu placed a hand on Ozcahar's shoulder. "This one. But he is so keen on your hospitality, I doubt he'll give you any trouble."

Phiazola looked him up and down and shook her head. She tapped the butt end of the hammer on Ozcahar's chest and warned: "You'd better not bring me trouble, boy. Or, By Keeper's Grace, Caizhiu will be the least of yours."

Ozcahar muttered a mangled "Good morning" in response and glanced at Caizhiu. He may have understood the threatening tone, but nothing else. 'Good morning' seemed to be the only Uayathi term he knew, and Caizhiu wasn't certain he knew what it meant.

Phiazola's mouth fell open when Heort introduced himself. "A cervitaur that speaks proper and a man who does not. Trueso, the world's in a jumble."

She set down the tool bag and used her fingers to whistle so piercingly Heort folded his ears back. There was cursing and stumbling from inside the tavern, then a younger woman appeared in the doorway and greeted them with a beaming smile. "Guests! What a welcome surprise."

"I'll need to prepare an evening meal. Would you ready the rooms, Zojia?" Phiazola said and turned to Caizhiu. "Have you horses to be stabled?"

"No."

"Your journey must have been arduous." Zojia clapped her hands together. "Through misfortune or choice you have left your journey late, gentlemen. But you are most welcome at the Silver Rose."

Her eye fell on Ozcahar. She cocked her head and beckoned him to approach. "Please, come on in. You look like you've had a terrible time of it."

When the dragon gave him the nod, he followed their host in.

"Put that one upstairs and lock his room," Phiazola shouted after her daughter. "He's a miscreant!"

Zojia smiled at Ozcahar. "Is that so, sir? Can't recall we've had a proper miscreant before."

Caizhiu wondered how long it would take the woman to figure out Ozcahar couldn't understand a word she'd said.

***

Night had fallen when Caizhiu walked up the stairs. The steps groaned beneath her feet no matter how carefully she placed them, and she wished she had taken the time to inspect the strength of the planks. She reached a narrow landing and unlocked the backroom at the top. Though the room looked empty, she could hear the man's snoring. An ornately decorated door drew her attention. By the flickering of the candle, the carvings gave the impression that the bedstead doors were alive with movement. Caizhiu squatted and opened the closeted bed. The fragrance of Ozcahar wafted out and filled the room. Delicious. She'd known prey scent before, the smell of her target that haunted her until she received payment. But it had never been mouthwatering before. Then again, she'd never hunted a human before. Caizhiu shook her head to rid herself of the notion.

Ozcahar had draped himself over his bag and pulled the heavy quilt over his head. When she touched the foot that stuck out from under the quilt, he awakened with a start.

"Be it morning?"

"No," Caizhiu said over the sound of her growling stomach, "but we require evening-food."

He got dressed and followed her to the taproom. In the small tavern, it held the middle between a bar and lounge. The lack of other guests made the meal feel more intimate, with only the proprietor's family sitting with them at the long communal table. Phiazola had indulged her hospitable nature. A large copper pot of a pulse and rabbit stew stood in the centre, surrounded by dishes with breads, steamed apples, and baked root vegetables.

Caizhiu studied the wooden benches on either side of the table and was relieved to find the Silver Rose's sturdy but basic furniture worked in her favour. Enviously, she glanced at Heort, who'd managed to wrangle a collection of twigs and dried apple slices out of their hosts. She sighed and made sure she ate enough of the human food not to cause offence. At least her foreshortened tongue couldn't taste the full range of disgusting flavours.

Phiazola's husband, Veiloz, appeared and sat next to Ozcahar, opposite his daughter. With a hunched posture and gnarled fingers, he appeared significantly older than his wife. Generously, he filled their glasses with spiced cider. Ozcahar took a sip and coughed. The old man had clearly added a spirit. He winked at his guests and smiled a toothless grin.

"You like?"

Ozcahar nodded. His cheeks had a rosy glow and there was a sparkle to his eyes. For the first time since she'd seen him in the moonlight on the top of the Ice Bird Falls, he didn't look on the edge of death.

"You better can walk later," Caizhiu grumbled. "I no carry you upstairs."

Veiloz nudged Ozcahar and, pointing the butt end of his knife at Caizhiu, chuckled. "Looks like he's eaten your share of provisions along the way."

Though he spoke Uayathi, his miming and puffed-up cheeks left no doubt of his meaning, and Ozcahar laughed. He cast Caizhiu a mocking grin, held out his palms in agreement, and pointed at his own skinny midriff.

Zojia placed a dessert of preserved pears layered with buttered crumbs in front of him and Phiazola scoffed.

"You are muddleheads, both of you, to trust a miscreant like that. Never trust a blue-eyed man."

"We don't trust him," Veiloz said and raised a glass at Caizhiu. "And no offence was meant."

"No offence was taken. Your liquor is as excellent as your cooking."

Heort struggled with the glass but managed to drink most of the cider. He licked some spillage off his hand.

"Do you have cervitaur here?" he asked.

Phiazola mopped up the last of the stew with a piece of bread. "I once saw a satyroi. They look a little like you, but they walk on two legs and have large horns. And of course, they do not speak. Did the Magistrate of Bladrid teach you…"

She didn't finish her question but bent towards Ozcahar. She put her hand on his arm and whispered so loud everyone around the table heard: "You no require thief food."

Blushing, Ozcahar took a piece of bread out of his pocket and put it back on the table. He flinched when his darting eyes found Caizhiu's.

She pinched the bridge of her nose. "Kind hosts, I apologise for his shameful action."

Zojia glared at her from across the table. "What kind of place is Aumegoa that they teach their people they need to steal food? And then send bounty hunters after them?"

She stood up to clear the table and patted Ozcahar's shoulder when she left his plate so he could continue eating. He looked bewildered, evidently expecting punishment.

"Aumegoa is a large land with as many cities, towns, and people as Uayath," Caizhiu said. "I cannot answer what they teach about feeding people."

She eyed Ozcahar. "I do not know what this one is wanted for. But I wager it is not for stolen bread."

***

T he morning sun struggled to penetrate the clouds that obscured the mountain peaks, as if an upturned ceramic bowl covered the valley. From time to time, a shower blew in and pelted the tavern. Despite her reluctance to climb the creaking stairs, Caizhiu had locked Ozcahar in his little attic room herself and released him in the morning. He looked healthier, unhampered by his bruised ribs or shoulder. The only thing that still bothered him were his feet. He walked down the staircase, carrying his boots in his hand. Heort sat him in a corner to make sure none of the blisters and scrapes had turned septic.

"Can he travel day-after-dark?" Caizhiu asked.

The cervitaur looked up from rubbing a balm into the man's raw heels.

"Please another rest-day?" Ozcahar suggested, glancing from his feet to Heort and Caizhiu.

Heort bobbed his head. "He can travel day-after-dark. But another rest-day may be good-thought."

Caizhiu frowned. The weather was not likely to improve and the longer they waited, the worse it would become. And that would make the journey harder on the human.

"We travel day-after-dark," she said and frowned at Ozcahar. "Use day-dark to rest and eat."

Feeling restless, she offered to help the family prepare for the rainy season. Since the inhospitable weather didn't bother Caizhiu or Heort, they helped Zojia and her elderly father bring in the early soft fruit harvest from the little orchard.

Caizhiu could only imagine that Phiazola's poor hearing protected her from Ozcahar's constant questions while she worked in the kitchen to transform the fruit and root vegetables into preserves. The hotelier seemed to tolerate him well enough. Caizhiu had offered to lock him in the attic room, but Phiazola said she liked the company. It was curious to see him among his own kind. He seemed like any other young human. Nothing about him indicated what a Keeper of Sinuation might want with him, and it seemed less and less likely he had had anything to do with the death of Ingrirath. Caizhiu reminded herself that it was not her business what he was wanted for. All she needed to do was hand him over to a Magistrate.

From his appetite, she would never have guessed the size of the meal Ozcahar had consumed the evening before. He attacked the food with a dragon-like ferocity she found almost admirable. She herself ate as little as good manners allowed, finding the meal just as revolting as the previous night. Mercifully, Veiloz kept their glasses filled. It was a potent and sweet drink that left a pleasant burning in her throat. Caizhiu wasn't sure what spirit and spices the man had added, but it surprised her how quickly it caused her head to spin.

"Drink up." He pointed at Ozcahar's full glass. "You'll be leaving tomorrow, and you don't know when you'll be able to have another drink."

Heort blinked, sighed deeply, and shook his head. Zojia had given him a clay flagon instead of a glass so he could drink easier. Caizhiu had a feeling that before long she'd get to see what a drunk cervitaur looked like.

"Excuse me," he said, struggling more than usual to shape his tongue around the words. He stood up, but his legs did not keep pace and he reeled backwards. His legs jerked to straighten up, but his hooves slipped on the stone floor. Caizhiu would have joined in the laughter around the table had she not caught the look of panic on her friend's face.

"Steady your feet, friend." Veiloz stood to reach out to Heort. The old man bumped the table and laughed at his own clumsiness. "Trueso, this is a strong batch."

Caizhiu felt a deadened sensation around her stomach. When she looked, she saw the tip of her tail had dropped to the floor and seemed far away. Her caudal blade lay limp and blunt against the table leg. She blinked to focus and recoil her tail around herself. It wouldn't move. The skin rippled and reverted to her scales. Veiloz's laugh caught in his throat. He leant heavily on the table, and his hands slipped off the edge as he tumbled away from the dragon. She reached out to help him but jerked back in shock at the sight of her taloned claw.

Her face elongated, and the tavern whirlpooled with the movement of her eyes. She stood up and extended her wings to prevent herself from toppling over. As she gasped for fresh air, her fangs sprung from her jaws.

Ozcahar was halfway to getting to his feet and gaped at her. A hump of chewed bread rested on his tongue.

Caizhiu lost the fight for her balance as her legs altered beneath her. She crashed onto the bench, which hurled Zojia and Veiloz across the room. Her tail lashed through the air as she toppled sideways, her vision filling with flashes of light, and her wayward tail struck the table. Crawling onto the carpet, Caizhiu could no longer lift her head. In front of her, Phiazola sank to the floor and lay still. Heort lay somewhere out of sight. She tried to find his heartbeats among those of the humans. They all thundered in her ears. She wanted to call to him, but her soul song reverberated through her skull without finding the way out. As it bounced around, it seemed to wipe the content from her mind. Her eyes rolled inwards. The world went black.

TWENTY-EIGHT

ACROSS THE MARSARIN MASSIF

Bodies were strewn around the room, and Ozcahar feared they might be dead. He had only intended to send his captors into a sleep deep enough to make his escape, but he did not know how much of the potion each had consumed. The cider had seemed perfect to mask the flavour, but Veiloz had been even more generous with it than yesterday. If they were dead, it was the fault of the old man, and of that deer-thing he had pilfered the potion from. But they weren't dead. They couldn't be dead. That couldn't happen to someone twice.

The only thing he knew for sure was that the monstrosity in front of him – the size of a horse and covered in scales – was still breathing. The grotesque head lay on its side, revealing rows of dagger-like teeth. Its wings stretched from one wall to the other, wider than the room itself. Caizhiu, his sluggish brain reminded him. Then he remembered his idiotic question: like the dragon? Ozcahar clamped one hand over his mouth to keep his jagged breath as quiet as possible and his other brushed over his crotch to make sure he hadn't wet himself. Jorganyon had been right to tell him to run, and he would have to run much faster now.

He snatched his hat and coat off the hook. The door was locked, but with a firm kick, he bust the screws out of the doorframe. A gust of wind extinguished the chandelier and Ozcahar ran out into the rain. The tavern's auto carriage was a sturdy vehicle, with a small globular cab topped with two carapaces and a dumpy trailer. He uncoupled the trailer, opened the door, and hoped the controls would be similar to Darjani's. Scooting to the middle of the spring seat, he felt around for the levers needed to start the thing as well as the steering sticks. He pumped the handle and pressed it the way Darjani had shown him. The carriage coughed to life, rattling as if reluctantly waking from a deep slumber. He pressed the handles to move the vehicle forward, but though the engine purred louder, after an initial jerk, it didn't move.

"Please move, please, please move," he cooed to the vehicle and frantically fumbled for a button or lever he'd forgotten. There was nothing. Biting his knuckles, he tried to calm his mind to think through the problem. Chucks. He remembered K'Netta kicking chucks under the wheels to keep their wagon in place. He jumped from the cabin and found similar wooden triangles. The vehicle rolled forward after he kicked them from under the wheels. Clambering to the controls, he moved the levers to veer the carriage away from the tavern. Ozcahar increased speed to move uphill, and the carriage jerked forward. The engine found its rhythm, and in a puff of steam, it sped onto the path.

***

Caizhiu regretted her yawn, not only because of the terrified cries around her but also because of the surge of nausea it caused. The air was thick with fear, but she felt too queasy to hunt. Was this feeling what humans called hungover?

{Caizhiu.} Heort's soft song felt like a cool drop of water hitting a hot stone. *{I could use your help.}*

She opened her eyes. They felt as if they'd dried up and were too small for their sockets. The red of a rug flung itself at her, followed in quick sequence by other colours that assaulted her. Heort lay between the staircase and the door. His front and hind legs were folded beneath him, and his arms hung by his sides. A boot rested on the withers where his spine curved into his upper back. Zojia had his antlers in one hand, pulling his head back so far that he could do nothing but look up at her. In the other, she held a bread knife.

Caizhiu lifted her head, and her stiff legs raised her belly off the floor. She wanted to draw in her wings from where they'd flopped to the ground, but Zojia pulled Heort's antlers back, causing him to grunt in pain.

"Don't move, monster!" The woman's heart thumped in her chest as she placed the knife's edge against her friend's exposed throat.

"D-dragon," Heort corrected her. His voice sounded distorted as Zojia pressed the knife into his skin.

Caizhiu stifled a warning growl. Normally, she could have knocked the woman's knife out of her hand in the blink of an eye, but not while the house was spinning. She didn't want to risk crushing Heort or Zojia. If she was too slow and the woman opened Heort's throat, the dragon could easily kill her and her parents, but the cervitaur would still be dead. Her foggy mind struggled to think of a way to alleviate the situation. Transfiguring into her human form was as likely to terrify as reassure them, but in her own form the human language was beyond her.

Zojia glanced at her parents, who stood behind her. Veiloz held a cleaver, both hands wrapped around the short handle, and Phiazola held a broom. Six be praised, none had thought of fetching a rifle. The three looked as bewildered as Caizhiu felt.

"Will you permit my friend to adopt her human form?" Heort asked.

"I permit it," Veiloz said in a quivering voice, "but if the dragon approaches, you die."

Caizhiu transfigured her rebelling muscles and bones. Every movement, from the smoothing of her scales to the restructuring of her skull, was a painful and slow fight to get her body to obey.

"Where is Ozcahar Nitt?" she asked as soon as she could.

Veiloz shrugged. "He was not here when we awoke."

"I assume you will claim you had no hand in the poison that sedated us."

Phiazola gripped the broom and stepped forward. "There was nothing amiss with that food. Surely, you do not believe that we would poison ourselves."

{Apologies, I'm afraid the poison was mine. Not so much poison as snukorat, the slumber root.} Embarrassment permeated Heort's song.

Caizhiu nodded at Zojia. "You can release him."

The woman loosened the grip with which she held Heort's head back. He brushed his fingers over the line the knife had drawn in his sleek fur. Zojia let go of his antlers and stepped back but tightened her grip on the knife. Heort got to his hooves and took wobbly steps. Caizhiu bent to pick up her bag, as well as Heort's coat and harness. Her friend joined her by the door and gave her a pointed look, directing her gaze to the bag in her hand. She took out fifteen sempanee as well as a few golden pieces from Nellepeth, placed the coins on the edge of the tipped-over bench, and backed out of the door. Munificence might, just might, lessen the hosts' recall of the harrowing end of their visit. In time it could be a story to regale travellers: the night a dragon came to stay.

***

Auto carriages left no trail of manure to show how long ago the vehicle had passed. The contraptions weren't as fast, but the humans could run them almost consistently. There were no regular stops to water, feed, or rest animals. It took a long time for the effect of the snukorat to wear off and Caizhiu moved slower than usual. She had been on the trail for a day and a night and still not caught up with Ozcahar.

Heort looked up at the surrounding cliffs and broke his embarrassed silence. *{Perhaps you could spot him from a higher vantage point.}*

Sight had never been Caizhiu's primary hunting sense, but it wasn't a bad idea. She transfigured into her true form. Through his own foolhardiness, Ozcahar had already seen her like this. What did it matter if she terrified him once more? It would serve as a valuable lesson to refrain from such impertinence.

With her wings safely tucked in, she could scale the mountain quickly. Soon Heort was reduced to a pinprick making his way along the road below her. She extended her wings, catching the wind but not unbalanced by it. She jumped off and soared, watching her shadow rush along the landscape below. As she approached the next peak, she moved her wingtips down, pushed her legs forward, and grabbed hold of the rocks, causing boulders to clatter to the ground below. For a fraction of a second, she thought she would follow them, but she strengthened her grip and kept hold of the mountain. She repeated her jump and glided to the next rocky spire. This time, the landing was more controlled, and Caizhiu planted her four claws around the outcrop.

The altitude of the hills diminished, and the mountainous terrain descended into undulant gullies and plateaus. She would have liked it better if the Marsarin were as hot as Jitren's peaks, but these were the days that fed the thirst of Uayath. Still, if her quarry led her further south, the cool air would give way to the warmth of the Tookigrok Plains, and she could bask in the sun. She glided from pinnacle to pinnacle; every time she could pay more attention to the surrounding landscape than her next landing. The further she dared look, the easier controlling her glide became. Since she had never seen the landscape from this position, it took a while before she identified the dark patches into which the fingers of the mountain range disappeared as forests. In the distance, rivers flowed into expansive golden lakes of a setting sun. It was so beautiful she almost forgot to look for her prey.

She tilted her head to turn when she spotted a glimmering in the valley. Something reflected the sunset the way water would, the way bhodine carapaces would. She swooped from her perch for a closer look, confirming that the speck was an auto carriage. Then she had to bank to the left to avoid the treetops. The wily human had left the road, descending so fast he'd propelled the carriage into the woods, where there was no clearing for her to land. Caizhiu returned to the mountains and discovered that flying up, against the wind, made the journey far more arduous than the descent and took every bit of concentration to keep her wings in tandem. She rushed her landing, and it was almost as ungainly as her disastrous attempt at flight in the Keeltois. Regretting her earlier burst of confidence, she crawled down the cliff face.

The mountain winds scattered all scents, filling the southern air with the aroma of rainwater as the rivers carried the remnants of the wet season to the parched landscape. Letting the air roll around her mouth, it dismayed her she couldn't find any trace of Heort. He might be fast, but he couldn't keep up with her flight. Before she walked away from the road to follow the auto carriage, she sprayed the cliff to tell Heort which way she'd gone.

She flapped relaxation into her wings, stretched and cricked her long neck before adopting her human form. In woodland it was the easier shape to make progress. As she broke into a comfortable trot, she ducked between the juniper trees to shortcut the track the carriage had created. The track sloped downhill and rounded a stony outcrop. Beyond it, the vehicle had vaulted off the hillside. As she surveyed the scene, it occurred to Caizhiu that it probably had not been by choice. She picked up one of the large cartwheels that lay against the uprooted bush and muttered curses so softly she felt sure none of the Keepers would hear. All that effort to catch the human only for him to end his life through his own stupidity. She had thought it would be her clumsiness that would cause his death, not his own.

Should she make amends with the Six to atone for her failure? Would her next iteration be a punishing?

Caizhiu clambered towards the collection of wood and carapaces that had been Silver Rose's carriage. She ripped the carapaces off the roof and tore the side of the vehicle away. Ozcahar's scent was all over the wreckage. Caizhiu's stomach rumbled. To quell the noise, she pushed her hand against the place she kept her stomach. Instead of bhodine guts, the wooden body was filled with handfuls of leather belts, long copper hairs, and an assortment of wheels with interlocking teeth. Even though she tore the vehicle apart, she couldn't find any part of Ozcahar's body. Had she been so fortunate that her prey had come out of this accident without injury? Could he be living still, heading downhill on foot? She closed her eyes and sucked in the night air, unpicking the odours. Then it came to her, a subtle but familiar scent. It clung to the wreckage. It told her that her prey had not jumped out of the carriage before it had careered off the road. Ozcahar didn't get thrown, nor did he walk away from the crash. He had been stolen.

TWENTY-NINE

THE TREZZOHL TRAP

The evening had turned to night and still Heort had not caught up to Caizhiu. He regretted his suggestion she leave him behind. It had been glorious to see her take flight, but he had been surprised by the unease he had felt as her shadow passed over him. He'd thought their friendship had expelled the terror of their first meeting, and yet, as he'd watched her eclipse the sun, he'd felt an echo of that certainty that he was about to die. He'd seen that fear in Ozcahar's eyes at the Ice Bird Falls. He thought of the painting in Euvie and Myrta's reception room. Iterations changed dragons. To what extent had this latest one changed Caizhiu? She had always claimed that her personality remained constant, likening the process to a growth spurt, but everyone knew the tragedy of Ujojen the Conflicted.

Though darkness shrouded him, he knew he was leaving the massif behind him. The air filled with the heady scent of conifers and olive trees. His stomach had finally recovered from the poisoning and the aromas made it grumble. He left the human road to pick some bark from a conifer tree before bounding into the forest and sniffed the air looking for his friend.

He froze with a piece of bark between his teeth, struck by the same sense he'd had when Caizhiu's shadow had flown overhead. Something large was close by. And it moved.

He pulled his jacket free from the prickly branches and darted along the alley of trees, vaulting over a row of bushes. As his hind hooves touched the leathery leaves, a flash of night fay billowed around him. He chronochi'ed past them, leaving the creatures whirling in his wake, and bolted towards the safety of the shadows. Trotting towards the taller pines amid the conifers, he felt safe enough to glance behind him. Nothing pursued him. Heort slowed his breathing, relieved Caizhiu hadn't seen him jump like a foolish fawn. Just then, his hind legs were flung upwards so violently he somersaulted through the air. Before he could hit the ground, his outstretched hands were knocked back, and whatever had hit them smacked him in the face. Netting bashed against his belly and ripped open the bottom of his jacket. His stomach lurched with the rush of swift elevation. The net nearly bent him double with his hind legs stuck above him. One arm was trapped behind his back and his entangled antlers prevented him from moving his head. He wasn't sure how far off the ground he was, but his front legs trod uselessly in the air as he swayed backwards and forwards.

The air changed with a scent that, though unfamiliar, reminded him of rain through shale. Unable to see anything beyond the rope, he pivoted his ears backwards in the direction of rustling caused by the large being that approached. He squirmed to free himself, ineffectively kicking as the net above him squeezed tight and someone lifted him higher still. Despite his terror, Heort reached out to find a soul song. The response he found in his captor was a wordless turmoil of menacing imagery: bloody paste and shredded organs. The mind sound of shattering human skulls enveloped him as much as the net had. He took hold of the rope to keep his hand from shaking and closed his eyes.

Death was tardy. When his hand was pried off the net and pinched between a powerful finger and thumb, Heort took his chance. He grabbed hold of the finger and filled his soul song with all the calming cordiality he could muster.

{Greetings, friend. I appear to have sprung a trap. Would you be so kind as to help me out?} He shared the Keeltois landscape, the scent of the woodlands, and the sensation of walking through the babbling brook. And he drew in the barely hidden thoughts of his captor. 'Trezzohl', he found, and caught glimpses of mottled brown, green, and grey bodies walking through elaborate cool structures, loving relations, and gardens with delicious plants. The thoughts of offerings sent a shiver from his neck to his tail. Ever so hesitantly, the menacing imagery faded from his captor's song, replaced by curiosity.

{Stinks of human.}

Heort was spun round and turned over. He groaned when his hindquarters, middle, and upper chest were prodded and squeezed.

{But it isn't one. Let's have a look at what type of otherkin you are.}

Heort hoped this would mean his release, but a large hand opened the net and fished him out by his harness. He hung upside down, and as he untangled the netting from his antlers, he had the curious sensation that he was losing a layer of protection.

{We've not had one such as you here before.}

Up close, the creature's face was dominated by an enormous nose with six nostrils. The quivering tip wriggled as if searching independently for interesting scents. A flurry of brown curls with green and orange patches filled the rest of Heort's limited vision. The strands had dark ends and a lighter base that matched the skin tone so that it was difficult to tell where the hair ended and the face started. Eyes the size of the cervitaur's hands blinked at him from beneath a pronounced brow. Orange stripes in the fur above them gave the face a quizzical and affable appearance. But two sets of conical tusks that stuck up from the triangular lower jaw on either side of the beak-like nose undid this impression.

{You can cease your trembling.} The stranger moved the tip of its nose over Heort's antlers and face, palpating and possibly tasting him. *{Not even our hungriest mother would stoop to eating otherkin.}*

{My name is Heort from the Keeltois,} he sang as serenely as his terror would allow. *{Would you honour me with your name, friend?}*

Finally, his captor's curiosity seemed satisfied. *{I am Tyrzinein, Third Upholder of the Bol Badihr Commonry. Why would a little cervitaur from the Keeltois be traversing our lands?}*

{I was not aware of your claim on the land, nor that travel was forbidden. I meant neither offence nor harm to you or your people.}

Tyrzinein chuckled, a throaty sound more terrifying in its volume than reassuring in its gaiety. *{I shall forgive the theft of the bark you took, if you tell me what brought you here.}*

{Would you consider setting me on the ground before I answer?}

{You move faster than my eyes can see, friend. I will put you down if you would give me your word that you won't bolt the instant you are free.}

Tyrzinein knelt and gently lowered the cervitaur's hooves onto the ground, though he kept hold of his harness. Heort licked his nose, considered how fast he could unbuckle his harness, and decided it would not be fast enough.

{What do you want with me, Tyrzinein? As you say, I have done you no harm and you claim you do not intend me any. You call me friend. So why do you keep me prisoner?}

To calm himself, he smoothed his jacket and folded the collar back into place. He cast a perfunctory glance at the forest floor but couldn't see the torn-off buttons.

{Sentry duty is tedious work, and you are an interesting distraction.}

{But am I free to leave should I choose to?}

Tyrzinein let go of the harness and moved his hands away. He seemed to expect the cervitaur to disappear, but Heort managed to suppress his instincts.

{There,} Tyrzinein said with a broad grin. *{You can see I will not keep you. But you should be careful not to trip our traps. Some are deadlier than a simple net.}*

The highest tip of Heort's antlers barely reached up to the trezzohl's knee. The creature stood on two legs like a human but was almost twice as tall as Caizhiu's human form. Tyrzinein appeared larger still because of the wild manes that cascaded over his shoulders and blended in with his thick pelt. He had long arms ending in, as Heort had gathered, enormous hands that counted eight fingers and two thumbs. Now that he was further away from the creature's face, he could see the elegant upswept ears ending in orange tufts.

Tyrzinein narrowed his eyes, picked something from the net, and held it out to Heort. *{Why have you surrounded yourself in human things? That is not a clever thing to do. You were correct that the net was not for the likes of you, but you can hardly blame me for mistaking you for vermin when you reek of their stink.}*

If Heort had bolted, he would have completely forgotten about Caizhiu's bag. That would have led to an awkward conversation with the dragon. He accepted the bag and took a few steps away from the pile of rope.

{Am I right to assume that the net is intended to capture humankin?}

Tyrzinein spat on the ground. *{Human... kin? They are not kinfolk! They ruin our plants and steal our crops. You were fortunate, little friend, that I was heedful. Stinking as you do, I'd as likely have stepped on you as finding out you were not one of those vermin.}*

Heort had never been happier not to be human, but wondered if Caizhiu would be as lucky. She would probably have taken her human form. He had antlers and four legs. If the trezzohl nearly mistook him for a human, it was almost certain she would be.

{I was separated from my travel companion, and given your animosity to the human creatures, I fear you may have encountered her.}

Tyrzinein grumbled and straightened up with an eye-obscuring scowl. *{You travel with a human?}*

{Not quite. We were tracking a human. That is the scent you detected. But though my friend has a human appearance, she is not one.}

{You are most foolish travellers.} Tyrzinein shook his head. *{I cannot guarantee your friend's safety, nor that of the human you were hunting. If it ran into one of us, it is likely dead. As for your friend, what fool would choose to resemble such loathsome beings?}*

Contemplating his own death was one thing; imagining Caizhiu's was torture. He needed to find her, warn her. *{Please, will you help me find my friend?}*

{I'll try but regrettably, it's possible she is dead. We have no patience with vermin.}

{She's not human, I promise.} He gave Tyrzinein the image of Caizhiu's human form, transfiguring it in his soul song to her glorious dragon body as she soared through the sky.

{Your friend is the dragon Caizhiu.}

Heort looked at the staggering trezzohl, ready to chronochi out of the way if he needed to. The creature whirled his enormous hands through the trees, faltered, and fell onto his backside. A small conifer snapped beneath him. He sat shaking his head, pulling first at the branches around him and then his own pelt. His nose paled in the moonlight and stared at Heort. *{Do you mean to say that we may have enraged a dragon?}*

Reeling from his captor's change of mood, Heort stepped forward. It had not occurred to him that an otherkin as formidable as the trezzohl would fear a dragon.

{She's only a small dragon.} He hoped Caizhiu would never learn of this reassurance.

Tyrzinein shook his head in despair and buried his face in his hands. *{Size is immaterial. A dragon's grudge lasts for their entire lifetime. Please remember how I did not harm you, friend, the care I took not to damage you.*

Advocate for us. You must help keep my commonry safe from your dragon's wrath.}

Part IV

THIRTY

EIMSIFF OF THE BOL BADIHR COMMONRY

E imsiff looked up at the stronghold of the commonry, carved into the Runei mountainside. It had taken all night to make his way back, but judging by the early morning's silence, his absence had gone unnoticed. Most of the fathers were still asleep. In the distance, the night sentry stood calmly on the eastern viewpoint. Two more patrolled the woods, but he had easily avoided them. Especially this morning, with his brilliant offering, he did not want a father's interference. Aside from the sentries, the only ones awake were his year-siblings, enjoying the freedom of the sunrise. For a few precious hours, the commonry was theirs.

Bobusgeh sat on her usual outcrop, leaning back against the wrong side of the balustrade of the western balcony, and dangled her legs over the gorge. She had done it since they were cubs, despite having been reprimanded more times than Eimsiff could count. But, as the fathers said so often, there was no reasoning with women. Bobusgeh was the embodiment of disobedience, and he would miss her very much. Silhouetted against the pink of the nearly risen sun, he noted how tall and muscular she had become. He stepped out of the woods onto the commonry bridge. She spotted him at once and fanned her hand in greeting. It was delicate, with long fingers, and the sky reflected off her claws. By comparison, his hand was broad and stubby, with none of her elegance. Sweat had matted the fur under the straps of his basket and Eimsiff wished he had time for a dusting.

Bobusgeh cocked her head and sniffed the air. Zevreityr followed her gaze to Eimsiff and snorted as he tried to smell what had caught her interest. Thalvur, the fourth nestling of their year and Bobusgeh's twin, stood on the bridge, close to the commonry entrance, blocking his path.

{Where have you been?} Thalvur asked. He frowned at the scents he could pick up and looked to see if there was a father to report Eimsiff to.

Eimsiff readjusted the basket straps over his shoulders to straighten his back. It wasn't as if there was a law against leaving the commonry at night. The fathers would not be happy, but what would they do? At worst, he'd be rebuked. He wasn't as rebellious as Bobusgeh, but he could be when he wanted to. Thalvur was a worrier. It was as if he already had taken up the mantle of Prime Upholder of the Commonry, like he was determined to prevent anyone from breaking the rules or have any fun. If his year-brother were ever to take leadership of the commonry, Eimsiff vowed to leave and live in the mountains like a woman.

{I've been hunting.} He stared proudly up at Bobusgeh, who poured her glorious laugh over them. *{Come and see if you disbelieve me.}*

Thalvur shrieked when his sister did exactly what Eimsiff had thought she would, though she did it more gracefully than he had imagined. She stood to balance on the outcrop and let herself drop. Catching the outcrop with one hand, she swung herself in his direction. Her claws sparked as they scraped over the rock, and she cleared the abyss.

Up in the commonry, Zevreityr gasped and disappeared from the window. Eimsiff could hear his footsteps run along the balcony towards the western exit. As per usual, poor Zevreityr had to take the slow road.

Bobusgeh landed on the bridge between her nest-brothers, her manes bouncing as she jumped to her feet with more panache than was necessary to be impressive. None of them had the athleticism that came so easily to Bobusgeh. His year-sister had outgrown all of them and looked down at Eimsiff with a mocking smile that showed off her newly grown fangs. Before the next sparse season, all her cub teeth would be replaced with female ones. Her pelt was already showing streaks of female grey, and her scent was more intoxicating than the flowers. She would come into season soon, then her nest-brothers would have to say goodbye to her. Even now, despite all her manifest changes, that seemed an impossibility to him. The commonry would never be the same without her. Even when she would make her annual return, he could feel in his gut that she would be different then; they would be different. Their siblingship was ending.

His confidence wavered, but he couldn't back down, so he loosened one of the shoulder straps and heaved the basket off his back with such speed that momentum propelled the content onto the bridge. He had wondered how he would tackle getting the human out, and this seemed the safest way. The carcass slumped onto the stones and lay still. Eimsiff was pretty sure it was dead.

{You caught this?} Her song dripped with admiration and wonder.

Eimsiff nearly burst with pride. He couldn't fathom how one could find anything appetising about the foul-smelling beast, but he guessed you had to be a woman for that. Bobusgeh took a few tentative steps towards the prone creature. She reached for it, feminine claws extended just in case, but Thalvur intervened before she could touch it. She snarled at her brother and shook him off.

{It's not dead. I saw it move,} Thalvur said and glared at Eimsiff. {You brought vermin to the commonry. I will tell the fathers about this.}

{If it's not yet dead...} Bobusgeh's eyes sparkled, and her grin stretched the breadth of her face. *{Let's kill it.}*

Her flash of enthusiasm quickly dimmed as the three stared at each other and realised that none of them knew how to do that. Eimsiff had seen plenty of dead humans, but none of the fathers had shown him how to despatch one. He now regretted having never been interested in learning, thinking it would be a more suitable lesson for a woman. What an impression he would have made if he'd confidently been able to... he wasn't sure what, but it would have established his superiority over his year-brothers.

He twisted a branch of a nearby tree and used it to prod the lifeless heap between them.

{You imagined it, Thalvur. That thing is dead.} His planned scornful laugh turned into a nervous bark.

Finally, Zevreityr joined them, wheezing and spluttering as he leant against the commonry wall to catch his breath.

Thalvur harrumphed. *{I don't believe you killed this thing. You wouldn't even know how to catch it. I wager you found it dead or stole it from a trap.}*

He searched for a father to back him up and tell tales of Eimsiff's misconduct. Bringing humans to the commonry was not celebrated. They all knew it was too early for offerings. None of the mothers had descended from the mountains yet. Suddenly, his brilliant idea seemed silly. He could not argue that he had found the human instead of capturing it. Alone, in the dark, it had been scary to approach it, to touch it, without being certain the beast was dead. But now, among his year-brothers, with the sun about to rise, his adventure didn't seem so heroic any more. He'd lugged the carcass all the way up to the commonry only to be made a fool of, and he hated Thalvur for it.

Zevreityr waved, and they all looked in his direction before noticing he was pointing at something behind them.

{You'd better figure out how to kill these things quickly. There's another one, and it looks angry.}

The sun breached the crest of the mountains as Eimsiff spun round. The light obscured his vision, but he could make out the human stepping out from the shadows of the trees. He started. The thing was bigger than the one he caught, bigger than any he'd seen. How could it have crept up on them without betraying itself with the human stench?

Eimsiff gripped the branch in one hand and unsheathed his knife with the other. Behind him, Thalvur screeched and waved his arms to intimidate the creature into retreat. To his shame, Eimsiff could think of nothing better than to join him and he swung the branch wildly at the human.

{*Calm yourselves,*} the human said in a soul song that carried as much authority as that of an Upholder of the First Order. {*And shut up!*}

The four fell quiet, bobbing from one leg to the other. Even Bobusgeh seemed uncertain what to do. As the human stepped into the light, Eimsiff could finally make out its features. None of this made sense. The creature should be frightened. It should be running for its life, especially when they had all screamed at it. But it wasn't afraid in the slightest. Eimsiff wondered if it had gone mad with terror.

{*Are you one of those halfkins?*} he asked. {*The fathers have told us of you. Don't think that will save you, vermin. We will kill you as easily as your soulless brethren!*}

{*Don't talk drivel. You will kill no one. You haven't even managed to kill him.*}

The human pointed at the one face down by his feet. It hadn't moved since he'd dumped it, regardless of what Thalvur thought he'd seen. Eimsiff prodded the prone heap with his foot and had to concede that the body was still floppy and warm. It had been hours since he'd found it, and though he might not know how to kill one, he knew that by now a dead human would have been stiff and cold.

{*It is dead,*} Eimsiff lied and pointed at the standing human with his knife. {*As you will be if you don't run away.*}

He could hear the others gasp admiringly, but he daren't take his eyes off the human to look at them. Instead of backing away, the creature stepped towards him. It stood so close that Eimsiff would only need to take one step forward in order to slash it. It was almost as if it was daring him to attack. That step seemed to be impossibly large, and his legs were unwilling to take it.

{What's your name, Cub?}

{Eimsiff,} he answered before realising he'd been insulted. He couldn't retreat, so he straightened his back and added pompously: *{I'm Eimsiff of the Bol Badihr Commonry.}*

The cloak unfurled from around the human and its body expanded. The head grew and rows of sharp teeth sprang from the elongated jaws. Eimsiff blinked and staggered backwards. When the transfiguration had finished, the head of the dragon was eye level with him.

{I am Caizhiu the Wayward, the dragon of the plains of Jitren. I am bounty hunter to the Six Keepers of Sinuation and their Magistrates. And I have a prior claim on this human.}

She stood over the unconscious human and placed a proprietary claw on it. This, Eimsiff realised, would be the moment to give ground. But it wasn't fair.

{I found it,} he sang. *{And I claim this offering for the woman Bobusgeh.}*

Bobusgeh gasped in surprise and then grunted approval behind him. He felt a burst of confidence. Caizhiu looked from him to her and sighed wearily. They stood in silence for a few minutes, and Eimsiff's confidence faltered.

{Very well. I recognise your claim on the human,} said the dragon and she looked from Eimsiff to Bobusgeh. *{However, forgive me for saying this, but you have not yet come into season, have you?}*

His year-sister shook her head.

{So what would you do with this offering?}

Bobusgeh highlighted her grin by running her tongue over her new teeth. *{I have my fangs already. I will kill the human, even if I cannot yet eat it. It is a fine offering.}*

She winked at Eimsiff.

{*A fine offering it may be, but your first kill is special.*} Caizhiu's song filled with empathy. {*Trust me on this. You don't want to waste that on something you cannot fully accept. Wait for the mothers to return from the mountains and then take their counsel. They will teach you when you are ready.*}

Bobusgeh cocked her head. What Caizhiu said was correct, but it pleased him she was hesitant to reject his offer. Eventually, she relented and shrugged at him.

The dragon turned her head to Eimsiff.

{*It is a fine offer, but since I have a claim on the human and the woman can't accept it, would you consider trading it for something more useful?*}

{*The Nuzazog.*}

The speed of the response and the source surprised Eimsiff. He turned to Zevreityr, who seemed to regret his outburst.

{*Don't talk trash!*} Thalvur scoffed. {*The Nuzazog is lost. Has been lost for eons.*}

Eimsiff nodded his appreciation at Zevreityr. Imagine if he were the one responsible for bringing back the sacred object.

Thalvur was in line, however many years in the future, to take over as Prime Upholder of the Commonry. All he had done to earn the position was to be born as a woman's twin. But returning the Nuzazog, the Mother's Claw, was a true accomplishment, and 'He Who Returned the Nuzazog' would likely be honoured and would be so desired he'd have his choice of women. And if he returned it in her name, Bobusgeh was sure to return for him and no one else.

{*Eimsiff.*} Caizhiu brought him back from his reverie. {*You have the human I want. Is the Nuzazog something you would accept in his stead?*}

{*I would accept that.*}

He described the famed Nuzazog dagger and spat on the ground as did all the others when he told her of the dastardly humans who had stolen the weapon from the late Honoured-Upholder Risradyl and how they were said to have taken it to their infestation by the Noxious Water.

Caizhiu gave it some thought and said: *{It is agreed. You have my word that I will travel to the town by the coast and that, if what you have told me is true and the Nuzazog dagger is there, I will retrieve it for you. And in return you will give me the human.}*

{Agreed!} Eimsiff crossed his arms. *{But you shall only have the human once you have returned the Nuzazog, and our agreement stands for as long as Bobusgeh is unable to accept the offer.}*

The dragon growled ominously. *{I hope you do not mean to doubt my word, Cub.}*

{The Noxious Water is far away.} He hesitated before continuing. *{You may fail to retrieve the Nuzazog, and we will not want to keep the stinking vermin around forevermore. Once the mothers are here, it will not be long before Bobusgeh becomes a woman. The human will be a fine offering then.}*

It sounded like thunder rolled towards them from the commonry. Thalvur smiled as, at long last, the fathers were arriving. At the prospect, the wretch seemed to swell. The first to reach them was father Tyrzinein. The air in their midst filled with Thalvur's soul song, but before he could give the Upholder of the Third Order a rundown of Eimsiff's foolishness, Bobusgeh's recklessness, and whatever he could accuse Zevreityr of, their attention was drawn by the deer-like creature at the father's side.

{Caizhiu!} In the blink of an eye, the being that looked like a deer cursed with a human visage moved to the other side of the group, next to the dragon. With barely an acknowledgement of the creature's arrival, Caizhiu rolled the human over onto its back. The limbs flopped, but the groan that escaped from its lips was inescapable. It was definitely alive.

{Honoured dragon,} Tyrzinein said, kneeling with a deep bow. *{Forgive these cubs. Be lenient with them, for they are young and new to the ways of the world.}*

{They seem to know enough. Though not that it is unwise to insult a dragon by doubting her word.}

Tyrzinein's nose paled, and he pulled at his fur. *{What did you do, Eimsiff?}*

{Your cub negotiates well,} the dragon said and bobbed her head.

He had expected Thalvur to jump in, but Caizhiu's compliment, or maybe the arrival of the father, had knocked the fervour out of him. The other nestlings, even Bobusgeh, seemed to retreat into their tyro status.

{Please say you have not made a bargain you cannot live up to. Not with a dragon.}

{We'll see if he can live up to the agreement we've struck.} Caizhiu nudged the little deer thing. *{Will he live?}*

{I don't know how badly his brain was rattled, but his sleep is snukorat-induced.} The creature took a jar from a pocket of his harness, rubbed the content between his fingers and held them under the human's tiny nose. The human twitched but didn't wake. *{Fortunately, there is no swelling inside his skull, and he has no obvious broken bones. His heart is strong, and he breathes well. He should live.}*

Caizhiu fixed Eimsiff with an intense stare and widened her wings. *{There you have it, Eimsiff of the Bol Badihr Commonry. Today, you have acknowledged my claim, and I have understood your terms to trade him. But I warn you; if I reach the town and there is no Nuzazog dagger and I return to the commonry to find my human is dead or missing, it will not go well with you, or your woman, or your commonry. Do you understand?}*

Eimsiff felt the urge to kneel too and tug at his fur like father Tyrzinein did, but he couldn't do so in front of Bobusgeh or Thalvur, so he meekly bobbed his head.

More fathers were arriving or looking on from the commonry balustrades, recently awoken and confused by the rumpus. Eimsiff looked back at the dragon, but both she and the deer creature had vanished. If it hadn't been for the human at his feet, curled on its side like a bird in its egg, he might have thought he'd been dreaming.

Thirty-One

Journey to the Noxious Water

Solitary bushes fought for survival in the winds. The landscape of the Tookigrok plains was as empty as the wastes of the Marsarin Massif. It was drier and its rivers were reduced to underground streams from the mountains to the narrow sea. Sporadic plant life showed where one ran close to the rocky surface. The winds were considerably warmer, and at various times Heort flapped his frock coat to cool down. Caizhiu caught him looking at the missing buttons with a sorrowful expression. After the rain and the cold, she would have liked to bask her scales in the sunlight, but the thoroughfare between the coastal town and the North Bergiu region was teeming. The scents and the noise had reached them long before they caught sight of the stream of human traffic, so she had twisted herself into her human form.

The road was broad enough for carriages to pass or overtake, but still travellers bunched together in impatience. A rider on a black mare cursed as he tried to get past a Sarfi caravan that had stopped. The driver ignored his expletives as they continued to exchange familial greetings with another caravan coming from the other direction. Following the lead of other travellers, Caizhiu walked on the rough verge along the road. Occasionally, they had to step over the conduit next to the road; a simple hop for Heort, but Caizhiu had to take care she wouldn't leave a line of cracks in the stone duct. The Tookigrok towns relied on these ducts for the water from the wet season in Marsarin Massif, and although it was only a trickle now, the rainwater would soon run down the mountains. Even this sparse flow was enough for life to burst from the thoroughfare as it formed a fattening snake of green through the sere landscape. Between the boulders, small ephemeral plants turned from their dry yellow colour to the luminescent green of the wet season. Palm trees lined resting areas. Caizhiu suspected that the traders who sold refreshments from their carts had planted the trees to attract travellers to shelter in their shade.

Heort stopped, sniffed, and gave Caizhiu the happiest smile she had seen from him since Wexede Crossing. *{Is that the sea?}*

Devoted to their commonry, trezzohl were loath to travel. If they were aware of a human settlement by the coast, outside of their territory, it was probably the closest one. As the friends approached the town of Basinwade, the scents of salt hung in the warm air, as did the pervasive stench of drying fish. It seemed to please the cervitaur.

{Have you ever seen a sea?} Caizhiu asked.

{Only in Gostawa's mind.}

Gostawa had crossed an ocean when she came from Aumegoa, but that had been a long time ago, and memories did not equate with experience. Though Heort's curiosity was boundless, most of the knowledge in Bladrid came from the tales of the Sarfi travellers. Her friend was in for a shock.

{I advise you not to drink the water.}

{I'm not a complete fawn.} He gagged at her memory of the taste. *{Suppose that's why the trezzohl called it 'noxious'.}*

Heort gleamed with enthusiasm as he darted between the moving carriages to the resting area on the other side of the road. Caizhiu sighed and, with difficulty, followed his lead. She wanted neither to waste the energy on chronochi nor draw attention to herself, so she lumbered between the carriages, mumbling apologies to the drivers that addressed her with profanities.

She found her friend by a haberdashery stall beneath a palm tree. Its stock contained practical spares for use on the road, and also some needlecraft bits and pieces that had caught his eye. He raised his hand to draw the merchant's attention, though he was the only person at the stall.

"I require buttons like these," he said in his most perfect Trader and pointed at his jacket. "Have you these?"

The woman behind the stall glanced at him from under her bonnet and shrugged as if she hadn't understood. He pointed at the two missing buttons and held one out as an example.

"Have you such button?"

Caizhiu walked over and stood next to him. *{Sewing supplies? You are ruining my reputation.}*

The smile the woman cast Caizhiu was missing a front tooth and faded when her eyes wandered over the dragon's bulk. The merchant pouted her lips and when her smile returned, it was taut, revealing none of her broken teeth.

"What say it? I no understand."

"My boss," Caizhiu replied pointedly, "require buttons for his coat."

She couldn't understand how the woman could have misconstrued Heort's meaning. The topics of conversation at a merchant's stall were limited and his pointing at the missing buttons was self-explanatory.

The woman straightened her bonnet and jutted out her chin. Despite the assortment of colourful buttons in the jars behind her, she said: "I no have buttons."

"You no have buttons like his?"

"I no have buttons."

Caizhiu shrugged. "Then we will find trade in Basinwade."

"It no find buttons in Basinwade," the woman said. "Go elsewhere."

Caizhiu shook her head, casting a last scowl over her shoulder before following Heort. The merchant pretended to look for other customers.

{I think I must practise my Trader.} Heort adjusted the dragon's haversack on his back. *{The humankin here don't seem to understand me.}*

Caizhiu laid her hand on his shoulder. She hadn't intended to use him as a beast of burden, but he had rebuffed several offers to take her bag from him. It was as if, after Ozcahar poisoned them using his snukorat, the cervitaur felt he needed to prove his worth. She resolved to make the human apologise to him for that.

"What be Basinwade like?" Heort asked, but Caizhiu couldn't remember whether she had ever visited the town.

For a long time, it had merely been one of many fishing villages that lined the coast of the Telereni Sea. Because of its extended harbour and large market squares, it had grown into a major route for trade from Ucral and the Zari lands. It had never risen to city status. Once Bladrid had received its Magistrate, it was decided that Basinwade was too close, and the honour had gone to the more southerly positioned city of Aerahan. It had been decades since she last visited that city too, and she wondered if Zel Zesen was still the Magistrate there. She ran the memory of the man's soul song through her senses. He had been young then, barely into adulthood, and eager to meet her with his insatiable curiosity. Human lifespans were short, so if he lived still, he must be an old man. His region was sparsely populated but spanned the hot and inhospitable lands from the Tookigrok plains to Udnar and even as far east as Tanokabei. If that were not enough to occupy Zel, on the other side of the Telereni strait, and visible on a clear day, were the Mospium peninsula and the Fire Isles. She knew little of the intricacies of a magistrate's life. Some, like Gostawa, regarded it as a calling; others, like Yullorik, regarded it as a curse. Still others hoped to be noticed by the Six. She didn't know what kind of Magistrate Zel had grown into. Perhaps once she'd recovered Ozcahar from the commonry, she could take him to Aerahan. The quicker she could get rid of her human, the better.

Heort stopped so suddenly that Caizhiu nearly bumped into him. As he looked out at the glistening Telereni Sea, he blinked and pointed with a shaky finger, forgetting his plan to use spoken words. His soul song dripped with amazement and awe. *{Are they humankin ships? Do they float all over that?}*

{That is only a small piece of the sea. Humans sail further than you can see. They sail south from here to Uha'Zari and all the way north to Aumegoa.}

Heort swallowed. "We won't be doing that, will we?"

"Not if I can help it," Caizhiu said. *{Let's get that damned dagger and we'll sort out our onward travel afterwards.}*

Welcome Gates were typically represented by a standalone arch or poles beside the road in many human settlements, but in Basinwade, it was a physical gateway built into a thick stone wall. Though Wexede Crossing still had remnants of its city walls, its dwellings had spilled out into the surrounding marshes. Around Basinwade, there were no buildings - no houses, shanties, not even any allotments. The town wall appeared to rise out of the landscape like a humanmade mount, or as Heort pointed out, like a beehive, with a crowd that swarmed around the gate.

Though the Welcome Gate dwarfed even Caizhiu, the stream of travellers compressed as everyone tried to get through simultaneously. People had either finished a long journey or were beginning one. Nobody wanted to wait for a turn that may never come. Humans jostled into Caizhiu, but they bounced off her gut. She was barely aware of them as she looked up at the portcullis overhead. It made a pleasant change not to have to stoop to get through a human door. She turned to look for Heort, who dawdled backwards and forwards at the edge of the crowd.

{Why don't you nudge them out of the way?} she asked, trudging back through the throng.

{There are so many of them... and it's not polite.}

People elbowed each other to make their way in or out of the city. The noise of carriage horns and people screaming as their feet were crushed beneath steel-clad wheels was deafening. She wondered where Heort thought politeness featured here. What she wouldn't have given for the cervitaur's ability to assert just that little push towards desired behaviour. She wasn't sure, and wasn't certain if even he knew, how far he could willhex others. He claimed he could only nudge someone into a decision they were already willing to make. If the ability had been hers, she would have known precisely to what tunes she could make people dance. Heort wouldn't even use it to move them out of his way.

Caizhiu knelt, lifted her friend over her head, and draped him over her shoulders. He ducked, though there was still plenty of room beneath the portcullis. The disproportional size of the gate reminded Caizhiu of the Magistrate's manse in Bladrid. It probably served a similar purpose: giving visitors the appearance that Basinwade was more impressive than the overblown fishing village it was.

Though it was late in the afternoon, without the plain winds, the air in the streets was sweltering. Moist bodies pressed up against her, and her nostrils filled with the aroma of their sultry sweat. Carriage wheels kicked up clouds of whirling dust that covered and stuck to the crowd. Heort squirmed. She felt how he abhorred being carried, and as she moved aside to let a carriage pass, she looked for a widening of the street where she could set him down. When she stepped into an alleyway, someone placed a sweaty hand on her elbow. She turned to see a young man with a wide-brimmed hat and an ornately embroidered shirt that was lightly frayed around the cuffs. He had the amiable smile of a street pedlar, and she was going to tell him to get lost when he pointed at Heort and asked: "What price?"

The man's eyes widened in alarm when he caught the confusion on her face. Before Caizhiu could ask after his meaning, the young man had darted through the throng and disappeared from view. She lowered Heort to the ground.

"What was that about?" he asked, straightening his harness and coat.

"I think," Caizhiu said with a deep scowl as she scanned the crowd to see where the man had gone, "that someone tried to buy you."

He laughed until he realised she wasn't joking. Nervously, he took a few steps back from the crowd. "They... they buy and sell Fabled here?"

"For the sake of this town, I really hope they don't."

Heort shook the dust off his ears. "Did you at least get a good price?"

They were attracting stares from the windows that lined the alleyway and Caizhiu led her friend back towards the stream of people to head to the market square.

"You don't have to keep hold of me," he muttered, but failed to jerk free from her grip. "I'll be fine."

Caizhiu snorted. "I'm holding on to my gold. You just happen to be attached to it."

THIRTY-TWO

SYMBOLS OF BEAUTY AND PRIDE

Nightfall changed Basinwade, bringing silence, but not darkness. Even in the alleyways without streetlamps, light bled from between the shutters of the houses, so that Caizhiu could make out her surroundings without difficulty. The streets were deserted save for stray dogs and the cats that slunk from shadow to shadow, hunting for rats and abandoned fish heads. She wasn't hungry yet, but it was good to have options.

They passed the Fish Gate, which, unlike the Welcome Gate, was not shut at night. The town guard had only lowered its portcullis. A man swayed as he helped another squeeze through the lattice on their way from a shanty tavern on the docks into the town. They reeked of beer and fish. Both ended up in a heap on the ground and guffawed at their intoxicated clumsiness. They pointed at Caizhiu, puffed up their cheeks, and found hilarity in their observation. As the drunkards staggered off, Heort stopped by the portcullis to stare out at the water.

Caizhiu guided him up the steps to the top of the town wall, where the view was better. The lights from the houses and taverns danced peacefully over the ripples of the water in the bay. It was hard to believe it was the same town without the hullabaloo of the daytime. On the square behind them was a wooden tower, and Heort observed that their view would be even better from up there.

"Perhaps," Caizhiu said, "but let's orientate ourselves on the layout of the town, see if we can narrow down the places where this Nuzazog might be."

They circled Basinwade along the unbroken town wall, attracting odd glances from the solitary guards that sat on the battlements by the fortified towers in the wall. The woman guarding the Western Gate by the Fortune Tower seemed glad of their company. Full of enthusiasm, she pointed out where she'd grown up, her voice betraying both pride and regret when she said that part of the town had over the years been transformed into a renowned factory for auto carriages.

"Sibrand's Mechanised Carriages." Heort turned to Caizhiu excitedly. "The Hilleram brothers trade with them. Can we visit it?"

"Oh, we have better things to see, sirs," the guard said and took delight in describing the Stand. Caizhiu realised she meant the wooden tower by the Fish Gate. It was only five years old and, according to the guard, a superior attraction to the Townhall or the factory. Caizhiu decided it was probably the best place to start.

In the daylight, the splendour of the tower became evident. The town wall was tall, but the Stand was at least three times that height. It looked imposing, yet airy. Constructed of iridescently painted wooden planks over a steel trellis, it perfectly reflected the style of building in the town. Interlocking planks formed a colourful spiral up to the sky. The guard had explained how each plank had been engraved by local artists. Above the height where humans could reach, the carvings were still gilded in a layer as thin as a fay's wing, causing the structure to glimmer in the sun. She walked around the tower, but it seemed to serve no purpose other than to be the pride of Basinwade. Around it, traders had filled stalls with paintings, tapestries, jewellery, and charms with symbols similar to those carved in its wooden planks.

{Let's see if we can catch any trezzohl scent in that thing.}

The cervitaur's usual reluctance to enter an enclosed area was close to his surface. *{In there?}*

{Humans display objects in places like this, like the paintings in Gostawa's manse.}

They waited for people to exit the structure, and a thin man beckoned them to come forward. His official outfit looked too elaborate for the weather and perspiration soaked the collar. Before they could enter, he stopped them and asked for coin.

"Why for?" Caizhiu asked with an incredulous smirk.

"To see the Stand, sir. It be tallest tower in the world. You can see far way to Aerahan from up-top."

Caizhiu shrugged and handed him two coins.

Inside of the tower, sunlight played through the gaps between the higher planks. The bottom of the structure was encircled with an iron panel with delicately cut out shapes, and an iron sheet with speckles of coloured glass was suspended from on high, casting shade but not enclosing the visitors. The aroma of metal and wood permeated the interior. Caizhiu stood for a moment with her eyes closed, drinking in the heat and the delicious hint of gold.

Around the iron circle, steps twisted upwards, following the walls up and up. She had seen humans struggle to pass each other as one was descending and the other climbing up. That would not be possible with her bulk, so she waited.

"It is very pretty," Heort remarked. He walked carefully, but the iron mesh floor wasn't wide enough to lose his hooves through. He ducked underneath Caizhiu's arm and preceded her up the winding staircase. She pressed a foot on the wooden runs of the staircase to see if it would take her weight. It would not go well if the first thing she did was to wreck the humans' pride.

"Better than that," Caizhiu said and followed him. "It's sturdy."

{Any sign of trezzohl scent?}

Heort sniffed, shook his head, and continued upwards.

"Then why are we still climbing?"

The cervitaur skipped on up. "I want to see the view."

"I'm not climbing all the way up there," she called after him. The step groaned when she turned. At the bottom of the staircase, a gathering of people waited, none of whom could begin their ascent until she had moved out of the way. Caizhiu walked past their scornful glances.

"Be long way up," the reedy man taking the coin called to her and laughed. "Lose weight, try again."

Seeing him, she remembered humans perspired, and she pretended to wipe sweat off her forehead. Instantly, a merchant rushed towards the dragon with a collection of garments. Caizhiu politely declined, but she couldn't blame him for trying. Her appearance looked as out of place as the man in the uniform. She had adjusted the colour to a pale beige, but she still looked overdressed in her layers of wing cloak.

Eventually, Heort reappeared at the entrance. Even over this distance, she could sense his delight.

"Pretty?" she asked and arched an eyebrow.

"Mock all you want. You can fly any time you wish. I have to take my opportunities of such vistas when I can see them."

It occurred to her that had probably been the first time Heort had got a proper impression of the scale of the sea.

"Glad you enjoyed the pretty view. I hope our human friend is still in one piece."

She instantly regretted teasing her friend because his mood dulled, and she caught a memory fragment of hard trezzohl hands prodding him.

"Don't be concerned. They'll be careful to keep him alive. Maybe we'll have better luck in the Townhall."

They crossed the crowded square, passed stalls with gleaming trinkets, but none were made of gold. They wandered through the maze of tiny alleyways of the old town that led them in a meandering way to the hall. The guard had been correct; compared to the Stand, the building was unimpressive. It was constructed from stone, probably from the Marsarin Massif, and the roof was covered with bhodine carapaces. Two rows of small, squared windows hinted at only two storeys. It looked like there had been a square in front of the Townhall at one point, but it had long ago been usurped by dwellings and the only remnant was a large rectangular well. Shaded by a timber shelter, it attracted thirsty travellers and those with animals to water. People sat on the edge to enjoy a moment of respite in the cool shade. Heort joined them.

Caizhiu would have liked to have quenched her thirst, but remembering what happened in Wexede Crossing, she took it easy on the fluid intake. And if she were going to have a drink, she'd rather it was beer.

They walked into the Townhall. For a moment, she thought the sea breeze had made its way into the building, but then she noticed a trio of curious spinning devices. The humans had suspended three bulbous copper bodies with rotating wooden blades from the ceiling to generate indoor gusts of wind. Caizhiu could hardly believe it when she caught a whiff of trezzohl. Heort gave an almost imperceptible nod. The blades made it hard to pinpoint where the faint scent might originate, but it was unmistakable. Part of her had doubted Eimsiff's tale of a mythical dagger. She knew he had spoken the truth as he knew it, but he was only a cub and myths tended to distort over generations.

They faced two corridors. Since Caizhiu guessed they probably met up on the other end of the building, she picked the one without a queue of people waiting. One side of the hallway was lined with offices, the other was decorated with paintings, draperies, and ornaments. The hallway widened into a room where people fidgeted on wooden pews, waiting for their appointment. On the other side of the room, facing them, was a marble pedestal with a white sculpture that resembled a bodiless spider with its legs wrapped around the grip of a long blueish blade. The weapon curved towards the ceiling like the talon of a gigantic raptor. A human would need six hands just to hold the grip and she doubted any one human could lift let alone wield it. Dust had gathered in the markings that were etched into the blade. Here and there, the pattern was broken up by scratches of yesteryear's battles. But it wasn't the weapon that held the trezzohl scent; it emanated from the mount, constructed of the bleached bones of a hand. Perhaps it was a remnant of Risradyl, perhaps some other unfortunate father.

Heort went to speak, but Caizhiu enfolded his snout in her hand.

{I admire your commitment to verbal speech, but this is not the time to practise it.}

The cervitaur nodded and moved her hand away from his face. He looked around the waiting room and back to the entrance hall.

{I'm curious to know how you plan to steal it with all these people watching.}

{That bit is easy.} Caizhiu smiled at him. *{They are only human.}*

THIRTY-THREE

LORD DOLT AND LADY TOCSIN

Sitting against the wall with his arms resting on his knees, Ozcahar watched daylight creep into his dark corner. Every time one of the hairy giants who'd captured him entered the room, he expected they'd come to kill him, but they hadn't yet. They seemed incapable of speech or at least unwilling to talk to him. Nevertheless, he'd named the larger slow one with the green-striped brown fur with orange tips 'Lord Dolt'. The shorter giant, the one that screamed at him whenever he did anything the creature considered wrong, like moving or talking, he'd named 'Lady Tocsin'.

They put food, of a sort, and water out for him, but if anything, the couple seemed unhappy at his presence. Why then did they hold him captive? He wondered what they kept on the shelves that lined the room, but the rope that attached him to the wall didn't allow him to investigate. In darkness's solitude, he worried they were keeping him with the other food in their storeroom.

Whatever their reasons, Ozcahar would not just wait to find out what they were. Would Jorganyon just stay huddled in a corner? And besides, he had escaped a dragon; he should be able to escape two hirsute giants. He'd given up trying to undo the buckle on the belt around his middle, but perhaps he could climb to the ring to which the rope was tied. There seemed to be little scope to make his situation worse, so he might as well try. As he got to his feet, it became impossible to ignore the cramping of his innards. His captivity had already forced him to relieve his bladder at the far end of his tether a few times, but now he had a more serious issue. Pearls of perspiration coated his hairline, and he doubled up with the spasms of his insides. He didn't have a choice, so he hobbled to the piss-stained edge of his tether and dropped his trousers. He was emptying his bowels when Lady Tocsin entered the room. Both froze in mortification as they stared at each other. Then, as Ozcahar had expected, the creature shrieked. He had always retreated, but this time anger trumped humiliation. Ozcahar stood up and, while sorting out his trousers, walked towards the giant.

"What did you expect?" he screamed at the top of his voice. "You tie me up like an animal!"

He kicked over the food and water saucers and picked up a tuber. "You want me to eat this? This isn't food! This is dirt! And if I do eat, I shit. If you don't like it, set me free!"

He threw the tuber with every bit of strength he had. Astounded, he watched it hit Lady Tocsin on her enormous nose. The creature flinched and rubbed her face. Ozcahar picked up hands full of the inedible vegetables and pelted the creature into retreat. Buoyed by his unexpected success, he gathered the scattered tubers still within reach. But then the giant returned with a besom. Just in time, he crouched into his corner before the bundle of branches was brought down on him. Most of the besom's branches clattered against the walls, but his arms and back took enough of a lashing for Ozcahar to cry out.

The beating stopped, and he was yanked into the air. He landed on his front. Dazed, he rose to his knees and reached out to Lady Tocsin. "Apologies."

She untied the rope from the wall and dragged him behind her as she walked through the archway out of the storeroom. He rolled towards her when she suddenly stopped. Sore and groggy, Ozcahar staggered to his feet. He could smell burning wood, and his eyes darted around the room. From his low viewpoint, he spotted diced tubers on the worktop and an earthenware cauldron next to it. He was in a kitchen. If he didn't want to end up as dinner, he had to escape.

He kicked Lady Tocsin's ankle. While she hopped on one leg, Ozcahar pulled the rope out of her hand, turned to run but stared up at the hairy wall of Lord Dolt's thighs. The enormous creature sniffed the air and scowled at Lady Tocsin. She pointed from the storeroom to Ozcahar and back.

"N-not my f-fault..." He wasn't sure it would be understood, but Ozcahar shook his head vehemently. "I couldn't help it."

Lady Tocsin took a few steps back and it looked as if she'd received a scolding. Ozcahar felt a flicker of satisfaction as he watched her walk to the storeroom. Although he was about to be killed, the creature having to clean up his shit caused a faint smile. It wilted when Lord Dolt grabbed the belt and lifted him into the air, dangling him at arm's length before laying him on a worktop in the centre of the room.

Ozcahar tried to get up but was forced down. Lord Dolt squeezed the back of his coat between his thumbs and fingers and raised him slightly off the bench to undo the buckle. This would be his only chance. Ozcahar slipped his arms out of his coat, rolled to the edge, and dropped to the floor. The bench and the large clay pot blocked Lord Dolt, and by the time he'd rushed around them, Ozcahar had reached the exit. He ran headlong into the middle of a long hallway. The structure was far larger than a mere house, more like a city. The hall ran in either direction, seemingly unending, with lights streaming from rounded gaps in the ceiling, but no other way to the outside. Since he had seen no others, he had assumed Lord Dolt and Lady Tocsin lived on their own, like the hoteliers of the Silver Rose Tavern. The hallway proved him catastrophically wrong. It was as if he'd suddenly ran into a busy Thirdburg street, surrounded by towering buildings, except that here, the buildings moved. Giants with different hues of brown, orange, and green fur walked in either direction. More and more of the creatures turned and seemed as startled to see him as he was to find himself in their midst.

Lord Dolt tried to take advantage of his bewilderment, but Ozcahar ducked from under his grasping hands and zigzagged across the hallway. The only direction he could go was to run down a stairway. It led to a balcony running parallel to the hallway, but beyond it, he could see the gaps in the carved pillars of the balustrade. There were likely more of the creatures there, but if... if he could dodge them, he could at least get out of the stone complex.

He hurtled down steps that were not meant for his legs and his stomach lurched when he lost his balance. He only remained upright because he was still moving at speed. It did not matter that one of the creatures appeared in front of him, spreading its arms to block whichever direction he'd dodge to. But Ozcahar couldn't change direction. Nor could he slow himself. He was falling and slammed straight into the soft fur and solid body beneath. The creature cried out in surprise as it doubled over, and they sprawled across the balcony floor. It was a softer landing than Ozcahar had expected. Together they tumbled across the balcony and landed against the balustrade. The ornately carved balusters were too fat to squeeze between, but the top of the rail was only slightly taller than him. He took a run at it and, using the body of his foe, launched himself onto the top.

He couldn't even see the bottom of the ravine before him. The prospect of falling to his death had to be preferable to being butchered. He should jump, but he couldn't do it.

Sharp claws ripped into his doublet and shirt, scraping over his back as he was hauled backward. This creature was even more terrifying, with sharp claws and pointed fangs. It flung him into the air, and he landed on the floor of the balcony. He tried to crawl away, but he was surrounded. A creature grabbed his arms, squeezing his biceps, and he was unable to break free. The pain paled in comparison to the terror of the creatures closing in, hollering and screeching. Someone picked him up and held him above their heads. Recognising the green-striped pattern on the orange-brown fur, he felt relieved to be in the hands of Lord Dolt, as if familiarity alone would protect him.

The kitchen seemed dark and hot after the clarity of the outside air. Lord Dolt put him back on the stone bench. As soon as he could move slightly, Ozcahar grabbed the creature's hand with both of his.

"Don't kill me," he whimpered in a language he knew the creature didn't understand. "Please, don't kill me."

Puzzlement and disgust fought for dominance on Lady Tocsin's face as she waved Ozcahar's coat at Lord Dolt. The larger giant snuffled and shook his head with a snort. He freed his fingers and pressed Ozcahar prone against the table surface. Ozcahar watched Lady Tocsin walk to the fire and toss his coat into it. The sight of the expensive object reduced to ashes caused him to groan, but his dismay turned into terror when he saw her grab a knife the length of a sword from the table with diced tubers and hand it to Lord Dolt.

Blood from grazes on his face mixed with tears as he struggled and failed to get out from under the giant's hand. The more he squirmed to get free, the harder Lord Dolt pressed him onto the table. His teeth scraped over the stone. Lady Tocsin grabbed his calves. The cold steel of the knife touched the small of his back. How long would he live when they cut him in half? Would he have time to witness his legs being diced up?

Lord Dolt nicked his belt, splitting it and leaving a long gash in the yoke of his trousers. He slid the knife underneath the shirt and halved both the shirt and doublet in one cut. Wrapping his hand around Ozcahar's head to keep him still, he peeled the clothing off him, tossing the rags of the doublet into the flames but struggling with the cuffs of the shirt that caught on his wrists. Ozcahar almost admired the way Lord Dolt placed the tip between the inside-out cuff and his wrist and cut it without breaking the skin. If the giant was going to gut him, at least it would be over in seconds. Lady Tocsin was less skilful. She'd pulled off his trousers and undergarments, but the trouser legs caught on his boots. Roughly jerking to free them, she dragged Ozcahar out of Lord Dolt's grip. He dangled upside down and cradled his genitals with his torn shirt. Shrieking, she reached for the knife, but to his immeasurable relief, Lord Dolt refused to hand it to her. She shook the trousers violently until Ozcahar landed on the floor.

"W-wait!" He raised one hand. "I... I untie b-bootlaces."

Sat bollock naked on the floor, he struggled to undo the laces one-handed. Eventually he managed it. Keeping his eyes down, he offered his boots to Lady Tocsin and hoped that wouldn't antagonise the creature. She hurled them too into the fire. Ozcahar untied the string of his cuff and removed the sleeve, looking up to see which of his keepers would want the pleasure of destroying the last vestige of his personhood.

Lord Dolt took the rag and grabbed his arm to haul him to his feet. Casually, the giant dropped the shirt into the fire as he walked past. Ozcahar could only reach the ground with every other of the giant's steps and he was dragged to the clay cauldron in the corner. Lord Dolt let go of his arm and grabbed his neck. Thumbs pinched beneath his armpits, and his hair was trapped between two of the giant's fingers. As he was lifted off the ground, he saw the faint curls of steam that rose from the cauldron.

"No, no, no! I'll be good. Wait, please!" Ozcahar clawed at the fingers around his neck and kicked the hot clay rim. Lord Dolt dipped his hand into the cauldron and poured a near bucketful of hot water over Ozcahar's face. The shock caused him to gulp for air and resulted in a coughing fit. He wiped the water from his eyes, only to have another bucket-load scooped over his head. Lord Dolt squeezed his ankles between the fingers of his other hand. Ozcahar wasn't strong enough to prevent having his knees folded against his stomach. Lord Dolt plunged him into the cauldron. The water was painfully hot, just off scalding, and the hand on his neck kept him under despite his desperate thrashing. Ozcahar twisted his hips upward until he kicked the air, tried to hook his knees over the clay rim and lever himself up. But his legs were pushed back into the water. He clawed at the thumbs digging in his sides. His torso shuddered with the need to exhale. At last, Lord Dolt let him go. Ozcahar pushed off against the bottom and hooked his arms over the cauldron's rim. Spluttering for breath, he tried to haul himself out, slipping before he could raise himself high enough to get his waist onto the edge. The giant picked him up under his armpits. Wet strands of fur stuck around Ozcahar's middle, and his skin prickled with the heat of the water.

He was deposited on the bench next to the cauldron and he scrabbled around, searching for anything he could grab to fight back. He kicked the tubers off the bench, cut his fingers on some debris, and then Lord Dolt grabbed him by the neck to force him to lie still. The giant picked up a brush and scrubbed his feet and legs. No matter how much Ozcahar tried to curl into a ball, he couldn't stop his tormentor from spreading him out and the stiff bristles scouring his reddened skin. No amount of screaming, sobbing, or squirming prevented them from reaching every tender crevice of his body.

Lord Dolt lifted him by his arms and Ozcahar closed his eyes when he was dunked in the hot water again. It was even more painful on his tortured skin, but he was too worn out to kick. He wasn't strong enough. Now that he'd been scrubbed clean, they would cook him and eat him, and there was nothing he could do. Trembling but helpless, he watched Lady Tocsin walk towards him. She fixed the belt around his middle again. Were they not going to kill him? He wanted to ask, but they wouldn't answer him if they understood him at all.

They carried him to the storeroom and once Lady Tocsin had retied the rope to the wall, Lord Dolt set him down. His arms felt like they were made of lead, and he couldn't even wipe the wet hair from his face. He stumbled to his corner, where he sank into a shivering mess of misery. Without lifting his head, he watched Lady Tocsin put out the usual dish with tubers, leaves and a saucer of water.

And that, Ozcahar, he thought, *is how you make a situation worse.* He opened his hand to examine the sharp fragment of stone he'd cut his fingers on.

Thirty-Four

A Mysterious Disappearance

A solitary woman sat on the bench in the waiting room, curly silver hair peeking from under her headscarf. She sighed and ran her fingers over the embroidery along the seams of her dress. Finally, the door opened and the administrator, wiping his forehead, cast his weary eyes on her before the man that left his office had said goodbye. The woman sat up and glanced around the room. She was almost certain there had been another person waiting, a man who had stood in the corner. It had been uncomfortable with that many clammy people on one bench. Though they had not spoken so, they had all been relieved that the fat man hadn't sat down. Petitioners had come in and jumped to their feet at their turn to see the administrator or left in frustration at the long wait. Diligent cleaners had scurried past with friendly words and assurances that everyone would be seen. She couldn't recall seeing the big man leave, but now there was no sign of him.

The administrator signalled for her to come in. After three hours of waiting, she spent but a few minutes in his office and walked out with a relieved grin. Locking the door behind him, the administrator walked the woman to the front lobby. The air rotators had already stopped for the day, so there was no relief from the heat until they stepped out into the evening air. As the Townhall emptied, the building became quiet, as if it had exhaled.

Caizhiu folded back her wing hood and opened her eyes. Without humans to spook, there was no need to keep her rear eyes closed. She cricked her shortened neck and stepped into the centre of the room. If any human had been watching, it would look as if a piece of the wall had decided to go for a stroll.

The Nuzazog gleamed in the glow of a single bhodine lamp that hung between the hall and the waiting room. Caizhiu carefully extracted the weapon from the trezzohl's skeletal hand. Delicate iron bars through the centre of each bone fashioned them invisibly together. When Caizhiu was finished, the collection still looked like a hand, an empty one, reaching up to the ceiling. The Nuzazog was awkward, both in size and sharpness. It was clear why the fathers had named it the Mother's Claw. How the foolish Risradyl had come to lose this symbol of strength to a band of humans was beyond her.

She turned the weapon sharp-side down and tucked it under her arm to walk to the lobby. The Nuzazog stretched from her armpit to her ankle and walking with it was not straightforward. By the time she had reached the entrance of the building, she'd found a rhythm that to an observer might look like a limp but did not hold her up too much. The lobby was well lit despite the late hour, and she peered around the doorway to watch the night porter leave his desk. He picked up a verve lantern and walked down the other corridor to do his rounds. He would first circle the upper floor, then the ground floor, and it would take him half an hour to return to the lobby, though she guessed he might be quicker if he noticed the weapon had gone.

The front of the Townhall had a large window on either side of the exit and no curtains, so Caizhiu had to move across it in stages to reach the desk. She didn't open the door. Not that the lock would have posed a problem, but the outdoors was an uncontrolled environment. The town was quiet at night, but she could not be sure there wouldn't be a beggar, brothel-goer, or even town guard who might pass by at the wrong moment. Based on what she had observed earlier, she found a space near the front desk where people didn't stand and the rotating air caused little disturbance. She moved, froze, moved again until she reached her position. There, she let herself blend into the background, and she waited.

It took the night porter two more rounds before he stumbled back into the lobby, visibly shaking and moving his hands to petition the Six for strength. It was the other reason she had not broken open the front door to make her escape. If she made it look like a burglary, the man would take the brunt of the punishment for failing in his duties. He was less likely to be blamed if they saw the disappearance as miraculous.

The night porter pulled out his pistol. He paced up and down the lobby, walked back to the waiting room to verify the Nuzazog was still missing. His movements were erratic, near to panic, when the First Attendant arrived. With excessive gestures, the man tried to explain what had happened, but because he didn't know, he kept repeating that one moment the weapon was there, the next it was not. By the fifth retelling, he'd convinced himself that it had vanished before his very eyes. The lobby flooded with people – administrators and town guards, but no town folk or traders. A woman dressed in the Burgomaster's whites stood in the lobby and gave whispered instructions to her inner circle. They, in turn, spoke with their underlings, who searched the building several times and questioned the night porter over and over.

Caizhiu stood and waited. Drawing into herself, she tempered her breathing and heartbeat until only someone as sharp of hearing as Heort could discern them. In her own shape, she was able to keep a quiet watch for months. That was how long it had taken to wait out a band of particularly observant kobolds. Several seasons had passed before they stopped noticing her and she had been able to capture their king. By comparison, humans were easy. Most of the time their own eyes did the fooling. Even with the restriction of her human form, she could keep this vigil for days if required.

When the sun had neared its zenith, the Burgomaster gathered her five subordinates around the front desk. She didn't shout, but her face showed her displeasure, a sentiment highlighted by her angular features. One by one her underlings expressed in more and more elaborate ways their confusion and regret that, despite searching every office, storeroom, and lavatory, they could not find the weapon. Nor had they been able to find evidence of an intruder.

"The night porter insists he was looking straight at the sword when it vanished. I have questioned him myself and could smell neither liquor on his breath nor discern madness in his eyes," one of them, short of stature and with his back to Caizhiu, said.

The Burgomaster sighed angrily. She was taller than most of her underlings but lessened the effect of towering over them by leaning against the desk. She smoothed the ruffles in her long silk skirt and thoughtfully tapped her lips with a finger.

"Very well then," she said. "The ornament will either return, or it will not. But I see no reason to further delay the business upon which we rely."

She had addressed all five. Then she concentrated her attention on a thin man with a white stripe of a moustache. "Sheriff Olyre, we cannot have the town guards concentrating their attention on the Townhall while leaving the merchants and populace unprotected from common thievery, swindles, and extortion. However, have your informants scour their haunts for whispers of this theft. If it is Talent trickery, then so be it. We have no appetite for such things in Basinwade, but there is little we can do about it for now. If it turns out to be common thievery, I'll see the culprits strung up by their ears."

Olyre bowed stiffly from the hips, and with a wave of the Burgomaster's hand, her entourage disbanded. She lingered only a moment longer and headed for the Burgomastery at the back of the Townhall.

The lobby filled with people, not only the petitioners, but scores of curious sightseers. It would appear that, for a little while at least, the Stand had been usurped as Basinwade's principal attraction. Caizhiu joined the crowd and left the building, hobbling into the radiant afternoon sun. At last, she could go get her human.

THIRTY-FIVE

HE WHO KEEPS HUMANS

Tyrzinein couldn't help envy the ease with which young Eimsiff darted around the kitchen. Once upon a time, he'd had that same energy, but the long days in the clammy chamber were taking their toll. Ordinarily, nobody would be expected to observe kitchen duties for more than a day or two. It was without doubt the worst commonry duty one could be laboured with, and he was nearing his seventh day of it. His fur looked frizzed, and his manes were matted so badly he doubted that even the most rigorous dust bath would restore them to their former glory. He felt certain that when they came, no mother would look at him. It was a great grievance that his punishment was so much worse than the one inflicted on Eimsiff, who was responsible for this mess. It was true that they had chained him and the cub to the same duty until the dragon returned, but it hardly affected the youngster. Despite what the cub himself believed, Eimsiff was not old enough to be of interest to a mother, and so it mattered not if his manes were dishevelled and that he smelled of boiled tigga roots.

With a wave, Eimsiff darted out of the kitchen to spend time with his year-siblings. He was still riding on his pride at having brought the vermin to the commonry, and he seemed uncomprehending of the dangerous situation he had created. This blindness, too, was something Tyrzinein envied him. Yet he couldn't bring himself to punish the cub for his youth. Would he have been any different when he was that age?

He hoisted himself to his feet and stretched his aching limbs. The damp played havoc on his joints. Eimsiff might have finished his duties, but Tyrzinein was not that fortunate. He took a deep breath, closed his nostrils, and walked to the storeroom. The vermin slunk in his corner when he entered. The casual glance Tyrzinein cast at the dish prompted the human to dart over to it. He fell onto his knees, tore up the leaves, and stuffed them into his mouth. He filled his cheeks and glared at Tyrzinein with hate-filled eyes. After that one day the human had refused to touch his food, Tyrzinein was relieved to see him eating again. It had only taken one evening of pressing pre-chewed leaves into his mouth until he'd swallowed to persuade the wretched creature to eat again.

The human gagged but dare not spit out the food. Tyrzinein waited for him to eat a few more leaves. He couldn't hold his breath any longer and took a gulp through his mouth, so he'd be spared the full impact of the sickening stench. Washing the creature had helped, but even after peeling the filthy layers off him and scrubbing him clean, the scent returned, diminished but still awful. He couldn't conceive of any preparation method that would turn the human into a toothsome meal. The thought made him heave, and not for the first time, he thanked the Keepers of Sinuation he had not been born a woman.

The human finished the leaves, chewing a long time before he swallowed. He stayed crouched on his knees and wrapped his arms around himself. After the first few days, he seemed to have lost his aggression, but Tyrzinein wasn't taking any chances. He held up the stick and although he'd never had to beat the creature, the human obediently dropped onto his stomach. Tyrzinein placed his foot on his back when he untied the leash from the wall. It still felt strange not to crush a human underfoot. He stepped back, sat on his heels, and lifted the human by the rope. Before he had to tap the stick against the suspended body, the creature stood on his own feet and held out his arms. It was the third evening since they'd started this routine, but already the creature had learnt what was expected. Tyrzinein held up the stick anyway to let him know not to try any bad behaviour as he grabbed the human's arms in one hand. The creature winced when he squeezed them between his fingers. It probably hurt, but after the incident on the balcony, Tyrzinein couldn't afford to be lenient.

Carrying the human at arm's length, with the legs turned away from him in case he kicked, Tyrzinein walked out of the kitchen. It wasn't enough that he had to spend all his days in the horrific room; he also had to traipse through the entire commonry with the wretched being. He'd have preferred to keep him out of sight, but they could hardly have the unhygienic thing pissing and crapping everywhere. Though the time between dusk and dark was a quiet time, with the night-time sentries taking their positions, the halls were not empty. With everyone they met, he had to remind himself that the disgust in the eyes of his brethren was directed at the human, not him. And yet, he knew that from now on, every time he'd speak to them, they would recall him like this. They would try not to, but they would smell the residual stench, even if it were no longer there. To make matters worse, he spotted Keakrea walking towards him. It was too late to turn and find another route to avoid the Prime Upholder of Bol Badihr.

Tyrzinein halted and squeezed the human's arms a little tighter to tell him to behave. As if to embarrass him deliberately, the creature wailed and kicked. The Prime Upholder raised his hand and turned his head away in disgust. It wasn't just the human he was offended by. Tyrzinein knew his name would forever be synonymous with the disgusting thing. He could already hear the whispers: Tyrzinein, 'He Who Keeps Humans'. Yet, if the dragon retrieved the Nuzazog, Eimsiff would get the praise for his cleverness. Tyrzinein struck the back of the human's legs, and, after a pained yelp, the creature kept quiet.

Keakrea dismissed him with a gesture, as if he were a tyro. Tyrzinein bowed and walked out of the commonry. As soon as they were outside, he placed the human on the ground. The creature stood swaying for a moment with his arms loosely folded across his chest, then he slowly dropped them and rubbed the red stripe on the back of his legs. Tyrzinein waited for him to massage his armpits before leading him over the cliff path to the bridge and further into the woods. The human kept the rope in his hand as he jogged to keep up. His exertion was probably the reason he had been more compliant over recent days, and Tyrzinein decided to walk a bit further than was strictly necessary. It would exhaust the human, keep him docile, and it would keep his faecal stink away from the commonry.

At least here, the air was thick with the heady fragrance of oubethyre flowers. Almost half the valley was in bloom already. It wouldn't be long before the mothers would be drawn from the mountains by the scent. The further he walked, the more frequently he had to stop to let the human clamber back to his feet, until at last the creature didn't get up. He held one arm wrapped around the rope and his face, the other clasped over his unretractable genitalia. Tyrzinein stopped. The human sat on one knee and, gasping for breath, pulled juniper needles out of his elbow. Then he wobbled to his feet and met Tyrzinein's eyes, who nodded at the surrounding shrubbery. The creature disappeared in the bushes and Tyrzinein looked away, closing his nostrils and swaying backwards and forwards on his heels. How long would it be before the dragon returned? Would she return before the mothers descended? When they did, Tyrzinein would have the longest dust bath of his life and roll in oubethyre bushes. What would the Upholders do if the dragon did not return before Bobusgeh came into season? He knew the cub would insist on killing the human the moment her stomach turned to desiring meat. That she would not be impregnated until the following year did not matter to her. Cubs no longer had any patience.

He gently tugged the rope, expecting an indignant wail from the human, but instead he met resistance. Yestereve the creature had wound the rope around a branch to prevent Tyrzinein pulling him off balance while he squatted. He felt a glimmer of admiration for the creature's ingenuity. He tugged a little harder but couldn't free the rope, so he whipped it. The end flicked up. He had to look twice to believe his eyes. Though the belt was still tied to the end of the rope, the human was gone. He examined the belt in his hand and ran his finger over the tear in the clasp's fold. The belt had been cut, fibre by fibre, with a stone blade. All those days he'd thought the creature was subdued, tired from running... the despicable thing had sat quietly tearing into the belt and he had done it in the natural groove where it had gone unnoticed. He hadn't learnt to stand up, or offer his arms to be carried, or hold the rope to obediently run after his keeper; he'd spared the belt so it wouldn't break until he wanted it to. Until he could make his escape.

Tyrzinein sniffed the air for a trace, but the flowers drowned out any other scents. He held back a howl of frustration. The noise would attract the sentries, and if there was one thing worse than to be known as 'He Who Keeps Humans', it was 'He Who Was Fooled by Humans'. He could still salvage this. He could still recapture the vile little monster. And when he did, he would break his cursed legs.

Thirty-Six

Tonight We Thief You

Ozcahar ran. He didn't care where, just followed the slope down for no more reason than that the monsters' keep was on higher ground. Concentrating on his stride, so as not to repeat his tumble on the stairs, he zigzagged between prickly trees. His legs burned. The stitch in his side got worse, but he kept running. He barely registered the stones, the sharp needles, and the twigs that stabbed the soles of his feet. The ground shook, causing him to lose his rhythm. He rolled down the slope until he landed in flowery bushes. A puff of pinprick lights exploded around him, and he gasped in horror. His position was as visible as if he'd carried a verve light. He fought free from the branches and leapt to his feet without checking for injury. He didn't need to look behind him to know that his pursuer was closing in. A growing vibration rumbled through the ground. Trees and bushes whooshed and splintered with something enormous that thundered past them.

He wouldn't be able to outrun Lord Dolt. The woodland was thinning out, leaving him with less and less cover. He needed a place to hide, small enough so the giant couldn't get him. A fallen tree perhaps, or a crevice between the rocks, but the landscape was too sparse. The ground lifted beneath his feet as the tree to his right was pulled out. He ducked between a group of conifer trees. Twigs and prickles scraped his skin, but he slipped through and turned sharply to avoid the tree Lord Dolt threw at him. From the tumult and the rain of dust and needles, he guessed Lord Dolt had not been so agile, had overshot, and ploughed into the trees. He didn't have time to catch his breath. Behind him, the giant rose.

He pushed his fist into his side to quash the increasing stitch. Gritting his teeth, he kept running, fearing with every step that his legs might falter. The ground beneath his feet sank. He tried to stop, skidded, and fell on his back as the ground gave way. His fingers tried to find purchase on the rocky dirt. For a moment he laid there, gazing into the hole before him, and then the ground dipped again. Helplessly he slid, without even the breath to scream at the sight of the long spikes that faced him. The trapdoor tilted and slid into the pit, taking him with it. Its corner landed between the spikes and Ozcahar fell face first into the dirt that had collected in the bottom. He coughed and gasped before he could push himself up. He rolled onto his back, scarcely believing he was unhurt. The trapdoor had meant to break beneath him, impaling him onto the spikes, but as it had tilted, he had slid in between them.

The hole was not that deep. He would have been able to climb up, but at that moment, the shadow of Lord Dolt obscured the moonlight. Ozcahar tried to crawl backwards, but he was trapped between the spikes. He made himself as small as possible, but that wouldn't save him. If he could hide behind the fallen trapdoor, perhaps the giant wouldn't see him. But before he could move, Lord Dolt lifted it out of the hole.

The sound of a blast cracked through the sky, and a halo of blood surrounded Lord Dolt's head. It rained blood. It rained brain. It rained Lord Dolt. The creature fell on his knees, folded, and toppled forward. Wedged between the spikes, Ozcahar couldn't get out of the way. He could only hunker when the remainder of the grotesque face rushed towards him. Three spikes skewered Lord Dolt's nose. His eyeball burst, and as his mouth opened, his tongue dropped onto Ozcahar's knee. Hot blood gushed over him.

Ozcahar screamed. His feet slipped in the mush of mud, needles, and blood, but his hands found purchase on the posts around him. Scared that any sudden movement would cause the carcass to slip, he edged backwards into the triangle of starlit sky between the gigantic head skewered on the posts above him and the enormous hand that had dropped after it.

"Hey you!"

Ozcahar flinched, and only then realised it had been a human voice. When he wiped the blood from his eyes, he saw a man standing at the edge of the hole with one foot planted on Lord Dolt's arm. The stranger motioned with increasing urgency for Ozcahar to get up. "Grab! Climb! Quick!"

The man grabbed the fur of the giant to indicate that's what Ozcahar should do, and he reached down encouragingly. Ozcahar glanced at Lord Dolt's mangled face. It could not be possible that he was alive, and yet, when he began to climb, he expected Lord Dolt to stir and grab his legs.

The stranger took his hand, seizing it with reassuring firmness, and pulled him up. Someone took his other elbow, and they yanked him forward onto firm ground.

"No-harm," he mumbled. "No-harm…"

"We no-harm you, friend," one of the men said and squatted next to him. It took a few attempts and the assistance of the strangers before his legs were steady enough to stand.

"What name have you?" The man snapped his fingers in front of his face before Ozcahar answered. The other removed his coat and draped it around Ozcahar's shoulders. They hooked their arms under his and marched him downhill. Despite stumbling, he kept up with their pace. He sensed others joined them, but it took too much effort to remain upright to look. They reached an auto carriage, and he was bundled inside with the others. The vehicle set off immediately, leaving the last man to run beside it before jumping on board.

The whispers that swirled around him were excited but muffled, in a language that sounded familiar but he couldn't comprehend. He had seen many escape attempts dissolve with daylight, and as he hunkered in a corner, he waited for the jolt of consciousness that would tell him he was dreaming. The sun rose, the carriage clattered over steadier roads, and the voices increased in exuberance. Hollering and whooping, the little band punched the sides and ceiling of the carriage in triumph. Though they perspired with the increasing heat, Ozcahar couldn't stop shivering. The person seated across from him leant towards him and placed a hand on his shoulder. He pressed himself against the small round window, as if it was an escape route.

"Hey, friend," the stranger said gently and pressed a small clay flask into his hand without letting go of it. "I think you require some drink."

He guided the flask to Ozcahar's lips. The liquid set his throat aflame and cleared his sinuses. The taste seemed to scour his tongue and Ozcahar expected his breath to be smoky when he exhaled. Like a dragon, he thought, and chuckled. His laughter came in loud, sobbing spasms. It took a while before he willed his body to stop. The carriage around him fell silent. Ozcahar straightened up and rubbed his throat. The man opposite grinned and wiggled the flask.

"Sand gin. Be good, trueso?"

Even though his mouth and throat felt raw, he smiled politely. He hugged the coat around him as he looked around the carriage. Three men sat on the bench facing him, and one sat next to him. They had suntanned faces, and each had their dark hair tied in a long braid bleached to brown at the ends. All but one looked a few years older than he. Smiles and curiosity played on their expressions. To a man they wore quality garments: pantaloons, shirts, and waistcoats. Each had a pistol by their side, but nobody wore an insignia on their coat. He noted that a beardless man in the opposite corner was dressed only in a ruffled shirt and waistcoat. Ozcahar fingered the collar of the coat around his shoulders.

"Grateful..."

The lad gave a half-smile and blushed. He tipped his hat and said in a breaking voice: "Be no trouble, sir. No you walk round town butt-naked."

"Town?" Ozcahar looked at the wasteland rushing past the window. Carriages and riders passed them going in the other direction, and they overtook a few. Suddenly, the world was filled with people again. But he saw no evidence of a town.

"No concern, friend. We find you clothes and..." The man next to him chuckled and sniffed. "A bath."

The carriage erupted into laughter. Ozcahar caught sight of his hands, sticky with congealed blood and his fingernails caked in mud. If the rest of him was in the same state, it surprised him they hadn't ditched him by the side of the road.

The man opposite pocketed his flask, leant back in his seat, and said: "We reach Basinwade by day-end."

Ozcahar tried to order his jumble of thoughts. A town was good. He'd learnt that in Uayath they called places with a Magistrate 'cities', so a town would be perfect – civilisation but without a Keeper's lackey. If he could keep out of the way of the local law enforcement, he should be fine. Before anything else, he needed to find out what his new companions had in store for him.

"I be grateful, but I ask who be you that save me?"

The lad without the coat piped up. "We be the troll killers of Basinwade!"

The others whooped in support and for several minutes they punched and slapped each other's arms, and Ozcahar's too. They went around the carriage introducing themselves, taking it in turns to bow so they wouldn't bump heads.

"Be that your… ehm… task… your work to kill… trolls?" Ozcahar asked the man opposite him. He was the only one who hadn't joined in with the jollity and was introduced by his friends as Handras.

"No. We be…" Handras searched for a term but gave up. "It no be work."

"But we kill them nonetheless," said Persis, the man next to him. "And thief from them if we can. Tonight we thief you."

The men roared with laughter and Persis softly punched his arm.

"Grateful." Ozcahar pulled the coat closer around him.

Persis pointed at the beardless lad. "It be my son's first along on hunt. Trueso, he do good tonight."

Ozcahar bobbed his head at the young man, who again blushed. His attention had been on the men opposite, but now he noticed that, between his knees, Persis held the biggest blunderbuss Ozcahar had ever seen. He rested the butt comfortably on the floor of the carriage and stroked it lovingly from time to time. The carriage filled with the image of the corona of blood around the troll's head. Ozcahar blinked to get rid of it.

"You be helpful too, Osk-Har," Persis added, "but next time run on, no stopping. Then we no require pull you from hole."

The carriage erupted in more laughter. Again, he noticed Handras didn't laugh with his comrades. The sullen man did offer Ozcahar a flagon of water and they all shared bread with him. The frivolity in the carriage lessened as they approached the large walled town. Several of the men fell asleep and were jostled awake when the carriage slowed to a bumpy halt amid the crowd at the Welcome Gate. Though he was curious, Ozcahar refrained from looking out of the window, lest his bloodstained appearance attract attention.

THIRTY-SEVEN

HANDRAS AND GAVALLIA

Caizhiu had hoped it would be quieter later in the day, but since everyone knew the Welcome Gate shut at sundown, merchants and travellers came and went continuously. Those leaving the town were locals, heading to one of the smaller villages on the plains, rushing to reach their destination by nightfall. Caizhiu walked with great care. It had been fine for people to bump into her before, but now she was carrying a large and very sharp blade tucked under her wing cloak, and in the chaotic swarm of humans, it was tricky not to stab either the surrounding people or herself.

The crowd smelled of sweat and sunburned skin. It had been four days since she'd last eaten and her stomach gurgled. She regretted not indulging in a few of the town's stray cats. She caught a whiff of trezzohl, and several people bumped into her when she halted in the middle of the mass. A woman raised her foot to rub her stubbed toes. A man cursed and held the side of his face as if he'd walked into a wall. An auto carriage bumped into her leg and, since this did not move her, tooted its horn repeatedly. The driver, trying to enter the town, raised his hands in frustration and screamed obscenities. Caizhiu turned to look around over the crowd. It was almost as if she could smell her quarry, but that was impossible. Hunger must be playing with her senses.

***

Ozcahar ran and jumped, fighting the bedding until he landed on the floor. The thud reverberated through the planks. He screamed as he pulled at the cloth that had wound tightly around his legs. He couldn't find Jorganyon. Something chased him. He thought it was a group of trolls, but it was the dragon stalking him along a never-ending tabletop.

Blinking, he squinted around the boxroom. No dragon. No trolls. No Jorganyon. He pushed himself into a sitting position and exhaled slowly, his hair and nightshirt soaked in sweat. He tried to rub the nightmare from his eyes. When the door opened, he edged into the corner between the bed and the wall, but it wasn't Caizhiu who entered.

"Be you hurt?"

Gradually, the events of yesterday came back into focus. He had been introduced to the woman who spoke. She was Handras' wife, and she had given him food. He was in a house. He was in a town. She had asked him a question.

"Unhurt," he said croakily, and he stood.

The woman was lean, with a dark brown face and hair that was piled on top of her head in a traditional Uayathan braid. Several times she had to dip her head to keep her hair from colliding with the ceiling beam. She opened the round window to let a dusty heat flood in.

As she looked him up and down, he hoped that the dampness of his bedding was due to sweat. He pulled the nightshirt away from his privates to save her embarrassment. Gavallia, he thought, that was her name. Gavallia and Handras. This was their house.

She opened a wardrobe in the corner, took out some clothes, and hung them over the footboard of the bed.

"You wash." She pointed at the bowl, jug of water, and washcloth she had put on the chair by the bed. "Hope you fit this clothing."

He bobbed his head, blushing at the similarity of the gesture to the one he'd made to appease Lady Tocsin. As soon as she had left, he relieved himself in the chamber pot and peeled off the nightshirt. He was covered in cuts and grazes.

The clothing was familiar only in that there was a kind of shirt, pantaloons, and a waistcoat, but the materials were strange, softer and shinier than he was used to. They had extraneous folds that created ridges in the fabric, as well as elaborate floral embroidery around the cuffs. He held up the shirt and wondered if it was meant for a man or a woman. The fabric seemed too lightweight for a man's attire, but he had seen the men in the carriage wear similarly puffed shirts. The pantaloons were wide around the waist, but with the colourful cloth belt, he could hold both shirt and pantaloons in place. Gavallia had waited for him on the narrow landing. From her impassive expression, he couldn't tell if he was wearing the outfit correctly.

"When you follow for morning-food," she said, "my daughter require no-know of you and my husband. You no-speak."

"Handras and friends save m..."

"I require no-know also." Gavallia turned to precede him down the staircase. The narrow stairway and dining room felt cramped. At every doorway, the woman had to dip her head to allow for her towering braid.

The breakfast, spread out on a round table that was too small for four people, was simple but filling. The youngster at the table, he assumed, was Gavallia and Handras' daughter. She was young, maybe fourteen years old, and as her mother forced her black curls into a proper braid, the girl stared at Ozcahar without saying a word.

"Much bad-dreams?" Handras asked.

Ozcahar shrugged. "No so bad."

The girl snorted and said something to her father that Ozcahar couldn't understand.

"What say she?"

"You scream in dark." Handras scowled at the girl. "Dreams be no concern to you, Hantine. Leave guest be."

Ozcahar wondered how loud his screams had been. Dread gnawed at his insides, and all he wanted was to leave the house, leave the town, and keep running. Reason fought with fear as he reminded himself that, without means, he would not get far. He did not even have shoes on his feet. Handras followed his gaze and grimaced. Eventually he found some footwear. It had straps and Ozcahar struggled to tie them so they'd stay on his feet. Hantine sniggered and after Gavallia tutted at her, the girl showed Ozcahar how to tie them by donning her own sandals. She giggled at his failures and bent to make sure he wore the pantaloons over the straps.

Handras took Ozcahar by the arm to lead him out of the house, though not before slapping a hat on his head. The tiny house led into a narrow street, packed with similar tiny houses, and within two corners, Ozcahar knew he would not be able to find the street again, let alone the right building. Despite the early hour, Ozcahar was thankful for the shade the hat provided. Now he understood why the fabrics were lighter than in Thirdburg and how their design kept the fabric away from his skin.

He struggled to keep up with his saviour. More than once, he slipped in the too large sandals and when he tried to speed up, his leg muscles threatened to shoot into a cramp. Every step reverberated in his shoulders, especially the one he'd hurt in the river. By the time they got to the harbour, he was hobbling.

"Grateful for help-me," he said to Handras in a low voice so the girl wouldn't hear, "But I no have repayment."

With a sly look, Handras scoffed: "Trueso? A naked man in woods no has repayment? This no be surprise."

He turned Ozcahar's hand palm up and studied it.

"You have working hands, friend. We find work for you, but no this day. You rest. Hantine and I work on boat."

"I work on boat before," Ozcahar said. "I be helpful. Get coin. I travel away."

Handras told his daughter to go on ahead. She ran off to a small fishing vessel barely half as large as the *Wexede Wanderer*. Handras placed a solemn hand on Ozcahar's shoulder. "Friend, you be injured. You have no coin for travel away. You require rest. Meet us here at day-end. Have no concern over repayment."

Ozcahar cast his eyes to the dusty stones. He wasn't sure how to voice his biggest objection without insulting his host.

"Your wife," he mumbled, "she no happy."

"My wife be Good Woman." The way he said the phrase didn't make it sound like a compliment. Handras, who until that moment had held Ozcahar's gaze intently, looked out to sea as he continued quietly. "Gavallia be no happy with much I do. She be no happy, but she be my wife. She be silent. You no need concern about her. Best no speak of trolls though. There be many Good People in Basinwade still."

Thirty-Eight

Fresh-fresh Jungle Fay

It amazed Ozcahar that only a short while ago he had shivered on the rocky ground in the mountains, begging for a fire to be lit. He wasn't certain how long the trolls had kept him prisoner; sometimes it seemed to have been a day, sometimes a year. It seemed a lifetime since he had left Thirdburg, and now he found himself in the bustle of civilisation again.

The heat was too intense, and he retreated into the town to find shade in the narrow streets. At first, he dared not stray too far from the harbour out of fear he'd get himself lost, then he noticed that close to the harbour's gate stood a tower tall enough to be visible from most of the town. He relaxed and slowly loosened his stiff muscles by wandering between the stalls on the squares and the street pedlars' carpets with their curious wares. His pantaloons had only shallow pockets, not big enough to hold more than a few coins or the smallest trinket. He couldn't rely on his legs to carry him should he need to run, and though he wanted to repay Handras and his wife for their kindness, they would know that whatever he gave them, he must have got through thievery.

He found stone steps that led to the top of the town wall, and he climbed them like an old man. He'd spent so long cast into the maelstrom of life he'd forgotten how good it felt to look down on it. As he looked out over the town, the lazuline sea, and the plains that in the distance undulated into hills and trembling mountains beyond, the homesickness hit him. How he missed the walkways, the towering buildings and, most of all, knowing every route, every cut-through, every hiding place. Sheltering in the shade of one of the sentry towers, he let the sensation wash over him. He was not in Thirdburg and would likely never see it or any of the people he'd left behind again.

With an increasing number of rests, he walked along the wall towards the harbour and the spot where Handras had told him to meet them. The little ships looked identical to him. Jorganyon had taught him to read the Aumegoan script, but Uayathi looked nothing like it.

He waved at Handras and Hantine walking between the ships when a commotion at the middle pontoon caught his attention. One of the fishing vessels collided with two already moored up. It caused no damage, but Handras rushed to aid those on board to secure the vessel and help carry a crewmember off the boat. As they lay the injured person down, a red stain spread along the pontoon and tinted the water in dissipating clouds. After only a few moments, the gathered stood up, shaking their heads. They carried the body to the harbourside and assisted the distressed crewmates with the boat.

"What happen?" Ozcahar asked.

Handras sighed and said something to Hantine. The girl's eyes lit up, and she waved at a group of other youngsters on the wall. After a confirmatory glance at her father, she ran towards them. Handras wiped his hands on his tunic and stretched his back before he answered. "Naiad attack."

He looked at the gate where Hantine met her friends and watched his daughter slip into the town streets. "Gavallia be more happy if daughter work at carriage factory. Sea be safe no longer..." He shook his head. "Even for Good People."

As they walked towards the town, Handras asked: "How be your injuries?"

Ozcahar pouted and said he was feeling much better. He expected to return to the house, but the man smirked. "No requirement for hurry. We get some drink."

Ozcahar had not eaten since breakfast and his stomach let him know. Handras opened his hands. "Food before drink, I guess."

They joined the crowd around a long stall with a jovial holder who flamboyantly cooked his wares to the delight of his customers and attracted curious onlookers. His appearance alone drew attention. He wore a red and gold kaftan and had adorned his black beard with small golden rings. After some jostling, Handras and Ozcahar made it to his street stall. The tables of the kiosk folded around the holder with a large copper pot directly in front of him. The fire underneath the pot radiated even more heat into the already hot air, but it didn't dissuade the crowd from lingering. A variety of bizarre-looking foods covered the tables. The scent was a confusing mixture of fruit, fish, and olive oil.

The man's eyes met his expectantly, but Ozcahar didn't know what to order. Fortunately, Handras shouted something, and the stallholder took a wooden skewer to load it with different coloured foods. Deftly, he unscrewed the lid off a barrel with one hand, waving the skewer like a sword. He gave a knowing smile to the crowd, who whooped with delight. Ozcahar seemed to be the only one who didn't know what was going on, but even he was drawn in by the man's flair. The stallholder dipped his hand in the barrel, quickly withdrew it and ensured he screwed the top back, which was an even more impressive one-handed manoeuvre. He turned to his audience and walked over to Ozcahar.

"See," he said and held out his hand. "Be only stall with fresh-fresh jungle fay."

Between his fingers he held a creature that looked like a night fay, complete with flailing limbs and fluttering wings, but ten times larger. He pressed the tip of the skewer through the fay's inner thigh until it emerged through the neck. The squirming slowed but didn't stop. As the body spasmed, the head bent back, and the feathery antennae quivered in the heat. He dipped the skewer in the oil. Ozcahar stared at the rim of the pot as the oil sizzled and spat. It was all he could hear, and it was all he could smell. People jostled him, held him captive. Their bodies surrounded him like hot water. He couldn't breathe. It felt as if his insides were melting. He stumbled backwards. People grabbed him as he tripped over their feet, angry shrieks rose as he trod on toes. The taste of dust, oil, and stone coated his tongue. At last he was spat out of the crowd, and he fled into an alley. He staggered along the wall, bent double, and gasped for fresh air to stop his retching.

Handras seized his elbow and hauled him up. Ozcahar's fist connected with the man's nose before he realised that he'd punched him. Blood sprayed over Handras' sun-bleached tunic. Ozcahar tried to run, but the fisherman had hold of his collar. He wiped his nose with his free hand, grimaced with the pain, and glared at Ozcahar.

"Apologies," Ozcahar mumbled, and not just because Handras held him up against the wall. He had punched the man who had showed him nothing but kindness. What had come over him?

"Come-with," Handras ordered and Ozcahar meekly let himself be led through the maze of alleyways. He expected to be marched to the Sheriff's office, but the alleyways became narrower and quieter. As they reached the dead end of a lane, his mind turned to darker outcomes. Handras checked his nose had stopped bleeding. Gently or warily, he patted Ozcahar's shoulder. "No hit me, yes?"

He pointed at the building at the end of the lane. The colourful wooden cladding had worn and faded and there was a signboard above the door. He couldn't read the name, but it looked like a tavern.

"Someone require meet you." Handras tapped his knuckles against the door. After a few moments, the peephole slid open. Quickly afterward, the door opened. When his eyes adjusted to the gloom, Ozcahar faced a horseshoe-shaped bar with several partitioned booths lining the walls on either side of the room. From his position by the entrance, he couldn't peer into the booths, but over the rhythmic squeaking of the ceiling fans, he heard muffled voices. Handras leant his elbows on the bar to speak to the bartender. The woman, who looked older than the building itself, pointed her thumb at a booth in the back. A girl who accompanied her behind the bar poured them four drinks in wooden tankards.

Ozcahar followed the man to the booth. Whatever he would do with him, at least it looked like he'd get a drink. After a day in the heat, there were few things Ozcahar craved more. He relaxed further when he recognised the man at the table.

Persis recognised him too. "Well met, Osk-Har. You look better in clothes."

Handras slid the drinks over the table and manoeuvred Ozcahar into the seat opposite Persis. His back rested against the booth board and Handras sat next to him. Though he intended to sip the beer, once it hit his tongue, he kept swallowing until he ran out of breath.

Persis nodded at Handras tunic. "Naiad?"

"No." Handras poured a bit of the beer onto the bloodstains to draw them out of the fabric. "Be Osk-Har's punch."

Persis' eyebrows shot up and he laughed. "So, no only be trolls you fight, eh?"

There was a knock on the door, and the girl leapt gracefully over the bar. She was slight of stature and wore pantaloons like Narastien had. The older bartender tutted and light-heartedly rebuked her as the girl went to check who was at the door and let them enter. The newcomer wore a sandy-coloured robe, and the girl looked up at him with shining eyes and flushed cheeks, the way Narastien had looked at him that night.

As the man turned towards their booth, Ozcahar noticed the town guard insignia on the robe. He looked into his tankard. His heartbeat sped with the footsteps that approached the table. His companions greeted the newcomer enthusiastically, and with a hint of reverence. Persis removed the hat Ozcahar had forgotten to take off and Handras lifted his chin towards the stranger.

"Rogza-Riz, this be Osk-Har, newest troll killer."

The town guard glowered at Persis, who stretched his lips into an embarrassed grin. Rogza-Riz took his time studying Ozcahar. Unlike the others, the guard's beard was short and skimmed his jawline rather than covering his cheeks. Without taking his eyes off Ozcahar, he removed his robe, turned it inside out, and folded it over the back of his chair. He sat and picked up the tankard in front of him. Ozcahar eyed the holstered pistol.

"You be man who treks naked," the guard said and, after a sip, continued. "As Persis say, I be Rogza-Riz."

They way he'd spoken his own name made Ozcahar think he'd rather have kept that to himself for a while. Rogza-Riz didn't trust him.

"It be so; I lose belongings when troll attack. If friends no help, I lose life also."

"Your voice be Aumegoan." Rogza-Riz swilled his beer around his tankard, took a sip, and wiped the foam off his fine moustache. "I hear rumour someone look for Aumegoan."

Ozcahar felt the blood drain from his face and took the last large gulp of the beer to hide it. Was Caizhiu here already? Was he looking for him? Would this be the end of his escape? He forced his mind to stop spinning and think of something he could say that would help him. He swallowed the beer, and he looked at the men.

"Please, no give me back," he whispered.

Their look of horror told him his plea had worked.

Handras grabbed his wrist. "We be the Unanswered, True Humans. If Keepers themselves command us, we no give you back to trolls. This be human town. This be Basinwade. Trueso, Rogza-Riz?"

Ozcahar looked at the town guard. He was the only one he needed to convince. Even though without his robe he was dressed in a similar outfit to the others, they deferred to him. The man was not in service of the office and yet he carried authority.

"Let me leave," Ozcahar urged. "Let me take my trouble to elsewhere."

"Perhaps you say what be your trouble and we decide." With a gesture, Rogza-Riz instructed Handras to get more drinks. His friend left the table and Ozcahar felt his absence. He doubted that was unintended.

"Dragon Caizhiu pursue me."

The news came as a surprise to Rogza-Riz, but he could see that the man was immediately processing it, working out how much they'd be prepared to endanger themselves for a stranger, or how much his return would profit them. He looked at the others and added solemnity to his lowered voice. "If you who saved me no give me to dragon, you best let me be. No risk your life."

Handras nearly dropped the drinks he carried to the table. As Ozcahar had expected, the others looked at Rogza-Riz, their expressions adding to his plea. He needed to be allowed to leave and if these people could provide him with means to do so, all the better.

"You require protection," Rogza-Riz said and narrowed his eyes. "The Unanswered could give you this. I speak to boss."

This caused shocked excitement in the other two.

"Be it time to remove the shade?" Persis asked.

"That no be my decision, but trueso this may be what we await for so long." Rogza-Riz smiled at their enthusiasm; some gleamed in his own eyes as well. He took a drink and said: "But boss decide what she do about Osk-Har and his dragon."

THIRTY-NINE

CONFRONTATION AT THE COMMONRY

So as not to offend the trezzohl, Caizhiu assumed her own shape as soon as they were far enough away from the human road. With great care not to scratch its engravings, she carried the Nuzazog between her teeth. The climb was easy, but they had not reached the commonry's cultivated rows of junipers before they felt the erratic tremors of Bol Badihr in turmoil. The ground trembled with the movements of the gigantic creatures. Caizhiu breathed in the mountain air, for a moment concerned that she had misjudged her timing and that the mothers had already returned from the wilds, but she could not detect the female scent. Caizhiu felt her companion tense as they climbed, but not once did Heort suggest staying behind. Given the quaking of the ground and sporadic bone-chilling shrieks, she expected to find the commonry in a state of frenzy, but when they reached the narrow stone bridge to the cliff-side fortress, and Caizhiu formally announced her presence, the noise inside died down.

{Eimsiff of the Bol Badihr!} Caizhiu sang again as they stood before the entrance. *{Caizhiu the Wayward has returned, and I have fulfilled my side of our bargain. I demand you fulfil yours!}*

The door opened, and they were faced by a trezzohl father who had once been a giant among his kind, but now stooped with the weight of time. He was flanked by four others, one of whom she recognised as the cub, Eimsiff, who looked decidedly less boisterous than the last time she had seen him. The central trezzohl stepped forward and was helped into a kneeling position. He placed his palms on the stone slabs, spreading his fingers into near circles. He could not prevent his glance lingering on the Nuzazog as he lowered his gaze.

{Recognise me, Caizhiu the Wayward,} he sang. *{I am Keakrea the Prime Upholder of the Bol Badihr Commonry. I beg that you reserve your ire for me.}*

Though his words were meek, she caught the hint of defiance at the sight of the Nuzazog. His soul song betrayed memories of ancient stories, of a mighty trezzohl warrior, Risradyl, the defiant male, as ruthless as a woman. A flicker of desire for bravery stirred within his old bones.

{Take the weapon, Prime Upholder.} Caizhiu curled her tail over her front claws like a satisfied cat. *{Touch it, hold it, and take a swing. We'll see what becomes of you and your commonry.}*

Keakrea's forehead touched the stone, and as he bent forward, his mottled pelt parted along his ancient spine. *{Forgive an old father his foolish desires, Dragon. We would never further dishonour ourselves by breaking our word with such a betrayal.}*

Further dishonour? Caizhiu felt cold spread from her stomach. She looked over the Prime Upholder's prone frame to Eimsiff, who took a step back.

{Where is my human, Cub?}

Desperation dripped from Keakrea's soul song as he kept his head to the stone. *{The one who spoke for us had no right to do so, but still our word was given. If vengeance must follow, we beg you to spare those who spoke in youthful haste.}*

{What you beg for is irrelevant to me!} Caizhiu roared her anger through the valley and felt even Heort shudder in response. *{I have no wish for vengeance. I only wish to have the human returned to me. What have you done with him?}*

{The vermin murdered father Tyrzinein and escaped.} The Prime Upholder's soul song filled with grief for the murdered trezzohl, feeling his life from when he was a cub to the moment his maimed body was discovered.

Caizhiu tried to reconcile that account with the image of the pitiful human shivering in the back of a cave. What was this creature that could kill a Keeper of Sinuation, kill a trezzohl five times his size, and yet, when faced with her on a cliff, could do nothing but jump down a waterfall? If he was just a human, as neath as a deer or a dog, how was it possible he had overpowered the commonry?

{We have many fathers hunting for him, Dragon, but we have not yet found him. Should you spare us, we will find him for you.}

Caizhiu placed her fangs on either side of the Prime Upholder's neck, felt the old father shudder, and heard the collective gasp of Bol Badihr. The anguish from Eimsiff was a particular pleasure, but she resisted the urge to bite down.

{Find him! And when you catch him, he had better be returned to me in one piece.}

{His life is only yours to take,} Keakrea conceded gladly. *{And our service is yours for as long as the Bol Badihr Commonry stands.}*

Caizhiu released him, spat tufts of his manes onto the Nuzazog, and stepped back from the commonry.

{You let us keep our lives... and the Nuzazog?} Keakrea sounded incredulous.

{I spare you because there is no honour in taking the lives of fools. The dagger has no value to me. It is nothing but a symbol of your broken word and I insist you keep it. Let your Nuzazog be kept for all time to remind you of the idiocy of Bol Badihr.}

She turned her back on the commonry, hooked her claws through Heort's harness, and threw both of them off the bridge. She spread her wings and let the wind tunnel of the ravine catch them. The air propelled her forward, and she used it to soar up past the balcony of the commonry. She roared her frustration into the mountains and over the forest below. Drinking in the sweet scent of terror it invoked, she looped backwards, then beat her wings to turn and glided away over the trees. The air was fresh, and the sun stroked her long body.

{I'm getting better at this flying, don't you think?}

Heort's fingertips frantically searched for a hold on her smooth scales. Her sharp talons prevented her from holding him tighter, so all she could do was offer her other claw for him to grab hold of, which he did with a grip stronger than she'd thought him capable of.

{I thought you wanted the view. You'll need to open your eyes to appreciate it.}

How wonderful it would be if she could fly all the way to Basinwade. It would be so much faster and more pleasurable. For her, she conceded, less so for Heort. But if the sight of an approaching dragon would have caused consternation in Wexede Crossing, where at least they had the assurance of a Magistrate, it would be a poorer idea still for a town populated only with neath.

{Set me down, Caizhiu. I'm begging you.}

She found a narrow clearing at the edge of the woods. After dropping her friend as close to the ground as she could without crashing, she gave one final beat and landed with a greater thud than she'd intended. Even the travellers on the throughway would have felt the reverberations. Her flight was improving, but her landings needed practice. All the same, she swished her tail with pride, cutting down several saplings and causing Heort to chronochi out of the way.

{Please, never do that to me again.} He shook the trembles from his legs and approached her when she, somewhat reluctantly, donned her human appearance.

{Apologies, my friend. I wanted to leave a terrorising impression.} She took his snout in her hand, stroked her thumb over his cheek, and checked she hadn't accidentally cut him.

{That you did. On me, if no one else.} He flicked his tail. *{What are we going to do now that the trezzohl let Ozcahar escape? How did he do that? How did he kill Tyrzinein?}*

{I have an idea where he is.} Caizhiu scowled. She had called the trezzohl fools, but she was no better. She had thought it her imagination, but now it seemed her nose had been correct. Ozcahar had been in Basinwade, and in her arrogance, she had walked straight past him.

For the second time, they traversed the dusty road to the coastal town. With every step, Caizhiu's anger at her own incompetence grew. It was time she stopped underestimating Ozcahar and treated him like the adversary he was proving to be.

Part V

FORTY

CHASE THROUGH A CROWDED TOWN

Their eyes met across the Oval Market. Had Ozcahar left town, she might have taken longer to find him, but he must have assumed he could hide among his kind. He had donned local garb and hidden his face under a wide-brimmed hat, but even across the distance his sandy beard and blue eyes stood out, and though he was probably not aware of it, his scent was unmistakable. Recognition was mutual and instantaneous. Caizhiu smiled and gave him a slight nod. Beneath his sunburn, the rosiness left his cheeks. The wares he was holding dropped from his hands and he darted towards the edge of the square.

In the open, Caizhiu could have easily caught up with him. A few chronochi'ed steps would have done it. But higgledy-piggledy stalls and mats filled the space between them, never mind the milling public. Heort could move among them unobtrusively, but her bulk would not allow it.

Even running at normal speed would crack the pavers and rattle the tiles off the surrounding roofs.

Carriages and cargo cycles rushed backwards and forwards on the streets around the square. Ozcahar ducked between them and vanished from view. He was determined to make this as difficult as possible, but neither running nor hiding would save him. Amused that he had not realised this, Caizhiu shook her head and strode across the market. The annoying humans seemed unaware of her haste. With reckless disregard for their safety, they jumped in front of her with offers of food, clothing, and furniture. Her scowl did not seem to deter them with their supplicant smiles, confident that she would have a need of their products. Perhaps she would have been wiser to shout out. A cry of 'stop thief' usually got humans riled up, and Ozcahar might have found it harder to make his way through the stalls. Then again, she could not be sure what he'd do if they cornered him. He had escaped the commonry – if he could kill a trezzohl, what might he do to humans?

The Welcome Gate was behind her. Ozcahar could circle back through the side streets, but even if he evaded her, he'd struggle to get through the throng. He could try the Westerly Gate, but it was a long way from the square and there was nowhere to make a quick escape from in that direction. His only way out was via the harbour. If he had any intelligence, he had to be heading to the Fish Gate. Caizhiu finally managed to cross through the stream of traffic and took one of the smaller alleyways off the square. The main street was teeming with traders and traffic. She could move much faster in the relative quiet of the backstreets. Running was still impossible, but she could get around the stalls quicker and there were no auto carriages to get in her way. As she heightened her senses to avoid the dead ends, the town felt like an assault: a jumble of wheels rolling on stone, people shouting, footsteps, and heartbeats. She hurried around the traders and shop entrances to meet up with the main street. People looked around in confusion at the rattling windows.

When Caizhiu reached the junction, one of the town auto carriages, a train of doorless carts, pulled up in front of her. A fissure shot across the paver beneath her foot as she halted. She searched the street for her target. A few metres to her right, Ozcahar moved through the crowd towards her. He saw her, stopped, and bumped into the people behind him as he threw himself backwards to fight against the stream of people. Cursing and muttering, they closed around him like a mudslide.

She made more progress than Ozcahar. People pushed him to the centre of the street that was blocked by the train of auto carriages. He glanced over his shoulder, and, seeing how near she was, his eyes widened. Before she could seize him, he jumped into the town carriage. The hat was knocked off his head as he ran between the two benches, stumbling over the passengers' feet. He exited the cart on the other side and slipped into the crowd. Trapped on the wrong side, Caizhiu slammed her hand against the carriage. She had no choice but to follow him as the space between the carriages was too narrow for her. She grabbed the doorframe, ignored the protestations from the seated passengers, and hauled herself onto the carriage step. Objections of the passengers turned to screams as the vehicle lurched over, the rear axle groaning, spokes snapping, and the wheel buckling under her weight. A woman seated on the opposite side of the bench lost her grip and fell towards Caizhiu. The dragon landed on her back with half of the carriage on top of her. Feet trampled her face as she used her arm to shield the woman from the panicked passengers trying to clamber out of the carriage. Caizhiu used her legs to semi upright the vehicle, propelling two people into the crowd. She got to her feet and placed the woman on hers. Shrieking obscenities, the woman hit Caizhiu with her feathered hat.

The driver, pale with shock, climbed from the first carriage and fought through the onlookers. He scratched his head, dislodging the hat from his sweat-soaked hair, and tapped his finger on her chest. "What were you thinking getting on, you flabby trollson?"

Caizhiu looked over his head to see if she could espy her quarry, ignoring the passengers who joined in with the verbal abuse. She felt Heort's amused mockery. From the moment she'd spotted Ozcahar, she had given Heort no thought. He had to be nearby, but she couldn't see him amid the river of people. Before she could ask him where her quarry had gone, she saw the man cross the road and run into one of the side streets. She turned to the alleyway she'd come from to head him off when a town guard confronted her.

"What happened here?" the man asked and pointed at the bent wheel with its dislodged and split spokes.

"Your town carriages are of poor construction."

Glancing at the crowd and the devastation that littered the street, the town guard held his hand up at the driver in a pacifying manner. But the man kept shouting about compensation and his reputation. He tried to push Caizhiu, but only shoved himself backwards. "There was nothing amiss with that carriage!"

{I hope you are not counting on me to halt your quarry.} Heort couldn't have gone far for his soul song to reach her, and Caizhiu responded with misgivings. The last thing she needed was for her friend to get himself hurt.

{Just let me know where he is.}

Beneath his officious appearance, she could smell the town guard's fear. Not nervousness, but deep dread. The aroma was so intense that Caizhiu checked herself in a shop window. She looked perfectly human.

{He's running to the square with the pretty tower.}

As she had suspected, Ozcahar was heading towards the harbour. No doubt he intended to blag his way onto, or steal, one of the little fishing vessels. Maybe he'd get to a larger cargo ship. She hoped she wouldn't need to retrieve him from the sea.

Caizhiu looked down the street. The hindrance caused by the collapsed carriage held up the flow of people. Bi-wheeled velocipedes wobbled and cast their riders into the crowd, causing a chorus of insults. Auto carriages tooted their nasal horns, but she could see gaps forming in the stream as people moved into side streets to avoid the hold-up. She bent down to the town guard, sensing his desire to step back, though the crowd behind him prevented it. She wasn't about to make the same mistake she had with Wylthren and wrapped her hand around his, holding his pistol in place to prevent him drawing it.

"I don't have time to deal with this," she whispered with a glance at the driver and the wrecked carriage. "And I don't have time to deal with you. Stand aside or I'll move you aside. I understand that someone in your position would find that embarrassing."

The guard shuddered, and he opened and closed his mouth with the effort to think of something to say.

Caizhiu took the opportunity to walk around him. "I'm grateful for your assistance."

She reached the Fish Gate and turned towards the Stand square. Her eyes darted over the stalls. About halfway down, Ozcahar walked among them, rebuffing a man trying to sell him a hat. He turned towards her, or rather the Fish Gate behind her, and stood frozen, as if he couldn't believe she had beaten him to it. Then he bolted for the Stand tower. Caizhiu shook her head. What did the idiot think he was doing? She had him as good as cornered. He might as well save his breath.

He quarrelled with the officious little man in the uniform and darted past him. Other visitors stopped to tut at the spectacle and the swelling crowd got in Caizhiu's way. When she approached the Stand, the man walked over to her to tell her it was closed. After one of her scowls, he backed away, moving others in the crowd with him. At last, she could get to her prey. Ozcahar zigzagged through the crowd and ducked into the Stand. Caizhiu tensed. Now he had truly trapped himself. Would it be better to wait outside or follow him into the structure? She walked slower. She didn't want to have to catch him if he jumped from the tower, but she was preparing to.

From inside the Stand she could hear Ozcahar's heart hammer in his chest. His aroma wafted through the iron and the wooden slats, and Caizhiu swallowed the saliva it provoked. She should have hunted after her flight from the commonry.

"We are well met, Ozcahar," she said gently. "I'm pleased, though somewhat surprised, to find you living still."

He hadn't got far up the steps. They were steep and there were a lot of them. By his laboured breathing, she guessed he'd given up climbing.

"Go away," he gasped., "Leave me be. Please."

Caizhiu tried to see him through the gaps between the slats, but she couldn't. Not wanting to underestimate her prey, she sniffed the air. She remembered their first encounter as she cagily rounded the corner of the tower entrance. He had shot her before, and he might get luckier this time. The Stand had a stormy scent, but she couldn't detect the smell of pistol powder. In response to her appearance, there was a movement on the steps. As he ascended the spiral, she could only make out his form through the ornamental gaps in the iron cylinder. Placing her hands on either side of the doorway from the iron cylinder to the stairs, she leant in and tried on her friendliest smile.

"It's not in my nature to leave you be once I have been tasked to capture you. But I don't relish the thought of chasing you further. There is nowhere for you to go. Come down." She extended a hand to him. "My word stands. I won't harm you."

"This..." Ozcahar climbed up further. "This wasn't my idea."

Forty-One

The Stand

Pain jolted through her legs. The skin on her arms rippled and her scales gleamed in the flecks of sunlight that danced around the tower. It was as if a hand had wrapped itself around her, burning her skin, freezing her blood, and squeezing the breath out of her. Caizhiu forced her rolling eyes to look down. It was her tail that constricted her. She couldn't stop it, couldn't move her muscles or release them. Her gasping faded to a quiver of her jaws. The world dimmed.

The pain ceased as suddenly as it had come. A spasm of her own leg muscles threw Caizhiu against the wall. Blisters scarred the palms and soles of her claws. Her wings jittered. After a few coughs, she greedily sucked air into her lungs. Then she noticed the sound of iron over iron. The world was turning, swirling; the iron cylinder enclosed her. Layers twisted round, blocking the exit of the Stand as well as the way onto the stairs. The bright shapes of humans, flowers, and fish swirled before her eyes. The ceiling landed on her head. It was a light blow that caused her to flinch at its suddenness.

{Caizhiu!?}

She wanted to answer Heort, but another current of pain moved through her. Thankfully, her tail was no longer wound around her, and she only needed to fight her chest muscles into expanding. Her head felt heavy as each pulse of pain pounded her senses. When it released her, she crumpled, too disorientated to figure out where her various limbs were, concentrating only on gasping for breath.

{Caizhiu, please answer me!}

A clean burnt smell surrounded her, reminding her of a thunderstorm. It troubled her to find it emanated from her own body.

{A moment, please.}

{I'd give you all the moments you want, my friend. But I think you are about to have company.}

Caizhiu blinked her four eyes and lifted her snout off her metal mesh on the ground. She had to get back into her human shape.

"Stay still, Creature. Or it will be the end of you!"

The Six be cursed and she along with them; she did have company. Why did humans always insist on her motionlessness? How did they imagine she would speak to them, reassure them, when they only had their primitive verbals?

Compared to the shade in her prison, the square outside was bathed in sunlight. Three human silhouettes stood where the tower's exit had been.

Caizhiu reached her soul song out for any Talented humans, but it did not surprise her when she found none. The human on her left looked familiar, and it took her a moment before she recognised the town guard who had confronted her at the crumpled carriage. The guard looked at the place on the stairs where Ozcahar huddled. He seemed to know exactly where he was.

"No move, Osk-Har." The guard's voice was a lot more forceful than it had been when Caizhiu had met him in the street. "We release you soon."

Her quarry sat on the wooden staircase. His forehead touched his knees, and he had wrapped his arms around his head as if he expected to be beaten.

Or for the environment to strike him... like it had her. He'd known! He'd led her into a trap.

Caizhiu didn't recognise the man on the right, but he too wore the garb of a town guard. She briefly wondered if it was a trick of the light, but both guards seemed to have grown in bulk, and they smelled like auto carriages. Caizhiu snorted to get rid of the confusing scents and looked again. Each of the guards wore a merchant's basket on their back. With their wooden panels and copper flex, they looked like wheelless auto carriages.

Her attention fell on the third person who walked up between them. The woman, tall, with broad hips, was familiar. Or rather, her costume was. The white dress covered her shoulders, flowed into a tight fit around her hips and then smoothly to the ground. It covered her arms to just above her elbows; similarly to the men's uniforms, the sleeves were a loose fit. The golden adornments on the large belt around her middle drew Caizhiu's attention, as did the bejewelled bracelets that jingled when the woman moved her arms. Caizhiu's breathing settled to a steady rhythm. She wasn't entirely sure what had happened, but she welcomed the sight of the Burgomaster. She would soon clear up this misunderstanding.

Human vision was akin to her own, so there was little point in pretending to be human; they already knew she wasn't. That would make it easier on her uncooperative body. As far as transfiguration was concerned, all she needed to achieve was getting to a state to enable verbal speech. Slowly, so as to not alarm her captors, she shrank into herself and forced her jaws to shorten. Her muscles prickled and spasmed as she forced them to reform. Stubbornly, her skin refused to give up the scales. It reminded her of her reaction to the nixe's tendrils. As a precaution, she left her tail on the floor.

"Don't be alarmed, Burgomaster." Ill-formed Uayathi words dropped off her tongue. Her lips felt swollen over her stumpy, square teeth. For the first time, she realised how exasperating it had to be for Heort to hear his voice, feel the painful distance between what the sound should be and what came out. "A mistake has been made, but I will not hold it against you or the people of Basinwade."

The fright on the faces of the Silver Rose family was fresh in her mind and even Morailo, who knew her as well as any human ever had, had been terror-stricken when she'd emerged from her cocoon. She renewed her effort to force her appearance to reform, to look as human as possible upon her imminent release.

"Ah, there is the famous dragon arrogance." The bracelets tinkled when the Burgomaster placed her hands on her hips. She lifted her head so that her dish-shaped hat tilted, deforming her silhouette, as if she, like Caizhiu, were changing her shape.

"You are aware of what I am, who I am?" Cold confusion halted her attempt at transformation. "And yet you have the audacity to treat me such?"

The Burgomaster's shoulders shook with her laughter. It was full-throated, with a razor's edge.

"You, a creature who has no qualms about deceiving others; you dare call this audacity? Do you not know where you find yourself, Monster?"

It struck Caizhiu that she must have missed something. She had looked at the town merely to find the Nuzazog and then to find Ozcahar. Basinwade seemed nothing but human, but it couldn't be. There had to be something she had overlooked. She reached out for the Burgomaster, trying to figure out what kind of creature she was. Whatever it was, it was far superior in its mimicry than Caizhiu's own abilities, and she couldn't figure out how to distinguish it from a neath human.

{Heort, I need to know what I'm dealing with.} She tried and couldn't keep the pain from her soul song. {Take heed. It is possible that Ozcahar is one of the same kind... and there may be more. I have not encountered this type of otherkin before.}

The Burgomaster strode towards the iron cylinder and looked at her with unbridled contempt. "Perhaps you fancy yourself in a city where you'll be able to impel some pretentious Magistrate to do your will."

Caizhiu touched the metal between them and instantly regretted it. The stinging flared up from her fingertips and up her arm once more. Her hand stretched, swelled up with extended talons. What kind of enchantment had been placed on it? It had to be powerful, and yet she could not recognise it. Straining to keep standing, the dragon waited for the pain to subside as she rubbed her misshapen arm. She was relieved to find she could still speak. "Basinwade falls under the protectorate of Zel Zesen of Aerahan, does it not?"

{Whatever Fabled you expect to find, Caizhiu, they are deeply hidden. I can find no trace of them.} Heort sounded scared. *{You and I are the only ones here.}*

{Keep looking. I'll try to distract this one.}

"Perhaps you imagine yourself more important than you are," Caizhiu said. "Perhaps this fishing village imagines itself a city."

The Burgomaster turned to look at the crowd of spectators that were packing the square around the Stand. She completed her revolution and faced Caizhiu with a triumphant half-smile. When she spoke, she did so at a volume intended not just for Caizhiu, but the onlookers as well.

"You find yourself in Basinwade, Dragon. We bow to no Magistrate!"

The square cheered.

"We bow to no Fabled!"

More cheers.

"Nor to the Keepers of Sinuation?" Caizhiu asked quietly.

The Burgomaster squeezed her lower lip and gave the slightest of conciliatory nods. But she said: "If the Six have business with Basinwade, they can take it up with us directly. We, who stand between mountains, plains, and sea, speak for ourselves. And if they ignore us, we will have to speak louder."

The square erupted in waves of cheers that pulsated from the tower to the edges and into the streets beyond.

"Burgomaster, you are like a crab in a bucket, thinking herself queen of the ocean. You are in charge of a small human town. A town that, your childish impudence notwithstanding, stands or falls by the grace of the Six. Release me this instant and I will forget your folly."

"You do not command us!" the Burgomaster yelled with meticulous anger. "We will not bow to Aerahan. We will not bow to Monsters or their puppet Magistrates. It is you, Dragon, who will bow to us."

Caizhiu sighed and rubbed her temples. "Don't be absurd."

Upon a sideways nod from the Burgomaster, the town guard fished under his robes as if he would draw a pistol. The man would have a job to get a shot through the cylinder, but she hugged her wings around her, slackening them to catch a lucky shot. Instead, he pulled out a stick attached to the auto carriage basket on his back. The apparatus whined, increasing in pitch as he approached. The black stripes of his neat moustache and jawline beard highlighted the guard's smirk as he stepped towards Caizhiu. It had been years since she'd last seen a human wield a rapier, but the stick he held looked somewhat like the weapon of old, though a bit thicker and without the sharp point. Caizhiu doubted it could penetrate her skin.

"Aren't you brave now that you think you have me cornered," she said and answered his smirk with her own. "You may want to rethink your distinctive facial hair, little guard. I might just remember you."

"I doubt you'll be able to remember your own name, Monster." The town guard jabbed the rod through a gap in the iron. When it approached the metal, sparks flew from it to the cylinder. When the two touched, pain throbbed up through her feet, legs, and tail from the mesh flooring. But it wasn't until the prong made contact with her thigh that the full agony hit her. All at once, everything hurt.

{Caizhiu!}

She latched onto Heort's soul song. The single isle of relief in the sea of pain. She couldn't answer him, but by concentrating on his presence, using it as a focal point, she could shift her attention onto a single part of her body.

{Breathe!}

She tried to move the sensation of pain to the rest of her body and fought to expand her lungs. With an anguished howl, she managed to get air into them. Using the sound as a foundation, she bounced into exhaling and inhaling. Screaming every breath. Every beat of her heart hurt and had to be fought for.

When the pain ebbed away in receding waves, she concentrated on keeping her breathing and heart going and the rest of her collapsed. The only noises that reached her were the forlorn laughter of seagulls, the steady rhythm of the sea, and distant carriages, velocipedes, and pedestrians moving around the town. The square had quieted to a hush in the wake of her screaming. She heard the whispering of the Burgomaster and her guards, but her mind was too muddled to make out what was said. It was as if she were buried in her own body. Several silent minutes passed before Caizhiu trembled into movement.

"Was that enough of a lesson for you, Dragon?" The Burgomaster drawled the last word with joyful disdain and nodded at the town guard. "I think it requires another."

Before she could catch herself, Caizhiu cried out. Even as the sound left her throat, she felt relieved that she was not capable of speech. Her anguished howl was immeasurably more dignified than the pathetic "please don't" she had, for that unguarded instant, intended to shout.

The town guard thrust the rod through the gaps and pressed it against her scales. Caizhiu screamed for breath as she concentrated on keeping her heartbeat going. She disgusted herself, screaming like a tormented banshee. But it was preferable to death.

The agony receded when the town guard pulled back and stood panting with a satisfied grin. Droplets of sweet sweat stained his cloak. Caizhiu tried to concentrate on the scent and waited for the world to stop spinning. Heort reached out for her, his soul song faint with fear. From his over-sharing, she learned, with some relief, that he was hiding in a shaded corner of an alley.

{Still alive...} It wasn't her usual facetious response, merely a stunned observation. Though it churned her stomach, she closed her eyes to lose herself in his soul song. *{What is this enchantment they're using?}*

{I can find nothing, my friend. They are all human. Neath human.}

"We are the Unanswered." The dragon directed her unfocused attention towards the woman in white and, as if to validate Heort's words, the Burgomaster continued: "Basinwade is a True Human town. Magistrates, and especially your ilk, no longer hold sway here."

The square erupted again in hollering and cheering. Caizhiu couldn't reply but was certain words would do her little good even if she had them. Instead, she loudly sighed her derision.

"Bridle your scorn, Creature. We have brought you to your knees and you will never get to your feet again."

The ceiling dropped further until it touched her wings. With it, a debilitating tremor spread through her, top to bottom. Her claws gripped the steel mesh on the ground, even though it made the pain worse. She resisted the urge to flinch. If she did, the ceiling would be lowered to follow her, and she doubted they would raise it again.

"It is time for the Unanswered to be heard!" the Burgomaster hollered. Though she looked and pointed at the dragon, she was addressing the surrounding crowd. "For years we've kowtowed to Fabled and their human lackeys. How many of you have cowered in your homes, praying to the Six for protection from the horrors in the sea and the horrors of the mountains? Have we been heard? No, we have not. When we speak to the Magistrate to give us the sea or ensure we can pass over the mountains unmolested, are we heard? No, we are not. Well, we have had enough! Basinwade must stand up to be heard."

Thankfully, Caizhiu didn't need to lift or even move her head to shift her gaze to the staircase. Ozcahar remained motionless and gazed ahead blankly. When she caught him glancing in her direction, she flicked out her tongue. It eased her stomach to seek solace in his flavoured scent. He was the only human who was appropriately fearful, and she let the aroma of it linger over her tongue before she breathed out.

"We will send a message to the Magistrate, Lord Zesen." The Burgomaster spat on the ground as she said his name. Some in the crowd did the same, prompting disgusted cries from others. "And if the Six take issue with this, let them tell us themselves. We, the Unanswered, demand to be heard. So our message must be loud. It must be bold."

The woman paused for emphasis or to catch her breath. The sun had not quite descended beneath the hills of the peninsula, but the town lights along the wall lit up.

"Therefore, I must ask something of you," she said. "I must ask you to gather your verve. What you would have paid in town duty, pay it in verve. To save it up, the town carriages will only run by carapace. That means only in daylight, unfortunately, and the town lights will not light our streets."

The lights along the town wall dimmed and faded out. It was too early in the evening to get the full effect, but the crowd understood the message. The Burgomaster folded her hands. "I ask you to do the same, to light your homes by candlelight and contribute your verve for the good of Basinwade."

Her last four words echoed among the crowd, at first purposely by guards, but then the cry was picked up by others and resounded around the square.

"Like this monster, all of their kind will learn to give us the respect we deserve. The example we set will echo around the world. They may be the Keepers of Sinuation, but we are the Keepers of the Verve, and it is time for humans to take our rightful place. Together we will send a message even the Six can't ignore."

The guards directed people away from the tower, encouraging them to participate in the Gathering of the Verve. When the square had all but emptied, the Burgomaster walked towards the Stand. She removed her hat and wafted it towards her face. Her aroma carried an odd blend of exhaustion and excitement.

{What can I do, Caizhiu? How can I help?}

{I need you to go to Aerahan, see Zel Zesen. He needs to know what is happening in his region.} She didn't mean to but answered Heort only with the whimper of song.

{I can't just leave. They are going to kill you!} Her friend was desperate.

She scoffed to reassure him, unsure if he could hear it. *{They are only humans, Heort. They might be a little over-excited, but I'll be fine.}*

Forty-Two

The Factory, its Owner, and the Inn

The bay window of the Hornet Inn looked out over the darkened square. Normally, the Stand tower was lit from the inside with verve lamps. Tonight, the darkness was interrupted only by the periodic sparks of current passing through the iron tower and the prisoner within. Unsure what would happen once he was no longer needed, Ozcahar had half-expected that they would leave him in the tower, trapped with Caizhiu. Instead, the guards regarded him as a hero. He looked at the row of tiny glasses on the table. He nudged Handras, sitting next to him. The man seemed just as uncomfortable as Ozcahar amidst the exuberant town guards in the inn. His illicit status of Troll Hunter had suddenly become one of reverence.

Ozcahar raised his eyebrows at his friend and nodded at the line of shots. "Help drink these," he whispered from the corner of his mouth, "or I no be alive by sun-up."

Handras gave a lopsided smile, and when he was sure nobody was watching, he knocked back one of the glasses. "If Gavallia find out I be involve with this, *I* no be alive by sun-up."

Suddenly, his demeanour sobered. When Ozcahar looked up, he saw Lady Lendoline and Sheriff Olyre making their way to the table and tried to keep despair from his face. Surely, he was not going to be arrested now. Lendoline's white dress stood out against the dark tavern interior and the tiny jewels woven into the seams of her outfit gave her a spectral appearance. As one, Ozcahar and Handras went to stand, but she raised her hand.

"Stay sit, gentlemen. Osk-Har, we be grateful for help-us. Trueso, we no trap monster with no your courage."

"Glad to be help," he said with a slow nod, hoping he got the Trader words right. "If you be kind to offer return-help, I require go-by-boat or go-by-road."

Even before Rogza-Riz had described their plan to, as he had put it, protect Ozcahar from the dragon, he had wanted to get out of Basinwade. Every moment since then he had spent in quiet terror. He had feared their plan would fail, and even now his water told him he needed to leave as quickly as he could.

Lendoline smiled at him, but it was clipped and didn't reach her eyes. "No, no, Esteemed Guest. You mustn't travel now. Man-who-capture-dragon be safer in Basinwade. You must be here to celebrate with us. On their name day, when the Six be most heedful, we do slay dragon."

"Respectfully, Lady," he said, fretfully fondling the embroidery on his cuffs, while trying not to let his eyes drift to the tower on the square, "a week be long time."

"You must no longer fear your foe. It will die. But I have query. We think dragon be alone, but Stand Warden say no so."

Ozcahar furrowed his brow in bewilderment. He was in trouble but had no idea why. Eventually, with the impatience of someone unaccustomed to having to repeat herself, Lendoline said: "You no tell Rogza-Riz of cervitaur. What be reason?"

He had forgotten about him. Remembering how the cervitaur had cared for his injuries, his heart sank at the thought of Heort being trapped in Basinwade.

"Apologies. It only be a little creature, and kindly in nature."

"Kindly?" Lendoline tutted. "Humans live by our own ways, with no requirement of monsters' kindliness. With no wish for monster mercy."

The Burgomaster directed her attention to Sheriff Olyre, who glowered by her side. That man would have had Ozcahar in a cell, not a tavern. The two stepped away from the table, and Ozcahar deduced from her gesturing that she ordered the Sheriff to oversee the search for the cervitaur personally. He sipped at the sand gin. She was right. If Heort was in Basinwade, he would attempt to free the dragon, and that would mean the end of Ozcahar. Would they kill the little creature on sight or drag him here onto the square? What if they wanted Ozcahar to kill him? He threw the liquor down his throat. He did not want to be here. One killing was enough to last him a lifetime. He wiped the tears from his eyes and downed another shot.

Handras elbowed him, nodded at a gentleman who'd walked in, and said with reverence: "That be Herp-Tura Sibrand."

The gentleman's face looked withered, but with a self-satisfied smirk and a twinkle in his hooded eyes. The fancy suit and the raised heels of his buckled shoes increased his stature, both in height and breadth. He walked with a gilded cane and made a beeline for the Burgomaster. Ozcahar couldn't follow the Uayathi conversation, but he sensed the power play that bounced between the two. Eventually, with the slightest of head nods, Herp-Tura acknowledged that he was at Lendoline's service. Ozcahar expected that service would cost her.

"He owns carriage factory." Handras slapped his arm and sighed. "I wish Hantine to work there."

He went to get up, but Ozcahar pulled his friend back. "No be good time. Ask day-after-dark."

Handras rested his head on Ozcahar's shoulder. At the bar, Rogza-Riz grinned at them. "Time to take friend home, I think."

Ozcahar agreed.

***

Heort headed towards the Western Gate through the alleyways, bracing himself in case it, too, was locked. If it was, what options were then left to him, the sea? The humans had boats and nets. He would not make it out of the harbour before they'd catch him. In the distance, he could see the dark shape of a wall tower. Next to it, a little further away, the light on the Sea Sentry, the only wall tower still lit, cast its gleam across the town in a slow rhythm, like a calming breath. Heort pressed himself into the shadows every time it passed over.

All of a sudden he ran out of alleyways. Before him was a Caizhiu-high fence. He remembered the guard on the wall had said there used to be houses behind it, but that it now contained the auto carriage factory. He checked both directions of the broad street along the fence. Four guards and a dog headed towards him. He contemplated if he could backtrack and find another route, but from the footsteps that resounded in the streets and alleys around him, he knew he would soon be cornered. There was no hiding from dogs; he was not Caizhiu. An acrid smell wafted through the slats of the fence, but there was no scent of dogs. Heort looked up, gauging the height. If he took a run at it, he could jump it, probably. Then he could hide in this factory place and wait for the Westerly Gate to open.

He backed up a little, ran, and leapt up. His hooves ran up the wooden slats. Clearing the top, he landed as quietly as possible. Like humans, dogs couldn't see him when he chronochi'ed, but they sensed the wake he'd left in the air and heard his rapid heartbeats. Without realising what he had noticed, the dog barked. A chorus of barking erupted across the town. Amid the barking and shouting in the street, Heort counted two different human voices. Despite the curious accent, he understood that two guards weren't where they were supposed to be and received a scolding. The tumult covered him as he crept into the shadows.

The light from the Sea Sentry illuminated the sky above, glinting through the top windows, but it failed to reach the area where he walked. Behind him, he heard a hound scratch and whine at the place where he'd scaled the fence. With trembling hands, he felt around in the darkness and found the hinges of a door in the wall before him. Just when he reached for a handle, he heard a noise from the other side. He tucked himself to the side when the door swung open.

"What by Sinuation's Grace is going on?" The voice of the man who exited the building sounded thick with sleep, but he was dressed in a uniform and carried a lantern. Heort ducked, squeezing his eyes shut so the light wouldn't reflect in them. He chronochi'ed faster than he ever had to scurry past the man and into the building. The floor inside was slick, and he pirouetted as his hooves skidded with his haste. He almost choked on the stench of verve and rotting flesh as his hands grabbed a curved board. It swung when he slid against it but didn't fall. He pulled himself up. A slimy substance dripped over his hands and up his sleeves. Gagging, Heort wiped his hands on his jacket. He backed away from the disgusting thing. A row of bhodine carapaces hung along the wall, a few tendrils still attached so the humans could fix it to their carriages. The rest of the creatures had been discarded. He'd never thought about the fate of the animals whose carapaces the humankin used to bring illumination to their houses and movement to their carriages.

Warily, he moved further into the cavernous factory. With every shaky step, his hooves threatened to slip, and he had to hold both hands out to feel if the space ahead of him was empty. Though as soft as he could make them, the resounding of his footsteps against the stone walls told him he was walking into a larger area with lofty ceilings. A building this size would have multiple entrances. There was bound to be another way out. And if he tried really hard, in the dark, he could pretend to be in the open air. He heard the hinges of the door squeak behind him. Louder footsteps than his echoed around the hall and lantern light flickered across his surroundings. Heort stood between rows of workbenches topped with a collection of half-formed auto carriage guts. Light danced over coils of copper threads, interlocking rods, and jagged wheels. He squeezed himself between the benches. His jacket caught on the machinery and his feet slipped when he tried to pull free.

"I'm not sure about this," he heard Sleepy Man mutter at the two guards who followed him in. The hound with them whined with excitement, and his nails tapped and scraped on the slick stones.

Heort jerked his jacket free and cringed at the ripping sound of the fabric. He licked his nose and skulked to the back wall. There was nowhere to go, no doorway. All he could do was hide between the tall cabinets with tools. To keep his white backside from view, he backed into the gap between a cabinet and the wall. The dog, a tall creature with short fur that ridged over his back, pulled the shorter of the guards forward in his eagerness. The other one, thin and with a rigid posture, carried a rifle and one of the torture backpacks. Heort shut his eyes and regulated his breaths, making sure not to let out a groan of despair.

The town guard turned to the night warden and, with a sprinkling of amusement in his deep voice, said: "I am the Sheriff of Basinwade. How much more authority do you require?"

"I intend no disrespect, Mr Olyre, but I'd feel happier if I knew Mr Sibrand had knowledge of your presence."

There was a moment of silence. Curious to find out what was going on, Heort squinted through his long eyelashes, ready to close his eyes should the lantern light find his corner.

"Though he might consider himself to be, Mr Sibrand is not above Basinwade law. Besides, he is currently meeting with Lady Lendoline, and I wager you wouldn't care to disturb them."

Sleepy Man shifted his weight from one leg onto the other. "Trueso, I don't think it'd be appropriate."

"I dare say you are right at that." Olyre looked the man up and down, running his fingers over the line of his moustache. "Would you mind lending us your lantern?"

"Odd turn of affairs, is it not?" Sleepy Man shook his head as he handed the lantern to the Sheriff. "We are surrounded by verve, and we can't keep the lamps lit. I tried to turn them on when I heard the commotion outside, but—"

"That would be the reason Mr Sibrand is meeting with the Burgomaster," Olyre said with a scowl that told the man the conversation had finished. "The sooner we can get this done, the sooner you will be rid of us."

Heort heard the door close as the night warden left. The shadows folded, melted, and melded around him when the lantern was raised. The town guard kept a firm hand on the lead of the impatient dog and the Sheriff adjusted the pack on his back. A shiver shot from the nape of Heort's neck to the tip of his tail as he recalled how they'd made Caizhiu scream with those. Would it shortly be his turn?

Forty-Three

Experimentations

The sunny square was bustling with people, but Caizhiu could neither see nor smell Ozcahar. She cursed silently. He had probably left town by now and was making his way to... There were too many escape routes to guess.

Two guards stood at a safe distance with their backs to the cage and busied themselves by keeping curious onlookers away. The longer these idiots delayed her, the longer it would take for her to catch up with her quarry. These two at least lacked the cruelty of previous pairs, and this had provided Caizhiu with the two hours of relative comfort she'd needed to regain her human form.

Her good fortune was about to worsen as she noted, beyond the guards, the parting of the crowd for the approach of a vision in white together with her entourage.

"As you recommended, we have reduced the number of lightning jolts," Lendoline whispered to a man at her side. "We're limiting their use so we have reserves, should the monster try to escape."

The man scratched his precisely trimmed grey beard. The hat he wore was tall and similar to Myrta's. It barely shaded his face, and from the deep grooves in his tanned skin, Caizhiu guessed he'd worn hats like this for years. Not just the impractical hat, but his whole attire set him apart. Most people wore loose-fitting garments from thin, sandy-coloured material. This man wore a suit that included a fully buttoned waistcoat. It was as if the suit held his wiry body rigid. Together with the cane the man leant on as he walked towards her, it gave the impression that the suit wore the man and not the other way around.

Walking around the Stand, he cocked his head from side to side to peer through the gaps in the ironwork. Caizhiu tried to snort out the stench of verve that surrounded him. A pair of gold spectacles peeped over the rim of his breast pocket, and he took them out with theatrical particularity to examine her.

"I see what you mean." A smile spread across his face, and his fingers opened and closed over the head of his cane. "The creature looks in inopportunely good health, given the treatment your guards have bestowed upon it."

"And who might we have here?" Caizhiu asked and opened all her eyes so she wouldn't have to move to keep him in her line of sight. "Do I understand correctly that Lady Lendoline isn't in sole control of this little performance?"

"G-goodness, it speaks." Emotion gripped his throat. "My name, Creature, is Herp-Tura Sibrand."

He looked over his shoulder at the Burgomaster, who raised her eyebrows and gave him a lopsided smile.

"Be my guest, Mr Sibrand. None of this would be possible without you. Please, don't let formality stand in your way at this point. It doesn't suit you."

She chin-nodded at the guards. "Follow whatever his instructions might be."

"This is extraordinary! I never thought I'd get to speak to one of them. I thought they only spoke to those so-called Talented."

"I'm open-minded," Caizhiu said. "And *my* name, Creature, is Caizhiu the Wayward. You'd find me a lot more talkative if you'd cease whatever enchantment it is you've endowed your tower with."

Herp-Tura guffawed and knocked the ferrule on the flagstones in the rhythm of his laughter. "Truly, it is as you say, Burgomaster. Its sense of superiority is astounding. Even now, it thinks there is some sort of Sinuation Talent at play. Can you not conceive, Monster, that it is our ingenuity that ensnared you, not some Talent? That you are at the mercy of human-folk."

Caizhiu rolled all four of her eyes. "What mercy?"

"Quite so." Herp-Tura pursed his lips. "It's almost a shame to kill you."

With some impatience, he indicated for the guards to approach. "I have not seen a proper dragon before. I need to know the true nature of this beast, so I can work out what we will need to slay it. Please give it a brief jolt of direct verve lightning."

Caizhiu heard the pitch of the apparatus rise, and she wasn't going to wait for the guards to immobilise her. Even though her legs were folded too harshly to allow her to put her full force behind it, she should be fast enough to break out of the confinement. She pushed up and spread her wings. Her muscles jerked the moment she touched the metal. When her legs threatened to buckle, she threw herself forward, grasping the cylinder with her transfiguring hands. And then the prongs found her flesh. One sent a burst of white-hot pain through her thigh, the other through her chest. Tremors shot through her body; her neck curved back. Her head bounced off the ceiling, sending a torrent of pain from her snout to the bites of the prongs. It felt as if those three points were fighting over her body, each tearing at her scales to gather them into their individual points of pain. Her skull felt like it was splitting, a sensation that moved along her spine, all the way into her caudal blade.

"That will do for the moment."

Caizhiu slid back, jerking helplessly while trying to regain control over her movements. She shut her eyes to avoid accidentally gouging them out with her claws as she tried to get up. Her talons speared the pattern of dancing figures, and in response to the metal's bite, her claw spasmed to lock it in place. One prong jabbed into the base of her tail. Caizhiu's eyes snapped open, and she screamed. Sparks rained from the ceiling, where her blade scraped along the metal.

"Short jabs," Herp-Tura instructed. "Lots of short jabs. We don't want it to get used to the sensation, because then we'll have to use more power."

The guard carefully handed him the rod, and he pressed the tip against her skin until her scales blistered. He repeated it several times, repositioning the point of impact with every stab, so they formed a burning track of pain from her back, around her tail, over her buttock.

"Like this, you see. Watch for the reactions to see which are its most sensitive spots." Her body jerked and her wings thwacked against the ceiling, sending competing pulses into her core.

Herp-Tura handed the rod back to the guard. He snapped his fingers and shouted at one of the bystanders, who came running. "Get me one of the technologists. You'll likely find Foxtine on the shop floor. Tell her to drop whatever she's doing and come to the Stand."

Caizhiu tried to turn and prevent the next jab landing further underneath her tail, but she wasn't fast enough. She couldn't even move herself out of reach of her tormentors – humans, as fragile as their stupid tower – and she wailed her frustration over the square.

"Now we are getting somewhere," Herp-Tura said, walking to the other guard, who handed him his rod. Because the rod was attached to the pack on the back of the guard, the men had to stand side by side.

"Hit it again," he ordered, and Caizhiu groaned despite herself.

The stiffening of her legs had wedged her against the biting metal. Both of her wing-thumbs were hooked through the dancing pattern, and she couldn't pull her claws out. The side of her face, her neck, and chest burned as, with her caudal blade trapped in a gap in the ceiling, the prison sent a permanent series of enervating pulses to every nerve ending in her body. She could only watch the guard methodically place the prongs around her body. In between the jabs she gasped for breath and stared at Herp-Tura. How could something so frail cause her such pain? She screamed, then choked when Herp-Tura pressed the other lightning rod on her tongue. In another betrayal of her body, the forks coiled around the metal, grasping it, as if to embrace the torment. Even back in the Keeltois, when Brekranez had vomited its firestorm over her, the burning sensation had not been this intense.

Herp-Tura's eyes widened when he realised he couldn't pull the rod back, and he let go of it. The guard didn't have that opportunity, because the pack on his back was attached to the rod. A sudden spasm in her neck jerked Caizhiu's head back and pulled the guard against the cylinder. His fingers clawed at the metal and his legs juddered. Faeces filled his trousers and a few hairs rose off his head. His beard curled into minuscule spirals and the air filled with the scent of roasted flesh and scorched hair.

As if he only now realised that the pack on his back was harmful, the other guard jumped backwards, and he threw the rod on the floor. Using a lull in the waves of pain, Caizhiu closed her jaws and snapped the rod in three. She spat it against the metal and tried to push herself to the centre of the cylinder. Though she longed to sink to the floor, her tail was stuck in the ceiling, sending juddering pulses down her spine until they slammed into the back of her skull.

The guard slumped against the cylinder. His skin showed the reddened pattern of dancing people, fish, and flowers. A gasp rose from the crowd as his corpse peeled off the metal and landed on the pavers.

Herp-Tura tugged at his beard. Looking from Caizhiu to the fallen guard and back, he muttered softly to himself. "On the right track, I think. Obviously, will need some refinement and more power. Where, by Six's perdition, is Foxtine?"

"The right track?" Lendoline strode towards him. "You call this the right track? Has it escaped your notice that one of our town guards is dead and that damnable dragon is still alive?"

"Of course, Lady Lendoline. But look at it."

Caizhiu wanted to get up from her crumpled position, but her limbs refused. Herp-Tura let his eyes glide over her twitching body, and a grin spread across his face.

"What we can hurt, we can kill. Have no fear. We will avenge..." He nodded at the fallen man.

Finally, Caizhiu freed her tail from the ceiling and coiled it beneath her. She curled into a ball, tugging her front legs against her stomach as if to keep her insides in.

"We'll avenge him, and all those poor buggers who've fallen to the naiad, have fallen to the trolls. I promise you, Basinwade will have vengeance and we will send a message to all Fabled, Magistrates, and the Six. It is time to show the world that it is ours for the taking."

Lendoline hesitated before returning his smile, her previous confidence returned. "I shall leave the details in your capable hands, Mr Sibrand. And you shall have all of Basinwade's resources at your disposal. The monsters will think twice once they learn what we can do to them."

Something behind her caught her attention, and Lendoline turned to see the crowd part to allow Sheriff Olyre and one of his guards to approach her. He wore one of those damned packs and it surprised Caizhiu that she recoiled at the sight. She cursed her cravenness; they were just humans. Nothing but weak little neath. Though there seemed to be nothing she could do to stop them for the time being, she would find a way out. She would haul the Burgomaster to Zel's office, maybe Herp-Tura too. Ozcahar would have to wait. She'd allow him a while longer to find a hidey-hole. And then she would dig him out.

The Sheriff looked dejected when he stepped up to the Burgomaster. He and his guard smelled of verve and lack of sleep. Something else tugged at the edge of her senses, something soothing. Its mere scent eased Caizhiu's tender insides.

"Apologies. I bring bad news." Olyre turned to his guard, who trailed behind. With some reluctance, she walked over and held out her hands. Where Caizhiu's insides seemed to have been on fire, now it was as if they froze. The guard handed her boss a jacket. It was tiny in Olyre's hands. Caizhiu recognised the blue belt, the stitching, and the soothing scent.

{*Heort!*} Frantically, Caizhiu searched for the song of her friend, though she doubted he'd be foolish enough to be near the square. He was likely already outside of the town walls. Mercy-of-Six, let him be out of the town.

The town guard glanced in the dragon's direction and then lowered her gaze as she handed Olyre two further objects. Caizhiu closed her eyes, but it was too late. Her nostrils confirmed what she already knew; the guard had handed him Heort's harness and her bag of gold.

"We were not able to capture the creature," Olyre said. "I take full responsibility, Lady Lendoline. We are unused to these new-f... these new types of weapons. We did not intend to kill it."

"Well, that is most unfortunate, Sheriff." Herp-Tura stroked his beard as he observed the dragon. "It would have been interesting to compare the reactions of both monsters. Then again, we designed the packs to be powerful. I should like to examine the cervitaur remains."

"There are none." Olyre shook his head. "The whole thing was over in a flash, completely burnt up. I never saw anything like it."

The blood blisters on her tongue burst as Caizhiu roared. It did not matter that they had her trapped; the humans instinctively recoiled at the sound.

Forty-Four

Breaking the Stand

From the beginning of this iteration, Caizhiu had thought it arduous to maintain her compressed state, but it was countless times worse here. It was impossible to expel her body heat. She guessed the Stand wasn't designed as a trap for her kind. It was likely meant to kill naiad. The drying heat would be intolerable to one of them. But it was effective at tormenting a dragon too. The floor sent enough prickling up her legs to keep her scales from disappearing, and she couldn't get rid of her claws. She sat on her haunches, keeping her front paws off the ground. Even so, she couldn't get them into a hand shape, hindered by the talons she couldn't retract. But none of it compared to the pain of losing Heort.

Guards sauntered around the tower, looking bored, more interested in the construction work around them than in their prisoner. They straightened up when a familiar visitor approached the entrance. Caizhiu recognised her vivacious gait.

As per usual, Betni Foxtine was laden with her large leather bags. When some threatened to escape from under her arms, she stumbled and lost her hat. Herp-Tura had called her a technologist, which meant nothing to Caizhiu. Whatever Betni was, she seemed to enjoy herself as she cast an appraising gaze over the Stand and the structures that were being erected on her instruction. She pushed her thick round glasses up her nose and her attention skimmed over the dragon within. She instructed the two men on either side of her to insert a pole into the hole they had made in the pavers. It held a strap on the top, and Caizhiu felt a tautness settle in her chest. They had killed Heort. And they intended to kill her.

In their previous attempts to do so, her thrashing had bent the walls of the cylinder and loosened the rivets. Her tail blade had punctured the ceiling. If only she could control a bit of that strength, she could slice the ceiling open further and snap more of the rivets off the sliding entry. No doubt they'd hurt her to stop her, and they would succeed. But once she had weakened the structure sufficiently, she would be able to break out the next time or the time after that. She just had to persist.

"It will be a shame to lose the Stand," the technologist said to herself, as seemed to be her way.

"Perhaps, Betni Foxtine, you'd consider saving your beautiful tower by letting me out?"

Betni jolted at the sound of her name and took a step back. "Speak again, Monster, and I'll have them burn out your tongue."

"Such harsh words," Caizhiu said. "Do you fancy yourself on a par with the Lady Burgomaster? Or perhaps you are the legatee to Mr Sibrand?"

Betni blushed and turned brusquely to snap instructions at her assistants.

Caizhiu decided there was no point in delaying any longer. She threw herself forward, pressing her fingers against the rivets that kept the door shut before the pain could disable her. She whipped her tail up and let her blade slice into the pliable metal. A shower of red and blue glass jangled on the floor. The metal bit into her skin. Her tail jerked, chafing on the ragged metal, but it broke through the ceiling. Painful pulses tensed her muscles and forced her body to elongate into her own shape. She screamed even before the guards added the intensity of their lightning rods. Her feet hooked through the mesh and her front claws crunched the metal of the door. Her neck extended and her head smashed into the metal. It stung, sparked, and scorched her scales. Her wings flicked up and quivered against the walls. The convulsions wedged her body between the door and the wall, and finally the mechanism buckled. Her scream became triumphant as much as one of pain. The humans shouted around her. She heard Betni's voice above them: excited, scared, tense, but elated.

A sudden heat gripped her tail as if lava had pinched it between finger and thumb. Her whole body became rigid, her limbs jerking uncontrollably, and her neck curved back until the top of her head skimmed her back. This was the end of her escape attempt and she surrendered to the agony. It would not last. She just had to endure. Concentrating on her breathing, she waited for the pain to diminish. When it did, Caizhiu sank to the ground. It took a moment to realise that her body was hers; no pulses haunted her nerves. The trap was broken. This was her opportunity. She had to recover before the humans could repair it. Caizhiu lurched forward through the gap where the door had bent away from the wall. Blinded by sunlight, she reached for freedom. A chorus of screams erupted around her, a sweet sound when it was not her own. She was about to roar to set the humans aflutter when a sharp tug on her tail stopped her and she lost her balance. One of the door hinges jabbed between the scales of her throat and her jaw hit the flagstones. The expected sting of the metal didn't come. She snorted the dust from her nostrils and shook the grogginess from her head.

Betni shouted something. It sounded like a growl, high-pitched but with implacable precision. The technologist was standing nearby and Caizhiu, detecting the smell of human excitement, looked around suspiciously. When she had burst out of the cylinder, bystanders and stall owners had retreated to the edges of the square. But Betni, her builders, and the guards were still crowding her. She snarled to chase them away and snapped at the guard closest to her. He jumped back, wielding the lightning rod as if it were a sword. Thankfully, he wasn't close enough to touch her, but he yelled a barrage of taunts at her. As long as her shoulders were stuck in the cylinder, she couldn't reach him, but she tried anyway. Her attention was on his hateful lightning pack. She had no desire to fill her mouth with disgusting verve, but the anticipation of crunching the contraption under foot elated her. If the man still wore it, all the better.

She squeezed one front claw through the opening when the tugging at her tail increased. Instinctively, she tried to pull back, but to no avail. Her tail was stuck. How could she have been so stupid as to trap the barbs of her blade? She didn't want to withdraw back into her prison, but after a few attempts to pull herself free, she had no choice. She growled menacingly, hoping to frighten the humans to keep away, and she moved her head so her crest wouldn't catch on the jagged metal. Sunlight glinted off spun metal ropes as they twirled through the air. Caizhiu jerked her head but could only avoid two of the lariats. The third tightened around her neck, quickly joined by the other two that were thrown again. Caizhiu pushed her front paws against the cylinder to pull it apart and pry the ropes from her neck. She froze for a moment as her ears were assaulted by the hum of a dozen auto carriages. Vibrations shuddered the square, causing more red and blue glass to cascade over her back and wings, and though it didn't hurt, it reminded her of the pulses they'd run through her body. Only now did she notice how quiet the town had become over the days she'd been incarcerated. The diminishing number of carriages passing by had gone unnoticed.

Caizhiu tried to grab the mesh flooring but found that her hind legs could no longer touch the floor. She jerked to free her tail from the iron grip around the base of her blade, but she was steadily and inexorably ratcheted upwards. She stared at Betni. This was no enchantment and yet humans were not this strong; they couldn't be doing what they clearly were doing.

Beneath the platform in front of the Stand, two auto carriage hearts hummed to life. They added to the judder in the ground and the restraints around her neck tightened. It was as if Betni had disembowelled several carriages to use their entrails as a dragon's restraint. No, Caizhiu thought, not 'as if'; it was exactly what the technologist had done. She had attached the hearts to the ropes around Caizhiu's neck. From the sound, she had more hearts on the other side of the Stand, pulling on her tail. Caught in a tugging war between the two sets of auto hearts, Caizhiu whacked her wings against the ceiling. She bucked to get out of this grip and scrabbled around the inside of the cylinder, uselessly slicing the metal with her claws.

Betni stood next to the whirling hearts. How could a creature so small lift her off the ground? Her hands moved the type of levers and knobs Caizhiu had seen in Raccio's auto carriage to adjust the tension on the ropes. They moved Caizhiu's neck to align it with the restraint the humans had placed before the platform. She clawed at the twisted iron of the door, pushing it away from the cylinder until at last it gave way and clattered onto the flagstones. Betni nodded at the town guard Caizhiu had snapped her jaws at and shouted to the others: "Stand back!"

The guard held the lightning rod against the rope. Caizhiu gulped her lungs full of air before the pain hit, before breathing became a life-and-death struggle. Her wings stretched against the remnants of the ceiling as if they were glued to it. She felt the membranes push through the decorative patterns, leaving patches of blisters with each pulse that methodically rushed from her tail to her nose.

At the behest of the technologist, the guard removed the rod from the rope and the pain ceased. Caizhiu struggled to get control of her disobliging limbs, tried to push against the metal. But they were no longer hers to command, and she had little strength left. The humans used her weakened state to clamp the restraint around her neck. Wary guards shackled her legs together. Despite having her paws shackled in irons and being lifted off the ground, it surprised her when the humans opened the back of the cylinder. It no longer functioned as a cage, but they had to be very confident in their restraints. Caizhiu forced herself to calm, despite her body's instinct to fight. The humans had hurt her many times over the last few days, but it had always stopped. Once the pain eased, she would take her human shape and squeeze out of the restraints.

A hubbub at the edge of the square caught her attention. Her heart sank when she saw Herp-Tura toddle over the cobbles, tapping his gilded cane. The man let his eyes wander from the platform to the dragon. He circled the Stand. Caizhiu kept her gaze on him as long as she could. A shudder travelled up her spine; she was watching her executioner.

Herp-Tura drew out the moment to maximum effect before saying: "Nice work, Foxtine. You've done well. As I knew you would."

The technologist straightened her glasses after her little bow. "It was quite the challenge, sir. I'm flattered that you've allowed me to be part of this. Let me show you the controls. I assume you will want to do the honours tonight."

Herp-Tura placed a hand on her shoulder. "By all means, show me your work, but I'm content to let you work them at the glorious event. It was you who designed them. Besides, I believe Lady Lendoline wants me on the platform, conducting events."

The technologist blushed and nearly skipped towards the table with levers and dials. Herp-Tura examined them, grunting his satisfaction. Each grunt caused Betni's cheeks to glow. She pointed at something, and with a broad grin, he looked at their captive and flicked the switch. Caizhiu's back tensed, and from her tail to the tip of her nose, her scales twitched with the arcs of pain that moved through her body. The effect was not as intense a pain as the touch of a lightning rod, more akin to the continuous torment the mesh flooring had caused. But this time it ran through her whole body, not just her feet.

"This is linked to the three bhodine carapaces," Betni said, bouncing on her toes with enthusiasm. "We will easily maintain it all day, certainly until sunset. And it keeps all our carefully gathered verve reserves free for tonight. So, we're as ready as we can be."

"How long would you say the generator will need to run to charge for maximum power output?" Herp-Tura eyed the equipment around the tower.

Betni pursed her lips and moved her head from side to side. "A couple of hours – three to be on the safe side. Any longer and we'll be burning verve for no good reason. Once we begin, we'll want to keep the output going as long as we can, so we'll need the verve then."

Herp-Tura seemed pleased and ambled over to Caizhiu's face. He gave the dragon's suspended body the once-over and chortled. With both hands on his cane, he rocked on his heels, and he licked his chapped lips like a cat observing a glued songbird. Gazing into Caizhiu's eyes he said: "It would appear that the reputation of your hypnotic stare is undeserved."

Unable to give a rejoinder, she determined to remain as impassive as she could. The pulses kept her in place, causing her scales to blister beneath the shackles and the ropes around her tail and neck. She might not be able to escape this new form of captivity, but she wouldn't show him how much pain she was in.

"Have you no supercilious answer, Creature?"

He stood so close to her head that his bitter scent was overwhelming. The fingers of the one hand rhythmically drummed a lazy pattern on the knuckles of the other that rested on the golden handle of his cane. If only she could break out of her restraints...

Herp-Tura directed his attention to Betni again. "What is the maximum power output, and how long can we maintain it?"

"Five hundred and seventy tura. And we'll be able to keep that running through the creature for half an hour. I can't believe it will take that long, but if we have to cook it, we can."

Caizhiu forced her jaws open, only a fraction but wide enough to flick her tongue out. She couldn't stretch it far enough to grab his hands, but she could slide one fork over the tip of Herp-Tura's little finger. At the moment of touch, the man squealed and jumped backwards with a force his legs didn't normally have. He landed on his back and his head hit the ground.

Herp-Tura's screaming was audible over the tumult of people rushing to aid him.

"Are you unhurt, sir?" Betni caught herself. "I mean, obviously, you are hurt. But... but... ehm... Do you require a physician?"

Caizhiu chuckled a low rumble across the square. It sent a ripple of anxiety through the humans.

"Ensure we can run the maximum turas through the monster for an hour," Herp-Tura coughed as they helped him to his feet. He tucked his injured hand under his jacket, and, with his other, he pointed from Betni to the Stand structure and back. "I don't care how we do it, but I want to maintain the maximum output for an hour, at least."

"We'll need more verve for that, sir."

"There is no sense in doing this by half, so tell our Burgomaster that if she wishes to oversee the slaying, if she wishes to send its neck bones as gifts to the Six or whatever she's planning, then her guards had better get every last drop from every last household of this town. This monster will die tonight. It will die screaming."

FORTY-FIVE

DO DRAGONS REALLY EAT CHILDREN?

During her long life of dealing with them, Caizhiu could count on one claw the times a human had seen her true form, and now she found herself on display. By trying to escape the humans' trap, she had merely stepped into their next one. As they ogled her, the smell of their fear made her stomach rumble. Despite their revulsion, they couldn't resist coming closer to take a look. It was incomprehensible. The guards' primary task was to keep curious onlookers at a safe distance.

The strain of her weight and the prolonged spasms in her muscles caused a growing ache in the base of her tail. It had started as a dull niggle, but now it felt like her tail might tear off. The sharpening pain spread up her back, through both sets of shoulders, and into the nape of her neck. Occasionally, competing bolts would fork around her scales, travel from her tail and nose, and cause itching sparks to jump from her wings to the iron, which would elicit a cheer from onlookers. Every pulse that was sent through her body stiffened her muscles. Tiny but repetitive, they drained her. Worst of all, the pulses solidified her scales and forced her to stay in her own shape. Unable to squeeze or break out of her restraints, Caizhiu was beginning to think that she might not get out of this on her own.

To distract herself from the pain, she focused on a woman who struggled towards the Fish Gate. She was carrying not only a heavy basket on her back but a package slightly too large to hold under one arm, while the other held a small child who had sunk to her knees on the cobbles and refused to walk. The girl wailed in protest when the woman tried to lift her onto her feet. Suddenly the woman dropped the package and then, with the young girl by the arm, strode towards Caizhiu and stood tantalisingly close to her head. She wore an old jacket over her dress, stained in fish guts. Her sweaty aroma wafted into Caizhiu's nostrils, craving knotting her insides.

"You know what happens to naughty girls who won't help Mummy with their chores?" the woman asked. The girl squealed and squirmed to free her arm from the pinched grip. "They are eaten by dragons."

The child was about Moro's age, perhaps a little younger. Her eyelashes glistened with tears. The rapid heartbeat thundered in Caizhiu's ears. She was plump and smelled delectable. The dragon's stomach gurgled and twisted painfully with a hankering for food. If only there would be a gap in the infernal pulses, the tiniest break in their hold, and Caizhiu could snap the bonds that held her. She wanted to sink her teeth into the squishy flesh. Her arms twitched as she imagined holding the child down, and she swallowed back more spit than she'd thought she'd been able to produce given her dehydration. There were so many humans. Surely, they wouldn't miss this tiny one.

"Good woman! Have you lost all reason?"

The authoritative voice snapped Caizhiu out of her daydream. The sight of Heort's murderer quelled her hunger momentarily.

"Step back! If the monster will not kill you, the weapon of its execution will certainly do for you."

Caizhiu attempted to snap at the child. She wasn't sure if she had merely wanted to scare her away or, if she could have, she would have caught her. Either way, the restraints around her neck made it impossible. When the woman shrieked and pulled the little girl behind her, Caizhiu expected the agony of a lightning rod pressed against her neck. She breathed in to prepare for it, but the pain didn't come. Sheriff Olyre held the rod in his hand, but the contraption on his back didn't whirl and whine in readiness to inflict its torment.

The girl pulled the woman's sleeve. "Is he going to hit it?"

"I will if it moves again," Olyre said in a low and threatening voice.

"Do dragons really eat children?"

Olyre's eyebrows met as he scowled at the woman. Then his voice softened as he addressed the child: "Rest assured, little one, after tonight, this one won't."

The woman bowed politely and dragged the girl towards her dropped package and onwards to the harbour.

Helpless, Caizhiu growled her hatred at the Sheriff. Since he'd claimed he had murdered her friend, she'd convinced herself that the man must have been lying. The guard died after being pulled against the metal, but there was still plenty of his body remaining. Even though Heort was slighter than a human, she couldn't believe he would have burned up. Yet, as she glared at the Sheriff standing by her side carrying a lightning pack, these thoughts seemed vain hopes. If hunger hadn't flooded her senses, she could have got an impression of Olyre's mood, but the scent of his blood was overpowering. Though not as tender as the child, she bet the Sheriff would make a tasty meal.

Olyre stroked his lips and whispered: "There is nothing I can do for you, Esteemed Dragon. Please know that not everyone in this town feels as Lady Lendoline does. I can't expect you to understand, but... I want you to know that your friend lives and he has made his way outside of the town wall. I wish there were more I could do."

Dizzying relief engulfed her, but she pulled herself to order and tried to catch his eye, to guide it to Betni's controls. What she would not give for the hypnotic stare people assumed she had. She willed him to go to the controls, willed him to switch off the controlling pulses. Without them, she'd be able to break out of the irons as if they were paper. He didn't move. Then another voice pierced the moment.

"Ah! Sheriff Olyre!" Betni gave him an excited wave. "How fortuitous that you are here. I wonder if you'd be so kind as to lend a hand."

Caizhiu saw despair flicker over the Sheriff's face. "How may I be of service, Technologist Foxtine?"

Her movements were quick and clipped, like a scurrying rat. The technologist beckoned for Olyre to follow her. Rather than walking round the Stand, they squeezed past Caizhiu, through the gap in the cylinder. The small woman easily slipped between the shards of torn metal and Caizhiu's twitching body, but Sheriff Olyre stepped carefully and had to twist so the lightning pack on his back didn't touch either. They moved out of her line of sight.

"Don't look so perturbed, Sheriff. I realise this looks strange, but the technology is no different from the internal workings of an auto carriage."

Caizhiu could hear Olyre grumble.

Betni giggled. "Oh dear. If I guessed you've never driven an auto carriage, would I be correct?"

"You would. But truth be told, it's been quite a while since I last drove any carriage myself."

"Well, do not be concerned; I shan't ask anything of you that should tax you." She spoke to the Sheriff with friendly condescension. "You see the spike up there? We've connected it to the generators, but we'll need to ensure it's aligned so we skewer the monster properly."

Caizhiu heard Olyre's intake of breath and the discomfited tone in his voice. "Seems excessive. Is Lady Lendoline that determined to demean one unfortunate Fabled just to send the Magistrate a message?"

"No, not excessive at all, Sheriff. It's a tough creature." Betni lowered her voice. "Between you and me, we will have to give this everything we've got for it to work. According to Mr Sibrand's findings, the scales deflect most of the reined lightning's power. Did you know we're running seventy tura over the thing, just to keep it in place? That's almost as much as it takes to keep the lights on in the Townhall. In order to kill the creature, we'll have to get to its insides."

Before he had answered, Betni swanned around the tower towards the controls.

"May the Six forgive me." Caizhiu couldn't tell if Olyre's whispered words were meant for her, or if he was muttering to himself.

He cleared the choke from his throat and shouted directions to the technologist. His instructions were followed by clicking and whirling sounds that sent shivers along Caizhiu's spine. She was dealing with creatures utterly beyond reason. They had boasted that they could kill what they could hurt. And they had certainly proved they could hurt her. They were going to kill her. They were truly going to kill her.

"Well, that's it. Preparations made." Betni beamed at her impromptu assistant. "Will you be there tonight?"

"It's unlikely I'll have a choice."

Betni laughed, mistaking his words for jest.

"In fact," he said, "I'll have to accompany the guest of honour."

Caizhiu twitched. Ozcahar, she thought. He was still in Basinwade. He'd stayed to watch her die.

"I should like to meet him." Betni sighed. "He must be the bravest of men, and from what I hear, quite handsome too." She giggled and straightened her glasses to hide her blushing. "I suppose you'd better collect him, Sheriff. Wouldn't want to be late, not if you want a good view. You'll not have seen anything like it before, I promise you that. And you'll likely see nothing like it again."

"I certainly hope not," the Sheriff muttered as he walked around the tower and past Caizhiu. He didn't look at her and breathed the words more than he spoke them. "Keepers' Mercy. I hope you can forgive us."

Caizhiu wanted to shout after him, curse him for the coward he was, but it was all for naught. Without help, she couldn't get herself out of this. But if Heort had made it to Aerahan, which would be a challenge even for someone as fast as him, it would take the Magistrate time to travel to Basinwade. More time than she had left. The only possible aid would be here. And what hope was there if even a powerful man like the Sheriff considered himself unable to give it?

Had it been like this for Ujojen the Conflicted? According to the legend, they had lived so long they had believed themselves placed outside of Sinuation's rule. So, despite numerous warnings by the Keepers, Ujojen had rampaged throughout the lands and eventually Sinuation had caught up with them. Their last iteration had been their undoing. The dragon had emerged from their cocoon with uneven wings, earthbound. While the two heads fought over which one of them was to blame, Ujojen was set upon by those they had terrorised. The same fate awaited her. She had failed to retrieve Ozcahar Nitt. Or was this punishment at long last for her role in the Great Blaze of the Keeltois? Had nothing she had done since counterbalanced that mistake? The painting in Myrta's living room had shown humans upfront of the army coming for Ujojen. Perhaps it was always humans that did for dragons when they failed the Six. A last humiliation.

FORTY-SIX

UNEXPECTED AID

C rackling laughter cascaded over Caizhiu, and her four eyes flitted around the square for the source of the soul song.

{Are we feeling sorry for ourself, Dragon?}

Despite the glow of the lowering sun, she could make out the fleck of flame that drifted on the air currents circulating in the Stand's spire. The connection, fiery and familiar, was like an elixir - welcome like a flagon of ale.

{Take heed not to touch me!} She sent the warning with more detail of her torment than she'd wanted to, considering who the voice belonged to.

{So you do have a smouldering place in your heart for me. You can't know how much that pleases me.}

The fleck was the size of a night fay, too small for Caizhiu to make out Brekranez's features. Alarm caught a breath in her throat when the drake landed on the tip of her caudal blade.

{I am quite familiar with lightning bolts, sweet Caizhiu.} It danced on the edge of her blade, then leisurely slid towards the bond that was fastened

underneath her barbs. *{But I'm not flesh and blood like you, and it will not harm me.}*

Caizhiu reined in her relief as the fire drake crawled over the rope of iron that caused her tail scales to throb. She wasn't sure why she had even cared whether her nemesis would share her fate.

{But you, my darling dragon, appear to be in extreme discomfort. I hate to point this out, but I warned you about fraternising with food.}

Brekranez slinked between the ridges of her scales. It dawdled in a slow spiral around her tail, taking in the surroundings with amused curiosity. *{They're inventive, I'll give them that. Who'd have thought they'd be able to harness the lightning.}*

Despite its minute size, she could feel the path it left on her tortured skin as if the drake were a fine version of a lightning rod.

{I tried to tell you that you are fighting the wrong battle, glorious one. Don't mistake me for your enemy. I take it you know what they intend to do to you?}

Caizhiu grunted dismissively and tried to suppress a wince when the drake lingered at the bottom of her tail. Its pinprick presence burned, as if it would go straight through her scales. She grimaced, pressing her eyes closed to temper its burning touch.

{Apologies, sweetness, is this painful?} Brekranez asked without moving from its spot above her cloaca. *{If you wish me to move, you need only ask.}*

Caizhiu pressed her tongue to the inside of her teeth. It was all she could do to deflect the intensity of the torment. She panted and gave in. *{May the Six freeze your flames, Brekranez, get off me!}*

{Please?}

{Get lost!}

The fire drake tutted at her tone. *{If you think this is painful, you've felt nothing yet.}*

Caizhiu tried to concentrate on anything other than the intense burning dot that was the fire drake.

{I do believe your beloved humans are going to send a prolonged lightning current up your backside to fry you from the inside out. Now, that will hurt.

And, because the wretched creatures are not convinced this will kill you, and they may well be right, they then intend to cut off your head.} The fire drake strolled around the base of her tail towards her back. *{And that, sweet Caizhiu, most definitely will kill you.}*

Caizhiu let out a shuddering breath and suppressed her desire for a drink of water, but as she did so she remembered the rectangular well by the Townhall. It would be glorious to sit in it. She imagined its coolness sloshing against her sides. Instead of suppressing her desire, she shared her water dreams with Brekranez. It laughed in response.

{Defiant to the last, eh, Dragon?} It slalomed around the ridges of her dorsal crest. *{Count yourself lucky that the humans haven't figured out how much better their instruments of torture would work if they'd added water.}*

{It would make even the water burn?}

Her surprise caused Brekranez to add a spark of genuine sympathy into its song. *{You really don't have any idea what you're up against, do you?}*

The sound of a bell from the Fortune Tower interrupted them and Caizhiu lost sight of the fiery fleck that shimmied down her body. Then she glimpsed it crawl over her upper shoulders.

{I think you owe me an apology too, Caizhiu. Now that you realise how uncomfortable it is to be suspended by your tail, don't you think a bit of contrition on your part would not go amiss?}

{It's not the same. You have no muscles to bruise or nerves to trap. And, as I recall, you were about to eat my prey – I mean, my target. I couldn't let you do that.}

Brekranez gave a sullen chuckle as it gambolled between her useless wings. *{I was not going to eat the whole thing. It would not have killed the human to lose one finger, and it's not like you were going to eat him yourself.}*

{I am familiar with your hunger. You would not have been satisfied with a finger.} Caizhiu sighed. *{What do you want, Brekranez? Have you come to torment me, or are you merely here to rejoice at my demise?}*

{Rejoice?} It sauntered from between the blades of wing shoulders onto her neck. *{Do you imagine it pleases me to see you like this?}*

With some effort, she concentrated her rear eyes on it. She could discern the fire drake's thin body and the four claws that left scorching footprints on the skin between her scales.

{This is meant to be a warning to us, is it not? Well, the lesson is clear: this is what happens when you allow your food to become uppity. So, if you imagine I take pleasure in this affront, you are quite mistaken. I'm here at the behest of your little cervitaur friend.}

Caizhiu struggled against her restraints, and it sent a wave of lightning pulses through her. It took a moment for her to gather her thoughts enough to form a coherent soul song. *{What have you done with Heort?}*

{Calm yourself, sweetness. I've not harmed him. For once, he and I agree: this is not a worthy end for a dragon.}

The fire drake clambered over the iron-clad leather bond around her neck. She hadn't been sure why they'd fastened her to a pole in the square, but it made sense if they intended to behead her.

Brekranez stood on her crest and was close enough to her eyes that she could make out its grey body. The orange glow of its core that shone through the cracks as it walked along the ridge of her crest made the drake appear to twinkle. She could see its features and it met her gaze with its bottomless eyes. Brekranez ran its dazzling tongue over a grin so wide it was visible. *{I believe it's time to remind these creatures where they belong in the food chain. You know what I need to help you.}*

Her empty stomach lurched, and pain cut off her breath when she had instinctively meant to shake her head and angered her restraints. *{I can't. I gave my word to Sinuation.}*

{Look around you. Do you imagine the humans are doing this for a joke? They have it in mind to kill you and they have the means to do it.}

The square, bathed in the rose shimmer of the setting sun, was slowly filling with people. Guards politely directed them to keep their distance and give each other room. The whine of the apparatus chimed with a growing susurration of animated voices. The human aroma drifted over Caizhiu with the sea breeze. Had she not been starving, restrained, and about to die, it would have made for a pleasant evening.

{Caizhiu, please. One little flame is all I require. There is so much kindling it will be easy. I'll take care of the rest.}

{I won't break my word!}

The fire drake shook its head. *{Oh, Caizhiu, my dearest dragon. There was never anything to seek forgiveness for. These creatures are nothing. Most are neath as cattle.}*

Carefully, it made its way over her forehead and onto her face. For a moment it walked between her eyes, and she could no longer see it, only feel its threadlike trail of heat.

{Besides, if Sinuation desires your demise, what does it matter to keep your word?}

People parted to make way for someone. She wondered if the Burgomaster or Herp-Tura would appear, but it was the town guard with the distinct facial hair who emerged from the crowd. He no longer wore the insignia of the town guard, but his cape had the same clasps as the technologist's outfit. With theatrical flourish, he threw back the cape to reveal a short, rounded sword. Using both hands, he lifted the weapon over his head to elicit whoops from the crowd. The weight caused him to nearly drop the sword as he lowered it, the tip hitting the flagstones with more force than he'd intended. Caizhiu could hear a disappointed sigh from the tiny drake when the metal didn't spark. The guard hid his error by getting a whetstone from his pocket and demonstrably gliding it over the edge. It was purely to please the crowd, as the blade already sparkled with sharpness. Or perhaps he meant to intimidate her. Inquisitive youngsters mobbed him and ruined the menacing effect.

{Him?} Brekranez sounded appalled. *{You're going to let him end your life?}*

{I have no desire for you to witness my execution, Drake. Be away if its concept offends you.}

Brekranez reached the twin protrusions of the egg tooth on her muzzle. It seemed mere hours since she had used it to cut herself out of her cocoon. She could not have imagined then that this would be her last iteration, that death was so near. The drake snaked up the larger of the two mounts. Though a wisp of scorched horn reached her nostrils, at last its tiny claws no longer caused her skin to burn.

{Caizhiu, please!} Brekranez perched on the tooth and looked into her eyes. She had not thought its face to be capable of despair, but there it was. *{Damn your obstinacy. You're a dragon. Look at them! These neaths don't deserve your protection, and they certainly don't deserve your sacrifice.}*

The drake looked around at the humans with blazing hatred.

{Time for you to go,} Caizhiu sang with as much kindness as she could muster. She was grateful it had sought her out. Though it surprised her it had been her old enemy that had done so, it was still good to know that someone had tried to help. She drew in her breath and saw the excited glint in the fire drake's eyes. She was going to disappoint it.

{Try not to miss me too much.}

With one fork of her tongue, she flicked the minuscule creature off her nose. It tumbled through the air and, when it drifted over her one nostril, she closed the other and exhaled powerfully, hurling the drake up into the air currents. Heated by the crowd, they carried it away. In a little while there would be no reason for it to return.

FORTY-SEVEN

THE UNHAPPY HERO

Smooth as the silk of his shirt, the knife slid over Ozcahar's skin. He felt his throat push against the blade when he swallowed. The barber flicked foam from his fingers. He wrapped a warm towel around Ozcahar's cheeks and rubbed oils on his hands with total disregard for the impatient Sheriff in the corner.

"It no matter how pretty he look, if he miss this cursed show," Olyre snapped. "And if that happen, Lady Lendoline no just have his head and mine, Barber, but yours also."

"No be afraid, Sheriff. He be complete," the man said, slapping the oil on Ozcahar's cheeks. He winked at his subject and held up a mirror so Ozcahar could admire his handiwork. It was a relief not to have to contend with that itchy beard. He felt more like himself. The precise stripes of the moustache and the edging of his jawline looked different with his blond hair, but the style was clearly copied. More and more of the guards sported the 'Rogza-Riz look'.

Olyre handed him a jacket with the golden buttons and a pair of soft leather gloves to complete the fancy outfit the Burgomaster had given him. Ozcahar wasted little time getting dressed. The barber might not be intimidated by the Sheriff, but he was. He wanted to get this over with and leave town.

The Sheriff ushered him out of the building, where the street crowd cast him that reverent look Ozcahar was tiring of. He had thought that between Lady Lendoline, Rogza-Riz, and the factory gent, all eager to step into the hero role, they would leave him in peace. But as he followed Olyre into the throng, several people pulled on his jacket to speak to him. The Sheriff told them to scram.

Handras met them at the edge of the Stand square. It looked as if he, too, had donned his finest clothes. His regular clothing was sun-bleached, but this hip-length coat was a deep red. Though it was a little tight across the chest, he looked dapper in it. The top hat that went with the coat had at one point suffered a crushing incident, but he had bent it back into shape. Ozcahar would wager the man had not worn this outfit since his wedding day.

The Stand square had changed almost beyond recognition too. They'd cluttered the space between the spire of the tower and the wall with a collection of scaffolding, vats, and wires that ran along the wall and then tethered it.

Ozcahar gaped at the spectacle. When he noticed how the bottom of the tower was split open, his first thought was that the dragon had escaped. If it hadn't been for Handras' steadying hand, he would have fainted. But nobody was in a panic; on the contrary, the crowd seemed jubilant. Irrepressible entrepreneurs had set up stalls selling refreshments around the edge of the square. People drank and ate as they milled, chitchatting in their clipped dialect.

Olyre moved his shoulders back, and as he stepped onto the square, his back was so rigid Ozcahar thought the man might snap in half. In the shade of the town wall, they walked past three enormous copper vats containing, from their acrid smell, verve. They were raised at stepped levels along the wall. In sequence, a trio of men and women pulled ropes so each would tilt and pour the steaming green liquid from one to the other. This was the reason the town carriages hadn't ridden at night and Handras' wife had complained about the darkened streets. He wondered if there was any verve left in the town that was not in these vats.

Handras grabbed his arm and beamed him a smile. He couldn't hear what the man said over the drone of the open verve engines. Next to them, two coiled structures completed the hum that filled the square.

The trio made their way to the back of the Stand. Closer now, he could see that a crane, fixed to the wall, had got Caizhiu by the tail, and held him suspended in the air. The sight stopped Ozcahar in his tracks. He sniggered in disbelief and felt the blood return to his cheeks.

A dumpy woman with round spectacles that enlarged her eyes to bizarre proportions emerged from the steam at the base of the tower, giving orders to teams of people dressed in leather aprons. When she noticed the four men, she wiped her hands on her pantaloons and strode towards them. No, towards him.

"You be Osk-Har, man who catch dragon." She blushed as she struggled for the Trader words and genuflected. "I be Betni Foxtine. Honour to meet us. Come, come. I show you what I make for you."

The woman nearly bounced with enthusiasm and acted as though she wanted to impress him. At a pace he would not have thought her capable of, Betni led them through the melee of machinery and people, while shouting and gesturing instructions. Even Olyre struggled to keep up. The noise of the thumping engines was deafening.

As they walked into the clouds underneath the crane, Ozcahar stole a glance up at the dragon. He'd forgotten how large the monster was. In the tavern, Caizhiu had collapsed in a heap, but here he was stretched to his full length. If he got out...

Beneath the crane, Betni motioned at a modified catapult. Ozcahar remembered seeing such a thing in the museum in Thirdburg: a device used to protect the city in ancient times. Here, instead of a bucket, they had affixed a metal spike to the arm. It looked like it would be painful, but he didn't think it was substantial enough to kill the dragon. Betni caught his worried glance, and with her energetic movements, gestured to the wires that connected the large buzzing coils to the spike. She pointed at the lightning pack on a guard that patrolled the tower. Ozcahar nodded, though couldn't hear over the engine noise what she so passionately explained. He understood that the catapult's straining rope was ratcheted tight and that, at a single command, the contraption would skewer the creature and run the verve lightning through him. He had up close seen the effect one little lightning pack had on Caizhiu, but would this larger version be enough to kill the dragon?

As they walked away from the noise, he saw how his head was bound to a pole in front of the tower. Rogza-Riz stood next to it. The man had traded the guard's robes for employment in Herp-Tura's staff, and his one hand casually leant on a sword. Their eyes met. Rogza-Riz grinned and gave him an appreciative nod. Until that moment, Ozcahar hadn't dared to believe, but after tonight it would be over; he would be safe.

"That be where you stand with Lady Lendoline and Mr Sibrand," Betni said.

The podium they'd built to the side of the Stand had different levels; he presumed the highest would be for the Burgomaster. All levels would have a perfect view of the beheading. Sheriff Olyre and the guard had taken up position by the steps onto the podium in anticipation of the honoured guests. When Ozcahar glanced at Olyre's impassive face, he noticed it had a sheen as ashen as his moustache. He kept his eyes straight ahead, looking past the dragon.

Betni sighed wistfully and leant towards Ozcahar. "I be happy to get piece of scaly skin. It be much strong against reined lightning. Wager it have usefulness. Hope they no sell all to School of Pring."

Ozcahar chewed his lip. Should he too petition to have a keepsake? The thought of stripping a corpse, monster or not, was distasteful. But if anyone deserved something, it was him. If they were going to carve the thing up anyway, would it not be fair if he were to profit by it, rather than someone else?

Adjusting her spectacles, Betni nodded at the monster. "It watch you, Osk-Har."

Caizhiu's eyes were fixed on him as if nothing else existed, not the scaffolding, not the tower, not even the man with the sword, just him. Ozcahar straightened his shoulders and, before any of the others could stop him, he strode over to the dragon. In his haste, he bumped against one of the artists that were sketching the details of the hideous head. The easel wobbled, and the man grabbed his canvas. His collection of charcoal landed on the stones. The artist had adumbrated and embellished the scene, with a depiction of a burlier Rogza-Riz bringing down his sword on the writhing neck of the dragon. The sketcher looked up from retrieving the sticks of charcoal, but the fury in his eye softened when he saw who had knocked into him.

Rogza-Riz held up a warning hand, and Ozcahar stopped a safe distance away.

"This is not my fault," he hissed at the dragon, trying to morph the tremor in his voice into a laugh. "Your own hubris has brought you to this. I told you to leave me be."

There was no answer. The unfathomable black eyes bored into him. How certain was he that the dragon wouldn't shake off the shackles? He staggered backwards, but Rogza-Riz put his hand on his shoulder and his lips to Ozcahar's ear. "No have fear. I slay your dragon."

The muttering crowd parted to make way for Lady Lendoline and Herp-Tura. The Burgomaster's white dress left her shoulders uncovered, but a delicate lace scarf cascaded like a mist around her neck and arms. It was as if the steam clouds had formed her. Her gloves reached almost to her elbows. The tailored garment drew attention to her hips with a golden bow wrapped around her waist. She lifted the long dress to climb the steps of the podium. Right behind her followed the factory owner, overclothed in a tailored frock coat, and his wrinkled cheeks were flushed. Among his entourage, Ozcahar recognised Handras' daughter who waved at her father.

The briefest glance of Herp-Tura caused Betni to spring towards the control panel beneath the podium.

Rogza-Riz winked with a mischievous smile and side-nodded at Lendoline and Herp-Tura. "Be lucky, Osk-Har. Them two be more risky than any troll or dragon."

FORTY-EIGHT

DAY OF THE SIX

S hadows stretched across the square as the sun dipped below the town wall. When he'd first arrived, Basinwade had been brightly lit, but now the town's verve was used to restrain the dragon, and only the flickering of traditional torches lit the square. Lady Lendoline's voice had to carry even more power than before to be heard over the thumping engines. Ozcahar struggled to understand her Uayathi words. She mentioned "the people of Basinwade" a few times. Her cadence reminded him of Jorganyon, talking about how the days of monsters had to end. All the while, Caizhiu's stare unnerved him. The sooner that monster ended, the better.

Careful not to let the creaking of the wood interfere with the Burgomaster's speech, Handras' daughter climbed up the steps to the podium. She gave Ozcahar an apologetic smile as she reached over and lit a torch on the corner of his dais.

Lady Lendoline spread her arms to the crowd, Herp-Tura standing next to her. Leaning heavily on his cane, he showed the blistered palm of his hand to the crowd. According to the Burgomaster, the suffering the town had endured would end tonight. The people cheered.

With a start, he noticed that the dragon no longer held his eyes but looked at the torch by his side. Ozcahar let his eyes drift over the hundred flames that lined the square. When they had traversed the mountains, Caizhiu had not been keen on fire, had even kept the innkeepers from lighting theirs. Ozcahar wrinkled his nose at the sudden smell of rotten eggs. A vortex of comprehension caused his head to spin and his stomach to churn. The torch to his left bulged.

"Be you ready, brave Osk-Har Nitt?"

He gaped at the Burgomaster as if he'd only just remembered she was there. The woman gave the crowd a half-smile and raised her eyebrows. The people closest to the podium laughed at Ozcahar's confusion.

"I fear I speak too long for our foreign friend," Lendoline said in Trader, "and in a language he no know. Apologies to our guest from Aumegoa. Please, honour us by saying for us to start. We end the time of monsters now."

Herp-Tura laughed and cleared his throat. "The boy have no heart for it. I give start command."

Ozcahar grabbed the rail that lined the steps up to their higher platform, not knowing the words to tell them to extinguish the torches. With a loud crack, the torch to his side split and blazed. He ducked backwards in anticipation that the fire drake would leap for him. It didn't. Instead, leaving nothing of the torch but a shower of embers, it jumped to Hantine. Frozen in surprise, the girl didn't let go of her lighter but watched the cat-sized creature leap onto it. It swallowed the flames, regurgitated the fiery fuel over the girl's jacket, and wrapped itself around her arm. Hantine gave a high-pitched scream as her jacket sleeve disappeared in flames and ashen strips. The surrounding people backed away, but Handras rushed forward, snapping buttons off his red coat in his rush to remove it. He grabbed his daughter and wrapped the coat around her arm. Phalanges fell from the wrap onto the ground. Instinctively, Handras knelt to collect them, but then he noticed that his own shirt was on fire. He looked up at his daughter, but the burning girl was unrecognisable. Fabric and flesh were aflame, and the grey and orange beast shattered her skull between charcoal-black teeth. The drake stretched its jaws over the shoulders, growing as it lowered itself around the torso. Sparks from its voracious consumption caught bystanders, and batting at their clothes, they fell into each other in their desire to flee.

The platform shook, as did the rest of the square. Against the indigo sky, Ozcahar saw large hairy shapes climb over the town walls. One straightened up to its full height. The last rays of the sun glimmered off a curved blue sword. Sheriff Olyre pushed him aside as he ran up the platform steps and held out his hand to the bewildered Burgomaster. Herp-Tura reached him first and allowed the Sheriff to help him down, while Lendoline yelled instructions at the people below. The factory boss grabbed Ozcahar's shoulder and leant on it to steady himself, and when he pushed off him, Ozcahar could do little else but jump off the dais before he fell. He landed on a guard, bringing the man down with him. Ozcahar took the dagger from the man's belt and searched for his friend.

Handras pulled at a guard's lightning rod, held the guard by the back of the neck and forced her to walk forward. Holding the rod overhead, Handras rushed towards the fire drake, who stood up on its hind legs and spun round to embrace his attack. The lightning rod bore into its chest. Sparks and bolts forked over the elongated body, and then the creature's arms enveloped both Handras and the guard. They didn't struggle long. The green liquid in the lightning pack boiled, and when the glass cylinder exploded, a ball of flame engulfed the three of them. Only the drake emerged, swelling before the eyes of the terrified onlookers. It lit up the sky when, with one exhale, it set a path of people aflame all the way to the Stand.

Ozcahar stared at the restrained dragon. Though his arms trembled, Rogza-Riz still held the sword aloft. The light of the flames shimmered over the whetted blade. They had mere moments.

"Kill it!"

"I no can!" Rogza-Riz yelled and nodded at Betni, who stood motionless, as if she had been nailed to her controls. "Tell her; end lightning. I can strike then!"

Ozcahar fought through the panicked people. He pulled on Betni's sleeve to jerk her out of her stupefaction. She opened her mouth, but before she could speak, there was a crunching sound above them. Ozcahar hunkered to avoid the rain of splinters, wood chips, and planks. There was a wet noise as the body of the Sheriff hit the square. Something had cleaved him near in two, spilling his innards over the flagstones. Ozcahar looked up and saw a troll on top of the wall wielding a blue sword stained in scarlet.

He scanned the panel but couldn't read the marks next to the switches and dials.

"How end lightning?"

She shook her head and blinked tears from her eyes. "We must prove it work."

"No time!" he yelled at her. "Stop lightning, so sword can kill dragon."

Her eyes flitted over her beloved apparatus and Ozcahar saw the anticipation die in them as Betni realised she would never get to display its magnificence to Herp-Tura. Their hope rested on Rogza-Riz's sword. His arms trembled with the weight and sweat poured off his forehead. Regardless of the surrounding chaos, his eyes were fixed on the dragon. Betni flicked a switch on the controls.

"Rogza-Riz! Now!" Ozcahar screamed over the commotion, and the ex-guard let his arms drop. But, no longer bound by the lightning, Caizhiu pushed himself up and thwacked his wings against the inside of the tower. Rogza-Riz put every bit of strength behind the weight of the blade, but with astonishing speed the dragon twisted his neck and closed his jaws around Rogza-Riz's arms. The sword clanged on the stone, followed by the double splats of severed hands. The former guard tried to stagger back. One of his arms had gone, the other was trapped in the corner of the dragon's mouth. With a jerk of his head, Caizhiu tossed him into the air, flesh ripping over the fangs. The sinew in his elbow snapped, tearing Rogza-Riz free of his arm. A spray of blood trailed his flight. With nothing to break his landing, the man thudded onto the ground in front of Betni and Ozcahar. He wormed himself onto his knees to crawl away from the dragon, holding up his squirting stumps.

"My arms! It eat my arms!"

Ozcahar stared at the control panel. Which one had been the lever Betni had flicked to turn off the lightning? Which one did he have to switch to turn it back on? Would that be enough to stop the dragon? Ozcahar grabbed a handful of Betni's tightly wound hair.

"The reined lightning," he yelled in her ear, not realising he had reverted to Aumegoan. "How do I reactivate it?"

Her boot landed against his shin, and she fought herself free from his grip to find refuge within the frame of the podium. With trembling hands, he randomly moved switches, levers, and dials. Nothing he did immobilised the dragon. Caizhiu bucked and kicked as he held Ozcahar's gaze, desperate to get to him. One of his wings had escaped the tower and flapped, fanning the fires.

The fire drake had grown to the same size as the dragon, consuming humans and stalls alike. With gusto, it threw itself into the closest verve vat. Blazing orange bathed the square as a fireball rose into the night sky like a second sun. A rain of flames engulfed the wooden structures of the catapult and the Stand. The engines grouched as if pained when the flames stole their fuel and evaporated their lubrication. The restraining rope of the catapult caught fire, snapped, and the arm shot up. Where the intended assembly had kept the dragon stretched tight to ensure the metal spike would impale him, in his efforts to escape, Caizhiu had pulled the arm of the crane down. The area of the arm above the spike took the brunt of the impact as it clanged against the crumpling crane, sending tremors through it, and pushing the structure through the wooden cladding of the tower. The iron mesh inside bent. But the dragon had not escaped yet and, though at a fraction of the original force, the lightning spike hit his backside, eliciting a howl of pain. When the catapult slammed into both creature and crane, it propelled them forward. At last, the strained metal of the crane buckled.

Momentum flung Caizhiu towards him. The wires yanked the tip of the spike out of the dragon and the creature crashed onto the remnants of the podium over his head. Ozcahar crawled to escape the rain of planks and poles. He risked a backwards glance. In an attempt to right himself, Caizhiu writhed on top of the collapsing podium, the barbed tail whipped through the air. The part of the crane still attached to the tip smashed into the wall, scattering chips of stone all around. One of the trolls was knocked backwards off the wall.

He saw Betni scamper to get out of the trap that had formed around her, but the dragon too spotted the movement and tried to get his head through the wooden mesh. Ozcahar averted his gaze, unwilling to witness what would happen next, and hid behind the controls. The wall was to his back, and both sides were blocked by the dragon and the fire drake that frolicked in the verve. His only way of escape was through the remnants of the Stand.

The ground shook when three trolls landed between him and the tower. Before they could turn and see him, he ran towards them, dodging the hairy knees, clubs, and blades. How he wished he could slash their tendons, but it would take too long. He couldn't believe his luck when a guard saw him and charged the trolls. She was a tall woman, though dwarfed by the monsters, and she still carried her lightning pack. Holding the rod like a rapier and with frantic fury, she rammed it into the crotch of one of the trolls. The creature gave a honking shriek and jumped into his comrades. The three toppled into a jumble as they tried to evade the guard's repeated jabs of reined lightning. Ozcahar didn't get the chance to admire the woman's tenacity as a flailing troll foot hit him in the back and sent him flying. He landed hard, but then quickly rolled out of the way. He picked up his dagger and fled into the Stand.

Upon entering, he noticed others had the same notion. A guardsman, flintlock drawn, huddled against a woman with a little boy clinging to her skirt. Above them, two girls in matching festive dresses hunched on the remnants of the staircase. The woman beckoned him to come closer, hoping that if they kept quiet, they might hide until this attack was over. But Ozcahar had no intention of getting trapped in here. He would take his chances with the crowd, try to get to the relative safety of the alleyways. He edged towards the exit on the other side.

The square was a tableau of pandemonium. People clambered over each other to get out of reach of the fire drake. A troll held a woman by the legs and used her to swat other people as they ran for their lives. It took Ozcahar a moment to realise that her red outfit had once been blazing white.

The fire drake grabbed the last of the vats of verve and glugged the contents down its throat. The creature was so large it could, without having to stretch, snatch people off the town wall. Drinking the verve fuel caused it to grow larger still. It belched and regurgitated part of the verve in a spray of vomit that set aflame half of the fleeing people and several trolls. Its reach was such that even buildings at the square's edge caught fire. The drake roared and Ozcahar could have sworn it sounded like laughter. He could scarcely believe this was the same being as the dog-sized menace of the mountains. Was this why Caizhiu had been so keen to avoid it? He glanced back at the other opening in the tower. A troll's heel crushed the skull of the fallen guardswoman. He couldn't see the dragon, but Caizhiu wouldn't have gone far.

He had to get out. Sweat stung his eyes, and he wiped his gloved hand over his face before he pressed himself against the wall and peered around the corner over the square. The drake turned towards him, and he'd jumped back from the opening before realising his mistake; it had only looked in his general direction. If he'd held his nerve, he might have gone unnoticed, but now the blazing blue eyes focused on the gap in the Stand. On him.

The drake crouched and slithered along the cracking flagstones towards the tower. Ozcahar ran to the people on the stairs. The girls burst into tears and the guard called him a Six-cursed fool.

"Why you bring them here, Aumegoan? Bringer of monsters, of death!"

Slipping and tripping in their haste, they hoisted themselves up the steps. The drake was too large to get in here, Ozcahar told himself. *Please, let it be too large to get in here.* A jet of glowing cinders washed across the floor. Flames licked up the wooden struts of the tower, and the whole thing shuddered when the creature reached through the opening with one of its smouldering arms. Birds, fishes, and dancers of red and blue showered them. As they ran up the spiral of the Stand, Ozcahar glimpsed black teeth and the splintering of the planks that lined the tower. His thigh muscles cramped with the hurried climb. Smoke stung his eyes and his lungs. Ozcahar stopped for the briefest moment to orientate himself. The Stand was toppling. If they could get high enough, if they were lucky enough, they might get over the wall. If... if... if... They might land on the rocks, or they might land in the sea – either way, it would be better than to end up between the drake's jaws.

Smoke seeped from the planks of the outer layer next to him as they blackened and splintered. The drake's fang, almost the length of his arm, pierced the metal mesh inside. Ozcahar crouched as best he could while still climbing, scrambling to avoid the flaming saliva that set fire to the steps below. He pushed his shoulder against the backside of whoever it was above him to urge them to move faster. A sudden rush of fresh air told him the guard had opened the door to the viewing platform. There was an animalistic scream from above, followed by a violent shudder and the crunching sound of splintering wood. Someone stood on his head, pressing his face into the top step, and causing his feet to slip. He felt the heat on his legs. Suddenly, the weight on his head was gone. He hoisted himself up by the barren doorframe, clung to it so he wouldn't slide down the leaning platform. The door had gone and so had the entire top of the spire. From the tilt of the tower, he guessed it was mere moments from tipping over. Below him, the guard and the two girls were crouched against the remnants of metal mesh and shattered planks. The guard struggled to get to his feet. The woman and the little boy weren't on the viewing platform. He hoped they had fallen, but he knew they hadn't. Clamped onto the doorpost as if it were the last solid part of the world, Ozcahar followed the direction in which the guard pointed his pistol, and he watched the head of the fire drake rise beside the tower. The orange tongue flicked around the enormous jaws.

Almost gently, the drake reached over and picked the guard off the platform. It seemed to delight in letting the man sizzle before biting down. Ozcahar felt the heat on his face and smelled the roasting flesh. The creature played with the corpse on its tongue before swallowing. Ozcahar struggled to keep his balance, but holding on to the doorpost with one hand, he drew the dagger out of his pocket with the other. The weapon seemed comically small, but he braced himself anyway. For a terrifying eternity, the blue that was the drake's eye held Ozcahar's gaze, and then it winked.

The creature moved past him. It licked up the younger of the two girls by rolling her in its tongue and, as an afterthought, took the elder between the tip of its jaws. As it bent forward to do so, it bumped the tower, and the structure tilted away from the wall. The dress of the girl who squirmed and screamed between its jaws ignited. Out of options, Ozcahar ran towards the smirking monster that stood between him and the town wall. The floor moved away from his feet, and he jumped onto the balustrade of the viewing platform, launching himself at the drake. Instinctively, it ducked. Ozcahar ran over the snout, his soles sliding while he tried to keep enough speed to jump from the creature to the wall. Charred bones snapped between the jaws. Before he could jump onto the wall, the drake dipped its head, causing Ozcahar to fall on his back and slide down the long snout. Smoke billowed from his jacket, and he struggled to breathe in the scorching air. Plunging the dagger into the grey skin, he pulled himself into a sitting position. The hand around the glowing dagger registered the pain first. His glove blackened and shrivelled in the heat, and, in a reflex, he pulled the blade out of the drake. The skin on his backside and inner thighs reddened, blistered, and split. He caught a whiff of singed hair and screamed as the grilling rose up his body. He didn't know which way to move to escape the pain. His stomach lurched when the drake lowered its head to the ground. For a moment, he thought he might jump to safety, but the drake flicked up its snout. Speed pressed Ozcahar into the coal-hot scales, and then he was airborne. He caught a glimpse of the starry sky, the waning sliver of the moon reflecting in a churning sea, and the burning town below. The cool, fresh air was a relief. Then he reached the apex of his flight and grabbed at the air, though he knew there was nothing to catch himself on. He closed his eyes, desperate not to know if he was about to land between the onyx black teeth or if he would plunge straight into the fire pit of the drake's stomach.

Part VI

Forty-Nine

Flight

Caizhiu shook the giddiness from her head. Her crest had taken the brunt of the impact with the wall, but it still resonated through her skull. There was a liquid sensation to her insides, a weakness to her limbs, and her scales flickered, confused about which colour to adopt to conceal herself. She righted herself on the trembling mass of wood of the platform and gasped when a ring of agony spread from her cloaca down her legs and tail and up her back. Below her, amidst the struts and beams of the platform, she noticed a flurry of motion and the delicious aroma of fear. Crawling on hands and knees, the technologist, who had taken such an interest in causing her pain, tried to escape the structure. Caizhiu reached through the web of wood. The woman turned onto her back, her face greying with terror as she watched the dragon's jaws snap overhead. Caizhiu's neck was still attached to the ropes of the infernal machinery and the mesh of beams and struts prevented her from clamping her jaws around the woman's head. She tried to dig through the structure to reach its architect. Betni emptied her bowels, and she raised her arm in a pitiful defence. Caizhiu growled when the technologist whimpered a string of prayers. Did she not regard it even the tiniest bit false to beg for the protection of the very Keepers she had so publicly defied? Caizhiu's talons sliced through the woman's arm. However, when she tried to get a good hold, she hesitated. She might think Betni hypocritical for petitioning the Six for salvation, but she herself had barely got out of the Stand alive. Should she really squander the second chance the Six had given her on this worthless human? Could she afford to fail them? She left the technologist to her prayers and looked around for Ozcahar.

The smoke-filled air was thick with the scents of terror, trezzohl, and the nauseating mixture of sulphur and hot verve. Her eyes flitted over the bodies strewn between her and the Stand. She searched for his unique scent. Was she already too late? Shakily, she clambered from the podium and circled a couple of trezzohl that were pulverising the broken body of a guard, while a third rolled on the ground with his enormous hands clasped around his genitals. Suppressing her creeping dread, she approached the entrance of her former prison. The elation she felt at finding Ozcahar's scent distracted her, and she only just avoided a stream of cinders Brekranez blew through the tower. She watched the drake sidle up to it, hungrily snapping off the wooden planks. It crackled with delight at the chase. There was little chance of reasoning with Brekranez mid feeding frenzy, but she had to try.

{The human is mine.}

Brekranez lodged its teeth into the tower to exhale a hot breath that ignited it below the humans within. {I would have shared him with you, but you didn't want to.}

It reached up and snapped the spire off the top, sending a shower of sparks into the night sky.

{Feast on the others if you must, Brekranez. There's a stringy one named Herp-Tura to which you are most welcome. But this one is mine.}

The fire drake flung two humans into its mouth and licked its chops. Caizhiu felt sick at the thought her life might have been spared in vain.

{Not if I catch him first, sweet dragon. I'll race you for him.}

She was not too late yet. Despite her backside pain and shaky legs, she tried to leap onto the town wall, but tripped over the wires tangled around her neck. Brekranez chuckled as she hurriedly clawed at them, struggling to pull them over her crest. She snapped the belt from around her neck, freed herself from the wires, and looked up at the drake, who winked at her.

{You should be glad that I will free you from this obligation. I'm sure your pitiful little Magistrates will understand. If not, I can always pay them a visit.}

It was impossible to tell neath apart when they screamed the way they did when subjected to torture, stripped of their culture, their language, their humanity. But Caizhiu jolted when the scent of roasted meat carried the flavours of her quarry.

{Want to say farewell to your morsel?} Brekranez lowered its head. Teasingly, it balanced her human on its muzzle, as if inviting her to grab him. Before she could, it threw its head up and flicked Ozcahar into the air.

Caizhiu propelled herself along the stones of the town wall, beating her stiff wings with every leap. She lifted off the ground, but it was not like leaping into the wind. With no time to find a path in the currents, she struggled up, battling gravity with every beat of her wings. She gasped through the smoke, suppressing her instinct to cough, and dodged the remains of the Stand that crashed to the ground. The drake batted a lazy claw at her, causing her to bank towards the town. Hot air currents boosted her rise. At last, she found a rhythm and climbed the sky with sturdy beats – but Ozcahar fell too fast. Brekranez's enormous jaws opened and surrounded them. She hooked the talons of one claw into her human's leg, the other through his jacket. The drake's teeth ran scorched trails along her body, but with a forceful beat, she slipped past the corner of its mouth, escaping the closing jaws. Brekranez swirled round and jumped onto the wall in pursuit. Its tail whipped across the square, scorching human and trezzohl alike, and she felt its fiery breath on her back.

{Never doubted you could do it, earnest little dragon. Come back and we can have some fun. I promise, I'll let you keep your human.}

Caizhiu panted as she forced her wings to stretch out and soared past the rocks. The air was as choppy as the water that crashed against the shore. Every beat of her wings caused an ache through her shoulders, every breath angered the burns along her sides, but she fought her way up. The water rushed by beneath them, churning with youthful naiads that darted past the harbour's edge, pulling down humans trying to escape to sea. Brekranez jumped after her, but it was too large to let the winds carry it. It wasn't foolish enough to try its luck over the expanse of water. Laughing, it returned to the town.

Away from the inferno, the night seemed as black as ink. Only the sloshing of the water told the dragon where the sky ended and the sea began. Ozcahar weighed noticeably more than Heort and he didn't have the sense to keep still. He flailed and kicked, forcing her to swerve to compensate. Pain exploded in her left front paw, disrupting the rhythm of her wings. She plummeted, tasted the salt in the air, and struggled to climb back up. A stinging in her paw overshadowed the ache in her shoulders and she smelled blood – dragon's blood. She let go of the human's jacket to shake the pain from her paw. Ozcahar wailed and pulled at the talons buried in his thigh. He twisted to pull himself up and, unable to reach her proper, stuck the tip of a dagger in her nail bed.

If she dropped him, she'd lose him in the roiling sea. Did he want to end up as naiad food? She attempted to grab his jacket, but he flailed his arms and cut her with the blade. Once more, she had the stomach-churning sensation of plummeting towards the waves. She envisioned one of the larger naiad snatching them straight out of her flight, and she redoubled her efforts, but her struggle left her breathless. If she didn't find somewhere to set down, both of them would end up in the water. And with the trail of blood they left, she doubted the naiad would care enough to distinguish between dragon and human.

The darkness hid everything. How close was she to the land? How wide was this damnable bay? Panting, she let the air flow over her tongue, tasting it for the scent of sand. Cool air stung her lungs almost as much as the heat had, but among the smell of salt and seaweed, she found the dust and rock she was searching for. She heard the sloshing of waves against rocks and banked to the left in a surge of panic that she might be about to crash into the cliffs of the peninsula. Ozcahar yelped with the change of direction and for a moment ceased his efforts to get free. Caizhiu blinked repeatedly, trying to find enough moonlight to espy the cliff's surface. She could see the blackness of the land against the star-speckled sky but couldn't make out how far below them it was. She couldn't deposit her captive and crash as she had with Heort. He might land on the sand, but she could just as easily break him on the jagged rocks.

As low as she dared, with her nostrils filled with the scent of dust and rock, Caizhiu slowed her flight. She felt gravity's pull. As she began her descent, she pressed her squirming captive against her chest, firmly enough so he couldn't stab her too severely. She turned onto her back, curled herself around the human, and folded her wings around them. Stones scattered, and the rocks scraped her back as she rolled and tumbled along the ground. She reached out with a claw to halt herself and lost hold of Ozcahar. At last, she was free to use all four claws to slow herself and she skidded to a halt. The cloud of dust caused her to sneeze, and she sent pebbles flying. Taut muscles spasmed throughout her body, either from the flight, the landing, or the repeated assaults with the lightning rods. Dawn was still hours away, but by the flickering of Basinwade, their surroundings brightened to a dull orange grey. Even from this distance, the fire was awesome; the sight of its destructiveness robbed Caizhiu of breath. She forced herself to look away.

She'd landed on a ridge that cut deep into the cliff. The layer of shale gathered in the shallow bowl between the edge and the cliff had softened her landing slightly. Ripples of a nauseating ache throbbed within her abdomen as if someone were kneading her insides. She hoped she wasn't seriously injured, that there was nothing that wouldn't heal on its own, given time. If she kept her breaths shallow, at least she could lessen the scorching along her sides from the drake's teeth. She licked the pinprick wounds in her paw. They were shallow but painfully positioned in the sensitive flesh between her toes and the nail bed around her talon. She longed for something to eat. At that thought, the aroma of sweat, blood, and fear landed on her tongue and her stomach demanded to be filled.

Ozcahar stood, more or less, leaning on a boulder. She could hear his rapid heartbeat, his ragged breath, and how he held it to catch the pain of his next movement. For an instant, the ridge was lit up and she saw him as clearly as if it had been daylight. On the other side of the bay, diminished by distance, the town erupted as flames caught hold of the wooden houses and whatever verve people had squirrelled away.

Ozcahar squinted to make her out against the darkness. When the light faded, Caizhiu crept towards him. At every crunching step he adjusted the pointing of the dagger. Hunger keened her senses. She heard his attempts to swallow and his stifled groans. Closer she crept, approaching her prey in a lazy zigzag. Her footfall confused his sense of direction, and as panic took hold, his pointing of the weapon became erratic. Luxuriating in instinct, she let a prolonged growl rumble through her throat. Until her escape from Basinwade, she had never eaten human flesh. But now she knew how good they tasted, and what they were capable of – what Ozcahar was capable of. She wanted to sink her teeth into his flesh, tear the bones from his body, and lick his blood from her chops; she wanted to make him pay. Run, she thought and shook her head. If he ran, then what?

He staggered backwards, dragging his right leg. Caizhiu hooked the flat of her caudal blade behind his good leg. He tripped and before he could scamper into the shadows, she reached out a cautious claw. She caught more trouser than leg and she dragged him towards her. He rolled onto his back and waved the dagger blindly. She was as unimpressed by his screaming as she had been by Eimsiff's hollering. Irritating, not intimidating.

She clamped her jaws around his hand and squeezed his wrist between her teeth until he let go of the dagger. It didn't drop from his opened fingers. When she dislodged it with her tongue, part of his skin came with it. She trapped his hand under a claw and spat the weapon into the sea. Disappointed, she realised it was not skin that had stuck between her teeth, but the remnant of a leather glove. Still, it was marinated in his blood, and she swallowed it.

Hearing Ozcahar rootle in the gravel, she placed her claw over his other hand to prevent him throwing dirt into her eyes. She held his arms pinned and for a moment he lay still, then his heels scraped through the shale as he struggled to get free. Using her muzzle, she pressed his legs down so he couldn't kick her. Where she had pierced his leg during their flight, delicious blood had drenched his pantaloons. Her stomach gurgled and twisted, and she ran the forks of her tongue round his knee and over the inside of his thigh. Would she not be able to take one little bite? Scraping her teeth over his pelvis, she felt the pulsing of the arteries beneath, and she pressed her fangs against the softness of his abdomen. She curled her tongue over the burns on the back of his legs and buttocks, his flavour eliciting a rush of saliva that she quickly gulped back. Could she take off one of his legs, or maybe just half of one? Had Heort been here, he could have instructed her how to dismember her prey without killing him. Then again, he'd probably tell her not to.

"C-Caizhiu?"

Unsure how good Ozcahar's eyesight was, she hovered her muzzle close to his face. He shivered when a strand of saliva dropped onto his cheek. She licked it off, but that prompted a strangled yelp. He wriggled to move his head out of the way and then lay motionless. Opening an eye and swallowing a sob, he asked: "D-does your w-word still stand?"

She snarled, but he was right. Caizhiu the Wayward had given him her word she wouldn't hurt him. No matter how hungry she was, she had to give up on the idea of eating even the smallest part of him. She shook her head to blow his delicious aroma from her nostrils. Ozcahar misinterpreted her gesture, and blinking back tears, he inhaled sharply. He clenched his fists, bracing himself.

Caizhiu sighed and found another scent in the mix that was her prey, something she'd be able to concentrate on to take her mind off food for a time. She nuzzled his chest in search of it and let her tongue glide over his jacket. Wrapping one fork around a gold button, she ripped it off. Sucking on the sweet flavour calmed her. She was still starving, but the pangs lessened. She let go of Ozcahar's arms and took a step back.

Warily, as if waiting to see whether the dragon was toying with him, he rolled onto his side. He tried to move away, but she stretched out her wing and scooped the crouched man into the membrane. She folded her tail around her wing and rested her head on it, close enough to feel any escape the human might be foolish enough to attempt, but not so close she might accidentally eat him in her sleep. As her scales adopted the shading of the surrounding boulders, she placed the gold button in front of her nose so the scent would escort her into restful dreams.

FIFTY

Nowhere Left to Run

The pain was so intense Ozcahar thought perhaps the dragon had eaten him after all, swallowed him whole and was slowly digesting him. He tried to move, but he was squeezed too tight, which increased his terror. Then he heard the growling of Caizhiu's stomach and reassured himself that if it was rumbling, he couldn't be in it. What squeezed him like too-tight bed linen was the dragon's wing. As if in response to his futile fidgeting, the creature stirred. Ozcahar braced for a fall, but as the dragon unfurled his wing, he slid down smoothly until his feet touched the ground. The sudden brightness made his eyes water, and he squinted at his surroundings.

At first, he assumed the blackness that cleft the blue sky was storm clouds, but then the realisation struck him: it was a column of smoke still billowing from Basinwade. The image of Handras consumed by flames forced its way into his mind, as did the scent of roasting human flesh and the face of a girl turning to ash. Had he seen that, or was he imagining it? The tremor in his knees spread to the rest of his body. He doubled over and spat out a mouthful of bile. Propping himself up on a rock, he sank to his knees, angering his blistered and burnt skin. A wound on his thigh began to weep.

"This was not my fault!"

There was no response from the dragon, and he wasn't sure if he'd expected one. He repeated himself, but neither affirmation nor denial was forthcoming. It was the dragon who caused what had happened to Basinwade. Why should *he* feel guilt when it was Caizhiu who should have let him be? Through clenched teeth, Ozcahar muttered a string of expletives and forced himself to stand. He turned round and found himself alone. The fury evaporated on his lips. Overhead, only seagulls shrieked their mocking calls. He blinked in disbelief. How was it possible he had not noticed the dragon taking off?

"Caizhiu?"

All he could see were the grey cliffs, the shaley ground of the ridge, and the blue of the ocean beyond. Even without his injuries, climbing the towering cliffs would have been difficult. Jagged rocks led to the sea, and the thought of clambering over them and then swimming to freedom was laughable. No wonder the dragon had risked leaving him here. He had nowhere to run, even if he could. And if he couldn't find shade, the sun would finish him. Caizhiu's promise not to harm him would be worthless if the dragon left him here.

As he limped along the cliff face, he couldn't suppress cries of pain with every step. He hobbled to a shallow nook in the cliff, where, until the sun moved, the overhang would offer him some respite. Leaning on the rocks, he let his hand glide round to his backside, his fingertips finding the frayed remnants of the seat of his pants. So much for the most expensive suit he'd ever owned, the hole extended from his buttocks to the inside of his knees. Wincing at the anticipation of his own touch, he explored the landscape of sores and blisters on his intimate areas. He tore strips of charred fabric from the ooze of popped blisters and dried wounds. It made little difference whether he pulled quick or slow; it was as if he were flaying himself. His curses resounded against the tall cliffs, but the only response was the laughing of the gulls.

Ozcahar wiped moisture from his eyes and pretended it was dust. The fingers of his right hand rested in a claw-like position. He tried to straighten them, but the pain was sickening. As he struggled to unbutton his jacket one-handed, a thread snapped, and the button dropped between the rocks at his feet. He groaned. The ground was a long way down. Frustrated at his clumsiness, he tore the remaining two buttons off and pocketed them. Leaning the wrist of his bad hand on a boulder, he bent his knees. The back of them stung grievously, causing his eyes to well up. As he reached for the coin-sized button amid the shale, the white-green dropping of a seagull splattered onto it. Well, at least it had missed his head. Ozcahar wiped the button on his sleeve and put it in his jacket pocket. Taking a moment to catch his breath before attempting to stand up, he noticed a silver-winged gull trailing a black-headed one. The smaller bird held a fish the pursuer wanted, and the pair swooped along to the cliff face, banking this way and that in their energetic chase. Under the blazing sun, the landscape seemed to blur and distort, and then the rock face shifted. Two grey talons landed in front of him, and he stared up at the dragon. He had crushed one gull between his jaws, and the other shrieked and flapped as it tried to free its broken wing. The dragon gulped down the first bird, fish and all, and swung the second round so it too landed to be despatched between the sharp teeth.

Caizhiu looked down at him with black, impenetrable eyes and ran his tongue over his fangs. A shiver ran down Ozcahar's spine when a feather landed on his hair.

"That... that was a neat trick. Invisible dragon... While we speak of tricks, I don't suppose you..." He waved at his own face. "That you'd care to become human again, would you?"

He pushed himself up and let out his breath in brief spurts to catch the pain. When he'd recovered, he took off his jacket and placed it over a boulder. It was mostly intact, though slightly blackened on the back, and it had several new vents where talons had slashed the fabric. With his eyes locked on Caizhiu, he fumbled to undo his waistcoat. His painful ineptitude seemed to amuse Caizhiu, and Ozcahar had the eerie thought that, to a hungry dragon, he might look like a chicken plucking itself.

"Won't you do me the favour of looking human, or is it beyond you?" He wound the sleeves of his shirt around his waist. It wasn't great covering, but better than limping around with a bare bottom. He put the waistcoat back on, leaving it hanging open to avoid messing with the buttons, and swung the jacket over his shoulders. Humiliation made him reckless. "You think my predicament is funny, Caizhiu?"

The dragon stood up and Ozcahar regretted the tone he'd used. He held out his hands, partially in defence, partially as a wordless plea. With his forked tongue, Caizhiu grabbed hold of Ozcahar's good hand. It was the only part of him that was undamaged and cold sweat pricked in his armpits. He waited for the jaws to close on his wrist, for the teeth to cut through tendons and bones, but that moment didn't come. Instead, the dragon pulled on his arm and turned him round. He complied, but exaggerated his limping in the hope it might elicit a smidgen of sympathy. Did dragons feel sympathy?

When he was facing the right direction, the dragon let go of his hand and prodded his back with his muzzle. After only two shuffling steps, Ozcahar had to stop. The air reeked of the burning town across the bay, and with every gasp for breath, his queasiness increased. Caizhiu growled a warning, and with gritted teeth and closed eyes, Ozcahar stumbled forward. He howled when a glop of dried blood and exudate split, leaving his skin ragged. The dragon's breath dried up the perspiration in his neck as he was nudged to walk on.

"I... I can't," he whimpered. "Eat me if you must... I... can't..."

The dragon's teeth scraped over his back, scrunching and puncturing both jacket and waistcoat but leaving his skin unharmed. With a jerk of his head, Caizhiu hoisted him into the air and swung him onto his back. Landing hard on his stomach left Ozcahar winded. When the haze cleared, he saw the wings fold over him. The shade was welcome at first, but the sun was relentless and soon it felt as if he was trapped in an oven. As the dragon began his hobbling trek towards the coastline, Ozcahar had to hold on to the ridges to prevent himself sliding from side to side, or even down the tail.

FIFTY-ONE

THE DEPOSED QUEEN

Caizhiu could just espy the dust that rose in the heat over the Ostroize plains. That's where they should be: on the other side of the Telereni sound. She should have fled south from Basinwade. However, she had been disoriented and had needed the body of water to prevent Brekranez giving chase. How different it had been not that long ago when she had soared from the commonry, so confident in her wings she had teased Heort with their prowess. Yet, the time when she had really needed them... In her struggle to stay aflight, she had followed the winds and now she found herself on the Mospium peninsula. The coast looked near, but at the same time impossibly far away.

The seagulls had been a welcome snack, but her legs still felt wobbly. A pulling sensation that radiated down her back legs and tail threatened to unbalance her. Her wings were folded in an uncomfortable position to keep the wriggly human in place. She tried to ignore his delicious aroma, but he moved continuously, sliding his hands and feet over her scales to reposition himself. With his every movement, word, and whimper, her hunger intensified.

{Caizhiu the Wayward, Esteemed Dragon. I was informed it was you, but I was unwilling to believe that song.}

The soul song held her pinned to the rocks with its melodious beauty. Soothing, the voice carried the temptation to sink into it. Legend had it that the naiad song could be so powerful even neath could sense it. But Caizhiu had never witnessed that herself.

{I guess the naiad should thank you for what you did with the human scourge, though I'm surprised it was you who did it.}

Caizhiu recognised the singer and smiled warily, letting her attention glide to the shadows in the deep that writhed and swirled. One broke free and drifted past her, at a considerable distance, to stay in the deeper waters. It should not have surprised her that, like she herself, Oohnbrraayahee had grown since they had last met.

After a moment to gather herself, Caizhiu jumped onto a stack of rock a little further out, teetering on the precipice of the undersea cliff. It was near enough that she didn't need an extra push of her wings and she could keep her human secure on her back. She reminded herself that the rock structure had stood for centuries and would not likely crumble beneath her. But fortuity had not been on her side for some time, and she felt a rush of relief when the rock stayed solid beneath her.

{Oohnbrraayahee, Esteemed Ruler of the naiad people and the Telereni waves. It has been too long since we met. What is it of which you speak?}

She watched the naiad emerge from the shadows of the deep, rising straight up from the below. She took a few steps back and pressed her human beneath her wings so she couldn't accidentally drop him with the flash of awe that would follow. Oohnbrraayahee might have grown old, but she had lost none of her vivacity. When she breached, she burst from the waves in an explosion of droplets that soaked Caizhiu and her charge. It was water dragged up from the deep, and even to the dragon, its coolness brought a welcome relief.

As she sank back into the water, the naiad folded her arms and rested her elbows on the rock. With a broad cone-toothy grin, she blew a geyser of spray from the blowhole on her head.

Caizhiu could scarcely believe the enormous being was the same young woman who'd taken charge of the Telereni naiad many years ago.

With one hand under her chin, Oohnbrraayahee cocked her head. She leant forward and moved an apple-sized eye so close Caizhiu could have touched it. *{You have grown slender, Caizhiu. It saddens me to say you have looked better.}*

The human's fidgeting made Caizhiu adjust her wings to keep him from sliding off. She growled to tell him to keep still. Oohnbrraayahee folded her ear fins back and beat her tail onto the water. The sign of irritation reminded Caizhiu how short the naiad queen's temper had been. She hoped it had mellowed with age.

{You seem to have picked up a parasite. Would you like me to rid you of it?}

Oohnbrraayahee let her cool hand glide over Caizhiu's wings, squeezing the outline of her human.

{If he were merely a pest, kind Oohnbrraayahee, I would not be hungering today. Unfortunately, he is my charge. I aim to take him to the human city of Aerahan. The Magistrate is the only one who can rid me of him.}

Oohnbrraayahee glanced over her shoulder in the direction of the far-off city.

{All respect to Sinuation, Caizhiu, but that is a long trek for you, and I heard your flight across the bay was, shall we say, inelegant. You were fortunate the older among us know better than to skirmish with a dragon or you might have found yourself in deeper trouble still.}

Caizhiu wished she could deny that, but if she were honest, she was still surprised she had made it to dry land. There had been several moments when she'd expected both she and the human would plunge into the sea. Sheer obstinacy had got her across. She wasn't sure if she could do it again, especially because the sound between the peninsula and the mainland was wider further south. She dismissed walking all the way around over land. It would mean passing Basinwade, as well as many other human towns and villages. Every dwelling would provide Ozcahar with a chance of escape. Her body ached at the mere thought of taking human form. Would she have the energy to maintain it? But flying across the sound with the squirming human seemed just as unlikely.

{I'd appreciate it if you wouldn't take him from me should I drop him during the flight.}

Oohnbrraayahee laughed and licked her lips. *{Very well, if you wish, I will not touch him. But I am no longer in a position to speak for the naiad.}*

{You were deposed?}

Oohnbrraayahee looked in good health. Her skin had greyed somewhat but was still distinctly blue. It was tight and as sandpaper rough as it had been when she was a young woman. Her breasts had shrunk since she no longer had calves to nurse, but she was strong. Had Caizhiu not known her age, she would not have questioned that Oohnbrraayahee was in the prime of her life.

The naiad shrugged. *{It happens. If Sinuation wills it, one of my daughters or granddaughters will rule the Telereni one day.}*

She let herself dip to cool off before rising to Caizhiu's eye level again. *{Besides, I doubt even Anreeyani could control each naiad, just as even the mightiest of Magistrates cannot control all the humans. She couldn't guarantee one of our youths would not take the opportunity to drag a human to the Telereni depths.}*

Caizhiu shivered with discomfort. She had known blood would attract the naiad. Instinct was instinct. But did naiad kill humans just for the joy of killing them? Caizhiu thought those days had ended with Oohnbrraayahee's ascension.

{Anreeyani allows senseless killings of otherkin?}

Oohnbrraayahee let her eyes drift over Caizhiu's wings for a moment and gave her a queer look.

{Otherkin? I'll concede the Magistrates may be so, but the rest... Daily, humans kill naiad senselessly, without a word or care.} There was a coldness

to her song, and all her cheeriness had evaporated. *{With their powder sticks and nets. They act as if there are not enough fish in the Telereni for all. And these past years not even the winds or lack thereof contain them.}*

Caizhiu thought about the ship Myrta's sister had taken them on. A few years ago, most of the ships on the Wexede would have had sails. *Wexede Wanderer* had not. She ran on her bhodine carapaces and a boost of verve when needed. It had been the same for the ships in the Basinwade harbour. It made no difference from which direction the winds came. Humans could now sail at almost any time. Caizhiu tried to banish the scent of the green liquid from her memory. She must have leaked her emotions, because Oohnbrraayahee arced back in bafflement, pushing herself away from the rock.

{They... hurt you. That is why your flight was so broken. How dare they skirmish a dragon? No wonder they burn. May Sinuation's Keepers burn them all!}

{The will of the Six is a matter for the Magistrates. That is why I have to deliver this human to Aerahan.}

Oohnbrraayahee let herself sink into the water. For a moment she vanished into the deep, but then she returned to the rock. She didn't hoist herself up though, merely squirted water from her blowhole and looked at Caizhiu from the breaking waves.

{You will have my aid if I can give it, Caizhiu, but I fear you and your charge are bound for trouble before Sinuation is done with you.}

Caizhiu laughed but couldn't make it sound as confident as she wanted. Oohnbrraayahee had always been proud that she drifted with what she called the Currents of Sinuation. She had led her people because she believed it was commanded of her. Now she relinquished power without rancour for the same reason. She had never felt Caizhiu's need to carve out a fate. Caizhiu couldn't feel as scornful about that as she had in the past.

Large as she was, the naiad disappeared in seconds beneath the waves as if she had never been there and Caizhiu hopped back to the rocks along the coast. She followed the raggedness of the cliff to climb up diagonally along ridges and rocks. It took hours before she reached the top, and looking around the arid landscape, she concluded that their situation was far from good. The naiad queen had been right; it was a long slow road from here to Aerahan. But knowing it was bad did not change the situation. To ensure he was still conscious, she squeezed her wings and got a groan from the human. A scent urged her forward, traces of it running beneath her feet, through the rock. She walked with her nose to the ground until she found the stream. It was a pitiful tributary of the Penbo river. This far south, most of the river was below ground. They were lucky to find water at all.

She slid Ozcahar onto the ground. He landed on his stomach and raised his head groggily. It took him a while to push himself onto his elbows. Pressing his face against the hot rocks, he stretched his lips into the gully to slurp the gritty water. Either he had not seen the large pool up ahead or he was too weakened to crawl that far. Watching him struggle for a while, Caizhiu shook her head and picked him up by his jacket. The freshwater pool was too shallow to hide anything dangerous, so she dropped her human in. Deep enough to cool him, but not enough to drown him. Instantaneously revived, he splashed his way to the surface and stood up. His expression and vocalisations were a confusion of relief and pain. Caizhiu scooped up mouthfuls of water. It had been heated by the blazing sun and she found it much improved with the taste of him. She wondered if this was how humans had invented their soups.

They were well past midday, and, once she'd drunk her fill, she lay down to rest and watched Ozcahar drag himself out of the pool. He draped himself over the rocks. The sight of his pained movements caused her stomach to twist in frustration. Take a bite, it seemed to urge. He's as good as dead anyway. Just as she had doubted Brekranez could have restrained itself to only take one finger, she wasn't sure if she'd be able to stop at an arm or a leg. He tasted too good, and she was so hungry. She bit on the gold button to stretch it over and around one of her fangs. The dulcet metal ring eased the hunger pangs, but only somewhat, and it wouldn't last. It wasn't sustenance. She had to eat something substantial soon or by the end of tomorrow, she would be too weak to hunt. And then they would both perish.

FIFTY-TWO

RUKH BAIT

"Caizhiu?" Her human bleated in a quivering voice. "Are you doing that invisibility thing?"

As soon as he thought he might be alone in this unfamiliar landscape, Ozcahar's heart rate had shot up. When night fell, he cowered against a rock by the pool. The longer she kept her hidden vigil, the more jittery he became. He scrunched the damp fabric of his jacket in his good hand and bit slivers off his chapped lower lip.

"You hear me, Caizhiu? I'm going to escape."

He didn't. He couldn't. He could barely walk. Initially, Caizhiu had wished the human would put some effort into quelling his fear, but now she enjoyed his anxiety, the scent, the hammering of his heart, and his suppliant cries. And if she thought him an easy meal, perhaps something else would as well.

She let the night air wash over her, with all its scents and sounds. She felt the tremors of a steady stream of small critters seeking the solace of the night as they visited the watering hole. When one was large enough for Ozcahar to notice, he hunkered against his rock. Though he believed himself to be imperceptible, he was a focal point of activity in the darkness. Next to him, it was easy to mask her own presence.

The whooshing of feathered wings startled her, and she pressed her chest against the solid rock to quell the sound of her own heartbeat as the scavenger approached. If what her ears and nose told her was right, this would mean more opposition than she had hoped for. Incarceration had weakened her. Too weak to chronochi, she'd been slow when she had taken the gulls. One of the birds had almost got away. She had hoped her wounded human might attract a carrion eater, such as a giant rock spider or a pack of bone eaters, but with the approach of a whip-tailed rukh, she looked forward to a larger meal – if she was fast enough.

Cautiously, the bird settled on a stump of a dead tree on the other side of the pool. Despite the low light, Caizhiu could see it silhouetted against the indigo of the sky. It was an adult female, easily the size of her human. The rukh shook her head and opened her serrated bill to taste the air. Though most of the creature was shrouded in glistening feathers, the head, including the bill, was covered in triangular scales, as were the legs and the tail that snaked below the perch. She struck with the speed of a whip and lassoed a Mospium rock rat that had lingered too long at the water's edge. The rat shrieked, but the rukh pulled the animal back so quickly it snapped the brittle neck. Dropping the carcass, she hopped from the tree stump. The rat disappeared whole down her long neck.

The rukh sniffed at the water and drank a few gulps, probably tasting the injured human just as Caizhiu had. Her beady eyes blinked with wary interest as she swayed left to right, trying to locate him. She flew over the watering hole and, after landing, kept her wings spread to intimidate prey and rivals.

She was so close, but Caizhiu waited.

The rukh clattered her beak to ward off challengers. She took a few hops towards Ozcahar. He had shut his eyes, but could still hear the creature approach, and cowered behind his rock. And Caizhiu waited.

The rukh lashed her tail at her meal to determine how dead it was. Ozcahar howled and grabbed his buttocks. It unbalanced him. He fell away from the rock, and as he saw the rukh loom over him, he tried to scramble away. The creature wrapped her tail around his ankle and dragged him back.

"Caizhiu!"

She waited.

Frustrated, the rukh hopped around Ozcahar and clattered her beak. It was meant to make him flee, drive him over a cliff. But, of course, he didn't run. He curled into a ball, and the bird lashed at his back and legs. Ozcahar whimpered and wailed depending on where her tail struck. The air filled with the scent of blood and the rukh risked a jump on her human's back.

"Get off!" He tried to twist from under her claws, but the bird was heavy. She clattered her beak and reached down to tear off some meat. Her human screamed. Caizhiu let out all of her energy and rushed forward. It wasn't chronochi'ed, but the rukh was unprepared. Caizhiu clamped her jaws around the long neck and crushed it. The bird reflexively gouged at her, and Caizhiu tore off the bird's talon. She landed on one of her front legs as she held the rukh with the other and snapped the head from the body. Elation at the kill made her feel giddy, like strong wine. She heard a muffled yelp and looked down. Her human was curled up beneath her and the rukh's head had landed on his. With the rukh's carcass in her claws, Caizhiu laid down next to Ozcahar. She indulged herself and licked his bloodied backside as he crawled for cover. He tasted better, but she would make do with the rukh. She crunched the ribcage and dragged the lungs out through the throat hole.

She was so famished that she polished the creature off before the night had even reached its midpoint. After a little rest and with a satisfied sigh, she picked up the rukh's head and swallowed it whole. She licked the remnants of carnage off her chest and claws and stood up.

As Caizhiu folded herself into her human form, her insides wrung and churned in protest. Her body shook with the pain, and she had to lean against a boulder to keep upright. For a moment, she doubted she'd be able to finish, but she persevered and, to ease the pain, took a few deep breaths, at least as deep as her restricted lungs would allow. Her skin refused to cooperate. She'd have to live with showing scales. Because she couldn't bear to lift it, her tail dragged behind her, making it impossible for her to pass off her stumbling as nonchalance while she walked to Ozcahar. Every step of her bipedal gait was agony. She stooped to her human, but the movement was more painful than she'd anticipated.

"Are you hurt?" Ozcahar sat on his knees by the edge of the pool. He'd spent a long time washing the rukh's blood off, and he stared up at her with a ghostly pale expression.

She spat out the ringed button. "What do you care?"

He shuffled away from the pile of feathers and bones and the pack of bone eaters that slithered closer to look for a meal. "My survival depends on you."

"It would have been wise to think of that before you tried to have me killed."

"That may well be so, but you look hurt." He shifted his gaze away from her. "Are you injured?"

"Let's say that neither one of us will be sitting comfortably in the near future." Her lips curved into a crooked smirk. "But it'll be nearly a year before I need to lay my eggs. If fortune wills it, I'll be recovered by then."

"Wait... are you a... wo... ehrm... a she-dragon?"

Rolling her eyes, Caizhiu lifted him by his collar and placed him on his feet. "I'm a dragon."

She took his good hand and placed the button in his palm. He fingered the mangled object to figure out what it was.

"I'm no thief," she said. "I only needed to borrow it. To keep from eating you."

Ozcahar gave a tinny laugh that died in the night. "You're not joking."

"No."

He held out his hand. "Take it. It's a gift."

"That is most kind of you, Ozcahar Nitt. I'd almost forget that because of you, my entire hoard is a molten puddle in Basinwade."

He rummaged around in his pockets. "I... I have more."

"No need for you to be concerned." Caizhiu placed a hand on his shoulder. "Now that I've eaten, you're as safe as you are going to be."

FIFTY-THREE

THE ROCK SPIDER

The dragon had returned to her true form and deposited him between her wings before ambling through the night. Ozcahar couldn't see anything, but from the difficulty he had staying in place, he guessed the terrain was rough. Once the sun had risen over the horizon, Caizhiu stood on her hind legs and shrugged so that he lost his grip and slid down her back and tail. He landed on his stomach in a narrow and shaded gully. Moving as slowly as he could, he pressed his arms against the rocky walls to get up. His scabbed skin pulled as if there wasn't enough of it, but he managed to get onto his knees. When he looked up at Caizhiu, he only caught her fleeting shadow as she took flight. The sudden loneliness was crushing.

Though it wasn't deep, he couldn't hope to climb out of the gully. The walls seemed to close around him, and he told himself Caizhiu was probably nearby, hiding until some monstrosity would wander by to eat him. He studied his surroundings to see if anything looked out of place. Every rugged stone shape looming over him looked like all the others. If one were actually part of a dragon, he could not tell. Sagging against the rock, he resigned himself to waiting for her reappearance. He might as well save his strength, whatever was left of it. After a final wary glance round, he shut his eyes and tried to sleep.

A pitter-pattering guided him from dreams of rain back to consciousness. Hunger's nausea clashed with the conquering heat of the sun. Again he heard the pattering echo through the gully. As he inched forward towards the darker corner of the crevice to escape the heat, a cluster of eyes lit up before him. He wanted to hurl himself back, but his stiff limbs wouldn't obey. A cat-sized spider jumped into the light. It was as beige as the stones, and it raised its first pair of legs towards his face.

Ozcahar's scabs split, and he fell over his feet in his hasty retreat. There was nowhere to go in the narrow gully. Despite the pain shooting up his inner thighs, he kicked at the spider. It scuttled back, pattering its legs on the stones. It ran along the wall towards him with its fangs poised to strike, but Ozcahar was ready for it and smashed a rock onto the front part of the body – once, twice. He panted as he hit it a third time. The sky darkened and dust swirled up around him. He folded his arms over his head to brace himself for whatever death was coming. Something sharp, a fang or claw, he couldn't tell, scraped at the back of his neck, hooked his collar, and hauled him up.

The dragon dangled him from her wing claw, and he grinned with relief. It was not something he'd expected to feel at seeing the hideous head. But his grin melted when Caizhiu lifted him to her mouth. Dagger teeth filled his vision as she pressed her mouth against his. Locked in a lipless kiss, he was about to object when water flowed from between the teeth. It was the first fresh water since the pool, so he drank as much as he could.

Once it was spent, Caizhiu set him on the ground. The squidgy noise of her contracting muscles and shifting organs made him feel faint. It was as if his own bones ached at the mere thought of the distortion he witnessed. He winced at the snapping sound when her snout crumpled into a face.

"It's surprisingly hard to carry water without lips," she mused, and peered into the gully where the spider twitched. "Well, look at that. Not bad, little human. You've caught your dinner."

She took her tail in hand and used it as a living line to fish the spider from the crevice. The creature's legs helped by wrapping around her barbs, and Ozcahar grimaced. "It's still alive."

"It's fresh." She raised an eyebrow ridge at him and broke the creature in two. "It's safe for you to eat. At least, the humans of the Ucral desert manage it. You'll have to eat it quickly though, before it goes off."

She tore off a leg and demonstrated pulling out the snotty white meat. As she handed him the spider in manageable pieces, he thought of the roof runners in Thirdburg - similar sized creatures that he used to hunt when he was a kid. One hot season there had been an explosion in their numbers, and because Jorganyon had convinced some of his wealthy friends in the higher echelons that the creatures stole pets, Ozcahar had collected considerable coin per carcass that year. But he'd never contemplated eating one. Wincing, he put his tongue against a severed leg.

"You've smashed a couple of the eyes." Caizhiu pried the others out and rolled the squishy balls into his palm. "These are intact, though. They contain fluid. Eat."

Ozcahar hesitated only a moment before popping one into his mouth. The sourness caused his face to scrunch up and made it hard to swallow. He downed the other four without popping them. As long as he gave no thought to what he was eating, just kept putting stuff in his mouth, he could pretend it was food.

"No chance of a tavern around here, is there?" He dropped the empty spider carcass in the gully, wiped his chin on his sleeve, and squinted at the surrounding wasteland. As far as he could see were rocks and sand. The rare trees appeared burnt and shimmered in the heat. There was no sign of greenery or water, no sign of civilisation.

"Sadly not." Caizhiu stepped away from the gully's edge. "Considering how slowly we can travel, we're at least a week from any human towns, northways. So we head south... That's where the peninsula breaks up into the Fire Isles."

It didn't sound like a place he wanted to end up. "Good name to put humans off travelling there."

"The isles are the home of the fire drakes."

"There's m-more than one of those things?" His voice shrank with every word, as if it wanted to crawl back in his throat.

"Of course there are." She lifted him by his armpits, carried him to lower ground, and set him down in the shade of a large outcrop. "Most are content to stay in their volcanos. Only a few are parasites, following dragons around for their fire. If you thought Brekranez was frightening in the town, you should see its kind in their natural environment where there is nothing to limit their fire. Perhaps you'll consider this if you feel the urge to wander off."

Once they'd left Basinwade, he had assumed he'd escaped. But he had thought that before when the troll hunters had killed Lord Dolt. And the trolls had found him. He had neutralised Caizhiu at the Silver Rose Inn... and she had caught up with him. A whole town had tried to slay the dragon, and she had escaped. What if the drake too would find him again? No matter how much he wanted to stand tall, Ozcahar slunk against Caizhiu, and his stomach turned. Her smirk vanished. She clamped her hand over his mouth, forcing his head up so he couldn't double over.

"Swallow," she said. "I put considerable effort into bringing you that water. Don't you dare spill it."

He swallowed the spider meat again. To banish the memory of Brekranez, he forced a couple of deep breaths past her fingers. When the urge to vomit had receded, the dragon let him go.

"Why are you taking me there?" Despite clearing his throat, his voice was shaky. "I thought you wanted to take me to, what's it called, Arhan?"

"We don't need to go as far south as the Fire Isles. The city of Aerahan is around that headland." She pointed at the blurred horizon, seeing something he couldn't. "If fortune be with us, we'll make it to a village called Udivoli by next dawn's break. Then we can cross the sound."

"A human village?" Ozcahar couldn't believe anyone lived in this unforgiving landscape. "How can they survive?"

"Like I said, most fire drakes have little interest in human affairs. But after Basinwade... who knows? You have placed us in a difficult position. But that is our concern for nightfall. We'll use the day to rest."

Ozcahar shuffled to the darkest corner of the overhang. Was it true what Caizhiu had said, that he was the cause of all this? He laid on his side on the bumpy rocks. The shade was mildly easier to bear, but the day was still baking hot, and his burns throbbed. He moved to ease the discomfort, but it only became more painful. Several times he closed his eyes, only for them to snap open to check Caizhiu was still there. Lady Lendoline had been right; he was at the mercy of a monster.

Caizhiu, standing at the edge of the shade, looked more human than she had the night before. Her tail lay on the ground, and she held a steadying hand against the overhang, but her healing seemed to advance faster than his.

"Don't you feel the heat?"

"I do, but it is easier for me to cope with... as long as I'm not reduced to this shape." She stretched her arms and widened the cloak to turn it into wings.

"Wait! Can't you stay human a while longer?"

"Why?" Her surprised tone turned into a low growl. "Is my true form that offensive to you? In Basinwade, you seemed keen to force me into it... or was that only because you'd considered me trapped? Something monstrous to gawk at, but not so pleasing up close."

"It's just..." Ozcahar hesitated, not wanting to say the wrong thing, and asked: "Would you talk to me?"

"What do you mean?"

"I can't sleep." He stiffened when she walked over, and he pressed himself into the crevice when she squatted next to him. That movement still seemed to cause her discomfort.

"Why not?" She looked genuinely mystified. Perhaps dragons didn't suffer from insomnia. Did they even sleep?

He turned his face away from her. With his forehead to the ground, he mumbled so softly he wasn't sure she would hear him: "Because I'm in pain and... I'm scared."

"No need to be scared." Her sausage-like thumb traced the rim of his ear. "I won't let anything else eat you. I'll get you to Aerahan. You won't be fed to a fire drake unless it's the will of the Magistrate."

"Is... is... is that what they'll do to me?"

He pushed himself up onto his elbows, but she held him down. "I'm not a Magistrate. Based on how much of a nuisance you've been to me, I guess you're in a lot of trouble..." She let it hang before adding, "Not to mention what you've done in Thirdburg. If I were you, I'd start to do exactly what the bounty hunter bringing you in says. Go to sleep."

"Caizhiu?"

"Yes."

"Please don't let them... send me to the Fire Isles."

"Of course." Her fingers combed through his hair, over the nape of his neck, and ran along his collar. "That wouldn't be fair at all. If it's your fate to be executed, I'll ask Lord Zesen to give you to me. I deserve a decent meal."

"Is that what passes for humour among dragons?" He forced a feeble laugh at her cruel joke. "Which part of me would you eat first?"

"Your tongue," she said without hesitation. "And I never jest with food. Go to sleep."

He tried to ignore that she licked her fingertips, and he closed his eyes. How had he ended up here? How had he gone from innocently cheating rich uppers to being wanted for murdering a Keeper? Without meaning to, he'd committed a crime worse than any other. Jorganyon had tried to save him as he always had, had got him out of the city. But this time, it had been for nothing. He was caught and the Magistrate, after Basinwade, would not likely be lenient. Would they punish him for the death of Lord Dolt too?

"Caizhiu... Did you never... do... something bad, without meaning to... and then you couldn't... undo it?"

He heard the dragon straighten up. Grains of rock and dust rained on him from the force she pushed herself back from the overhang. Any friendliness he'd imagined was gone when she growled: "Be silent, or I'll remove your tongue right now."

The sudden shift in her mood caught him by surprise and he glanced up at her through his eyelashes. Caizhiu extended her cloak into her wings, and her back elongated. Her eyes repositioned themselves and when they fixed on him, his hope vanished. He could expect as little pity from her as he could from the Magistrate. Just as Jorganyon had said. No matter how impossible it seemed, he had to escape, or his end would be a grim one.

FIFTY-FOUR

UDIVOLI

U divoli looked deserted. Still, Caizhiu adopted her human form long
before they reached the houses scattered in the greenery along
a creek. It made her feel uneasy to rely on Ozcahar's honesty that her
appearance was passable. Both walked with careful regard of their injuries,
and they progressed slower than Caizhiu had wished. It was well into the
morning and her human was suffering in the heat. They were so close,
though. She didn't want to waste time on rest.

The dilapidated buildings had rusted rooftops and blackened wooden
walls. Ozcahar pointed his thumb at articles of clothing hung from a rope
tied between a hovel and a nearby tree.

"You think thievery will warm these people to our welfare?" she asked.

"Well, looking like a vagrant will not." Ozcahar tried to free his collar
from her grip. "And we will be gone before they'd notice a missing pair of
trousers. Trueso?"

She snickered and kept walking. Her human would have to make do
with his singed and tattered rags.

It did not take long before they reached the village centre and found a collection of the elderly and children sitting beneath a roof over the communal well, giggling as they worked. As one, they looked up from their netting to gape at the appearance of two strangers. A woman puffed as she put down the net and stood up. She took a moment to adjust the headdress to shade her face before stepping into the sunlight.

"You be unexpected." She waddled towards them and kept a distance she considered safe. "And you be small welcome."

Caizhiu noticed that two of her fellow netters had taken rifles off their backs. One was as wrinkled as the woman, the other looked younger but balanced awkwardly on a pristine pegleg.

Caizhiu held out her hands. "It no be intent to cause fear or harm."

There was little point in speaking to this woman in her native tongue. These people never saw faces they didn't recognise. And if she spoke broken Trader, the villagers might speak freely to each other in Uayathi.

The woman's dark eyes flitted to Ozcahar, and the lines on her forehead deepened. Caizhiu saw the recognition strike her face. "You be he from Basinwade. You be the Aumegoan." The last word she pronounced as if it were bile filling her mouth.

The gunmen flanked her, pointing their rifles at the strangers' heads. Ozcahar looked from the barrel to the old woman and gave a single nod. "He be me."

"We live between the palms of water and fire," the woman hissed at Caizhiu. "Why bring you him here, to us? Have you no mercy?"

"I give apologies." The dragon rubbed her thumb over her chins and gave the woman a sideways nod. "But I be choice-poor."

Caizhiu had given no thought to the impact of their presence in the tiny village until the woman had pointed it out. Now her imagination filled with images of their demise. Many people had perished in Basinwade, and though she found it hard to feel sympathy for them, these people had done nothing to deserve such a fate, yet.

"How do they know of me?" Ozcahar asked from the corner of his mouth.

"Rumours run faster than the tide. And they could hardly miss the enormous cloud of smoke arising from what used to be Basinwade."

"Trueso," she said to the woman. "He be the Aumegoan, and I deliver him to the Magistrate at Aerahan."

"Choice-poor maybe, but why you spread your misfortune? Aerahan be long way across sea, and we no require share of your choices."

Caizhiu bowed her head to acknowledge the fault was hers, but then she said: "If you give passage, we quick be gone. If not, we be trapped. Here."

The man with the pegleg bared his broken teeth and bumped the barrel of his rifle against Ozcahar's forehead.

"No be trapped if he be dead." He looked at the old woman for endorsement.

Though sweat pearled on his hairline, Ozcahar didn't flinch.

Caizhiu placed her fingertip over the barrel and guided it away from her human. "His fate be for Aerahan's Magistrate. Or be there no obedience to laws of the Six in Udivoli, like they no obey in Basinwade?"

"Threaten you us?" The woman's eyes widened, and with a jerk of her head, she got the men to lower the rifles.

"No, but I request aid."

The woman considered it for a moment. She spat at Ozcahar's feet and raised a knobbly finger at Caizhiu. "We aid. But people no die for the Aumegoan. If monsters desire him, we give him."

"That be fair."

Ozcahar glanced at her but said nothing.

"Be hasteful. Take the Aumegoan to where he no can be seen." The older woman chin-nodded at her henchmen and the elder of the two hung his rifle over his shoulder. The man grabbed Ozcahar's arm, while the other kept his rifle aimed at his head. A fresh flavour of nervousness infused his aroma and Caizhiu placed a proprietary hand on his shoulder. She followed the three men away from the square. Behind her she heard one of the children whisper to his companions: "Is that Caizhiu the Wayward? He's just a fat man. Doesn't look much like a dragon to me."

It was followed by the sound of a clip round the ears. It would seem that Ozcahar had been truthful when he'd said she looked human enough.

***

Caizhiu watched Pegleg fiddle with the lock and chain to open the door of the ramshackle lock-up. She watched him touch the metal, depress the handle to open the door, and still the thought of going inside caused her to pause. It was just a shed, she told herself. Was this sense of enclosure what Heort felt whenever he entered a human dwelling?

The air in the little room full of fishers' equipment was stifling. Fish overpowered a lot of smells. Was she certain there was no trap here? The building was rickety, and she'd half-expected Ozcahar to have made a run for it, but it seemed the Udivolians had had similar thoughts. Humans didn't underestimate each other the way she had.

"I see they've made a neat bundle of you," she said and gently prodded her human with her foot. His wrists and ankles were bound together behind him, so that he struggled to get up onto his knees.

"Come on, *Celerity* has docked, and her captain has agreed to provide us with passage." She tucked Ozcahar under her arm and stood up. His clothes and hair were drenched in fragrant sweat.

"Aren't you going to untie me?" Hung upside down, he fidgeted to right himself.

"I see no reason to." She exited the little shed, felt the immediate relief at the peach-coloured sky and the evening breeze, and walked towards the small quay.

Most fishing vessels were too feeble to be acceptable to Caizhiu. *Celerity* was twice the size of *Wexede Wanderer*. She had a round bow and relatively high stern. Likely, it was the flagship of the Udivoli fishing fleet. She was equipped only with masts and sails – no chance of reined lightning. The lack of engine would also make *Celerity*'s passing quiet. Caizhiu reckoned it was this ship or no ship.

She stepped onto the gangplank, which creaked under her weight, eliciting a falsetto intake of breath from her human.

"Wait, wait! Set me down! I mean, on land. Please, please, please, if you untie me, I'll be quiet. I mean, I'll come quietly."

Their escort, who was about to follow her onto the gangplank, thought better of it and took a few steps back. Caizhiu felt the wood bend beneath her feet.

"How about you being quiet now?" she grumbled. "Besides, I remember someone stabbing me so he'd be dropped in the sea."

It was only three paces to the deck, and the plank seemed sturdy. The wood groaned, and the ropes squeaked, as did Ozcahar. "But, but, but I wasn't hogtied then. Please. I can't swim like this."

"That should put us on an even footing," she said as the plank bowed beneath them. *Celerity* tilted towards the quay. "I can't swim like this either."

He was right. Caizhiu didn't want to consider the consequences if the plank gave way, if the ship proved less sturdy than she seemed, if the crossing turned out to be more eventful than she hoped. There were a lot of ifs to her plan. The Six had better watch over their journey.

Ignoring the creaking of the plank, the squirming of her human, and the expressions of alarm of the crew of *Celerity*, she warily walked over the wood and onto the deck. The captain frowned as the ship dipped beneath her. She couldn't blame the man for regretting he'd agreed to take her across the sound.

"I be Grastell." He was younger than she'd expected, tall and lean, with a full but trimmed beard. There was tension in his movements, fear reined in by determination and courage. She would have to make a point of finding recompense for him and the people of Udivoli, especially since she'd forced them into aiding her.

Grastell nodded in the direction of the man with the pegleg, who had untied the gangplank from the ship and tossed it to a comrade on the quay, and a woman who walked up from the stern. "They be Mortynn and Vroza, my crew."

"Two only?" Caizhiu asked and wished she hadn't.

"They volunteer. We no lose more hands than we require, if the Six so decide." The captain rubbed his beard. "I require at least two crew and I think you no have sailing skills. Trueso?"

Caizhiu grimaced an apology, but Ozcahar perked up.

"Zail?" He mispronounced the word he'd picked up on. "I go-by-boat before. I be zailor before."

"If you no be quiet, we bind your tongue." Grastell raised his hand as if he was going to strike him, but the backhanded slap didn't materialise. Instead, the captain clicked his fingers at Mortynn and continued in Uayathi: "The sun has set. Let's get this fool's errand over with."

Mortynn hobbled over and tapped his wooden leg against Ozcahar. "Do we sling him in a fish hold, Captain?"

Grastell sucked air through his teeth. "Nah, we'd better keep him on hand in case we need to ditch him smartly. Tuck him beneath the nets. That should hide his scent as well. Keepers willing, *Celerity* will sail us smoothly across the sound."

Caizhiu offered to help carry Ozcahar, but Grastell looked up at her. "Best you stay in ship's centre, so you no cause unbalance. If you no be help, keep out of crew way."

While the two men dragged her human to the side of the ship and wedged him between the balled-up netting and the gunnel, she moved carefully over the ship towards Vroza to ask her where the best place was for her to sit during the voyage. The woman wiped greasy hair from her forehead and hinted that Caizhiu should follow her towards the stern. A port wine stain reached from under her right eyebrow to her upper lip. Her lidded eyes observed Caizhiu for a moment. "Trueso you be dragon?"

Caizhiu gave a sideways nod.

"Can you..." Vroza searched for the right word to use. "Change into dragon? Maybe dragon dissuade attack, make other Fabled think twice?"

Caizhiu would have loved to ease out of the painful restriction of her human form. "Your captain require me out of your way. That be difficult in my dragon form."

Vroza shrugged.

Caizhiu tried to get comfortable sitting against the mizzenmast and listened to the muffled voices of the crew, the wind through the rigging, and the sloshing of the water around the hull. The crew worked quietly and quickly. *Celerity* left the harbour and raised her sails. Caizhiu moved only to avoid the crew. Her body ached and wanted to unfurl, but she managed to keep it composed. Her injuries made it hard to maintain her concentration, and it took a lot of energy to stay human. After a full day of it, she was exhausted. She knew how lucky she had been that *Celerity* had returned to Udivoli when she did. Despite herself, Caizhiu drew the triangular symbol of reverence to the Six with her finger on the deck.

The night was eerily peaceful. Without the light of the moon, the inky blackness of sea and sky was interrupted only by the pinpricks of stars. Further from shore, the waves swelled, causing a slow roll to the ship's movements as she cut through the water. It felt wrong, after Basinwade, for such serenity to exist, as if the night were mocking her. She relaxed and her colouring blended with the night and the ship. Though she was tired, she couldn't allow herself to sleep. She forced her skin to return to the human pigment and took a long blink. Thankfully, at that moment, she caught a whisper from the bow, a hushed voice speaking simple Trader in a heavy Aumegoan accent.

"Why have you angry with me?"

Caizhiu glanced over her shoulder to see who Ozcahar was talking to. She guessed it was Mortynn as the shadow that stood closest to the netting that hid the captive had a pegleg. She sat back, entertained by her human's prattling. It didn't seem so annoying when it wasn't directed at her.

"I no-harm you."

Mortynn ignored him and kept his eyes on the horizon.

"It no be me you need fear," Ozcahar insisted. "It be them."

At last, Mortynn scoffed. "Become quiet, or I quiet you. I live in Udivoli more than thirty year, we never have Basinwade problems. Basinwade also never have problem, before you."

"How you lose leg?"

Caizhiu could smell Mortynn's mood stiffen.

"I be careless."

"Be that what you be told; Six took your leg because you no have carefulness? Be that truth?"

Mortynn didn't answer. Caizhiu heard him take a few steps away from Ozcahar as his discomfort grew.

"If there no be monsters..." Ozcahar's whispers insisted, "you still have leg?"

Creepingly, it dawned on Caizhiu that Mortynn's silence might mean the guess had been correct. If it had been a simple accident, the fisher would have said so. Her human had an uncanny ability to weasel his way into a mind. He'd tried to get under her scales on the peninsula. For the briefest moments she had pitied his fear. It had reminded her of how it had felt when Ingrirath held her, spoke to her, the one time she had felt true terror. And then he'd asked her about irreversible misdeeds. How had he known about the fire she had ignited in the Keeltois? Even Heort didn't know. Ozcahar might be soulless, but perhaps he was Talented in a different way.

"I see your hurts and understand you have fear. See my hurts, trueso I have fear also. But I no be your foe."

"Become quiet!" Mortynn growled from the corner of his mouth.

Caizhiu scratched behind the skin flap she'd shaped like a human ear and wondered what she could do about Ozcahar; if she needed to do anything at all. She wouldn't have cared about his inane jabbering if it hadn't been for what had happened in Basinwade. Could he do it here?

Celerity's waterline was much lower than on the *Wexede Wanderer*. Caizhiu wouldn't be able to simply give him a quick dunk to keep him in check. Worse, she thought that might make his point. She wondered if she had made a mistake in the way she had treated Wylthren.

"Monsters keep us in fear." Ozcahar's voice didn't sound fearful. He sounded conciliatory. "But this be human world. We ought have no need for fear."

Mortynn walked over to the nets. He crouched next to Ozcahar. Caizhiu watched his movements intently, wondering if he'd make her human be quiet.

"Please, friend," Ozcahar pleaded. "I know you no can release me, but… loosen my bonds. Just a bit, so if I be thrown to sea, I have chance of life."

Caizhiu got to her feet, and that caught Grastell's attention. The captain shouted at her, but she hadn't yet moved from her spot when the bow of *Celerity* veered to the right. The sails flapped as they suddenly weren't set to catch the wind. Caizhiu held onto the mast, though the jerk of the ship hadn't been strong enough to unbalance her. She had a sense of something gigantic moving beneath the ship.

FIFTY-FIVE

ANREEYANI OF THE TELERENI NAIAD

A chorus of sustained low grunts pervaded the night. The surface rippled and broke with the rapid lunges of three naiad. They were young, barely two humans long, and vanished as quickly as they'd appeared.

Mortynn reached for the flintlock rifles hung by the mainmast, but Grastell whistled to him and yelled: "We're not here for a fight."

Mortynn reluctantly withdrew his hand from the rifle.

"They're just youngsters." Caizhiu wasn't sure if Grastell meant to reassure the crew or himself. "They might upturn a skiff, but we'll be fine on *Celerity*."

"I think Mortynn is more troubled by thoughts of their bigger brothers," Vroza said while she secured the line. "It wasn't those three that knocked the ship off her course."

"All the more sensible not to get into a fight, wouldn't you say? Let's not give them a reason to attack us." He paused and stared out over the ocean. "All the same, better get our cargo ready in case we need to ditch it."

With hurried movements, Mortynn and Vroza moved the netting to drag Ozcahar away from the gunnel. Grastell had been wise to hide him among the scent of fish. Though she'd been aware of him, it was only now they dragged him across the deck that his full aroma hit her, a scent beacon on the wind. Her human struggled to escape his restraints, but only made things worse with his futile efforts. The sailors dumped him onto the deck, and he rolled onto his side to look up at them. "Release me. I be useful. Please, no throw me into sea."

Vroza bent down and squeezed his throat. She reinforced her threat with a sharp blade against his jaw. "Become quiet or I throw you over now. We no die for you!"

Caizhiu cursed inwardly but couldn't disagree. It was the bargain she'd made with the people of Udivoli. If it came to it, she'd have to grab her human and attempt to make it to the coast on her own. She tried to espy land, but the night was too dark; a featureless sphere of blackness surrounded the ship. At least the volcanic scent of the peninsula indicated from where they had come. But the coast was still too far away. She'd never make it there, not carrying Ozcahar.

"You have my gratitude, Captain. You have more of it if you delay ditch of irritating cargo until it be necessary."

"Your gratitude no keep us afloat, Dragon."

She was tempted to make her way to the mainmast and the huddle that was her human, but she figured Grastell would not be happy about that. He needed his concentration on getting the ship as close to Aerahan as he could, and she did not want to distract him.

The naiad youth porpoised alongside *Celerity* and ran ahead of her moderate bow wave. The air was alive with their clicks, blows, and ghostly grunting. It seemed playful, but Caizhiu knew it wasn't. There was raw hatred beneath the youths' inquisitiveness. The humans might not be up for a fight, but she couldn't say the same for the naiad. The youngsters scattered, and the ship came to a halt. This time, the force knocked even Caizhiu off her feet. She landed on one knee and left a cracked indentation in the decking. *Celerity* drifted in an aimless turn, the wind causing her sails to flutter ineffectively. The captain had been thrown partially over the wheel and had pulled it round when he collapsed onto the deck. With his face twisted in pain, he tried to catch his breath. He massaged his abdomen, bruised by the impact of the handles, but when he tried to get up, his feet slipped. It took him a moment to pull himself up, but finally he shook the shock from his head and then carefully straightened up.

"Everyone... still... aboard?" he tried to shout but couldn't get enough force behind his voice to do so.

The sudden stop had flung Mortynn and Vroza across the deck like dice on a game of Long Shot. Though they glanced around anxiously as they scrambled to their feet, they both gave affirmative responses to their captain. The only one who seemed to be unhurt was Ozcahar. Something took hold of the rudder and spun *Celerity* all the way round twice, forcing the crew onto their hands and knees. Ropes thumped against the masts and snaked through the air.

{*Naiad!*} Caizhiu sang, and the ship bobbed unmolested.

{*I don't believe I've had the pleasure,*} a screeching song replied with a coolness that flooded Caizhiu foot to head. {*But would this little fat man actually be the dragon Caizhiu?*}

With a geyser of exhaled air, Anreeyani rose out of the water. She held her vertical position, exposing her head and chest, and was almost tall enough to peer over the gunnel. The new ruler of the naiad was not as large as Oohnbrraayahee, but she had a menacing air and a powerful build. A scar marked the side of her neck and ran past her breast to a point below the waterline. An infantile naiad – her youngest, Caizhiu guessed – clicked and chirped excitedly as he swam around her. The ruler placed a hand on *Celerity*'s railing, depressing the ship, and revealed a smile with tens of interlocking conical teeth.

Vroza had been thrown against the netting close to where the naiad queen had breached. She crab-crawled upwards to the middle of the deck until she bumped into Ozcahar, and both let out a cry of alarm.

{I am indeed Caizhiu the Wayward. The dragon of the plains of Jitren. As bounty hunter to the Six Keepers of Sinuation and their Magistrates, I seek safe passage to the city of Aerahan.}

Anreeyani pulled on the side of the ship, lowering it further and forcing Caizhiu to walk towards her. They were practically at the midpoint of the sound, and she could only imagine the watery abyss beneath them. If the ship were to capsize, she'd plummet straight to the bottom. Poor air eyesight notwithstanding, Anreeyani's action was rude and Caizhiu suppressed a growl at the insult.

{I am Anreeyani, ruler of the Telereni naiad. You may, of course, cross to Aerahan. We could not interfere with the business of dragons. After all, the entire sky is yours.}

The continued tilting of the deck caused Vroza and Ozcahar to tumble and slam into the netting. Vroza grabbed onto it for dear life. Her eyes were fixed on Anreeyani, and her port wine stain was all that remained of her natural complexion. The rest had paled to a sickly white.

{Let go of the ship, Esteemed Ruler of the Telereni naiad. You are frightening my crew.}

Anreeyani looked around the deck, removed her hand, and submerged. She doused the whole of the sound in her laughter. It was uncanny to know the enormous otherkin was so close by, yet completely invisible. Caizhiu's weight kept the bounce back in check, and though there was no danger she would capsize, the vessel still tilted over so significantly that any humans not trapped against the lower gunnel had to hold on to something.

"No-no-no! Please!" Ozcahar's voice was breathless with fear.

Vroza held him by the lapels of his jacket and, with greater strength than Caizhiu had deemed her capable of, lifted him up to push him over the side.

"Captain! I don't recall you giving that order," Caizhiu called out without turning towards him. It was a long way from the railing to the water's surface. She reckoned she would be able to transfigure herself and grab Ozcahar before he hit the water, but she would have to be quick.

Grastell drew a juddering breath and said with as much strength as he could muster: "We... won't die... for him."

"That may well be so, but at this point, you don't know if sacrificing him will save you. Act hastily and you may lose your one piece of leverage."

He called Vroza's name but couldn't manage more. She halted her attempt but didn't pull Ozcahar back. He was pressed against the gunnel, which had to hurt his backside. His fingertips were firmly hooked over the lip of the railing, and his heels scraped the wood in a desperate attempt to get himself back to safety.

{My predecessor has told me of you, Caizhiu. I see she was not mistaken about your obsession with the neath. What are they to you that you care about these silly creatures, too reckless to recognise their helplessness?}

{Your predecessor was wise to take my counsel in these matters. Are you wise too, Esteemed Anreeyani?}

The naiad ruler breached on the other side of *Celerity*. She waited for Caizhiu to walk across the deck. The ship rocked as the dragon moved her weight to the other side and caused Ozcahar to fall into the ship. He landed on his knees, slumped forward, and inhaled with relief.

{These humans are no enemies of the naiad people. Why do you harass them?}

The naiad queen floated on her back, flanked not only by her nursing baby and the three youngsters, but other naiad too. The night was alive with their clicks and grunts and their excited soul songs. Caizhiu closed her eyes, and feeling the vibrations of the naiad's song, she counted twelve of them.

{Is it not enough that they steal our fish all day long? Must they do so at night as well? And your counsel, after Basinwade, is not what it once was.}

Caizhiu wished she was dealing with Oohnbrraayahee instead of this hothead queen.

{What do you believe happened in Basinwade? Was its destruction not enough for you?}

There was a weariness from the naiad, anger too, but the lack of nets around had thrown them. It dawned on Caizhiu that their darting backwards and forwards was to test for netting deployed. Their anger had been directed at the thought that even the night would not give them relief, but it was waning now.

{That we'll grant you,} Anreeyani said. *{We owe you our gratitude regarding that carbuncle by the shore.}*

{We seek passage, and we are not here to fish, as you well know. The naiad have never troubled themselves with human passage. And the people of Udivoli have not bothered with the naiad.} Caizhiu sincerely hoped that was true. *{Would you not rather reserve your ire for those that do?}*

Anreeyani looped the ship. Her movements were leisurely, her calf at her breast, and she studied the humans on the deck. She was buying time and Caizhiu hoped she was considering what she'd said.

{I agree that the humans from Udivoli have not bothered the naiad, so they are free to go. But tell them to keep their ships to the daylight in future.}

Caizhiu bowed her head, relieved that the new ruler of the naiad seemed to have some sense at least. Her conversation with the naiad ruler had been inaudible to her human companions, so she tried to sound as reassuring as she could. "They'll leave us be, Captain. Though they'd appreciate it if you'd limit your sailing to the daytime."

She smiled at Grastell but stiffened when she saw how grey his skin had turned. He was injured worse than she'd realised.

"They'll leave us be, will they?"

Caizhiu turned round to the bow of the ship and saw that Vroza stood ready to chuck Ozcahar overboard. Mortynn had helped her lift the bound man onto the side. He stepped back and grabbed the rifles from the mast. One was over his shoulder, the other he held in his hands. Vroza precariously balanced Ozcahar on the gunnel, where he tried to haggle with them to at least cut a few of his bonds before they'd throw him overboard.

"Bind his tongue if you must, but there is no need to ditch your cargo," Caizhiu said.

It would help to have this affirmed by the captain, but though Grastell opened his mouth to speak, he could only groan, and no words came out. He held onto the wheel as if it were the last piece of flotsam left.

"Because they'll leave us be…"

Mortynn repeated the words with an import that Caizhiu couldn't place, but it sparked unease within her.

"That is most gracious of them. They kill our captain, but they'll let us be. Perhaps we should fall on our knees, thank them. Perhaps we should give them an offering." He nodded at Vroza and she shoved Ozcahar off the ship. "Go fetch, Dragon."

FIFTY-SIX

PERILOUS WATER

Caizhiu was reminded of her injuries when she leapt forward. Overhead ropes hindered her from unfurling her wings. She still couldn't chronochi, and the pain of her rushed transfiguration rippled through her body. As she watched Ozcahar fall, she realised her plan to catch him before he hit the water had been foolishly optimistic.

Her claws shattered the port side gunnel as she grabbed it, and finally free from ropes and sails, she spread her wings. Ozcahar plunged beneath the waves, and she soared past the ship, swooping down to pluck him from the water. Aerahan was still too far away, but if she could fish him out, she could at least drop him back on *Celerity*.

"The day of the Fabled is over!"

It was Vroza who shouted, and Mortynn who fired the rifle. Caizhiu felt the impact of the shot in her neck. Another gave a downward tug on her left wing. The tip hit the waves, yanking her wing back, and then she was submerged. Salt stung her wounds. Despite kicking wildly with her four legs, her wings dragged her down. Quelling her moment of panic, she got her body into a rhythm, rising her chest then following it with her abdomen, and it seemed to work. Her wings funnelled the water downwards. However slow and laborious, the movements were reminiscent of flight. Gasping for air, she burst through the surface. She sucked air into her lungs, and immediately, it became easier to stay afloat. Though she could not escape the waves, she could stay on top of them.

With increasingly confident strokes, she swam towards Ozcahar and dipped her head into the water. Her teeth scraped over his shoulder until she could clamp them through his jacket and haul him up. For a terrifying moment, she thought she might be too late, but once she shook the man, he coughed, inhaled, and coughed again. Carefully, she hooked a talon through his binds and slashed the ropes. Ozcahar scissored his leg through the water, kicking as if he wanted to climb out of it. His squirming made it hard to keep his jacket between her teeth and impossible to rip the bonds around his wrists without damaging him. A rush of cold water hit her chest, and the human was ripped from her jaws, when one of the naiad grabbed his ankle. In a reflex, Caizhiu exhaled and dived after him, her wings sleek against her body. She sank her teeth into the naiad's tail. The creatures screamed at her. Not just the one she had by the tail, but others too, as if all of them felt the pain of dragon's teeth in their flesh. No wonder their anger at the humans was so great. Whenever one of their pod was killed, they all felt it. Ignoring their pulses hitting her body and their voices bouncing against her mind, she hooked her talons in the naiad, climbing along his body. She grabbed his arm.

{Let go of my human!}

The pressure increased in Caizhiu's ears. With her teeth in the naiad's arm, she couldn't get her tongue to the point at the roof of her mouth she used to ease the effect in flight. She held back from grabbing hold of her human for fear of wounding him. When he was first pulled under, Ozcahar had tried to kick the naiad, but he was no longer doing it. Caizhiu hoped he was merely conserving his breath.

{Let go of my naiad!}

Anreeyani's hand wrapped around her upper shoulder, webbed fingers spread to envelop her wing, neck, and upper shoulder. Caizhiu's talons ripped through the flesh of the male naiad when she was pulled upwards. She tightened her grip, plunging her talons deeper into him so that should he continue his dive, she'd rip chucks out of his side. He gave up. The three of them were hauled up. Caizhiu saw Ozcahar surface and be pulled back down. She slashed at the naiad's arm with her caudal blade and at last he let go. Ozcahar frog-kicked to the surface and Caizhiu could concentrate on Anreeyani. She let go of the young male naiad and he fled to the company of his peers, singing a song of indignation.

{How dare you attack one of my pod – and for a human of all things. Have you learnt nothing, Dragon? They are not worthy of your protection!}

Caizhiu filled her lungs with as much air as she could and placed her hind legs against the arm of the naiad queen.

{He's mine and I'll not have him stolen from me.}

Ozcahar spluttered for breath, kicking ineffectively as he tried to keep his face above the choppy waves. Struggling to stay afloat in the water, he frantically scanned his surroundings, searching for escape.

{Even the humans reject him. How worthless he must be!}

Despite the darkness, Ozcahar spotted Anreeyani's hand rush towards him and he fled with desperately slow frog kicks. Before she could grab him, the human was lifted out of the water. He disappeared in the roguish smile of an enormous naiad. As the creature breached, she obscured the silhouette of *Celerity* against the star-sprinkled sky.

The breaching giant threw herself backwards against the ship. Though her bow wave pushed the ship away from her, she still caused it to capsize. When she righted herself, *Celerity* lay considerably deeper in the water. Caizhiu couldn't see the crew, and the sound of the rifles had ceased. The water was alive with excitement at new prey.

A column of spray bespattered the fluster of naiad, their queen, and the dragon. Surprised, Anreeyani slackened her grip. Caizhiu used Anreeyani's confusion to shrug off the hand from her shoulder and narrowly escaped having her wings trapped between the grasping fingers. She spun and briefly sank her fangs into Anreeyani's wrist. It was merely a warning. She was not foolish enough to imagine that she could win in a fight with the queen in her dominion. The best she could hope for was to make a fight too costly for the naiad.

{*What are you doing here, Oohnbrraayahee?*} Anreeyani's song betrayed her unease, a sliver of qualms that she was going to face a challenge. Caizhiu, too, hoped the former ruler of the Telereni was not just here to regain control of her people. Upturning the human ship had impressed them.

{*Fear not, my queen. I am merely here to help a friend.*}

Oohnbrraayahee placed her bulk between her leader and Caizhiu, who finally composed herself, finding a rhythm to her movements. She was no match for the grace of the youngsters and the speed of the older naiad, but she had broadened her tail blade and managed to propel herself forward without embarrassing herself.

{*And of course it would not be your intention to start a conflict with a representative of the Six.*}

{*Of course,*} Anreeyani reluctantly agreed. {*The dragon must realise that, while she may have reign over the sky, the sea is ours*}.

{*Pray the Six don't heed you too closely, Esteemed Anreeyani,*} Caizhiu sang. {*Or you may have to contend with a water dragon.*}

{*It's obvious that you're not one in this iteration, Caizhiu.*} Anreeyani raised her upper body out of the water, forcing Caizhiu to look up at her, but thankfully she had lost her desire for a fight. She hugged her wailful calf to her, and the pod spread out. {*When next you choose to defend the humans, remember that it was one of us who saved you.*}

The queen sank beneath the waves and joined her pod in tearing into *Celerity*.

Oohnbrraayahee blew a geyser as she surfaced beneath Caizhiu. Using her large body, the naiad lifted her from the waves and swam towards the coast at pace.

{Tell your human to stop wriggling. I've nearly bitten down on him twice already.}

{I can't.}

Oohnbrraayahee stopped and sank down to take a vertical position. Caizhiu looked up at her enormous friend. Her puffed-up cheeks gave the naiad a comical expression. She picked Ozcahar up by a leg and took him from her mouth as if he were a stringy piece of meat stuck between her teeth. *{He's not even otherkin? Just a neath, like a fish?}*

With a derisory snort, Oohnbrraayahee let him fall. His scream stopped abruptly when he hit the water in front of Caizhiu. She hooked a fang through his collar, hauled him up and slashed the bonds around his wrists. She wasn't sure what she'd expected the human to do, but his hugging her neck took her by surprise.

Oohnbrraayahee leant backwards, sinking until only her face remained above the dark waves. Having turned onto her back, the old naiad moved beneath them, and like Anreeyani with her youngest, she balanced Caizhiu and her human on her midriff. For her part, the dragon folded her legs beneath her to protect her friend from her talons. Trembling, Ozcahar pressed his face against her, and she folded her wing around him. As he snuggled against her warm scales, she could feel the fright melt from his body.

{Looks like you've gained a barnacle.} Oohnbrraayahee sounded bemused as, with slow but enormous movements of her tail, she sped through the water towards the coast near Aerahan. *{I hope he is worth all this trouble.}*

At daybreak, the coastline had changed from a line to a rugged outline of the mountains beyond. Most of the small fishing villages were barely larger than Udivoli. The protracted shoreface prevented larger ships from entering them, hence the growth of Basinwade as a trading town. *Celerity* had set a course for the town of Traveses, the nearest harbour to Aerahan, but Oohnbrraayahee was loath to approach.

{We are losing the cover of night, Caizhiu. I want to help you, but I have no desire to become trapped in the shallows, especially near one of the human lairs.} Oohnbrraayahee lingered over the deeper waters, following the coastline south. *{Would you be able to swim to the shore with your neath?}*

The waters might be too shallow for Oohnbrraayahee, but Caizhiu would have to swim for several hours to reach the shore. *{I should be fine, but if you could keep your smaller cousins off my tail, that would be helpful.}*

{I'll try my best. The tide is in your favour, and I suggest you head for a secluded cove ahead. Few humans come there.}

Ozcahar, suddenly finding his firm footing sink away beneath him as Oohnbrraayahee lowered herself, looked around in a panic. There was nothing Caizhiu could do to explain to him what was happening.

{Good luck, Dragon.}

The old queen of the naiad disappeared into the deep and Caizhiu began her long paddle to the coast. Whether it was Oohnbrraayahee's doing or Keepers' providence Caizhiu couldn't tell, but they were unmolested by naiad on her lengthy swim. As the sun rose, the sea bottom looked tantalisingly close through the clear water. Once in a while, Caizhiu tested the depth by letting herself sink a little to see if she could reach the bottom. When she felt the sand slipping through her toes, and enticed by the scent of dry land, she surged forward with renewed enthusiasm. Up ahead, a white sliver of sand glowed against the background of a dark green cliff. Beige clouds of dust rose in the heat. Caizhiu had set her hind legs on the seabed when she noticed a quint of humans on the beach. She lay low in the water. With every breath she rose and sank. Under the heat of the sun, keeping in the cooler water felt comfortable, as the burning trails of Brekranez's teeth still stung her sides.

Her scales had adopted the blue-grey of the water and sky. Only the top of her head, some of the ridges of her back and her human stuck out above the waves. The humans on the beach couldn't see her yet, but it would not be long before they'd be confronted with the sight of a monster emerging from the waves. Caizhiu considered her options: stay afloat until nightfall and hope no fishing vessels or curious naiad youngster would come by, swim further along the coast – though if there were a better cove, Oohnbrraayahee would have taken them there – or carry on and take her chances with these five humans. Her tail swished as she made her way to the beach, unsure if it was the right decision. Though she kept low in the water, she could feel her body grow heavier. She hadn't realised how tired her legs were until she tried to stand up. Ozcahar, who had been clinging to her, let himself drop. The water came up to his shoulders, so he could walk or swim on his own.

A cacophony of shrieking and shouting erupted from the beach, but Caizhiu walked on undeterred. She occasionally gave Ozcahar a lift through the water, but once it was below his hips, she found him too heavy. Both of them staggered through the surf. Caizhiu shook the water off her wings and winced. When she stretched the wing, pain shot up her fourth finger. She couldn't see an injury. Perhaps it was a sprain or a minor fracture; she'd need Heort to confirm, and hopefully, he'd be able to help her heal faster. For the moment, flight was probably not a good idea.

Ozcahar collapsed onto the warm sand and stayed there, panting, for a couple of minutes before slowly rising to his feet.

The beach fishers were unsure about what they were seeing. They approached cautiously, shaking rifles from their shoulders at the odd sight of Caizhiu and Ozcahar.

Caizhiu gathered what strength she had left and began to transfigure into her human form when pain exploded in her neck. She ceased her efforts. She felt a warm, sticky sensation and looked down to see blood oozing from the gunshot wound. Panting to cope with the rush of pain, she took a step towards Ozcahar and bent her neck for him to have a look. Hindered by his feet sinking into the sand, he stumbled backwards and turned towards the other humans on the beach.

"Require aid," he cried out while waving frantically at them. "Please. Require aid."

Somewhere during their ordeal, he'd lost the shirt he'd tied around his waist. He'd lost his sandals too and pranced to keep contact between his feet and the scorching sand to a minimum. He held his hands out in front of him, palms facing the humans, as he walked towards them.

Too late, Caizhiu realised what he was about to do.

Fifty-Seven

The Last Option

H er human hobbled towards the five fishers, each step sinking into the loose sand up to his ankles. "Please. Require aid."

Caizhiu was too tired for this nonsense. Her neck hurt, and her persistent hunger pangs worsened with the prospect of a chase. Exhausted, she lumbered forward and, with a shove of her muzzle, sent Ozcahar flying. He scrabbled up onto his hands and knees to continue his desperate crawl through the sand towards the other humans. Caizhiu grabbed the salty, soggy fabric of his jacket, but he'd been expecting it and slipped out of his clothes. He resumed his hobbling run, dressed only in half of his pantaloons. Caizhiu spat the jacket and waistcoat on the ground. Licking the gritty sand off the roof of her mouth, she wondered how she could recapture her human without cutting his skin to ribbons. She overtook him easily and placed herself between him and the fishers. He moved so slowly she almost felt sorry for him.

She heard the shot and turned towards the other humans as it ricocheted off her snout. The shooter was too far away to puncture her scales, but he had to be an excellent shot to hit her head from that distance, and he was running closer. At least two others had also loaded their flintlocks and were taking aim. Caizhiu was running out of options. While her back was turned, Ozcahar had dropped back on his hands and knees. She expected him to crawl away, but he slipped underneath her belly to get past her. Instinctively, she tried to place a claw over his back. He crouched to avoid her, but he was too slow and screamed as her thumb sliced over his back, leaving a bright red stripe. Caizhiu distended her jaws to get them around his waist. He was too broad for her to pick him up, but she hoped her teeth would persuade him to at least stay still. Ozcahar's screams turned into unintelligible pleading, part Aumegoan, part Trader. She had the eerie feeling this panicky display wasn't for her. The taste of his blood filled her senses. She breathed in to clear her head and had to suppress a sand-induced sneeze.

A gunshot hit her shoulder, and though it bruised her, it didn't break her skin. She growled but stayed put. Ozcahar's fingers interlocked with her teeth as he tried to pry them out of his sides. She folded her wings over them protectively and caught two more shots in her slack membranes, but her blood painted a target. The third hit her neck, dangerously close to the established wound. The shot lodged in her muscles and kept her from adopting her human form. It wasn't just painful – if she tried transfiguring, she might cause more damage, perhaps puncture an artery.

The next shot grazed her nose, sending a spray of blood along its trajectory. Caizhiu dropped Ozcahar and lunged towards her attackers. She knocked the shooter off his feet, but the fishers had spaced themselves far enough apart that she couldn't take them all out with one action. Before she could turn, another shot hit above her hind knee, and she roared. Had she been able to chronochi, she would be fast enough to snatch each rifle from their hands, but now she had only the options of retreat, leave her human behind, or cause the fishers serious harm. She cursed Ozcahar for his callousness.

A third option occurred to her. Ignoring the pain, she stretched her wings, and with forceful beats, she caused a dervish of sand to envelop her attackers. She hooked her fangs under Ozcahar's belt. Uncertain how long the fabric would hold out, she didn't bother to carry him, but threw him halfway up the beach. She roared again, knocked over the leader of her attackers. Despite the ache in her cloaca, she covered the five with a spray of scent urine. Its viscosity enabled the urine to stick to any surface, and in combination with the whirling fine sand, it formed a paste. It should take the fishers a while to wash off, and with a bit of luck, it would gum up their powder weapons.

Her human lay still on the sand, but when she rolled him onto his back and dropped his ragged jacket onto his chest, he sat up. He groaned at the soreness this caused and staggered to his feet. Shaking the sand from the garment, he stretched the jacket between his hands. She must have caught it in her spray, because sniffing the fabric caused him to heave. Caizhiu pressed her bared teeth against his back and let a long growl reverberate through his chest. He gulped, and though his face twisted in disgust, he put the jacket back on. With one fang hooked through his collar, Caizhiu fast-walked him into the forest. She considered hoisting him onto her back, but her upper shoulders stung, and she wanted to save her wings. She held them flush to her body, but every time fatigue caused her to slacken them, she winced when her wings caught on the vegetation. Her landing in the water had sprained her shoulder. At least she hoped that's all it was. The gunshot in her hip ached and caused her to lurch more with every step. She needed to rest, and so did her human. But what would the five fishers do when they reached their village? Hopefully, they'd seek help from the Magistrate, but, just as likely, they'd arrange a hunting party. Her stomach grumbled, and she noticed the bloodstained footsteps Ozcahar left. Together with the urine-stained jacket he wore, he left a bright scent trail through the woodland. She could mask her own odour, but not his. A hunting party would have little trouble trailing them. They could not rest until they reached Aerahan.

***

From her crouched position at the edge of the dark woodland, Caizhiu glanced up at the enormous Welcome Gate, careful not to let the city lights catch her eyes. The gate and the wall spanned the breadth of the crevice in which they'd built Aerahan. The settlement had existed for centuries, already an old town when it had eventually become a city. Had it not been for the natural limitations of the mountains, Aerahan could have grown as large as Thirdburg. But it was contained by the steep slopes of the Shunned Hills of Sakliom, offering rest and respite to travellers before they embarked on traversing either the Ostroize plains to the north or the Shunned Hills proper. Many had lingered and made the city their home. Cheery sounds and the aroma of a multitude of spice pallets from the myriad of taverns drifted over the wall onto the road. Below the music, Caizhiu heard the trickle of water from the conduit where the stream ran through the wall, and she smelled the verve of auto carriages and streetlights. When she had last travelled through the city, shortly after Zel Zesen's inauguration, the night had made the city indistinguishable from the mountains. This had changed. The Aerahan night was no longer dark, and it would be impossible for Caizhiu to remain invisible while in motion. To give her scales time to adapt to the pattern of the city's lights, she would have to slink so slowly climbing the gate would take longer than the night. Through lofty embrasures, guards watched the locked gate. She couldn't see them, but they were there.

As if he sensed she wanted him to keep still, Ozcahar fidgeted, slowly edging in the direction of the gate. Unable to take her human form, she could hardly knock. She relied on Lord Zesen or Heort. But what if her friend had not made it? What if he had, and he and the Magistrate were on their way to Basinwade? The town had taught her how humans would react upon discovering a Fabled at their gate. Ozcahar had easily fooled the fishers that he was the one in need of protection from her. Why would the guards of Aerahan be different? Caizhiu waited for a cloud to hide the moon before lifting Ozcahar by his belt and tucking him under her wing pit.

She could hold him there, out of sight, but not if she were to climb the gate. She had to find a different way in.

The rains only reached this far south once every few years. The people of the Shunned Hills of Sakliom called the downpours the Laving. When she was much younger, and much smaller, Caizhiu had partaken in the festivities when the rains had fallen. The deluge had flooded the streets so much that she saved a man from washing away. Despite that danger, the people had celebrated. The man she'd rescued had explained that rains washed away all past transgressions. His eyes had sparkled when he told her of the woman he would now be free to wed and how blessed their offspring would be. It hadn't occurred to Caizhiu to ask what the rain had cleansed. Back then she hadn't thought humans capable of much wrongdoing. She knew better now. This year the sky had shed most of its tears on the north side of the Marsarin Massif, but she was certain that a city the size of Aerahan, surrounded by granite, must have a way to prevent the entire population from washing off their mountain during a deluge. In the event of heavy rain, the gutters couldn't handle the flow of water, requiring alternative outlets to avoid flooding the road. If they were large enough, maybe they would offer her a safe way to reach the Magistrate's manse.

Moving only whenever a cloud dimmed the moonlight, she followed her nose. Rounding the side of the city, she was no longer visible from the front of the Gate. The Laving outlets were positioned in an aslant line along the city's height. When it came, the Laving caused a spectacular trio of waterfalls into the valley. Caizhiu squeezed her human closer so he wouldn't slip out from beneath her wings as she climbed to the lowest one. The wrinkles in the landscape that formed the Shunned Hills of Sakliom weren't as daunting as the Marsarin Massif, but the stone below the gate was worn by water and had become a slick, almost vertical drop to the trees below.

Caizhiu climbed around to the top of the aperture and peered into the blackness. Only a thin layer of sludge slid down a groove in the centre of the humanmade cavern. Rats lived amid the scraps of human life, and a colony of bats had made this their home too, but there was nothing so large it would pose a danger to her human. Flapping her wings for balance, she dangled Ozcahar over the abyss and swung him into the drain in one swift motion. She hurried in after him to block the sound of his horrified cries before it could attract the attention of an inquisitive guard. The last thing she saw of him, before her body blocked the light of the sliver of moon, was the white of his darting eyes. He stumbled about aimlessly in the pitch black. When his fingers brushed over her teeth, he retreated into the tunnel. If she could have spoken, Caizhiu would have told him to step out of the central trench. Her human could have avoided trudging through the slurry of bat and rat droppings by stepping on the narrow ridges on either side, but he was unaware. She guessed he could feel scuttling insects between his bare toes too.

"What kind of horrid place have you brought me to?" His muffled voice ended in dry heaving. It allowed her to locate him, and she could move forward without the worry she might step on him.

Ozcahar stopped still. She prodded him to continue walking. Much to her surprise, he hesitantly but insistently pushed back. "Where do you expect me to go?"

To prove his path was blocked, he hit whatever it was that had stopped him, and the sound resonated through the tunnel. Caizhiu detected the scent of rust, and as she skimmed the ceiling with her crest in her search for it, she bumped her nose against an iron grate. Fang-thick bars formed a lattice between ceiling and floor. Her nostrils flared frantically as she snuffled for the scent of another trap, but apart from the stink of verve in the residue of garbage, the scent of its lightning wasn't there. With a tail swipe, she proved to herself that, even though she couldn't turn around, she could still back out of the drain. She checked the grate for any gaps or movement, but it was firmly attached to the floor, ceiling, and sides, leaving her unable to so much as jostle it. Not a trap. The purpose was simply to keep anyone, Fabled or human, from doing exactly what she intended to do – avoid the Welcome Gate to steal into or out of the city. She took a step back and growled. Curse Zel's prudence!

Ozcahar gave a thin laugh, and the stench must have hit him with renewed intensity as he bent over to heave. Gagging, he limited his speech to short inhales. "I take it... you weren't... expecting this... to be here."

Caizhiu nuzzled his chest to calm her nerves, savouring his aroma amidst the overpowering stench. There was nothing to be gained by staying in this nastiness. Using the forks of her tongue, she gathered the lapel of Ozcahar's jacket and pulled him with her as she backed away towards the entrance. The wind caught her caudal blade, alerting her she'd reached the entrance before she stepped off the edge. Though it was unlikely someone would look in their direction, she took care to turn slowly and blend into the shadows. Her wing shielded her human from view.

Ozcahar took a deep breath of the fresh air. He ran his fingers over the membrane that separated him from the outside and cleared his throat. "Things just don't seem to be going your way, do they? I mean, you're a powerful dragon and me... Well, shouldn't this be easy for you?"

She expected mockery in his tone, but he sounded as sincere as a vocal voice could.

"You obey the Six, trueso? Do you think there's a chance you're not meant to take me to the Magistrate? Is it possible that the era of Sinuation's Keepers has ended, and you are meant to set me free?" He got onto his knees. "Please. I promise I will not set a foot wrong if you do. I'll disappear and you can too. You'll never have to concern yourself with me again."

He was right that this should have been easier than it had proven to be. She had lost her human form, and she couldn't sneak into the city. But he'd reminded her that she obeyed the Six. Ingrirath had chosen her – not just chosen but yanked her from her iteration to do this. Caizhiu was what

Sinuation needed her to be, and that made her remaining option obvious. she would enter the city like the dragon she was.

FIFTY-EIGHT

LIKE A DRAGON

In the pale rays of dawn, Caizhiu shook her scales and stretched her wings. Despite the ache in her upper shoulder, she was relieved to feel that it was stronger than the day before. Her wing wrist ached, but she could endure it. She would not have tried to take off from the ground, which would have required laboured wing beats to rise over the treetops, but with the outlet as a launch point, the air currents would take care of most of her flight.

She nudged Ozcahar, who shuffled backwards before he even opened his bleary eyes. Her talons pressing into his sides woke him.

"What are y—?" His eyes darted from her face to her wings, to the trees and rocks far below them. When she lifted him off the floor, his eyes widened further, and his hands clamped on hers. "You're not going to... Have you seen how high this is? I—"

Caizhiu jumped. She extended her wings and felt the wind pull on her sore shoulder. The dull ache wouldn't hinder her from holding her wings in position for the short flight she had to undertake. With a couple of strong beats, she increased her speed and, soaring higher, made a sweeping turn towards the city. At least the human held still in her grip. He wasn't the same aggressive creature she'd fished from the drake's jaws. This time Ozcahar seemed to realise exactly how far he'd fall if she let go of him.

The city was busier than Caizhiu had hoped. Guards opened the Welcome Gate to waiting vehicles. Traders unfurled their stalls. The shadow of the dragon caused the people to pause and squint towards the brightening sky. She hadn't realised how beautiful the city would look. In human guise, she had walked along its steep or staired streets before, but from the ground she'd not realised how the city had been built in rings of elevation. Aerahan's hooded alleyways looked like colourful snakes coiling up the hillside from the Welcome Gate. Bhodine carapaces shone like jewels between them.

Circling the city caused her to decelerate, and her human weighed heavier. When she tightened her grip, Ozcahar, who had until then remained motionless, writhed in pain. His movements caused her talons to slice further into his sides and he moved with greater desperation, worsening their situation. Caizhiu flew higher to give herself space, and though she wasn't sure it would work, she rolled. Hurriedly, she extracted her talons from his sides and squeezed the squirming human against her body, holding him in place with one arm.

She was tiring, the ache in her injured wing worsening with every beat. She had expected Aerahan to be easy to approach from the sky since its people had never faced attack from above. However, she wasn't attacking, and finding a place to land proved more challenging than anticipated. Unlike Basinwade, Wexede Crossing, or even Bladrid, there were few open spaces. The street awnings formed a false floor she couldn't land on – she wouldn't know who or what would be hiding below. There was nowhere she'd be able to set down and find cover, and the longer Caizhiu took to decide where to land, the more time the humans below had to panic and gather their weapons.

A growl rose up from the streets, rising in pitch and hitting Caizhiu like a punch to the gut. She almost gasped at the rush of terror. Beating her wings, she lurched from side to side as she fought against the paralysing fear, fought to keep it from dragging her out of the sky. The tops of the Shunned Hills of Sakliom stretched out before her. Ozcahar scrabbled at her scales but couldn't find a grip. Unknotted from round his middle, his jacket fluttered to the ground, and Caizhiu thought how easy it would be to accidentally drop him. She could let the wind carry her far from here, far from the cursed humans and their verve engines. Would she really allow herself to flee, like she had from Basinwade? There at least she'd been able to tell herself that she had fled to save her human. That was not the case now. This time, she would take her charge to the Magistrate of Aerahan. If that would damn her, then so be it.

Though below them the drone swelled in volume as more and more verve engines started up, she turned back and pitched towards the city.

The enormous Magistrate's manse jutted out of the mountainside, touching streets on several of the spiral tiers while overlooking the whole of the city. Halfway up the manse, she spotted a wooden platform partially protruding from the building. The flooring was constructed of sturdy planks with thick struts to the mountainside wall below. It formed an oval, with half of it enclosed by the building. Half of the extended section was adorned with a copper railing which gleamed in the sun and reached from the floor to the ceiling. A couple of people stood behind it and, with their hands on the bars, gazed over the city. One of them pointed at her, but they didn't move back from the barrier. The other side of the oval platform had an opening between the railing and the wall. Caizhiu doubted her eyes for a moment because it seemed made for her to land on. She passed the construction, trying to figure out why it might exist. Even Lord Zesen couldn't have had the foresight to think one day a dragon might want to visit. After the Stand, she was not about to enter a human structure without making sure it wouldn't harm her.

There was something disturbingly familiar to this construction. The wood creaked softly with vibrations. Below, the hum of the verve engines swelled, and the breeze carried a rigging song. Caizhiu noted the noise before she saw the ropes hung in front of the opening. She recognised the metallic scent. The last time she had smelled it, such ropes had also been attached to a verve engine. And they'd been affixed around her neck.

She only just managed to veer away before she'd committed to a landing that would have sliced her wings in half. Ozcahar gasped at the sudden change of direction, and he clung to the arm that held him in place. They rushed up past the building, while Caizhiu searched for windows and doors, any other way for her to get in. Where was Lord Zesen? One word from him would end all her trouble. Her wings beat steadily, but with each flap, the cramping in her muscles intensified, a reminder of her injuries. She couldn't find any opening big enough to pass through without hurting herself, but she had to land somewhere. The platform still seemed the best place.

Turning in a slow spiral, Caizhiu studied the constructions once more. A couple of pulleys extended out from the manse and were used to tie the ropes somewhere on the tiers below. There were several similar rope constructions that spanned over the roofs throughout the city. Small carriages dangled from them, and the verve engines on either end of the ropes pulled them to and fro over the heads of the pedestrians below. Just normal neath nonsense, she thought, not a trap.

Though the ropes narrowed the opening to the platform, if she tucked her wings in close and angled her approach, Caizhiu should fit through. Beyond the gap, the people on the platform were retreating towards the building, but they were not moving fast enough. It left her with no room to skid. She would have to come to a dead stop. The manse rushed towards her. Caizhiu twisted her body and kept her head low as she folded her wings out of the way of the ropes. Once she got past them, she opened her wings as far as the small area permitted. She bent her knees to catch the deceleration. The wood creaked as three sets of her claws splintered the planks. The platform sagged. People screamed. But the floor held. With a deep sigh, Caizhiu let her human slide onto the floor.

"Did we crash?" Ozcahar asked, unable or unwilling to move from his prone position. "Are we dead?"

Had she been able to talk, she would have cursed him over his assessment of what she deemed to be a flawless landing, the best she had ever performed. All she could do was growl her displeasure at him.

A shadow moved behind her. Caizhiu tried to turn before the steel brushing against her tail could trap it. But her right wing-thumb was caught in the railings, and she couldn't turn fast enough to face the threat. Her caudal blade scraped the copper, sending sparks flying around the platform. By the time she'd untangled her wings, a rope-way carriage had come to a dangling halt, blocking her exit. Caizhiu snarled, but as her caudal blade sliced through the rope, she noticed the carriage was ornately decorated in green and copper paint. The wooden panelling looked as flimsy as any auto carriage. Though it wasn't metal, Caizhiu leant forward cautiously and grabbed the rim of the carriage before the rope could snap completely. Her talons sliced through the wooden roof, and it wasn't until she peered through the window that she spotted the six humans hidden within. To make sure they didn't carry lightning rods, she shook the carriage, causing them to roll across the floor. As she watched them crawl on hands and knees to huddle in the far end of the carriage, she felt a fool. They had no weapons, hadn't intended to attack her; they were just travelling up the manse. And now they were at least as frightened as she was.

To make up for her mistake, she opened the carriage door, a similar construction as the cylinder in Basinwade. The carriage didn't line up with the depressed platform, so she angled the contraption forward to allow the humans to jump onto it. They remained in their corner. Caizhiu shook the carriage again to stir them from their stupor. The humans shrieked and scurried backwards to keep from sliding towards the door.

{I should have known it was you causing this ruckus.}

The people at the manse's door moved aside to allow Heort to pass. Caizhiu wanted to rush towards him, but he was flanked by a dozen city guards with guns. Though she worried for her friend initially, the guards' weapons were all aimed at her, not him. Her growl grew when she saw guards with lightning rods, and her muscles tensed as she prepared to defend herself.

{Where's Lord Zesen?}

{Regrettably, he is still en route to Basinwade... To rescue you.} Heort pointed at the sky carriage. *{It's probably best if we stop scaring the populace. It'll make our wait for his return easier.}*

{Not before they lay down their weapons.} She shook the carriage to indicate that should the guards choose to use their lightning rods, the humans inside would share her fate and then likely fall to their deaths.

Heort glanced up at the Sheriff who stood next to him and gave her a weary smile. The Sheriff grunted and the guards with the lightning rods reluctantly shrugged them off their shoulders to put them on the ground. But she kept her eyes and pistol trained on Caizhiu.

The cervitaur stepped towards the sky carriage. He licked his nose before telling the humans cowering within: "No be afraid. Come out. You no be hurt."

His pronunciation had improved and somehow it irked Caizhiu. She understood all languages known to the humans, and now she could speak not a word. He made it worse by adding: "Dragon no be wrathful, merely foolish."

One of the six people in the carriage was dressed in a tunic in the same green as the carriage with copper epaulettes. He'd sat on his knees between the dragon and the others. Caizhiu wondered if he was the driver. Finally, he straightened his rounded hat and slowly got to his feet. The assumed driver eyed Caizhiu warily, as if she might bite off the hand with which he grabbed the doorframe. With the other he helped his passengers get up and, one by one, walk by him to jump onto the platform. One of the guards who had laid his verve pack down readied himself to catch them and guide them towards the building. The driver hesitated only a moment before he too disembarked.

"They'll have to fix those ropes if I ever board that death trap again," he muttered to the guard in a quivering voice. "Bloody dragons. Whatever next."

Though the entrance to the manse was wide, the eagerness of the sky carriage passengers to get through the door caused them to throng together until none could move. Two guards tried to pull them apart. Taking advantage of the panicked people on the platform, Ozcahar crawled on his elbows and knees to follow them. The obliging guard squatted and held out a hand to him. Before her human could think of accepting the offered help, Caizhiu leapt forward. The platform shuddered, the empty carriage plummeted to the ground, and the guard fell on his ass. Caizhiu roared and Ozcahar curled into a ball to ward off the claw she placed over his head.

"K-keep him!" the guard cried as he scooted towards the manse. "Six's Mercy, keep him!"

"Esteemed Dragon!" the Sheriff said with a shaky solemnity. The other humans glanced at her as she got on one knee. "Would you allow me to take your charge into custody?"

Caizhiu growled. Heort stepped in between them.

{Becalm yourself.} He caressed the dragon's egg tooth with his fingertips. His touch flooded her with solace and stalled the rumbling in her throat. *{You are among friends.}*

Despite herself, Caizhiu closed her eyes and pressed the bridge of her nose against his chest.

He stroked her cheek. *{I understand you'd not be inclined to trust them, but they mean well. Sheriff T'oelo serves Lord Zesen.}*

{So did Sheriff Olyre of Basinwade.} She looked at the receding crowd and rested her gaze on the Sheriff. *{For all the good it did him. Or me.}*

{Well, it helped me.}

Her human whimpered and Heort glanced down at him. Ozcahar squeezed a hand between his face and her claw and, either in greeting or a plea for help, wiggled his fingers at the cervitaur. Heort ignored it and instead reached for the wound on Caizhiu's neck. His touch eased the pain.

{They've injured you. I wondered why you opted to approach the city in your true form, no matter how splendid it was. Let the Sheriff hold the human. They have sturdy prison cells. I checked. Please, let me heal you.}

Caizhiu struggled to disagree with him, and she raised her head to eye Heort suspiciously. *{You are not nudging me, are you?}*

He winked. *{I wouldn't dare. Besides, I think you're smart enough to realise I talk sense.}*

Caizhiu grinned, prompting a wave of anxiety to waft across the platform. She stooped towards the Sheriff. The woman's breath caught in her throat, but she didn't move and held Caizhiu's gaze. Sat on one knee, she placed her pistol on the floor. Though she held out her palms to Caizhiu, she addressed Heort when she asked: "May we take the dragon's charge into custody to await the Lord Magistrate Zesen's return?"

In response, Caizhiu lifted her claw off Ozcahar, who gasped for breath with what she deemed was a little more drama than required. He remained face down, with his hands held up over his head.

"You may, Sheriff," Heort said.

In one silky movement, the woman got to her feet, her powder weapon in hand. She aimed it at Ozcahar and glanced over her shoulder at her guards. "Take him to the inner cages, away from the public. Until the Lord Magistrate returns, his life belongs to the dragon."

Caizhiu reluctantly took a step back when a man and a woman came forward and lifted Ozcahar by his arms. He staggered to his feet but struggled to stay standing. She wasn't sure if it was exaggerated; there were four new red stains on either side of his waistcoat. The wince he gave when the guards twisted his arms onto his back seemed genuine. As they clamped manacles around his wrists, his eyes flitted from the Sheriff, to Heort and finally rested on Caizhiu as if he expected her to intervene. The entrance to the manse had been cleared of people, and the guards dragged him into the building. Several times Caizhiu could hear him, in his rudimentary Trader, ask where they were taking him. No answer was forthcoming.

Heort gave the Sheriff a sideways nod. "If you value lives of Aerahan, I suggest you no lose him."

"But lose those." He tapped a hoof against one of the discarded lightning packs and jumped back when a tiny air bubble drifted through the green liquid from the bottom of the glass cylinder to the top.

"Must we be defenceless, Honoured Healer?" the Sheriff asked softly, trying not to glance at Caizhiu. Before Heort could answer, Caizhiu swiped the hateful weapons off the platform.

The cervitaur sighed, winced at the cries from below as the packs found the ground, and placed his hand on the Sheriff's arm. "She be a dragon. If you require defences, you already be dead. When he return, ask Lord Zesen about success of lightning weapons in Basinwade."

FIFTY-NINE

RECKONING AND REMUNERATION

It surprised Caizhiu how small Lord Zesen's chamber of judgment was. In accordance with the rest of the manse, this room too was colourful and intimate. Behind the Magistrate's dais, the morning sun lit up a stained-glass window that depicted the joining of the Six. She quelled the alarm swirling around her stomach as she looked at the blue-and-red-coloured glass. Though she had hoped to use the quiet of the morning to make her way to the chamber, Zel was already sat at the dais. He watched her prowl between the benches.

{You honour me, Caizhiu. I'm told your arrival in Aerahan was magnificent and I was worried I might not get to see your true self.}

She draped her tail between the rows of pews that faced his elevated position and folded her wings so she wouldn't catch one on the gaudy chandelier. The Lord Magistrate wore a patterned garment as colourful as the mosaic on the floor and the stained glass. When she had last seen the man, Zel had been very young and very serious, with a corona of black coils that framed his face. Today he struggled to stand up straight and a thin layer of white down had replaced the corkscrew curls, but the strength behind his dark eyes was undiminished. Gostawa Azer tread her office carefully. Yullorik Veentar hid from it. But none embodied the enormity of the role like Zel Zesen. The diffidence of his youth had been replaced with a cool poise, making him a master of Sinuation conduction. Yet, his mottled brown skin was lined with grooves, his smile missed several teeth, and she caught his relieved sigh when he sat back down.

In his seated position, he moved backwards. Accompanied by the squeaking of turning wood, a puff of steam, and the acrid stench of verve, he rolled from behind the desk and down the curved ramp. Just in front of his feet, Zel's chair had a miniature carriage wheel, and two full-sized ones at the rear. He controlled the movement with a familiar panel of switches. Lazy bubbles rose in the green cylinder by his side. Caizhiu snorted and took a step back.

{Don't tell me a mighty dragon fears an old man like me?} Zel stopped his contraption mid-slope and gave her a lopsided grin.

{Actually, I'm fighting the urge to throw you out of that cursed thing, Lord Zesen.} Caizhiu lowered her head, careful not to get too close as she checked for a lightning rod. *{This mighty dragon has learnt to be wary of such devices.}*

{I take it you recognise Betni Foxtine's handiwork?} He continued down the ramp, until he sat before the dragon's claws, and he spread his arms to show her he was unarmed. *{She designed it for me a few years back. It saddened me when I heard of her involvement in your ordeal. And as I look up to you, I'm surprised I found her alive.}*

{You saw her... in Basinwade?} A nervous twitch of Caizhiu's tail caused the line of pews to scrape over the stone flooring.

{In a makeshift sickroom, with other survivors... Few as they were.} Zel knotted his bushy eyebrows, and the joviality left his expression. The vision of the ruined town, the scent of blackened and burned buildings, infiltrated

his soul song. *{She's become quite the devout woman, pledging her undying fealty to the Six for saving her life.}*

Disgust filled Caizhiu's song when she thought of the technologist who'd so pitiably crawled through the platform.

Zel's fingertips caressed the bridge of her nose, and he studied her with a deep frown. *{I trust your appearance is not on account of your injuries.}*

{Thanks to Heort's care, I can take my human form again. I am considering it since the size of your chamber doesn't appear befitting its standing.}

Zel let his eyes wander over the room, a quarter of which was taken up by the dragon, and he turned to manoeuvre his chair back to the dais. *{The worst moment of someone's life is an intimate affair, not one for grand spectacle and entertainment. There have been many worst moments in this room.}*

This wouldn't be Ozcahar's worst moment. That would come shortly afterwards when she... Only if he is condemned to die, she reminded herself, only then.

The Magistrate flicked a lever on his desk. The memory of Basinwade sent an icy shiver over her scales, but all that happened was that a bell rang somewhere in the adjacent hall. A side door opened, and the First Attendant entered. He bowed deeply to both Zel and Caizhiu.

"Lord Magistrate, are you ready to begin?"

Zel beckoned him to proceed, and Caizhiu adopted her human guise.

{That is quite the transformation. I suppose at least Ingrirath's intervention in your iteration offered you the extra flexibility to fit into such a small form.}

Caizhiu started at the memory of her early emergence. Had she wanted to request of the Keepers what they had already given her? Before she could ask Zel if that was what he had meant, a court scribe entered. The man bowed and scurried to a seat. No other spectators joined them. A guard accompanied Ozcahar Nitt, and she wasn't sure whether his shuffling was because of his injuries or the shackles that bound his feet. His eyes darted around the room. Only because she watched him so closely did Caizhiu notice his brief faltering when he caught her eye.

Her human's condition had visibly improved since she last saw him on the platform. His complexion had lost that sickly pallor, and he carried more meat on his bones. The aroma of his fear was so intense it made her mouth water. While waiting for Zel's return, she hadn't been able to escape the prey scent that permeated the manse. But there had been no need to hunt – Ozcahar was already caught – and it had left her antsy. Today at last, receipt of her bounty would release her from the hunt. Fortunately, the goat she had eaten earlier made having to sit through the process of justice bearable and kept the grumbling of her stomach at bay.

Heort entered via a side door. He had replaced his Keeltois outfit with a brightly patterned, silky tunic. The bejewelled sleeves only reached to his elbows, and Caizhiu noted the attire had no buttons. Respectfully, he bowed to Zel. That her human was well enough to appear before the Magistrate was due to his efforts. Caizhiu had expected her friend to take a seat beside her, but he followed Ozcahar to the dock.

"I have not had much need for my Aumegoan of late." Zel grimaced as he spoke the unfamiliar syntax. "But I'll try to remember what I can. No doubt, Caizhiu will assist if need be."

"In every way, Magistrate." She took a seat where she could enjoy watching Ozcahar. Zel might choose to make this worst moment private, but she intended to relish every bit.

"I hope to reach the hundredth year of my life soon." Zel's Aumegoan was heavily inflected but flawless. "And the murder of a Keeper of Sinuation is the gravest accusation I have ever had the misfortune to preside over. More than a murder, an attack on the very foundation of our world."

The webbing of lines on his face sagged. His expression grew harsh, the kindly old man gone from his features. "Had you not run such a long way to prevent appearing before a Magistrate, you would not find yourself in my court today. Your elusiveness would imply you are guilty."

Ozcahar gripped the balustrade around the dock. His lips moved, but it took a while for the words to trip out. "But I didn't mean to... I mean... I didn't know it would... I didn't know it was poison."

"Perhaps if you had, you would not have been able to give it her," Zel said thoughtfully. "However, the poison used could not have come to the cup by accident. Somebody added it. And if that was not you, young man, then who was it?"

"I... I don't know." Ozcahar blinked. He was quiet for a moment, and by the time he repeated his answer, it had become a lie.

Heort placed his hand next to Ozcahar's and their fingers touched. The man's cheeks hollowed, and he clenched his jaw as he wrestled to control his tongue.

"I think it..." Ozcahar vomited the words. Beads of sweat dripped down his face, and he grimaced as if he were in agony. He gasped, trapped his lower lip between his teeth, and fixed his gaze on his hands. Finally, he spat again: "I don't know."

"Are you absolutely sure that you want to carry the burden of this crime?" Zel entwined his hands. "That you are prepared to face the consequences that come with it? If, in truth, someone tricked or coerced you, you may end up regretting not disclosing their identity to me at this moment. Once it has passed, I won't be able to assist you. Leniency will not follow you if you hold your tongue."

Assist him? Caizhiu shifted in her seat. Zel had spoken in kind terms of the Betni woman. He was fond of her on account of his wheeled chair, but surely he would not let the murderer of a Keeper go free.

"I would rather pass judgment on the architect of the crime. But I have only you, the hand that held the poison."

Ozcahar's jaws tensed as if he were anticipating a punch, then he slowly exhaled and said: "Lord Magistrate, you said it was an attack on our world, but the Six are human. They are Keepers to guard us. Us! Therefore, should this not be our world? It isn't. I didn't understand that before, when I... When Ingrirath died." He looked down and a drop of sweat, or perhaps a tear, landed on his pale knuckles. "But after the wolf men, trolls, and sea monsters... and... after Basinwade... I understand now. Humans go unheard and unanswered. The Keepers of Sinuation may betray their kin, but I won't."

Zel let out a weighty sigh. "So be it, Ozcahar Nitt. I must carefully consider what punishment would befit such a serious crime. And without your contrition or cooperation, it is unlikely I can spare your life."

He turned to Caizhiu, who tried to suppress her grin. "We haven't yet discussed your payment, Bounty Hunter. As the representative of Ingrirath, I extend my appreciation for your exceptional service. Your hardship has been significant, not least because of the loss of your hoard. Tell me how I can reward you."

"I'd be grateful if you'd give me the life of Ozcahar Nitt."

There was a delicious whimper in Ozcahar's intake of breath.

Heort's head snapped around to her, his eyes wide and mouth agape.

Zel's eyebrows lifted. "That is a high price, Caizhiu. Are you certain you would not rather have a more conventional payment? We have enough gold in Aerahan to recompense you for the hoard you lost and double it."

"What else would you do with him, Lord Zesen?"

"That needn't be your concern." Zel opened his hands to her. "I urge you to ask for something else."

Caizhiu got to her feet and bowed. "If it pleases you, Lord Zesen. The payment I require is the life of Ozcahar Nitt."

Zel hung his head, slowly raised it, and rested his sad gaze on Ozcahar. "Since I know of no precedent, I suppose it is a fitting punishment for the crime of killing a Keeper of Sinuation. Caizhiu, you have fulfilled your obligation to Sinuation. In payment, the life of Ozcahar Nitt is yours."

She closed her eyes and let the relief of her fulfilment wash through her. Her hunt was complete. She would spare Heort and Lord Zesen the sight of... Her four eyes snapped open. Where was his prey scent? She saw Ozcahar standing in the dock, heard the jangling of his manacles and the shallow breaths he fought to control. But it was as if he'd left the room, as if she were looking at a nixe's mirage.

{*What trickery is this, Lord Zesen? What have you done to my human?*} The mosaic cracked as Caizhiu crossed the room until she stood before the dock. She looked from Ozcahar to the guard beside him. The man had impassively witnessed the proceedings, probably not understood a word of the foreign tongue spoken, but under the scrutiny of Caizhiu, he wet his lips. His eyes flitted to the Magistrate and a drop of sweat ran from his hairline.

{*There is no trickery, Caizhiu. You agreed to the payment. Thus, your task is complete, and you are free of your hunt. Ozcahar Nitt is no longer your prey.*}

Desperate to revive the allure of Ozcahar, she inhaled his fragrance deeply. She recognised her human's scent in the same way she recognised that of Zel, of the guard, the scribe, and Heort. But the tingle it had given her had gone. {*You mean he's just any human now?*}

{*Not at all. He's your human.*}

{*And I'm stuck with him?*}

{*I did warn you to choose something else.*}

She could still eat him. But why would she? The ecstasy she had longed for would not be there. It would be no different than if she ate the guard, no different than when she had despatched the Sinuation-mangled deer. She could kill Ozcahar, but it'd be nothing more than a practical execution, a cold killing, like humans did.

Unless...

She snapped the chain that shackled Ozcahar's ankles. A flutter of hunting lust stirred within her as he stepped back in surprise. It would work! She gave him a light prod. "Run. Let's see how far you get."

"Be no-motion," Heort warned him in Trader.

Caizhiu scowled at the cervitaur. {*Whose side are you on?*}

{*Yours, Caizhiu.*} Heort cocked his head. {*What kind of friend would I be to let you make such a mistake?*}

Ozcahar's eyes flicked between them before finally, pleadingly, resting on the Magistrate. "Does she mean I'm... Am I free to go?"

"Certainly not." Zel rubbed his eyes warily. "Allow me to explain your punishment to you, Ozcahar Nitt. The rest of your life, however long or short it may be, belongs to the dragon Caizhiu. If you act... sensibly, she'll take no joy in killing you. If you, however, return to your foolish ways, she'll not rest until she's hunted you down and eaten you."

For a moment it looked like Ozcahar would give a rebuttal, but he swallowed it and mumbled: "I can be sensible, Lord Magistrate. I promise."

"I'm not the one you'll have to convince. But to help remind you, and to prevent recurrences such as what happened in Basinwade, I'll add that you will carry the marks of your misdeeds. No innocent shall aid you, should you... fail to be sensible. None shall perish in your stead."

Though Ozcahar nodded his understanding, Caizhiu calmed herself with the notion that it would be a mere matter of time. Before long, he would try some foolish thing and then she would devour him. To emphasise it, she pinched his chin between finger and thumb and forced him to face her. The reflection in his water-blue eyes scowled back at her.

"The word I gave you has been fulfilled. From now on, if I go hungry, I will eat you. If you annoy me, I will eat you. If you run, I'll enjoy it more. You are nothing but provisions."

"Provisions." Hope tugged at the corner of his mouth. "So... you won't eat me today?"

"No," Caizhiu growled, "but an old friend once told me that sometimes compassion and cruelty are the same thing. We shall see whether that is true."

SIXTY

HER OWN DRAGON

The shutters rattled, and the rain lashed against the steamed-up windows. The humans called it cosy, but Caizhiu found the sitting room cramped. None of the armchairs would enable her tail to take her weight, so she sat on the floor. Though she had dried off, Wylthren's hair was still damp. Slumped in the comfy chair next to her, he struggled to keep his eyes open. He was not used to travelling, had learned to ride horseback along the way, and the weather had made it a gruelling journey. No wonder he was exhausted.

Raila entered, pushing the door open with her backside so she could carry a tray with chalkar. Since last Caizhiu had seen her, she'd forced her too-short hair into braids. With practised poise, she walked over to Wylthren.

He bolted up from his slouch and accepted a cup. "Grateful, miss."

The girl smiled at his northerly accent and blushed at his formality. Before it was offered, Caizhiu reached to take a cup from the tray and said: "I'm grateful too... miss. You're unusually helpful."

Raila shot her a daggered look. "I am helpful because my aunt has just had a baby." Her critical eyes drifted to her cousin, who was sitting at the writing table in the far corner of the room. "It's what you do, if you have anything about you."

Torbel glanced over his shoulder at Wylthren, then at Raila and, with a sly smile, said: "You weren't this helpful yesterday. And I *am* helping. I'm teaching Heort to read."

"How can that scribble mean dragon?" The cervitaur scratched his antlers. "It doesn't look like a dragon."

"Neither does Caizhiu," Wylthren said and Raila laughed, a little too loud.

She hiccupped as she caught herself and leant over Torbel's shoulder to see what they were studying. Pointing at something in the book, she explained that, unlike Trader symbols, Uayathi letters didn't resemble what they described.

Torbel read out the story of the Great Blaze of the Keeltois, his finger tracing each letter as he went along.

Morailo shook his head as he sipped his chalkar. *{How does Heort do it? That boy never reads, given a choice.}*

{I never read either.} Wylthren glanced at the children. *{Lord Veentar said I have to learn to enjoy it, which gave Heort the idea.}*

{Ah, so we have your good influence to thank for this.} Morailo lifted his cup at Wylthren. *{And your song was very clear. Well done.}*

Wylthren glanced at Caizhiu and hid his smile of pride in a sip of chalkar. She guessed that, by the next moon's life, it would be as if he'd never lived without a soul song. It had been the same for Morailo, though he'd had more time to get used to it. And his mother had helped him. And nothing had been at stake. He'd even had the freedom to refuse the honour of becoming a Magistrate. Then again, Morailo had never wanted to be invaluable.

Over the howling of the wind, an insistent knocking caused Morailo to frown. "More guests?"

"Don't worry, Grandpa. I'll see who it is," Raila said before he could get up, and she followed it with a grown-up: "I wonder who that could be at this late hour."

When she returned, her precocity seemed to have faded and her eyes flitted towards Morailo for help. Her sleeves were wet where she'd taken the topcoat from whoever she had admitted. Before she could figure out what to say, Gostawa followed her in.

"Lady Azer." Morailo sounded as surprised as Raila looked. He stood up and held out his hand to the chair he'd vacated. "Please come in. Have a seat. Can I get you a warming cup of chalkar... or something stronger?"

Gostawa removed her headscarf, and, with a handkerchief, she wiped the rain from her spectacles before looking around the room. Apart from the sodden hem of her skirt, the Magistrate looked immaculate.

"I do not believe I've ever visited your farm, Mr Hilleram. Or, as it is now, your hotel." She gave a tight smile, smoothed her house jacket, and sat. "I think that may have been a mistake. A cup of chalkar sounds lovely."

Raila offered to prepare chalkar for the Magistrate, but her grandfather replied softly: "It is getting late. Perhaps it would be best if you and Torbel made your way to your beds."

Torbel opened his mouth to protest but glanced at Gostawa and changed his mind. Silently, the children left the room.

{You must be Wylthren Mudridge.}

Caizhiu noticed the flash of panic on his face. Though it was improving by the day, he still doubted he could form a song. Wylthren rubbed the corners of his eyes in concentration. He was trying too hard, but pointing that out wouldn't help. On reflection, she wished she'd been more patient with him.

{We would have visited you, Lady Azer,} he managed to sing flatly. *{But we arrived late and thought it better to leave it until the morrow.}*

{Oh, I'm used to being kept in ignorance of our dragon friend's plans, such as they are.} Gostawa infused her song with a rare glimpse of humour, but the Magistrate had not come for pleasantries and had not wanted to

wait until the morning. Whatever the reason she had come, it had to be important.

Morailo returned with a cup of chalkar. Once he'd sat down, Heort walked into the circle. For a moment he took the critical focus off Caizhiu when he sat in front of the cabinet in the fireplace, the one housing Torbel's night fay.

{We are finding ourselves in unprecedented times.} The humour vanished from Gostawa's song. *{When a Keeper of Sinuation dies, it is rarely unexpected, and they quickly install a successor. Because of the circumstances, I understand the remaining Keepers will gather at the ancient place in Uha'Zari's heart.}*

{Lord Zesen has informed you well, Lady Azer,} Caizhiu said. *{He requested I travel there as well, should my assistance be required. Given my recent difficulties with humans, he advised me to find a Talented companion. Wylthren, without the obligations that bind Magistrates and with a body youthful enough to withstand the journey, seemed the best choice.}*

Gostawa gave a sideways nod to Wylthren as if to say she approved of the decision. *{Unfortunately, further grave news has reached us from Thirdburg. An object has gone missing from Ingrirath's chambers, a tablet called the Key of Sinuation. Since her murderer is an ill-famed thief, tell me, did he have it?}*

Heort stood up, but there was not enough room to pace, so he just stroked the stitching of his jacket in thought. *{Perhaps he sold it before Caizhiu caught him because then he possessed only a haversack. I brought this to Aerahan, and Lord Zesen would surely have recognised such an object. When I healed his burns, the man had neither bag nor rag on him.}*

Gostawa's forehead creased, and her cup rattled on its saucer. *{You healed him?}*

{So that he might give account of himself to Lord Zesen.}

The Magistrate sat back. Her unasked question hung between them until Heort licked his nose and said aloud: "He remains in Aerahan to finish healing, because... well, Caizhiu has decided to keep him."

Morailo glanced at the fireplace cabinet where a new tower of twigs leant against the glass, and his gaze moved to Caizhiu. "You mean as a pet?"

{He's not a pet,} Caizhiu reassured him. *{He's provisions.}*

The ensuing silence made plain that this was something her friend disapproved of even more. Caizhiu scowled around the room, daring them to voice their disapproval in defiance of Zel's judgement.

"Nah!" Wylthren sat back in the armchair and cocked his head. "I bet you won't eat him. You'll get attached. I can't wait to meet this guy who bested you."

The tension eased a little, and Caizhiu shook her head. *{Don't be absurd. He did not best me. And don't use your verbal voice.}*

{When I were a kid, I had a pet magpie. She stole everything I had, but it still broke my heart when she died. You have a dog, Mr Hilleram. Tell her. She clearly doesn't understand the idea of pets.}

"The lad truth-talks." Morailo glanced at Mitzer. The dog lay beneath the writing desk, occasionally raising his lip to Caizhiu but not going so far as to snarl. *{It doesn't matter how wayward or daft they are, or how much trouble they cause you. You get attached.}*

The men exchanged a glance, and a smirk played in the corner of Morailo's mouth. Gostawa did not partake in the joviality. She studied Caizhiu intensely. *{He may not have bested you, but if you'd permit me a word of counsel, Bounty Hunter: kill this man at the earliest opportunity.}*

{Lady Azer!}

Caizhiu and Heort shared Morailo's surprise. The Magistrate of the Keeltois had a reputation not only for aloofness but of one who was fair-minded and, more often than not, merciful. Caizhiu equally felt unease at this disagreement between two Magistrates. If they were interpreting the will of the Six, how could they differ in their opinion? Then again, Zel never said she shouldn't kill him. Perhaps it was she who had misunderstood him, anticipating compassion where there was none.

{Lord Zesen suspects Ozcahar was part of a greater danger and that ending his life would rob us of discovering what or who is behind it,} Heort

said and flicked his ears. Evidently, he shared Caizhiu's disquiet. After a quick glance at the dragon, he added: *{Do you not agree with him?}*

Gostawa held Caizhiu's stare. *{There may well be more danger. I dare say that is why Lord Zesen wants you to protect the Keepers of Sinuation. However, Mr Nitt has already proved he is a danger who dispenses with morality at will. As a result, we now experience a situation the like of which we have never seen, and we can't predict the consequences. End his life before he can do more damage. Or you grow attached to him.}*

Caizhiu trapped her lip between her stumped teeth and smirked. Part of her wondered if Gostawa was goading her. She had not truly expected the blessing from a Magistrate to eat a human, and she wasn't sure Gostawa realised the implication of what she suggested. She had never seen Caizhiu's true form. Morailo had, and he paled at the thought. Before long Wylthren would too, but Caizhiu would prefer that confrontation not to be with the image of her devouring one of his kind. She was determined to be gentler with him in future. Humans were resilient, but she wasn't sure he would be *that* resilient. If she was going to do it, she'd have to despatch Ozcahar quietly and eat him in a private moment.

Caizhiu looked around the room from one friend to another and finally grinned at Heort. "You had me going. But I will not get attached to my human. I'll eat him at a time of my choosing, not, respectfully, Lady Azer, at your command. I am my own kind of dragon, after all."

EPILOGUE

Ozcahar lay on the bed and picked slivers of skin from his palm to distract himself from his backside's insufferable itching. It took some restraint not to scratch at his healing burns. Heort's treatment had been excruciating at first. Believing he wouldn't live long enough to feel the benefit, Ozcahar had begged the cervitaur to stop. He had not expected to walk out of the chamber of judgment. When Caizhiu had grabbed his chin, he'd expected her to snap his neck and would have been grateful for the mercy of a quick death. She'd spared his life, but his relief had faded quickly. During the initial weeks of his imprisonment, he had cowered at any passing footsteps, certain that the dragon would have him for breakfast that day. But she hadn't come, and now the fear sprouted that she would leave him to rot, alone, in this tiny cell. His eyes drifted over the incomprehensible scribbles in the wall. If he added his name, would anyone be able to read his Aumegoan script?

It was too early for the wardens to bring his evening meal, so when the key turned in the lock, he bolted upright. Curse it! His eyes flickered towards the tray on the ground. The thought of being fattened up robbed him of his appetite, and he managed only a few mouthfuls of his breakfast.

To hide this disobedience, he would dump the leftovers into the shit hole in the corner. But he hadn't got round to it yet. Would they tell Caizhiu? He sat up straight on the edge of the bed with his hands on his knees to hide their shaking.

The Head Warden, a solemn woman who'd told him her name was T'uus, but that he was only ever to address her or any of her staff as 'Warden', entered the cell. She was flanked by a man and a woman he recognised, but whose names he'd consequently not bothered remembering.

"Stand, turn, and place hands on wall," the female warden said. He obeyed, relaxing a little at hearing the familiar command. But why was the Head Warden here? He'd not seen her since his first day. The male warden pulled Ozcahar's trousers and undergarments down. Ozcahar flinched at the application of the cold salve. Heort had insisted the wardens carry treatment out every day. At least he hoped it was treatment and not something to make him more appetising to Caizhiu. The warden wiped his hand on the back of Ozcahar's tunic, pulled his garments back up, and ordered him to turn back.

Clearing her throat, T'uus presented a piece of paper and pronounced: "Ozcahar Nitt, in accordance with the sentence as pronounced by the Lord Magistrate Zel Zesen, you are to be branded with the symbols indicating your criminal nature."

"W-what?" He'd not caught every Uayathi word, but that sounded official and not good.

The Head Warden cocked her head as if daring him to interrupt her again. Biting his lip, he watched her retrieve a piece of charcoal from her pocket.

"Namely: Liar." He knew that word. She drew something on his left cheek. "Thief." She marked his right and placed the charcoal against his forehead. "Murderer."

"Respectfully, Warden... What?"

T'uus repeated herself in Trader, and Ozcahar nearly slumped in shock. Her wardens grabbed an arm each and kept him standing. "Marks of his misdeeds," Lord Zesen had said. He hadn't realised that meant they would burn his face.

"To make sure you no give danger to people like those on the beach, like people of Basinwade."

It was not the first time he had been sentenced to branding, but today Jorganyon wasn't here to get him off, and no amount of tears would save him. He was no longer a seven-year-old caught purloining purses in a market square. Back then, the iron mark had been larger than his young hand and the court had taken pity on him. Could he possibly try for mercy again?

"Please, may I see my..." He struggled. What was their relationship? What did food call its eater? "My dragon? M-may I see Caizhiu, please?"

"You think dragon care you no be pretty no more?" T'uus shared an amused glance with her wardens. "She return in some days and require you be ready to take."

"Be Caizhiu no here?"

T'uus glanced at the tray on the floor and said to the woman: "From day-after-dark, check he eat food. He must be good weight for dragon. In case she return hungry."

They marched him out of his cell, along the hallways of the prison. T'uus opened a door. Screams and the scent of scorched flesh greeted them.

Ozcahar pressed his heels onto the flooring and twisted his arms to get out of their grip. They hadn't even bothered to bind him.

"Dragon return soon," the Head Warden said. "You want we tell you behave bad?"

He ceased his struggling and hung his head. They dragged him past three people who stood with their arms wrapped around themselves in a dejected hug. Relief flashed in the eyes of the other convicts as they realised his queue-jumping meant a few more moments of respite before it was their turn. The warden guarding them saluted T'uus and opened a door.

Heat rolled into the hallway, followed by a man who was unceremoniously shoved towards them. He stumbled against the wall. When he glared around, the blistering wound on his cheek drew gasps from Ozcahar and the others awaiting this fate. The branded man bowed to the Head Warden and slunk off, clutching his face. T'uus held out her hand as if to invite Ozcahar to enter by choice. He stiffened when he saw the smouldering hearth in the corner. The heat in the room was suffocating, and he heaved at the stench of scorched skin. As the wardens stepped forward, his legs lost all strength. Muttering curses, they lifted him up by his arms and ankles and deposited him in the chair in the centre of the room. The brander, a woman standing next to the fire, straightened the collection of irons and studied the charcoal drawings on his face. With a lopsided grin, she wiggled three fingers at Ozcahar. The flames sputtered and his lungs seemed to shrink in on themselves. He scraped his heels over the chair to try to get away.

"Becalm, friend." The brander spat on the glowing steel. "No yet be ready."

The woman poked among the logs and the room began to spin. If he didn't get out, he would die; they would all die. He needed to get away before the fire drake found him.

The brander took the iron from the fire and examined its colour.

"Hold him," she said to the male warden as she walked towards the chair. "This be a wriggly one."

The warden placed a sweaty palm on his forehead and grabbed his chin firmly. Ozcahar tried to catch his eyes. "Please, mark with knife, no fire."

The warden shared a nod with his colleague. She, standing next to the brander, took a dagger from her belt. Ozcahar wanted to close his eyes, but he couldn't. The warden swung her arm and planted the dagger in the brander's neck. Ozcahar recoiled as the glowing iron clonked against the chair and dropped to the floor. He stared at T'uus, already trying to convince her he had nothing to do with this. In a state of shock, she stepped back and the male warden seized her by the hair. In one smooth motion, he slit her throat, deep enough to open her windpipe. Whatever she had wanted to say vanished in a bloody gurgle.

The warden who'd murdered the brander grabbed Ozcahar's arm and pulled him off the chair and onto his feet. The other stepped over the body of his boss and cautiously opened the door.

"Come with us," the woman hissed.

Ozcahar's hands were pushed to his face as if he were clutching new scars on both cheeks. He didn't need to playact his stumbling as the warden marched him out of the room. He peered through his fingers, trying to read the face of the man, who again had a firm grip on his arm. The woman walked ahead of them. When they passed the guard in the hall, he placed his hand on her shoulder. He frowned at her blood-soaked uniform, but before he could do anything, her dagger pierced his neck. The man slid down the wall with a look of utter bewilderment. Huddled against the wall, the convicts waiting to be branded exchanged shocked glances. The warden turned to them and whatever she said led all three to follow them. Probably not much of a choice.

Ozcahar lowered his hands. "Who be you?"

"We be the Unanswered." The man held him close so Ozcahar wouldn't trip and answered without looking at him. "We hear the call of the Aumegoan. He say you be his brother. He be waiting for you."

Ozcahar blinked in disbelief. Jorganyon was here. At last, he had come to rescue him. He should never have doubted his big brother.

The End

Printed in Great Britain
by Amazon